Praise for Contemplating Oblivion

"A gorgeous vision of the future. Wiley creates a lavish galactic civilization in which computerized, immortal humans transmit their self-patterns in and out of simulations, and branch their minds to travel between stars, all as comfortably as we drive across town. But we see a culture stymied by the unsolvability of consciousness and horrified by the end of the universe. Inspiring philosophical fiction!"
—**ERIC KLIEN** • *President, Lifeboat Foundation*

"A unique vision of humanity's future. Wiley has created a world in which technology and biology are indistinguishable and people travel between the stars as beamed data streams. Consciousness itself has become the predominant curiosity, while survival has become the primary concern in a universe fated to die. A beautiful story of commitment and quest, both personal and societal."
—**ZOLTAN ISTVAN** • *Founder, the Transhumanist Party* •
Author, The Transhumanist Wager

"Contemplating Oblivion is the rare science fiction novel that imagines a truly posthuman future, where technology has transformed the nature of the mind and self. Wiley combines hard science and profound philosophy to grapple with the ultimate existential challenges that advanced civilizations may face. Prepare for an awe-inspiring adventure exploring the co-evolution of intelligence and technology."
—**JAMES J. HUGHES PHD** • *Executive Director, Institute for Ethics and Emerging Technologies • Author, Citizen Cyborg: Why Democratic Societies Must Respond to the Redesigned Human of the Future*

"A beautiful exploration of the possibilities of future minds and consciousnesses. It will give you deep appreciation for the gift of conscious experience and a new perspective on humanity, technology, and our individual futures and collective future in the universe."
—**JOHN SMART** • *CEO, Foresight U. • Founder, Evo-Devo Institute • Vice President & Co-Founder, Brain Preservation Foundation*

Continued...

Praise for Contemplating Oblivion continued

"A spectacular vision of the far future, in which the functioning of the mind is separated from the substrate of the brain, enabling light-speed interstellar travel and wild explorations of consciousness. Wiley depicts a society consumed with curiosity about the nature of consciousness, but also vexed by existential angst over the end of the universe, when even the immortals will perish."

—**RANDAL KOENE PHD** • *Founder & CEO of Carboncopies.org • Founder of Minduploading.org • past Director of the Department of Neuroengineering at Tecnalia*

"The opening sentence in the introduction in Keith Wiley's latest book, *Contemplating Oblivion*, immediately draws the reader in – 'This is a story about people who have long ago computerized their brains, which is commonly called mind uploading'. Succinctly written, sometimes challenging and complex but more often thought-provoking, it is not only an engaging and deeply moving sci-fi novel but also an important contribution to the ongoing discussions on the nature of consciousness and mind-uploading. I highly recommend it!"

—**RICHARD BRIGHT** • *Editor, Interalia Magazine*

Contemplating Oblivion

By the Author

Books
Available on Amazon

A Taxonomy and Metaphysics of Mind-Uploading

Articles
Available at https://keithwiley.com

The Preconscious Smart Home

The Stream of Consciousness and Personal Identity

Nondestructive Mind Uploading and the Stream of Consciousness

Mind Uploading and the Question of Life, the Universe, and Everything

The Fallacy of Favoring Gradual Replacement
Mind Uploading Over Scan-and-Copy

The Fermi Paradox, Self-Replicating Probes,
and the Interstellar Transportation Bandwidth

Contemplating Oblivion

Keith Wiley

Alautun Press

Published by:
Alautun Press
https://alautunpress.com
contact@alautunpress.com
Shoreline, WA, USA

Contemplating Oblivion
Keith Wiley

First edition 2024

This is a work of fiction. Names, characters, places, events, and incidents are the product of the author's imagination. Any resemblance to actual persons, living or dead, or actual events is purely coincidental.

Cover design by Keith Wiley with Mochi Diffusion

Starscape illustration by Keith Wiley

Milky Way depiction
NASA/JPL-Caltech/R. Hurt (SSC/Caltech)
https://spitzer.caltech.edu/image/ssc2008-10a-a-roadmap-to-the-milky-way

ISBN 979-8-9910135-0-5 (paperback)
ISBN 979-8-9910135-1-2 (hardcover)
ISBN 979-8-9910135-2-9 (ebook)
Library of Congress Control Number (LCCN): 2024912692

Acknowledgements

Thank you to my colleagues at the Carboncopies Foundation and the Brain Preservation Foundation (BPF). You are my tribe. Where others might find my ideas about the brain and the mind, the technification thereof, and the future of humanity in general, to be quaint at best and objectionable at worst, you simply understand me. With sincerity, I thank you.

Thank you to the early reviewers who braved the manuscript absent of prior validation—for they were the tip of the spear. They include my dad, my sister, Randal Koene (founder and CEO of Carboncopies.org and my long time colleague and occasional coauthor), the staff of the BPF (Kenneth Hayworth, John Smart, Michael Cerullo, Andy McKenzie, Oge Nnadi, Ariel Zeleznikow-Johnston, and Alan Ziegler), Eric Klien, Zoltan Istvan, and James Hughes.

Thanks again to my dad, and to my daughter Alyssa, for their unknowing assistance with the audiobook. My dad read to me when I was a child, showing me what spoken narrative can sound like, and Alyssa has provided me with many years of practice at that venerable art.

Also thanks to David Brin, who although he was too busy to read the manuscript himself, did take the time to exchange a few emails with me discussing both writing and publishing advise, the former of which yielded pleasant improvements I believe.

About the Author

Keith Wiley was one of the original members of MURG, the Mind Uploading Research Group, an online community dating to the mid-90s that discussed issues of consciousness with an aim toward mind uploading. He has written a previous book about the philosophical interpretation of mind uploading, various invited book chapters, peer-reviewed journal articles, and magazine articles, in addition to several essays on a broad array of topics, available on his website at https://keithwiley.com. When away from the keyboard, he can be found hiking the mountains and rainforests of the Pacific Northwest. He currently resides in Seattle, WA.

Author's Request

Thank you for purchasing *Contemplating Oblivion*. If you enjoy it, please rate and/or review it on Amazon and/or Goodreads. Authors are heavily dependent on public feedback of that nature.

Furthermore, since this book is self-published, you, dear reader, are my publicist. No grandiose publishing house has purchased advertisements or arranged tours and signings for me. The only way anyone will ever know this book exists is if you tell others about it—or buy it as a gift for someone. So yell it into the chasmic expanse of social media and whisper it into the tranquil chamber of friends and family.

In the immortal words of Leia, "You're my only hope."

Naming Conventions

This is a story about people who have long ago computerized their brains, which is commonly called mind uploading, but which in the story is called *fortification*. It is a topic I am quite passionate about, my having previously written a nonfiction book and several articles about it.

Computerized brains can be manipulated and maneuvered much more easily than biological brains. For example, they can be embodied physically, in a sort of robotic body, to interact with the physical world (called *corporealization* in the story), or they can be embodied in a virtual world (a *virtuality*), with no physical body and no direct interactions with the physical world (called *decorporealization* in the story).

Another task facilitated by computerizing the brain is recording the complete description of the current state of a brain as a sort of futuristic data file. In the story, such a brain state description is called an *etching*. Curious things can be done with brain etchings. They can be transmitted to a new location, either over a physical network (electrical or fiberoptic cables) or via an electromagnetic transmission (radio waves or perhaps laser beams). This is essentially a form of travel as far as the person involved is concerned, called *transiting* in the story. Upon reception—or arrival—in a new location, an etching can then be used to create a new computerized brain, which might then be embodied either physically or virtually.

When a brain etching is transmitted elsewhere and then used to construct a new brain, this can result in what philosophers call *branching*, with one remaining behind and the other traveling to a new location. Branching only occurs if the brain at the origin location continues 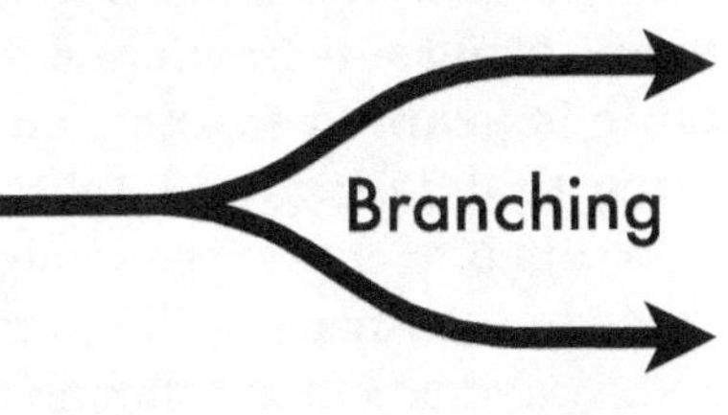

to operate. If not, the person has simply traveled to a new location without branching. In the society portrayed in the story, people are unconcerned by notions of bodily priority, continual neural function, or continual stream of consciousness regarding personal identity. Such concerns are utterly antiquated in the story's far future setting. A person's identity is simply indicated by their memories.

Another possibility is *reunification*, the opposite of branching, in which two people who previously branched in their shared past splice their brains back to- 

gether again, yielding a single descendent from two immediate ancestors, who themselves have a common mental ancestor. This new descendent will have the combined memories of both ancestors during their time apart, as well as the singular memories from prior to the branching event.

The reason for explaining all of this is to set up the following vernacular. We need a naming convention to keep track of a person's branching and reunification history. Consider the following table of vowel accents:

1st appear-ance	Branches										
	1st	2nd	3rd	4th	5th	6th	7th	8th	9th	10th	11th
a	á	à	ă	â	ä	ã	ȁ	ă	â	ā	å
e	é	è	ě	ê	ë	ẽ	ȅ	ě	ê	ē	e̊
i	í	ì	ĭ	î	ï	ĩ	ȉ	ĭ	î	ī	i̊
o	ó	ò	ŏ	ô	ö	õ	ȍ	ŏ	ô	ō	o̊
u	ú	ù	ŭ	û	ü	ũ	ȕ	ŭ	û	ū	ů

The naming convention for a branching event is as follows. The mental ancestor prior to such a branching event will already have a name in which the emphasized syllable has one of the accents shown in the table above, or no accent if they are the first introduction of that character in the story. For example, our protagonist begins with the name Lysandra. **By convention, when a person branches via transit, the next accent across the table is granted to the non-traveling branch and the next accent after that is granted to the transiting branch.** So, the first time Lysandra branch-transits somewhere, her non-traveling branch is renamed Lysándra and her traveling branch is renamed Lysàndra, as per the first and second accented columns of the table (pronunciation of the accents is irrelevant and ignored). If either of those people then branch-transits again later in the story, the next two accents, ă and â are used, and so on.

Reunification events are named differently. Accents are not used. The same syllable is once again considered. The emphasized syllable will have some vowel, potentially accented. **To name the descendant of two reunifying branches, the two vowels are considered and the latter such vowel is incremented in alphabetical order.** So in our previous example, if Lysándra and Lysàndra reunify into a single person, the new person is named Lysendra, advancing the vowel and resetting the accent traversal back to the left side of the table, with no accent. If the two ancestors that are reunifying have different vowels, say Lysăndra and Lysendra, then the reunified person is similarly named with the next vowel, in this case Lysindra.

Note that there are periods when characters transit, branch, and reunify without meaningfully impacting the story, i.e., without branching that produces plot-relevant differentiated characters (their incidental transits likely *do* involve branching and reunifying, but only one such branch is relevant or seen by the reader). These inconsequential branching and reunification events are ignored and the character names (accents) are preserved until an important branching event occurs later in the story. For example, all of the characters likely undergo almost countless minor excursions within their home stellar systems, or even to and from other systems, over the course of the story's extended narrative, but since these trips have no relevance to the story, their implied branching and reunifying character name alterations are discarded.

Note that there are character branching diagrams at the back of the book. Feel free to glance over them before beginning, but be aware that studying them in detail may provide minor spoilers. Rather, refer to them as you read along, if you find them helpful.

Additional supplemental materials at the back

Name pronunciation guide

Character branching diagrams

Stellar system diagrams

The Milky Way

Diagrams of each stellar system are at the back of the book

<u>The Center:</u>
Sol (Earth)
Ylorin
Yseldor (Icarion, Luminith {*Seraphi*})
Vimrei (Ermozara, Krasavitia {*Regenium*})
Oudara

Star
(Planet)
{Moon}
[Station]

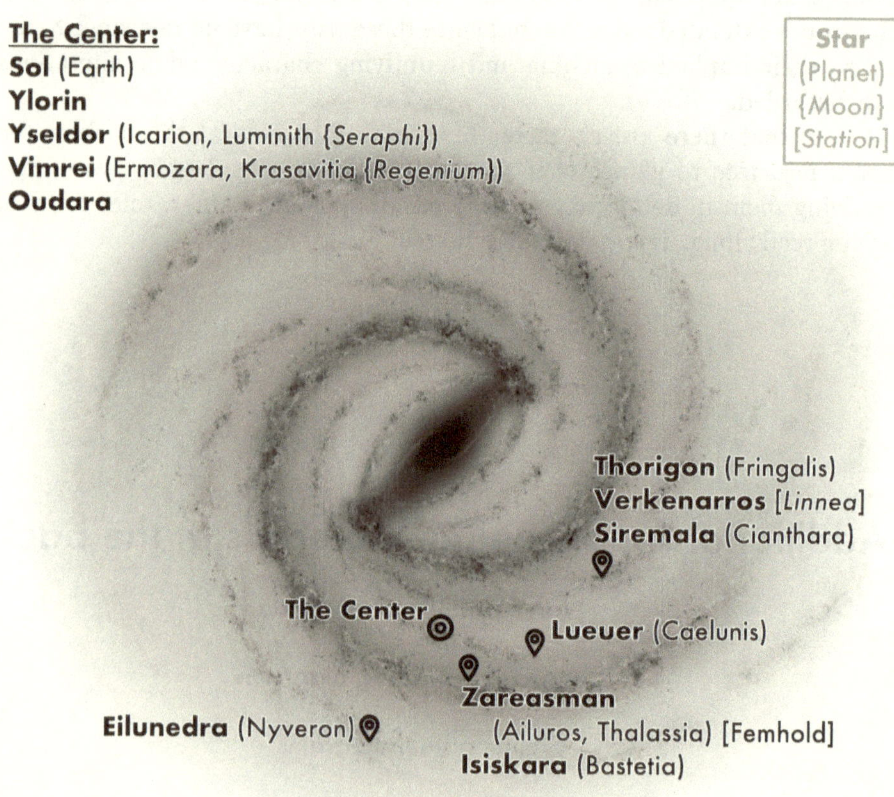

1

Qualia (s. quale): The intrinsic feeling of a conscious experience, e.g.,
The hue of sight, the timbre of sound.
The sensuality of touch, the agony of pain.
The splendor of love, the isolation of loneliness.
The grief of loss.
Qualia cannot be conveyed; they must be experienced firsthand to be known.

"**N**O NO NO! UNDO THAT LAST ALTERATION," exclaimed Lysandra with a twinge of urgency in her voice as a discomforting sensation swept through her mind from some unspecified source in thought-space. It arrived suddenly, allowing no time to brace herself, crashing across her awareness, some nondescript combination of physical ache and emotional dread, the latter an odd blend of fear and ennui that would not generally occur naturally. She squirmed in her reclined chair despite its active contouring to her shape moment by moment, veritably merging with her curves and surfaces. She tried to relax and focused on the warmth of the red sun against the skin of her current body, her corporealization, a construction neither biological nor artificial, or perhaps both. The distinction was negligible at the molecular level.

Ceolbur, sitting nearby in a similar neural interfacing chair, satisfied Lysandra's request by promptly manipulating the neural parameters under his mental control—within his own thought-space—directing them to their values prior to the experiment. Lysandra's neural configuration reverted to its previous arrangement, removing the unpleasant sensations. She visibly melted as the ill feeling washed away.

"Shall I erase the memory?" asked Ceolbur, his attention hovering over the interface of Lysandra's algorithmized hypothalamus, ready to obliterate her short term memory before it could be transferred to a more permanent representation.

"Yeah, no need to keep that one around." Ceolbur wiped the memory clean and Lysandra's expression immediately went blank. A moment later she flinched and sat up in her chair abruptly, confused at her surroundings. The chair, previously molded to her form so intimately as to practically bond with her, instantly retracted ever so slightly, releasing the physical connection. Her confusion almost immediately faded as she recalled where she was and what she was doing. She gazed pensively into the distance, reflecting on the sensation of brief—and very intentional—amnesia.

"Not a good quale, huh?" she said. She swept her fingers through her hair and huffed in mild annoyance.

"Nope. My turn next time. You need a break."

"We've only tested a few networks recently," Lysandra responded. "There's lots more we can do. I can go longer."

"Well I can't," said Ceolbur. "The day is lovely. Look at our mountain." The garden in which they sat resided between their home and a rocky cliff edge that plummeted to an endless forest painted across the valley below. Their mountain, as Ceolbur joked, broke the remote horizon, its snow cap reddened by the alien sun. The house was a balance of wooden beams and aquamarine glass that erupted from alpine ground-cover below a cloudless sky. Vertical window panes stretched upward from ground level, separated by the wooden ribs, reaching three stories, granting the interior an unimpeded view beyond the cliff and onward to the horizon—to the mountain.

"We haven't made much progress recently," remarked Lysandra as they both stood up and ventured indoors, their neural interfacing chairs shrinking and vanishing into the ground. "The recent network designs haven't revealed anything of value. I need to find a good network," she said with irritation. "A good perception, a good experience. It's been a dry spell lately." One of the window panes dissolved entirely as they approached, then rematerialized after they entered.

"I don't know," said Ceolbur in a reassuring tone. "I liked the quale we found a few days ago. It tasted like vermillion and smelled like melancholy with just a hint of nickel magnetism and circular polarization mixed in."

Lysandra rolled her eyes. "Must you do that so soon after an experiment? You know I dislike attempts to describe qualia. At least dwell on it for a while so you can be sure you've found the right words." Music began playing within the room. A moment later, Lysandra realized it was precisely the music she wanted to hear, as the neural pathway leading to her awareness of the desire had been intercepted while it still resided in her preconsciousness.

"I can't help myself," said Ceolbur. "Someone has to attempt to categorize the conscious states you discover. How else are we supposed to catalog our discoveries?"

"Can we really categorize them though?" said Lysandra. A glass of wine almost instantly appeared in Lysandra's hand, formed from the air itself, and she sipped, an act that was entirely recreational and cathartic, unnecessary for sustenance. Her body suffered no such need, but drinking and eating were just too pleasurable to give up. "Catalog yes," she continued, "but can we describe them? Can we do better than assign sentiment labels like good and bad? I think all we can do is record which neural configurations are worth keeping around and sharing, and which are better rejected and avoided."

She contemplated the network she had just tested, the sensation she had just experienced. She shuddered and the wine wobbled in the glass as she wondered if she had suffered. In what poor state had Ceolbur witnessed her? It could have been mild or it could have been horrible. And did it matter if it never transferred to long term memory? Was a forgotten suffering real after it was gone?

"Well, you could deliberately conflate one quale with another," said Ceolbur, standing in a wash of red sunlight from the window. It would have felt like twilight except that it was practically midday on their planet of Ailuros. "You could feel colors tactilely, taste echolocation, see magnetism, hear polarization. You could do that if you chose to, but you generally choose to experience them directly. Occasional ancient humans exhibited such traits of qualia interplay by sheer fluke of neurological wiring. Synesthesia." A matching glass appeared in Ceolbur's hand and he joined Lysandra in the social practice of shared chemical nutrient consumption, pointless as it otherwise was. "All this neural configuration design and consciousness exploration was your passion before it was mine, Lysandra. All I'm trying to do is put some rigor into recording our results. I'm surprised you resist tracking our progress."

"I do want that," she replied, somewhat pleading, "but I also acknowledge the practical limitations. No one has found a way to predict the quale that will result from a particular connectome. It's almost a blind search. Once we find a neural configuration of interest, we can refine it to some extent to see if we can alter or improve the qualia it evokes, but the initial search space is enormous. It takes ages to find a tantalizing new sensation." She saw Ceolbur nod thoughtfully and they both sipped at the same moment. She smiled at the timing.

"Well," said Ceolbur, "I still think that when we manage to find interesting conscious states, we ought to strive for some shared vocabulary with which to characterize them. You trade your network designs with other quale-divers all over the galaxy on a regular basis. And all of you lot are constantly confounded to describe your results to one another. I see the descriptions as you send your latest neural configuration off to your colleagues or receive new configurations from them. You're all so rigid and procedural, attaching the most boring labels to your networks, like, 'A pleasant quale that makes me feel good.'" He enunciated the quote with a goofy voice. "Really Lysandra? I think we can do better."

Lysandra approached Ceolbur and took his face in her palms. As she did this, she veritably dropped her glass freely into the air, but it simply vaporized away so quickly as to practically wink out of existence, wine and all. "Of course, that's what you're here for," Lysandra responded. "You're better at capturing these experiences in poetic terms than I could ever be. I couldn't do it without you. Tasting vermillion will do just fine." Lysandra planted a kiss on his lips and then crossed the atrium, its vaulted interior perfused with sunlight. Now she sought food: flavor and satiation, among the most pleasurable of experiences wired into her ancient network. And she realized, as a shudder ran up her spine, that her vexation had left her craving a more vibrant sort of release as well. Her drink reappeared in her outstretched hand, prior fingerprints and wine legs included. She glanced over her shoulder alluringly. "Are you joining me?"

"I hope documenting your experiments isn't the only reason I'm here," he teased, following her obediently. "We've been doing this for several thousand years after all."

2

"We may be alone in the darkness, but at least we're alone together."
—The great cosmological artist Rihon

RIHON SURVEYED HIS WORK ONE LAST TIME. He stood atop a pewter-toned metallic platform, a terrace really, raised several towering stories above the ashen surface of Seraphi. A moon, it was a naked chunk of rock with little to draw visitors, but it offered Rihon an excellent vantage point from which to stage his latest artistic creation. Seraphi was tidally locked to its host planet, the gas giant of Luminith, of no importance except as a resource of various elements. In this tidal locking, the platform on which Rihon stood faced directly away from Luminith with an unobstructed view of the cosmos, constellated with thousands of stars. Far more stars were visible to Rihon's eyes than had been accessible to the progenitor humans on Earth a million years ago. If he stood perfectly still—and he could stand *perfectly* still—his eyes could temporally integrate the incoming photons, gathering weak retinal illuminance that would otherwise be lost below the noise floor of even his bettered eyes, penetrating the darkness and bringing yet fainter stars, yet wispier nebulae, and yet fuzzier galaxies within reach of his photopic sensation, then perception, and then conscious realization.

But none of that was why he stood on the platform gazing skyward. Set against the cosmic symphony were three objects arrayed in a triangle, only a few lunar diameters above Seraphi, so large and so near as to dominate the view. First, there was an unnaturally bright scarlet nebulosity stretching across a large swath of the sky like a silk scarf, wisps spilling to its sides, fading into the stars. In another section of the sky there was an unambiguously artificial raw tetrahedron, metallic, gigantic, slowly rotating against the stellar backdrop. The tetrahedron had a fractal structure that faded to desolate blackness toward its center. Although the tessellated structure was considerably hollow, the black core permitted no stars to shine through, an utter abyss of discombobulating nothingness. The third object, completing the triad, was a myriad web of white tendrils, gently bobbing, gently morphing as the tendrils extended and shrank like springs that retained the overarching structure of the web. The web evoked notions of neural connectivity but did not appear brain-like in shape, just a bare connectionist abstraction. To Rihon's preternatural eyes there was also perceptually apparent—vision would be the wrong word—translucent ribbons of light polarization weaving the three objects together into a triangle of uniform composition. It would have been no more correct to say that he visually perceived a certain color in the ribbon than to say he heard a certain tone from it. Polarization granted its own intrinsic sensation, a unique conscious experience.

Rihon absorbed his creation in solitude one last time before inviting the gaudy masses. He glanced around its elements expertly, as he had done for centuries over the course of its design, construction, and refinement, but then he was interrupted by internal communication.

Rihon, came the voice, a thought really, a call for lack of a better term. *Your guests have begun to arrive.*

Thank you Ananda, he responded, issuing the return message over the same mental communication network. He took one last glance upward and then descended a long flight of steps off the front side of the platform, entered a small building, and rapidly rode the equivalent of an elevator straight through the core of Seraphi to the opposite side of the moon over the course of a minute or so. As he emerged, he saw people from all over the galaxy beginning to accumulate. This layout of the gala would permit him to unveil the art piece properly. No viewer could see his creation from the planet side of the moon, not until they transited Seraphi's axis as he had just done, to then suddenly behold the cosmic construction suspended above them for the first time. It had taken some people millennia to arrive for this event, scattered throughout the galaxy, and now everyone was converging at the same moment.

Rihon gazed briefly upward at the banded gas giant looming over him, its orange, gray and purple belts eddying across its surface. From here, the giant swamped half the expanse of the sky. The vertiginous sensation that the planet would simply fall on him stopped him momentarily, but then he looked around to see who was present. This side of the moon was also barren—untouched soot-colored rock, pocked with craterlets, but otherwise featureless. Everyone stood directly upon the frigid, airless surface, awash in radiation and magnetism from the adjacent planet. No wonder nothing biological could be found for cosmic distances in any direction.

Spread across the surface of the moon and stretching over the low radius horizon, he saw countless people gathering, milling, chatting—anxious. Dotted across the landscape there were transit stations, a common occurrence throughout the galaxy. Each station had the form of a glowing circular dais, raised slightly above the lunar surface. New arrivals would simply appear—or corporealize—on one of these platforms as their pattern file was received and rapidly constructed from the raw materials of the moon itself. Each person would then step off and blend into the crowd to mingle. Despite relative freedom regarding bodily forms, people were generally unremarkable in this fashion, the novelty of body exploration having worn off hundreds of thousands of years ago. All that really mattered about a person—and during a transmission—was the pattern file of their connectome, which prescribed the neurology of a given person's brain. A minor body addendum of preference barely even registered in the pattern file.

"Ananda, what's our head count?" Rihon asked. His assistant stood near where he had exited the intra-lunar elevator.

"A little over a hundred and thirty thousand. You said you wanted to keep it small for the grand unveiling."

"Right you are. Thank you as always." Rihon took a few deep breathes of lunar vacuum, closed his eyes, opened them again—and then abruptly elevated straight up off the surface of the moon by no apparent means—which shocked no one in and of itself—so that he could survey—and be seen—more easily. The crowd drew quiet. In the distance, as the throng stretched over the horizon, naturalistic depictions of Rihon were presented at a reasonable spacing, similarly suspended above the surface, replicating his appearance so everyone could observe and hear his speech.

"Welcome," he declared. There was no atmosphere to convey his words, but his voice was broadcast across the gala, received by every attendee's brain with their incorporated communications. "Thank you for coming to the grand unveiling of my latest creation." A version of applause and cheering spontaneously erupted. "This piece is perhaps more abstract than my previous works, but that is because I am tackling the trickiest challenge of our time. In the past, I have explored many aspects of the human condition, such as the strange sensation of having never found another sentient species in the galaxy with whom we could bond and share culture. And by contrast, I have depicted and considered the implications of our few contacts with sentience in other galaxies, so far away that we will never converse with them. And I have explored the dissonance of near-eternal existence with near-eternal companionship as challenged by ever-evolving personalities, compatibilities, loves—and loss thereof. Forever hurts, does it not, my dear companions?

"But nothing so grand as my latest work. Permit me to present to you Contemplating Oblivion! A work that explores nothing less than the EOUSP!" Rihon pronounced this as *yewsup*, the unanimous vernacular for the ubiquitous term. He made this statement with a flamboyant conclusiveness and at the mere mention of the word EOUSP the crowd reacted a thousand different ways, for he had not publicized this profound fact in advance.

"The End-Of-Universe-Survival-Problem is the defining challenge of our era!" he veritably yelled. "We have but one other great exploration, the nature of consciousness, the single remaining neuro-metaphysical relation that eludes us despite our having solved the brain a million years ago. We know how the brain does it, but not why certain neural arrangements produce particular qualia. But," he practically yelled again, almost in agitation, "I think the EOUSP is more pressing! We can spend eternity solving the mystery of qualia, but not if we perish first!" He was animated now, floating back and forth above the crowd in a frenzy, as if pacing but without the motions of legwork. "What have we learned since we emerged from our Earthly cocoon a million years ago? What is known and what is left, I ask you? Do we not already have the closure of physics?" The crowd nodded in unison. "Chemistry?" Murmurs of agreement. "Biology? Yes, we celebrate newly discovered ecologies—always hopelessly insentient—throughout the galaxy, its interrelations and behaviors the final source of novelty in our era. But we have nevertheless solved *physicality itself*, have we not?!" More agreement from the crowd. "From the smallest scale of matter to the largest structure of the universe, from the weakest force to the strongest. We have allied time and space, gravity and subatomics. We know the evolution of the universe from its origin to the present—and we also hold the model of its continuation into the future," he said in an ominous tone, pausing for dramatic effect. He then dropped to nearly a whisper. "And we know its fate as well, do we not?" This caused a wave of agitation to sweep over the crowd. "When you participate in Contemplating Oblivion today, and I do mean participate—" Rihon snickered momentarily "—remember the EOUSP. Dwell upon it. Let its angst pervade you. Do not run from it!" A final pause for his final delivery, as he recentered and faced the crowd. "For the EOUSP will not RUN FROM YOU!" he hollered. This sent the audience into a final uproar. Rihon hovered over his adoring fans, grinning briefly, and then descended back to the surface.

"Are you quite pleased with yourself?" asked Ananda. "They're already here, you hardly have to sell them on it." Rihon smiled and ignored her.

"Okay," he said. "The platform will accommodate about three thousand at a time. In the interests of granting access to everyone here today, we will confine each group to a brief duration and we will only grant a few primary observers per group before moving them on. Most attendees will have to settle for passive participation. That will heighten the excitement and keep them coming back for a long time. Everyone will want to return so they can be the primary observer at some point."

"Yes, yes, you're very clever," said Ananda, as she focused her attention on the task of organizing the guests into groups of a few thousand and herding them into the moon-traversing pods. The doors to numerous small buildings housing the elevator-like pods opened and people begin milling in. They were then whisked away through the center of the moon, where they emerged, and were guided to ascend the platform, and from there to engage in Contemplating Oblivion. If one listened carefully from the gala on the Luminith side of Seraphi, one could imagine hearing the concert of unified awe emanating from the first group as they arrived on the platform at the antipode.

A moment ago Satori had been standing on the transit station on the planet Icarion, in orbit of the star Yseldor. The next conscious experience he had was of standing on a similar transit station, a glowing white dais, on the moon of Seraphi, which orbited the next planet out, the gas giant of Luminith. The dais below him hummed and vibrated with gentle energy. He stepped onto the coarse regolith and took in the crowd. He had arrived early, having heard in advance that entry to Rihon's latest creation would be organized into small groups. For some reason, the art piece could only be consumed in batches. Others would have to wait until their turn came around. Satori was therefore near the front when Rihon emerged from one of many small buildings arrayed in rows in front of the crowd. Satori could actually see him exit and approach a woman, his assistant from the appearance of their private interaction.

I wonder if he remembers me, thought Satori, as he elbowed forward semi-politely. *It's been a few millennia, I suppose.* Satori had been the presenter and Rihon the audience member that previous time, as Rihon attended a public reading from one of Satori's latest rhetorics, one of his more popular arrangements of thoughts and ideas concerning the pursuit of wisdom and the nature of consciousness—enlightenment, in effect. Would Rihon remember him though?

Rihon was briefly chatting with his assistant. Satori pushed forward a little more.

"Rihon! Rihon!" Satori declared, but the crowd at the front was gaining energy in response to Rihon's appearance. No one could hear Satori, even as he broadcast his voice over standard mental channels to the area immediately around him. The next thing Satori knew, Rihon had rapidly ascended off the moon's surface to a mild height for the obvious purpose of presenting himself to the crowd. Satori's chance was gone. All he could do now was go along and await another opportunity.

"Welcome," began Rihon. Satori listened as Rihon's voice projected into his head, manifested in his auditory cortex and became the perceptual experience of sound and the cognitive experience of language. Satori reveled at Rihon's charisma as the artist gave his presentation.

The speech was short, culminating in a grandiose declaration. "For the EOUSP will not RUN FROM YOU!" Satori heard and observed, full of animation both on part of Rihon and the reactions from the crowd. Satori soon found himself being swept toward the row of small buildings, which all opened simultaneously to swallow as many people as could be held. The interior was revealed to be a pod that rapidly took him and a few other attendees through the moon's core to the opposite side of Seraphi.

Satori exited the transit pod, felt the same bare regolith beneath his feet, and immediately noticed strange objects in the sky: an enormous, brilliantly red nebula suspended far overhead. Then a completely unnatural, shimmering silver tetrahedron with a self-similar recursive structure and an uncanny darkness at its center. And finally a mass of bright filaments interconnected in some sort of snarled nest. He also clearly perceived bands of polarization connecting the three objects into a cohesive triangle.

As a few thousand people joined him from similar pods in rapid succession, the crowd was directed by a combination of illuminated markers on the ground and thought-insertions that manifested in everyone's minds, instructing them to move toward a large metallic platform clearly visible nearby. It rose from the moon's surface like a tremendous stepped pyramid, but stopped far short of ascending to a peak, instead leveling off low enough to offer an expansive raised terrace. Satori and the rest of the audience ascended the pyramid from all sides, up the steps that squarely, yet concentrically, surrounded the platform, and regrouped at the top. No further instructions were given.

Everyone milled around, confused. However, it didn't take long for people to notice that there was a focal point in the center of the platform where numerous golden rays inlaid into the otherwise featureless floor converged radially from the perimeter of the platform. Of the few thousand people who quickly found space on the platform, a few early arrivals couldn't resist the urge to follow the rays to their shared vertex. Satori was still taking in the arrangement of the rays and the general surroundings when he was suddenly overcome by a wellspring of emotion that clearly wasn't his own. At the same time, he felt a powerful urge to look upwards. His attention was drawn to the red veil in the sky as it drifted back and forth. Somewhere deep in his mind, he realized he was sympathetically receiving his emotional response from whoever was standing at the vertex of the rays in the floor. He forced himself to glance down briefly, following the nearest specular golden ray on the ground, trying to trace it to the center where the person responsible for his sympathetic emotional reactions was standing. However, the density of people provided him no visibility of the person in question.

He gave in to the pressure to look skyward and once again took in the nebula. He stared at it, stared *into* it. Through it. Its motion seemed to respond to being gazed upon by the crowd. No, that wasn't right. Somehow, deep within the crevices of his situational awareness, he knew the nebula was only responding to the primary observer standing at the vertex of the rays inlaid into the floor. No one else mattered. Satori gave into the sensation, presuming this was the intent and purpose of Rihon's art piece, that this was how it was meant to be experienced. The nebula meandered in the sky without wandering away from its position at one corner of the triad. It wasn't just *responding* to him—to the primary observer that is, but it felt like himself—no, it was *interacting* with him, dancing with him, writhing gently as if in the solar wind. Coupled with the visual interaction there was a penetrating emotional component as the nebula pressed an emotional sensation into his brain, into his mind. It was a soft verve of pleasure and relaxation, lovely to bask in. What did this beautiful veiled nebula and its calming invocation have to do with the horrible EOUSP, as Rihon had implied? In his inner dialog, he naturally pronounced the word EOUSP in the ubiquitous form everyone used, *yewsup*. The EOUSP was notoriously one of the most vexing and angstful problems facing civilization. What would become of humanity's galactic legacy when the universe finally succumbed? People had gone literally mad over the issue. For thousands of years, it had been practically the last remaining unknown to all of humanity, with the singular exception of the completely unrelated challenge that no one had found a way to predict the qualia that would emerge from a given neurological arrangement.

But this beautiful red veil, drifting gently in the sky, with its evocative emotions of relaxation and inner peace, seemed to have nothing to do with the EOUSP.

Satori felt his attention—that is to say, he felt the primary observer's attention—refocusing on the polarized ribbon leading away from the nebula toward the tetrahedron. His gaze followed passively along as the primary observer's attention traveled along the ribbon to the lustrous tetrahedron with its infinite, recursive structure descending inward to its center while also vanishing into the blackest nothingness Satori had ever beheld. How had Rihon accomplished such blackish black? It couldn't be a purely visual stimulus. Somehow the tetrahedron was pressing an even blacker black into his visual cortex, deep into his visual perception, forcing him to perceive an abyss no natural human eyes had ever beheld. The complexity of finding a visuo-cortical firing pattern that would evoke this stunning visual percept! How had he done this?! Rihon was a genius.

Satori felt the primary observer's attention being swallowed by the black core of the tetrahedron. He was drowning in it. While attended to, the tetrahedron rotated, stretched, shrank, contorted, as if alive. It seemed to gain strength from the observer's gazing into the center, animating more wildly as it pulled the observer's attention toward its abysmal core, around and around in a feedback cycle that made it impossible to determine who was responding to who, the tetrahedron or the observer. Such terror, such depth, such hopelessness. The core of the tetrahedron invoked it all. This was the EOUSP portrayal Satori expected.

Eventually, Satori felt the primary observer forcibly tear his attention away from this horrific engagement and follow the polarized ribbon to the third object, the tendril-web. The web was even more powerful. It immediately grabbed his mind with veritable claws. An overwhelming sensation of awe and fear, of simultaneous enormity and diminution, and of death was being forcibly pushed deep into his psyche. Of the thousands of attendees standing on the platform staring upwards, those whose bodies bothered to include tear-ducts found themselves helpless to such a response, which then had the peculiar effect of instantly vaporizing in the vacuum of Seraphi's absent atmosphere. The tendril-web gained a ferocious energy of movement as it was gazed upon, the kinetic manifestation of screaming Satori realized, so visceral he almost thought he could hear it. Satori, along with everyone else in unison, stood rapt in this horror, a physical crying out in the dark, unrelenting void, until the primary observer finally grasped the strength to attend along the ribbon once more, back to the scarlet nebula, where the grace of calm swept over the crowd to tremendous shared relief.

Satori then had a moment of freedom as he became disconnected from the artistry. The primary observer had clearly stepped away from the focal point, breaking the neural connection with the art piece. Satori breathed heavily, the instinctive motion of breath at least, not actual air of course.

A moment later, he felt the nebula's warm embrace as it drew him into its hues and shades and wisps once again, as a new person stepped into the primary observing position and established a neural connection to the art piece. And then he and the rest of the crowd were drawn through the tripartite cycle for another round.

This was an exhausting art piece. But there were over hundred thousand people waiting on the opposite side of the moon to experience it this opening night. Satori's group was only permitted a few trips around the cycle with various primary observers before everyone was shuffled off the platform and back into the pods, back to the gathering area. Upon their return, their group were sequestered in a slightly different area of the moon where any discussion of the experience could not give the show away to those still waiting to enter. This area had the usual furnishings of social interaction. Furniture of a wide variety, food if anyone wanted to partake in such recreation, trivial entertainers putting on simplistic performances, all this was scattered haphazard across the surface of the barren moon. Satori watched as people within the crowd shared their reactions to the experience in hushed tones of emotional recovery. Periodically, a new group of a few thousand people would join them. Eventually, everyone had transitioned from the initial gathering area to the after-party, of sorts. The opening gala was drawing to a close.

Rihon appeared last, but was not bombastic, as he had been at the beginning. He simply mingled with the crowd and engaged whoever could manage to push their way toward him. Of the thousands in attendance, Satori failed to reach Rihon, but that was okay. There would be plenty of time for them to reconnect later.

3

KAIMEA WAS THERMAL-SOARING WHEN THE ALERT CAME IN. Long slender wings, webbed with gossamer carbon, stretched to either side several times farther than her body length—not a body of any human form, however. A long, whip-like tail snaked behind her, terminating in a pair of orthogonal fins, cross-like. With the slightest deviation of wing or tail, she could swoop, plummet, arc, or simply spiral lazily upwards as a thermal lifted her ever higher above the ocean. The enormous rolling waves were reduced to gentle ripples at this height, a vast grating of parallel white lines moving in unison across the water's surface. She could glide for hours, with her home planet of Nyveron far beneath her, a large but underpopulated planet orbiting the star Eilunedra on the outskirts of the galaxy, the outskirts of civilization.

But the alert persisted at the forefront of her attention. She took in the view once more, then decorporealized into the planetary data network, disappearing entirely, and a moment later recorporealized in human form in a completely different region of the planet, inside her home. She emerged from the house she had designed and grown long ago, in the middle of an expansive savannah, its structure coalesced from the air at her mental invocation. Alien grass of a sort, thin fuchsia stalks with silver, pearlesque seeds running their length, stood in tight, waist-high bunches, spaced slightly apart. These grass bobs spread in all directions to the horizon, where distant hills rose up, rendering the savannah a huge bowl.

Kaimea mentally scrutinized the alert that felt as natural as sight or sound, but which was nevertheless a distinct sensation and perception. *Curious*, she thought. *Some sort of anomalous signal detected by the observatory.* She instinctively glanced upward toward the sky, where the observatory orbited Nyveron, but of course she couldn't see it in the middle of the day. She considered transiting to the observatory, but then thought better of it. The data was just as readily accessible from her current location. The observatory was little more than a reflective surface, a tremendous, yet diaphanous, atoms-thick sheet stretched across empty space, an area so vast that no gravitational moon or planet could have supported it. Only open space would suffice. She briefly confirmed that the observatory was operating properly, its precise curvature continuously micro-maneuvered and maintained to atomic precision. Any hole punched through its surface by cosmic dust or larger infractions immediately self-repaired with no seam or scar left behind. Upon her inspection, everything appeared to be performing flawlessly. The signal was clean.

As she mentally consumed the data, she gazed across the savannah. Breaking the homogeneity of the fuchsia grass with its silver beads, there were infrequent conglomerations of lavender roots that rose at an angle from a circle on the ground, meeting at an apex at head-height, as if around the sides of a cone, mangrove-like. At the apex of each such plantish lifeform, where the conical roots met, there was a broad circular disk, parallel to the ground.

She had chosen Nyveron not by sheer accident or wanderlust, but with great deliberation. It was on the perimeter of the galaxy, such that if the observatory's dish was aligned with the galactic plane but pointed away from the galactic center, it could observe extragalactic targets with minimal signal extinction by the Milky Way's distracting dust clouds.

She watched a flock of small shimmering fauna skim over the savannah at the height of the grass picking off invisibly smaller creatures in the air. Frequently, these flocks would alight and rest around the perimeters of the flat disks atop the multi-rooted plants, and then momentarily they would set off again, sweeping left and right as they veered into the distance. But once in a while, such flocks would crowd too closely on a disk, venturing toward the middle. The disk would then snap upwards, folding over on itself into a sphere for the briefest moment and then instantly unfold again. The bird-like creatures, no longer shimmering, now coated in matte lavender powder, would stumble away through the air, discombobulated, leaving a cloud of lavender powder in their wake that would slowly settle elsewhere on the savannah.

As she observed one such flock painting mesmerizing flight patterns, she mentally accessed the observatory's data feed streaming down from orbit. She first checked the observatory's target location, disregarding the alert until she could learn more about the circumstances. *It's been decades since I checked in with the observatory,* she thought, acknowledging that over the hundreds of thousands of years she had been surveying galaxies from Nyveron, she often left the observatory unsupervised for long stretches. *It could be looking just about anywhere. Ah, it is indeed pointed almost directly out of the plane of the galaxy. Wow, that is a very distant target galaxy.* She blinked with surprise. The signal was weak and Nyveron's spectacularly large observatory, positioned right at the edge of the Milky Way, had probably made all the difference in detecting the signal. Even if the signal would eventually be detected deeper within the galaxy—and it would take thousands of years for it to reach inward since the signal was coming from the opposite direction—it might be so corrupted in those inner regions that any actual data it contained would be unrecoverable. Humanity throughout the galaxy might detect it and still remain dependent on Nyveron to actually decode it. She smiled at the thought of her remote world becoming the most important planet in the galaxy for handling this momentous event.

What's the alert? she thought as she shifted her attention. *Multiple narrow power spikes, equally distributed across a suite of frequencies, like a perfect comb of fine lines...or like waves on the ocean,* she realized with a chuckle of recent recognition, *and in one of the spectral regions that is generally absent of natural cosmological sources, no less. That's definitely suspicious.* She studied it further. The multiple spikes indicated the likelihood of a multiplexed signal—sending numerous parallel streams of data at different frequencies to increase the total data throughout rate. *Ah! Look at that, both amplitude and phase modulation, likely indicators of data encodings. And is that—yes, the polarization is being modulated too! Less common. Fascinating! Definitely looks like a beacon, or more precisely, several beacons, one at each of the applied frequency bands, and each with an attached carrier signal! But what message is it carrying?!* That was the question.

Her excitement grew stronger. This was real. A sentient species had transmitted a data stream to the Milky Way, or at least to a range of galaxies along the same path and within a narrow trajectory. The certainty of it seemed more likely with every passing moment that she further scrutinized the signal. This had only occurred eleven times over the million years since Earth Exodus, the most recent more than 100,000 years ago. Only eleven sentient species ever discovered, all in far-flung galaxies, with no hope of communicating back and forth, much less of meeting them. She stared at the data, shock setting in. This was real.

Kaimea inspected the signal more deeply. *Clear signs of a stepped encoding in the modulations. Ah, it isn't a binary step though.* It appeared to be—she studied it momentarily, continuing to remark to herself. *The modulation in each frequency encodes not two levels, but seventy-two distinct levels.* So each sample actually encoded one of seventy-two values, not just a binary encoding of two values. That would further increase the data rate of the message. *Seventy-two,* she thought silently, *a multiple of twelve, which has a high density of prime factors, with all the mathematical advantages that provides. It makes sense that an advanced civilization would use twelve as the basis of their mathematics.* Humans had used base sixty for similar reasons at various points in its archaic past. But a signal with numerous modulation levels would have required absolutely colossal transmitter power given the source's distance. Whoever had sent this message had harnessed an incredible amount of power to send a coherent, decodable seventy-two level signal so far. Would a mere star have even been sufficient to the task, she wondered, or had they relied on—what was the alternative? A black hole perhaps? She couldn't even imagine the scale of power going into this signal.

Kaimea continued her investigation. The observatory had narrowed in on a tiny galaxy—by distance, that is—300 million light years away. It was by far the most distant galaxy anyone had received a message from yet. The eleven prior messages had all come from closer sources, some considerably closer. She stared at imagery of the galaxy from earlier visible spectrum sky surveys. Although she could not possibly resolve anything of a technological nature within the galaxy, she could still appreciate the fact that she was, in fact, looking directly at an alien species and its enormous signal transmitter. She was looking right into the communication rays of another kind of mind, another kind of civilization.

Could this be the one? she thought, feeling a tingle of anticipation run up her spine. *One of them must have solved the EOUSP. One of them will save us.* But after a brief moment of excitement she sobered up, realizing the unlikelihood of her hope. The previous eleven had conveyed nothing of the sort. Wondrous works of art, sure, in media of magnetic, quantum mechanical, and gravitational natures—and visual and auditory art too. They had sent their versions of literature, and their societal structure and politics of course, and their values and dreams. They had sent depictions of themselves, as beings, as families, as communities. And they had shown how they feel and express connection and companionship, and love.

But none had made any mention of the EOUSP. Kaimea's long quest seemed destined for failure.

Could this be the one?

4

*T*HE WATER IS WARMER TODAY THAN IT WAS YESTERDAY, thought Lysandra as her not-quite-an-Earth-whale form bobbed on the surface. *We should begin the migration soon*, she completed her thought to no one but herself. With a push of her fins, she turned to the left, then the right, looking for someone.

"Ceolbur?" she said, although not in such a fashion. The name emerged from her ferrous lobe, a region of her alien whalesque body located behind her head, along her dorsal region. The utterance produced a series of magnetic deviations that rippled out through the water in all directions. "Ceolbur?" she magnetized with greater strength. While she waited for a response, something food-like swam past her. The difference in size between herself and this prey was so incredible that the other creature probably regarded Lysandra as a rock formation. Lysandra scrunched and flexed her fins, building up power, and then released her fins forward with ultrasonic force, sending a lethal shockwave through the water. The little prey item ceased all motion as it was stunned. Lysandra opened her maw and sucked the little aquatic alien inside.

"Lysandra, have you felt the change in water temperature?" The magnetic communication buzzed through Lysandra's ferrous lobe, immediately translated to neural impulses and transmitted to her brain.

"Yes. Another year has passed. This is our eighth migration, I believe." Ceolbur's massive cetacean-like shape emerged into view through the water refraction and suspended particulates. *What a handsome alien whale thing*, thought Lysandra. *No wonder I love you.*

"It's funny," replied Ceolbur, "that I can never seem to recall what came before our first migration. Perhaps we are only eight years old."

"How can that be?" responded Lysandra. She barrel-rolled slowly, exposing her belly to the surface so it would absorb the warm sun. Now upside down, she continued. "We were this size eight years ago, so how could we have been born then? And I have no memory of parents. In fact, there are no other whales like us. We have never met anyone like us in these eight years. Where is everyone else?"

"Questions that have plagued me these many years as well," said Ceolbur. "It doesn't quite make sense, does it?"

The meta-level realization on Ceolbur's part triggered an exit condition and the next thing Lysandra knew, she was no longer a strange alien whale floating in the ocean. She found herself suddenly corporealized in her home with her original memories intact, but now with the retention of eight years of experience as one of the native whales of Ailuros, the planet on which she and Ceolbur resided much of the time. There was no particular discombobulation in this change of scenery. If she could remember what sleeping and dreaming had felt like a million years ago, she would realize her emergence felt much the same as awakening from sleep but with higher fidelity memory retention of the dream state. The critical difference was that until the moment she awakened in her house, she had possessed no sleeping body. The extent of her physicality had been a brain, a massive network of interconnected nodes, a veritable jumble of gallium, germanium, gold, silicon, argon—even a little carbon here and there. The corporealization upon ending the virtuality had granted her a newly formed body and here she stood.

The room was diffused with red afternoon light as the transparent ceiling far above permitted the sun, the star Zareasman, free entry. Crimson rays, containing billowing dust eddies, projected from smaller side windows diagonally to the floor. Chairs, tables, the architecture itself, were all the same golden wood as the exterior ribs that supported the house and separated the ascendent windows facing the cliff.

She felt the rock floor beneath her bare feet. It was cold and hard, but neither sensation had a negative sentiment to her. Her body was not one blindly evolved, naturally selected to impose physical discomforts—and pains—on an organism in order to motivate avoidance behaviors regarding potentially damaging stimuli, such as surfaces whose temperature might impart dangerous heat loss if one were to recklessly stand in one place for several days. But she could feel the coldness and the hardness nonetheless. And that gave her joy in fact, the mere physicality of the sensation, the knowing of its presence, the verisimilitude of the experience—the sheer intimacy of being in direct contact, not only with the floor, but with the entire planet. She laughed lightly as she recalled the first time she bent her perspective by performing a headstand and then reframing her perception of her circumstances as not of being upside down, but rather of being rightside up and holding the entire planet above herself on her tiny frame.

"Lost in thought?" she heard. Ceolbur had similarly corporealized elsewhere in the house and now entered the room. He walked through a dusty red sunbeam and approached her.

"A bit, yes."

"So, that was a new one," said Ceolbur. "I've never been one of the Ailurosian whales before."

"Just think of the number of species in the galaxy," said Lysandra. "Think of all those forms, all those ways of being, the niches filled, the existences felt. Think not only of the species, but of the individuals. How many animal minds are there in the galaxy, thinking and feeling at this very moment? Doesn't it practically bring you to tears to even contemplate such a notion?"

"So not just the humans and the de novos then?" Ceolbur asked.

"No, not just humans and the beings we created once we understood the mechanisms of the brain. I'm referring to every conscious mind out there, waiting to be found. Can you imagine the amount of sheer experience being felt everywhere, even as we stand here?"

"It is a daunting notion, no doubt," responded Ceolbur. "I'm reminded of the creatures on Henothras, with a strong collective and interconnected capacity, all sensing and feeling one another. We could tap into and experience their way of being. I found that sensation...alluring. Nothing else has quite repeated that sensation for me." They paused a moment. "Sooo, we were whales for eight years."

"Virtual whales to be clear," said Lysandra. "It's not like we were out there." She gestured imprecisely toward the vertically slatted window, outside of which they could see the rocky bluff, the cliff's edge, and the forest stretching across the untamed landscape to their distant mountain.

"My point is," responded Ceolbur, "eight years. Let's take the afternoon to get our senses about us and then—"

"—then," interrupted Lysandra, "we are overdue for some experimentation. Although we blocked our memories while in whale-space so that we could internalize the adventure, some deeper regions of my brain appear to have been processing other ideas the entire time—subconsciously it would seem. I find myself newly awakened with wild network configurations I never thought of before, but which I now want to try."

"You were intrigued by the magnetic communication, weren't you?"

Lysandra responded, "I think that's what did it, yes! Of course, we've had the connectome of the Ailurosian whales for thousands of years now, so it's no surprise that when we emulated those networks and attached them to our brains, we were able to tap into a semblance of the whales' magnetic communication."

"To be fair," Ceolbur said, "we've been able to create magnetic qualia for ages now."

"Yes, but subtle variations in the associated networks yield corresponding variations in the experiences. That was the first time we felt how the whales of this planet communicate."

"Sort of," said Ceolbur. "As I reflect on the experience, I'm not sure I felt entirely like a whale. In retrospect, it turns out we were communicating in a fashion rather typical of ourselves. I mean, it's not like any of the actual whales out there—" this time it was Ceolbur who waved toward the window, even though there wasn't an ocean view at all, "were having the sorts of conversations we were having."

"That is a strange realization, isn't it," responded Lysandra. "It would be difficult to retain the memories after awakening if we couldn't somehow tie those memories into our framework of understanding and language."

"That's the tricky part, isn't it?" said Ceolbur. "But for now, I'm going to reach out to some people. I'm sure everyone has been wondering when we would emerge. Remember, it's been eight years. And then we'll see where we left off last time."

"Agreed," Lysandra declared with finality.

Lysandra found her way to the garden between the house and the cliff before Ceolbur returned. She waited patiently for Ceolbur to make his appearance. Behind her, the wooden beams and narrow vertical windows of the house rose high above her. Surrounding her, she absorbed the surreal floweresque organisms and low shrubs growing out of the rock. Ahead of her, the cliff plummeted out of sight. Beyond it she could see the forest at a fantastic distance below, spread across the gaping valley, stretching to the horizon, where the grand distant mountain rose up with conical elegance, its upper half pink with red-sun tinted snow.

Ceolbur came outside and joined her at the view.

"Ailuros is pleasantly similar to Earth," Ceolbur said. "Not identical, but similar."

"True," said Lysandra, "although my memory is foggy at such a stretch, even though our brains have been fortified for so long at this point. Since memory retrieval is an active process in which the experience of the memory is intermingled with our current state of mind, the sensation of a memory therefore changes over time even though our fortified brains preserve the underlying data better than our former biological selves—and for some reason the changing is always a loss of fidelity, isn't it? Memories fade. I guess that's because we become increasingly distant from the person we were when the memory was formed."

Ceolbur nodded. "A valid concern. It's incredible we have designed memory circuits that so vastly outperform our original biological capabilities. Retaining million-year-old memories would be impossible the old biological way. Fortified brains do a much better job. But you're right, they still aren't perfect."

Lysandra sighed. "Still, I wish my earlier memories had been better preserved. I've lost a lot from then." She became pensive.

"You're thinking of him now, aren't you?" Ceolbur said.

"Anytime I start thinking about those first decades of my life I always think of him," Lysandra said. "That was before anyone had fortified. The process didn't even exist yet. Those biological memories are the worst preserved of all, not only because they are the oldest, but because their organic neural circuits were less precise than our later constructed brain architectures. It all feels so dim. I remember almost nothing about him except that he was there. It makes me envy de novos."

Ceolbur considered this a moment. "Their brains are better at high fidelity data preservation," he said. "Not so hung up on human structures, they are. Modeled heavily on human brains of course, but not impeded by any aspects of the evolved design that could otherwise be improved upon."

"We couldn't do the same for ourselves," said Lysandra, "because we would have lost too much of who we are in the process of such alterations. But the de novos are created from whole cloth. They have no biological history to try to preserve so they can start fresh."

"Still, they're mostly human." Ceolbur chuckled. "In all the ways that matter. They were designed on human brains, and fortified humans were augmented with many of the advances de novo designs offered. At this point, it's almost impossible to tell us apart, except that as you said, they tend to have slightly more precise memories." He squinted in thought momentarily. "Anyway, it's okay that you miss him, even after such a stretch of time. I understand your feelings on the matter."

"Really?" said Lysandra. "Because the full depth of it often escapes me, and then I really think about it and it lands on me like a mountain. The scale of what happened."

"He didn't make it to the Great Fortification," Ceolbur said.

"Look at that view," said Lysandra. "I have been watching sunrises on planets scattered across the galaxy for a million years...and he missed it by twenty years."

"Human bodies didn't last long back then," Ceolbur said. "Heck, they still wouldn't. That's why we use these bodies instead." He triumphantly beat his chest with his fist a few times. Lysandra smiled awkwardly and painfully. "I'm sorry," he said.

"You weren't there," she said. "You don't know how different it was."

"True, I came along after the development of fortification. I wasn't even born on Earth."

"Twenty years," Lysandra said. "He could have seen all of this, all the planets, the whole cosmos. He could've experienced all the states of consciousness we've discovered, learned of all the alien life scattered across the galaxy, learned of the few extragalactic communicating species we've heard from over the long years...all but for a twenty year gap. The loss is just unimaginable. He would have loved this view."

They gazed off over the cliff for a mutually silent moment which became longer than original humans would have tolerated, but which felt perfectly comfortable to their ancient selves.

Ceolbur finally said, "I know that's a painful memory. But let's go find a new network. Ready for another session?"

"Yes," Lysandra responded with conviction. "Let's find something new today."

"Who's first?" asked Ceolbur.

"If you have to ask, you lose. I'm first." Lysandra laughed and settled into one of two reclined neural interfacing chairs that rapidly grew up from the ground at a mental invocation. It subtly conformed to her contours while her very body responded by conforming to the chair. The two objects, chair and body, briefly interplayed like colliding waves and then settled into a stable state in which it was no longer clear where each ended and the other began. All Lysandra needed for the upcoming activity was her mind, so this merging of perfect comfort would eliminate any potentially distracting body-to-chair misalignments. Ceolbur joined her in the other chair.

"Let's pull up configuration 5299-585-19993-57," said Lysandra. In both of their minds, the layout of a vast network of interconnected components became apparent, partially as a visual representation but to a significant extent as a direct cognitive comprehension of the network's structure, an *understanding* of the network, raw *knowledge* of the topic at hand, not just a picture of it.

"I want to take another look at region 298," said Lysandra. The total neural configuration they were considering consisted of billions of neurons interconnected in various ways, but it wasn't homogenous. There were regions of higher connectivity and there were broad highways of connections between the regions, all essentially brain-like in its structure. Some of the regions would inherently fire with greater gusto than others. Some generated cortical waves at certain frequencies while others resonated at other frequencies. These waves would propagate between the regions, and in some cases over the entirety of the configuration, in complex ways. In many cases, the firing patterns of the neurons within the new configuration were strongly responsive to signals coming back from the brain, not just generative and pumping signals into the brain. In this way, when connected to Lysandra's brain, the module would no longer be an external object, but would essentially become part of her.

"Bringing it up now," said Ceolbur, and that region expanded, both visually and conceptually, to fill their respective attention.

Lysandra continued, "I'm going to play with the parameters a moment. Hold on." She proceeded to prod the billions of variables in front of her, altering both the topological properties of the network—the connectivity between the neurons—and their functional properties—how the neurons and synapses would behave and respond to one another. This went on for a while, with Ceolbur distracting himself by scrutinizing a different region of the same configuration.

"Okay," Lysandra eventually said. "Let's give it a shot." She relaxed her intentionality, letting Ceolbur take over.

"I'm establishing the connection now," said Ceolbur, "but I'll leave it disabled until it's fully integrated." It was Ceolbur's turn to work earnestly for a while as he guided the almost countless afferents and efferents of the configuration to their respective attachments on Lysandra's brain. As Ceolbur did this work in the abstract space of his thoughts, a very physical set of corresponding actions took place between Lysandra's chair and the back of her skull.

"Okay, we're all hooked up," said Ceolbur. "Ready?"

Lysandra squinted with thought. "Let me recall the quale of the previous experiment with this network. It felt...grand somehow. It felt, ummm, influential. That's why I wanted to alter it a bit and try again. I think there's something here."

"Now who's trying to describe qualia linguistically?" teased Ceolbur. "I thought that was against your rules."

"Fine fine, just do the damn thing already if all you're going to do is give me a hard time about it." Lysandra chuckled intentionally to make sure Ceolbur hadn't misunderstood her tone. At a thought from Ceolbur, the module came to life, frothing with activity, and instantly flooded Lysandra with action potentials, signals, patterns, waves.

And then came the sensation, the feeling, the raw unadulterated conscious experience of something immense.

"WHOA!" Lysandra's declaration was immediate and pronounced. Ceolbur instinctively disabled the module completely. "No no. Bring it back!" But Ceolbur hesitated. *Bring it back right now!* declared Lysandra.

"Ummm, okay. Let me bring it up slowly, if I can." This request made Ceolbur nervous. Lysandra was too carefree about this sort of thing. And it wasn't always obvious how to turn a neural module on to a diminished degree since any activity within the network was likely to rapidly propagate, self-reinforce, and refill the network's implicit firing patterns to their natural attractor state, but there were options. Ceolbur attempted to revitalize just a few regions of the network. They hummed back to life and Ceolbur could see a visual representation of their activity warming back up. Lysandra murmured incomprehensibly in response. The network rapidly resettled into its former state however, as Ceolbur expected, with complex patterns of activity sweeping over its surface and right through its volume. Ceolbur could see the bridge between the module and Lysandra, and could see that the bridge was flooded in both directions as the module seemed to take hold of Lysandra. Ceolbur watched nervously as information surged back and forth.

"Lysandra? How are you doing?" Lysandra didn't respond. Ceolbur hesitated, unsure what to do. "I'm going to turn it off again."

"No," declared Lysandra adamantly. Then she just quietly repeated herself. "No." Ceolbur checked Lysandra's vitals, which didn't consist so much of bodily functions as of long-established bounds on safe brain activity. As far as Ceolbur could tell, Lysandra was fine. There was no seizure-like cascade, no breakdown in synaptic or neural habituation. The action potential profiles of individual neurons, as well as large conglomerations of neurons, all appeared well within norms. Admittedly, various neural activity levels appeared to be pushed to the limit—notably what might have once been called gamma waves, but no longer in her postbiological design—implying that Lysandra was deeply engaged with some profound sensation, but everything was in healthy ranges. She was simply overcome with whatever experience she was having. Ceolbur waited.

"Ceolbur," came Lysandra's voice, as if from far away. "You have *got* to try this."

"You ready to disconnect?"

She hesitated, not wanting to answer, but eventually she relented. "For now...I suppose." At a moment's action on Ceolbur's part the module disengaged, not only in power but in connection. Although Lysandra's body remained melded to the chair, the interface with her skull was closed off. Lysandra lay there for a long moment, and then eventually rose from the chair, which peeled away from her as she did so. She stared off the high cliff toward the mountain, centering her thoughts. She loved the height, she had always loved standing right on the edge of the precipice, feeling the verticality just beyond her toes. The mountain in the distance felt like it was reaching toward her this time, like it had always known what she just learned for the first time—a rather curious quale she realized in the moment, the feeling of the mountain conversing with her. She watched the mountain for a while.

"You really have to try that, Ceolbur."

Ceolbur was up next. He watched as Lysandra returned to her chair and they traded roles. The module they were testing resided in an emulation being run by the computational substrate interwoven between the chairs, the house, the house's deeper infrastructure, and ultimately the invisibly thin, fibrous mycelial computing network that pervaded the planet's outer crust. To say *where* the emulation was being processed in such a pervasive computing system was a bit of a misnomer, and not something to which anyone gave much attention.

He settled in, expecting something profound given what he had just witnessed. The module interfaced to his brain in a similar fashion to its prior connection to Lysandra. Lysandra then took over the role of enabling or disabling the connection, starting or stopping the module's interior processing, mediating or even halting its propagation to and from Ceolbur's brain.

"This is more your adventure than mine," said Ceolbur. "I'm more interested in collective cognition and unified minds, not expanded qualia."

"There's plenty of time for that," said Lysandra, missing the earnest nature of Ceolbur's statement. "Here we go," she said. Ceolbur closed his eyes apprehensively. When Lysandra flipped the figurative switch, Ceolbur's expression instantly changed to raw astonishment. Ceolbur physically tightened as an overwhelming sensation of emotion swept over him. An out-of-body oddness rippled through his parietal region—usually perfectly synchronized to either a virtual or a corporealized body. Then a tidal wave of enormous awe crushed him like a physical weight. Ceolbur felt the awareness of time, of universal space, of the ancientness of it all, looming over him. He felt his minuscule size in the unending cosmicness of everything. But it wasn't an elated feeling. He felt the darkness, the universe spreading, thinning, cooling—dying. He felt consciousness withering away as one civilization after another faded out. Whole galaxies slowly went dark before his awareness as their energy ran down to zero. Infinitudes of minds, feeling their existence, feeling it slipping away from them, feeling their stars chilling, frigid interstellar space descending to true zero. Slow, inescapable death everywhere. Then, he felt the moment of finality. The last conscious being in the entire cosmos, certainly not from their galaxy at all, just some alien being in a far off galaxy, someone humanity would never meet or even know the existence of. But whoever that last person—alien—was, *wherever* that last person was, Ceolbur felt that last light of consciousness go out, felt the universe's capacity to *experience itself* sizzle away. This was the greatest existential challenge of humanity. Its quandary and its unease spread from one edge of civilization to the other. In a population of near-immortals, this question was the preeminent challenge of the era—and utterly vexing.

Ceolbur could make no reaction as this transpired. He was paralyzed by the sensation. But eventually he spoke.

"Okay then," he said, but then paused a while longer as if he didn't really have a complete thought ready. "So, ummm, what we have here is some sort of powerful EOUSP quale." He pronounced it in the universally common vernacular.

"Yes," responded Lysandra. She disconnected the module and Ceolbur steadily sat up. Lysandra did the same and they faced each other.

"Not just the usual quale of realizing the EOUSP though," continued Ceolbur. "We already had that, after all."

"No," Lysandra replied, mirroring her own recent experience and therefore truly *knowing* Ceolbur's experience. "No, it doesn't feel the same as our current comprehension of the mere fact of the EOUSP, or even our current knowing of the angst it already inspires. This goes beyond that somehow."

"Agreed. You have found something different Lysandra."

"We did it together."

"You found the network. It's yours."

"What are we going to do with this, Ceolbur?" Ceolbur was still in an emotional torpor, coming down from the intensity he had just ridden. But he offered a brief reply.

"I don't know Lysandra. I don't know what to do with this."

5

SATORI RETURNED TO RIHON'S CONTEMPLATING OBLIVION A FEW TIMES BUT eventually decided it was time to go home, an entirely different stellar system. It was time to reunify with his branchling, his psychological sibling in effect, with whom he shared a recent psychological ancestor before they branched during his transmission to Icarion to see Rihon's creation.

But first, he had just received an unexpected invitation to a party of sorts, hosted by Rihon, and so he found himself standing before a building fronted with a row of smooth black columns, each with a curled base and capital. The stone was slick with a subdued dark blue tint that came through under the dwindling sun. He ascended several steps to the landing and passed through a large doorway into a high-ceilinged foyer. A few people were in this first room.

"Welcome," one person said as he entered.

"Hello. I'm Satori. I received an invitation from Rihon?" he intoned questioningly, unsure of the circumstances.

"Yes yes, no need for such formality here. Come on in. Welcome." Satori nodded and wandered farther in, finding the building to be full of individual rooms, each splendidly furnished and offering endless comforts, entertainments, games, food and drink. As he peered into the various rooms, he glimpsed people in small groups engaged in conversation, game play, or artistic activities. One such group was rendering statues and sculptures from materials that appeared and disappeared out of thin air as per people's intentions, all while a sizable audience observed and expressed approval.

He explored deeper into the maze of hallways and entered one room in which people were, again, conversing in separate groups. They sounded like scientists, artists, philosophers, tinkerers—Rihon's sort of crowd.

His attention picked a group at random. "The evolutionary dynamics of that world are quite unheard of. Each of the major taxa appears to evolve into the other groups in an endless cycle. It's quite strange."

Satori turned to another group. "Remember when they called virtualities simulations? It was a derogatory term at the time."

"You mean a million years ago?" someone responded. "That terminology died out during the Great Fortification. Reality is whatever collides with your senses, inspires your perceptions, and gives rise to your conscious experiences. No one doubts that now."

"Oh they're still around," another person in the group responded. "Ardent in their belief that a mind operationalized noncorporeally by a virtuality lacks consciousness. They think the rest of us are constantly popping back and forth, conscious when operationalizing on brain orbs, and then some unspecified emptiness when operationalizing in virtualities."

Someone responded. "Nope, they aren't gone. They just haven't made it very far into the galaxy yet. Since they won't leave the cozy confines of their brain orbs they refuse to travel by beamed transit."

"Right," said another person with as scoff. "They insist on traveling by—" she snickered "—spaceship." She literally snorted at the outmoded reference, followed by the rest of the group. "Consequently, they're still trapped within a couple hundred light years of Earth, positively crawling their way between the stars."

"Leaving the rest of the galaxy to us," said the first speaker again. "They will never discover any place not already populated by us millennia in advance. It's sad, really."

"Ah, except," someone interjected, "for the true frontier explorers, steadfastly pushing transit infrastructure ever farther across the galaxy so the rest of us can zip out there at the speed of light. *To the frontier!*" Everyone cheered and drank to the toast.

Satori was about to turn to another group when a new speaker with a strong presence spoke up, bringing everyone else to attention. "Look, we're all operationalizing from brain orbs right now, right? Physical. Neural hardware, clearly conscious. But we were in one of Icarion's virtualities earlier, right? So standing here, now, we can consciously remember our experiences from that prior noncorporeal form. We can remember the events, the sensations, even the emotions—we remember the *conscious experience* of it, yes? So if we weren't conscious during that time, owing to some purported failure of the virtuality to invoke consciousness, then what are we remembering now as we reflect on that earlier circumstance? If we remember being conscious, the most logical conclusion is that we *were* conscious. Otherwise, what are we remembering?!" Murmurs of agreement burbled through the group.

Another group's sudden energy caught Satori's attention. "Yes yes, we all know he's crazy, but he's still the greatest artist of the last 200,000 years. *Are they talking about Rihon?* he wondered.

"Well, he's no Rihon, that's for sure," someone responded. "And nowhere near as crazy either." The entire group laughed.

He turned to the last group in the room. "Politics of the Center be damned. We're Ailuros! We can govern ourselves however we damn please. We're 9000 light years from the Center for Earth's sake! Who cares about Central politics out here?"

"Hello. Welcome," said someone who suddenly glanced in Satori's general direction.

He half uttered the response, "Thank you, I'm Satori," just as another person spoke over him loudly.

"Rihon!" The famous artist followed Satori in, then navigated around Satori, who had stopped near the entryway. Rihon made no pretense of stopping awkwardly however, instead strolling around Satori and coming up short in the center of room, as if undecided which conversation would be graced with his approach.

"Hello," Rihon said.

"Contemplating Oblivion is a masterpiece," said another person, as much to the room in general as to Rihon. Huzzahs of agreement rippled through the room's inhabitants.

"Thank you Nyris," he replied. "The reception has been mostly positive. Obviously, it has upset many people, but that's the point of course."

"Of course," said the same woman, Nyris. "What's the point of art that doesn't piss off at least a few people?"

The various conversations briefly dwindled and merged into this new room-pervading discussion. Another person spoke. "Is there interest in duplicating it elsewhere? I can think of several worlds it would be well received on."

Satori watched all attention turn to Rihon, who in turn scanned the room, permeating everyone's attention with his charisma. "The current installation will certainly be left in place for a good long while. Luminith can power the triad installed on Seraphi for longer than any of us have been alive, provided no one decides they need the moon for another project. Part of the reason I chose it is that it is a rather dull moon. I'm hoping no one will want to repurpose it for a while."

"Join us, both of you," said the person who had initially welcomed Satori. Satori walked up beside Rihon, who nodded to him stoically.

"Yes, but I still think you should recreate it elsewhere," the same person continued. "In fact, why shouldn't there be a Contemplating Oblivion installation in every star system of the galaxy? Everyone should be able to experience it without the tedium of interstellar travel."

"It would take 50,000 years to install it everywhere," Rihon protested. "Even if I branched to do it, I just don't think I would want to. My role was done as soon as I breathed it into existence. I leave it to others to spread its message."

"You said you're Satori?" said someone off to the left side of the room.

"Yes." Satori glanced around. The room was dim and warmly lit. The walls were of a nondescript soft texture, neither natural nor artificial, just a shave on the green side of gray. The ceiling was similarly toned, but without the soft texture, rather, hard and with a sheen.

"*The* Satori, who wrote the rhetorics on multi-dimensional memory formation?"

Satori grinned at the recognition. "Yeah, that was me. You liked it?"

"Some of it." The room laughed.

"Don't listen to her," said someone else, "I loved it. Your theory that memories include shadows of the collapsed dimensions beyond the primary three was fascinating. To think that memories might be ten-dimensional is rather astounding. Have you taken the theory much further since you last wrote on the topic?"

"Ah, um, no. Not yet, as yet. That was an early speculation. I haven't fleshed it out much, I admit. I'm afraid I moved on to other topics and never circled back to it."

"Well," said someone, "I hope you finish it. I want to know what lurks in the hidden dimensions of my memories."

"Thank you, I need to do that, I suppose." A little more of this banter led the room to return to its smattering of isolated groups talking in muted—and occasionally more energized—tones. Satori and Rihon had not yet fully integrated into any one group yet, still standing near the center.

"I remember meeting you," Rihon whispered, without taking his eyes off the room.

"Sorry, what?"

"We met once before—it was a while back, I believe—and then I spotted you at the grand opening recently."

"Oh! I didn't think you noticed me. It was such a large crowd."

"I did. Although it's a bit unfair. I'm de novo, did you know that?"

"I...I'm not sure if I had heard that before actually."

"So naturally," continued Rihon, "my brain, closely modeled as it is on our shared human progenitors, has some convenient advantages. Mine constantly scans everyone I encounter and stashes their semblance away for future reference. The vast majority of those people I never encounter again of course, anonymous strangers lost in a cosmos of faces. But if I ever have reason to connect semantic associations to someone, I can recall them perfectly at a later time. So even in that busy crowd, with its thousands of faces, yours immediately stood out to me, like a flame among dead coals, and my associations with you—your rhetorics, your mild fame, shall we say—were all instantly available to me, if I wished to attend to them."

"And why didn't you...attend to them? Why didn't you say something if you recognized me?"

Rihon chuckled. "I was a little busy with the speech I was about to give and then with the needs of running the event, shuffling all those people to the opposite side of Seraphi and back."

"Of course," said Satori. "I wouldn't have presumed."

"Psh! You *should* presume. Your audience is larger than you realize."

"Thank you."

"Work on your presentation, your style, your...grandiosity. Your message will be better received if you hone that skill."

"I have a message?"

"I've read your rhetorics. You definitely have a message. Your thoughts on the nature of mind and consciousness are not to be taken lightly."

They stood there and observed the hum of conversation filling the room momentarily. "Come on," said Rihon. "Let's talk." Rihon waved to the others, who acknowledged his exit, and he then turned on his heel and walked out, clearly expecting Satori to follow.

"I've consumed all your rhetorics," Rihon repeated. "I enjoyed your thoughts on the relation between conscious moments and conscious durations, and the relation between consciousness as a state and as a process."

"You have? How so?"

" 'There is no such thing as a conscious moment'," Rihon quoted in a jocular and stiff tone. " 'Consciousness is neither noun nor does it exist within an instant'," he continued to quote, " 'but rather it is a verb. One does not *have* consciousness, nor *is* one conscious, but rather one consciousates'." Here Rihon winced as he spoke. "I don't like that word, consciousate. I would have chosen consciate, or perhaps conscify. Consciousate is unwieldy in my opinion."

"A reasonable point," said Satori. Rihon was leading them on a meandering tour of the halls and rooms on offer, dropping in on various guests as they went.

As they walked here and there, chatting rapidly and with little direction, Rihon continued the previous topic. "I think you should focus less on the temporal aspect and more on the quality of it," he said. "The feeling of it."

Satori considered this momentarily. "Both fascinate me," he responded. "That we can utterly stop and restart consciousness is fascinating. That doing so has no effect on the person, in either inner psychology or outer affect, or the abstraction of identity for that matter, is equally fascinating.

"People once disagreed about that," remarked Rihon. "Before the first people fortified their brains, replacing the biological construction with hardier material, many felt that personal identity depended on a ceaseless neurological and conscious process, that if a brain temporarily halted neural function and then later resumed, the circumstances were that the prior person had died and a new person had emerged and replaced them. But even then, they knew that wasn't the correct interpretation, if they were properly informed that is."

"Yes, I quite agree," said Satori.

"Their medicine, even in that ancient and simple time," continued Rihon, "could revive a patient who had suffered hypothermia, stunting all spike propagation. And they routinely did so on purpose as well, lowering a medical patient's temperature to such a degree that all neurological processes and associated consciousness ceased. And they didn't regard such medical patients as new people upon later revival. There was so much confusion back then."

"Well, that problem solved itself," said Satori. "We all understand that these issues are unimportant now because everyone who felt differently about it self-selected themselves out of the population during the Great Fortification. People who feared it would kill them, or replace them with other people, whatever that meant, chose not to fortify their brains during that era, and so they vanished within a few scant decades as the fragile biological beings they were. Everyone who passed through that—philosophical filter, shall we call it—went on to build the next great human civilization and ultimately populate the galaxy."

"Hmmm," said Rihon pensively. "A philosophical filter. I like that."

They wandered off and found their way into an intimate chamber where six people had arranged themselves into a circle, with each person holding one hand in front of them fully palming a luminously busy sphere resting on a pedestal. The sphere swam and shivered with bright patterns of light that seemed to pool around the points of contact with each hand.

"A high bandwidth network," observed Satori. "I'm not too familiar with it, but each person has generated a thick axon bundle down their arm and exposed it against their palm, putting them into direct neural contact with one another."

"Quite," said Rihon.

"I wonder what sort of shared experience they're engaged in," Satori said.

Rihon scoffed. "Definitely sex. Practically nothing requires a direct physical network connection like that. But it can improve some aspects of sentiment alignment."

"Ah. Yes, that makes sense. I wonder why they didn't just make contact through the floor, through the planetary data network."

"Privacy, I would presume. The central sphere is isolated from the Icarion network embedded in the ground." They observed for a moment. Then, without warning, he blurted out to the room's inhabitants, rather bombastically, "Thanks for inviting me!" in a teasing tone. Three people opened their eyes languidly and glanced over at him. Upon recognizing him, they gained a more energy.

"Rihon. Join us!" one said, smiling and laughing at Rihon's absurd behavior.

"Bring your friend too."

"You wish!" Rihon replied. "I'll come back later." The three dismissed his response and promptly returned to their inner activity.

Rihon laughed and they left to find other surprises. "I also enjoyed your take on the temporality of consciousness. It is both temporal and also outside of time, temporal in that it occurs as a result of spike propagation, and network activity in general, but also atemporal in that it feels like a thing, an object almost, even if it isn't. As I quoted from your own rhetoric a moment ago, many of us recognize that consciousness is a process, but it still *feels* like a thing."

"Ah, the quale of consciousness itself. The ultimate meta-quale" said Satori thoughtfully. "It feels like a thing." He chuckled. "Perhaps the subject of your next creation?"

"I have my hands full dealing with this Deimos fellow at the moment. Have you heard about him?"

Satori shook his head. "Only in passing. A politician or public figure who is prominent in the Center. I haven't been that close to Earth in ages."

Rihon responded, "Apparently he has objected to the EOUSP for thousands of years."

Satori frowned. "Objected to the notion of it? The question of it?"

"He objects to trying to solve it. Quite vehemently. He has become a thorn in my side, I must say."

"Because of Contemplating Oblivion."

"Yes. Although I would say the piece is intended primarily to emphasize and invite contemplation about the raw angst of the EOUSP, not to necessarily prescribe a solution. But he has chosen to interpret it as a calling for greater investigation into the EOUSP's solution, if there is one. And now he's upset about it."

"I didn't take that from the piece."

"Thank you. I wanted it to be more abstract than such an overt call to action, but he has chosen to see it that way nonetheless."

"And now he's protesting it? How much trouble can he cause going around squawking about the cultural event of the century?"

"That's kind of you to say," said Rihon. "I'm too humble to see it that way myself."

At this comment, Satori visibly chuckled. "I saw your opening speech at the gala, remember. I'm not sure humility is your strongest suit."

"I suppose I get energized by the crowd. Apparently, Deimos can be quite troublesome. He has the ear of people who wield significant societal influence. He may yet prevail in steering public perception against Contemplating Oblivion enough to get the piece removed."

"That would be a shame. I felt that it showed something new about the EOUSP. It is an ancient problem, one that you were able to look at it a new way, and show to others, a badly needed shift in our perspective."

"Thank you." They wandered on again. "I hope you stay a while. The evening's festivities will continue for days, possibly weeks. It's hard to tell with these folks."

"I will explore. Thank you. But don't let me keep you. You seem to be the center of attention."

"Oh me? Nah...okay, well perhaps. You should barge into one of these rooms and start preaching your rhetorics. That will get you some attention."

"Hmmm...I'm consider it."

"Find your message Satori. Then go forth and spread it."

6

MINERVA GLIMPSED THROUGH THE FOREST, if that was the right word to describe it. The taxonomy of life on Caelunis didn't conform to conventional groupings like flora and fauna. Practically no species were fixed in place. Everything lumbered or oozed or rolled or hopped around to varying degrees, regardless of scale. So that gave all life on Caelunis a more animalistic feel. But the better represented kingdoms had nothing resembling a nervous system or a signal processing and associative learning organ, a brain in effect, so that made such Caelunisian branches of life feel more plantish. Caelunis required its own taxonomy.

As she stared off through the forest, the largest organisms were the most prominent feature, many stories tall, competing for high altitude winds to power their fin-like appendages, or perhaps reaching above the dead air below the canopy of their neighbors. These huge organisms had three trunks, or legs, wider than a person was tall. These trunks did not attach to the ground and so were not plant-like, but also did not lift from the ground and so were not leg-like either. They continuously slid along the ground, much slower than a person could walk, but persistent and covering considerable ground in a given day. Many smaller species resided on the same branch of Caelunisian life: three-trunked, wind-powered lifeforms that steadily skated across the landscape in similar fashion, but far below the towering monsters.

Minerva had determined via her investigations that this well-represented kingdom couldn't stay in one place because, in addition to relying on wind for movement, individuals continuously slurped nutrients up from the soil through their feet—as it were—and rapidly depleted the point of contact beneath their trunk-legs. The smaller species on this branch of life moved faster, about as fast as Minerva's comfortable stroll, but given that they lacked anything resembling conventional sense organs—to say nothing of lacking a brain with which any senses might be processed— they endlessly impacted other things in their path, such as boulders but just as often the larger trunks of the larger species! In this way, the smaller species steadily ricocheted haphazardly around the forest, heading off in random directions after an impact. As far as Minerva could tell, this seemingly inefficient behavior hadn't been weeded out by evolution because the very randomization that struck her as initially inefficient had the benefit of sending the creatures careening over fresh soil with fresh nutrients. As to how the largest species, towering over her like buildings, employed any such directional strategy, she hadn't figured that out yet.

As she marveled pleasantly at the scene before her, she felt a message come through in her head. "We're heading back with new samples." Minerva worked alone, but she had deployed a large team of insentient de novos that helped her efficiently comb through Caelunis's biology. They helped her collect samples, scrutinize biochemical structures, study physiological macrostructures, and patiently observe in-the-field behavior—this last area of study being the most interesting part since it was the only remaining source of novelty and surprise in the physical universe.

"Thanks for letting me know," she mentally responded. "I'll meet you at camp." She returned a short distance through wet undergrowth and over soft ground—much of the equatorial region was boggish—to a building she had grown while she was studying the local ecosystem. Only other de novo assistants were there. She was quite alone, one of the only people to take an interest in the planet as she steadily classified and studied the life of Caelunis, as she had done for a few hundred years at this point. A few colleagues scattered around the planet provided the bulk of her social interactions.

Soon after she returned, various de novos arrived. Their bodies varied wildly from one to the next since they were designed for specific purposes of investigation. Some had powerful visual and auditory acuity. Some had fractal, filamental appendages that could feel a surface with molecular precision, and even chemically taste the molecular composition of a surface by direct contact. Some were fairly large and accommodated imaging apparatuses that could look inside and through alien organisms. Some had vast, complex chemical laboratories incorporated into their bodies so they could analyze specimens on site in the forest. And a few had inner compartments for collecting samples to bring back to the laboratory where Minerva waited, like the one that had just informed her that it was returning with a new sample.

When it stilted through the doorway on its thin legs, she greeted it politely. It seemed almost proud of its discovery, but she knew it lacked the neurological and psychological apparatus for such feelings. It stood before here, waiting patiently for her to act.

"We have almost solved Caelunis," she said to the de novo. "But you appear to have found something new."

"Yes," it replied. "Nearly solved. Almost all lifeforms and interactions have been documented at this point, but we appear to have overlooked this one."

The day will come, she had thought many times and thought again now, as she scrutinized the de novo with its gathered sample, *when we will have categorized the last life form on the last planet of the galaxy.*

"This appears to be a new species," said the little de novo. The de novo stood a few feet tall on spindly legs for easily traversing the dense forest understory. Its body incorporated a transparent vessel that was currently completely sealed closed and contained some sort of organism inside it. Minerva looked closely.

"Are you sure it doesn't need to breathe the atmosphere? You have completely sealed it off."

"I have solved its environmental interactions. It makes no use of the atmosphere, although of course it depends on a narrow range of indigenous atmospheric pressure and temperature."

"Ok, thank you," Minerva said. "I don't recognize it. I don't think I've seen one of these before." She looked more closely. It wasn't much to look at, a radially symmetric body consisting of twelve soft spokes, almost indiscernibly grouped into four triplets, and several concentric rings connecting the spokes, so it looked slightly like a loose-mesh net. It was orange with yellow spots and had a soft texture, as if its entire body might be fluidly maneuverable. She watched as it gently explored its compartment without urgency, moving either on its radial tips, as if on twelve feet, or suddenly hopping by full flexion from one side of the compartment to the other.

"Honestly," Minerva continued, talking to herself as much as to the de novo, "I'm not sure I've seen anything particularly closely resembling it on the entire planet. I think this is a new major branch of life on Caelunis. Nicely done." The de novo gave no reaction, as it was carefully crafted to lack the sort of consciousness that would call into question the ethics of confining it to a vocation it might otherwise have chosen against.

"Let's do a full scan," she said. The de novo transferred the organism from its own containment vessel to a machine in the laboratory, which then proceeded to generate a full structural scan. Minerva mentally accessed the data as it became available and watched intently.

"Definite signs of a nervous system, this one," she mumbled as she studied the scan results. "The nerves appear to be auditory, or pressure-based in some fashion. That's rather nifty. Look at how this works," she said to no one in particular, as she had developed the habit of anthropomorphizing her de novos as a self-talk device. "Nerve signals from the extremities are passed along the nerves as pressure pulses in the liquid medium inside the nerves. I suppose that might transmit signals fast enough to enable moderate reaction times. It looks like the pressure signals are then transduced into electrical impulses in the central nervous system. That'll let it think quite a bit faster of course." She continued to watch the data coming in. "Oooh, I see, no need for rapid escape behaviors and therefore no need for a faster peripheral nervous system. This thing is utterly poisonous to the other indigenous life on Caelunis. This potassium-bismuth molecule in the outer membrane is devastating to the cell wall structure of other lifeforms. No wonder it gets by with this odd fluid-pressure nervous system. How does it not poison itself?...Oh, yes of course, that makes sense now." She continued to observe the data as the scan built an increasingly comprehensive overview of the organism's physiology and function.

"Oh wow! It has a little brain," she exclaimed with glee. "Can you think?...Oh, I see. You can't think can, you? Do you see this?" Minerva actively gestured in the air as if to point out a feature to the de novo, but of course there was nothing to see since she was merely experiencing the scan data in her own mind. Her instinctive arm gesture confused the de novo, who immediately became bored and wandered away. Minerva ignored it and continued talking to herself. "See? It doesn't have a brain after all. It has multiple neural ganglia, but no central brain, so it probably doesn't think in the normal sense, unless it's a sort of collective creature with multiple independently thinking ganglia. But they seem too tightly integrated to be independent. And yet I don't see a central brain either. Perhaps you don't have much consciousness after all," she sighed, rather disappointed.

She continued to study the data, steadily building up a comprehensive understanding of everything pertaining to the organism's fundamental functions: its molecular and chemical processes. There were two areas left untouched by this sort of scan. She learned nothing about how the organism lived in its ecological niche. How did it interact with other species? What did it actually *do*? That would require prolonged observational field studies.

The other thing she could not ascertain in the lab was what sorts of metaphysical abstractions might associate with its neural firing patterns. That is to say, she could model the nervous system and see signals passing around its neural network, but she could never comprehend the qualia—if any—that this organism experienced. Even if it couldn't think very deeply, as she had concluded, it still might have conscious experiences of some sort. She would briefly need assistance for that step, the next step.

Rassianel corporealized on the transmit station in Minerva's lab later that day, arriving from the far side of Caelunis.

"Thanks for coming," said Minerva.

"No problem. This sounds like a fairly straightforward neural configuration investigation. I'm glad to help you out."

"Did you branch?" asked Minerva, asking if Rassianel had left a waking version of himself at his research lab in the opposite planetary hemisphere.

"No, this seemed like a fairly short trip. I presume I'll be home in a few hours. I saw no need to branch for that."

"I just need your help integrating this new...do you call them animals on this planet? I don't. At any rate, this one has neural signatures, so I think calling it an animal is acceptable."

Rassianel said, "You want to try to integrate the brain of a Caelunisian organism with your own? That has never worked on Caelunis. I've tried with several species myself."

"It's worth a shot," Minerva responded. "I've been studying its connectome and its processing functions. As you point out, it's one of the most alien nervous systems we've encountered, but it's still a nervous system, and it is electrical—well, for the most part."

"We've found other organisms here," said Rassianel, "with what seemed like compatible nervous systems, but the signals have never integrated with our own neural functions." At a thought from Minerva, two reclined neural interfacing chairs grew up out of the floor.

"You're safely etched?" Rassianel asked, inquiring whether Minerva's brain pattern was recorded elsewhere.

"Yes. Even if this thing kills me, I'll lose an hour at most. People used to lose more time than that every night of their entire lives. Can you believe that?"

"Frankly, no." Rassianel said. "It is truly unbelievable that humans wasted such a high proportion of their terrifyingly short lives deliberately unconscious, and quite happily so at that. May I see this discovery?" Minerva nodded toward a tank in the lab and Rassianel approached it for a closer look.

"I've never seen one of these before. It reminds me of..." he trailed off.

"Genetically," said Minerva, "it's related to Vertipodae, but I think it's on a parallel branch, not a descendant."

"Not some sort of Shulobionta?" Rassianel asked.

"Not based on its genome. Weird, huh?" Minerva sat in one of the chairs and it immediately softened at her touch and then melded with her body. Rassianel did the same in the other chair.

"Everything look good?" Minerva asked. Rassianel worked with the control interface that had emerged in his mind when he sat down. He checked Minerva's neurological health, then checked the emulated model of the organism's scanned brain that now resided in the computational systems incorporated into the laboratory.

"The scan is clean, the emulation appears operational. Have you given any thought as to how you want to integrate it?"

"Let's try region F-54-B first," she said, indicating a particular area within her brain to which to connect the alien's emulated brain. Rassianel established neural connections between the emulation of the organism's brain-like organ, notably distributed multi-ganglia-style throughout its body, and structurally similar regions of Minerva's brain, to the extent that such similarities could be found, in the hope of invoking a related sensation instead of a complete failure of alignment.

"It should be ready to go," Rassianel said.

"Let 'er rip!" said Minerva with a laugh, which then became a nervous laugh. Rassianel invoked the emulation to turn on, in effect. It immediately began consuming signals from Minerva's brain while simultaneously emitting signals back to her brain, along with a complex arrangement of recurrent processing within the emulation. Minerva settled into the sensation. After a moment, she spoke again.

"That...is peculiar," she said. It is definitely integrating. It's working."

"Yes," Rassianel said. "I can see that the organism's signals appear to be compatible with your own."

"I think there's more here," said Minerva. "Let's see. Can you disconnect it from that region and put it," she began indicating visual and pictorial cues to Rassianel as if their thoughts resided in a shared workspace, "here and here," she continued. Rassianel made the adjustment. Minerva's reaction was immediate.

"Yeah, that's...profound," she said. "Increase the connection density at H3 and decrease it at N7." More changes from Rassianel. "Woooow," she said.

"What are you getting?"

"Ummm, hold on." Minerva soaked up the sensation.

"Are you attenuating the interface?"

"Yes, of course. We have to do this safely."

"Remove the attenuation please. I need a stronger signal."

"I'm not going to merely rely on the fact that you're etched," Rassianel responded. "That's for emergencies only. The goal here isn't to put you in danger."

"Fair enough, but please dial the attenuation back. I need more to figure out what's here." Rassianel tenuously permitted the emulated module to transmit signals to Minerva's brain with greater intensity. Minerva was silent for a while.

"You okay? Your vitals seem a little heightened, but mostly acceptable."

"I'm okay. Rassianel, this quale...it feels like the EOUSP."

"Seriously? That's fascinating."

"Yes, fascinating indeed. I don't believe I've ever encountered a natural EOUSP quale before. Have you?"

Rassianel replied, "In all the research, everywhere in the galaxy, I'm not aware of any naturally evolved organism whose connectome inspires a EOUSP quale when integrating into the human brain. We concluded long ago that it takes a human level of comprehension and theorizing and imagination, and, well, just bare intelligence frankly, to feel any emotional impact from the eventual death of the universe. No simpler organism would ever care about that sort of thing. It can't even comprehend the idea."

"Agreed, but there's something here. There isn't any clarity to it though, no structure. It just feels like the EOUSP. It isn't remotely specific though."

"Does it merely feel the same as the quale of pondering the EOUSP?"

"No, and it doesn't feel like the awe or the dread of it either."

"Well it can't feel like elation! The EOUSP is a horrible conundrum."

"No," Minerva responded. "It feels like something different. Something...something different. Can you alter the resonance modes? I think the module's cortical waves aren't perfectly synchronized with my own."

"Ah, I see that now. My apologies for not catching that sooner." Rassianel manipulated the controls some more.

"OK!" declared Minerva. "Now we're really getting somewhere."

"Increased clarity?"

"No, just increased intensity. It's really powerful. It really evokes a EOUSP quale. Something...deep, something...cosmological."

"What is a cosmological quale?" asked Rassianel.

"Think of what it feels like to deeply internalize the scope of the universe."

"Like gazing up at the night sky?"

"Now combine that with a realization of the universe's expansion, its ceaseless, irresistible spreading out, thinning, dimming, cooling. Everything slowing down. The helplessness of everything getting farther apart, and weaker, and deader."

"Yeah, I know what the EOUSP is. Thanks already. The question is what quale are you getting from this network that is any way different from a standard EOUSP sensation?"

"It's different. I'm telling you, it's different. That's qualia for you, I can't find any words for it. It indicates...oh wow! I found the words. It indicates *hope*! That's what it feels like. This quale feels like...hope. It feels like believing in a solution to the EOUSP."

"Don't be ridiculous Minerva."

"I'm not saying the quale says there actually is a solution. In fact, it invokes a strange discordance in that respect. I'm saying it feels like what believing in a solution would feel like, while simultaneously not preventing me from continuing to feel that a true solution is rationally impossible, just as it has seemed for the last million years. This is absolutely incredible."

"But it doesn't have any utility. You aren't saying we can do anything practical with it, are you?"

"No, I suppose not, although it could be use in a palliative way for existential dread I suppose." Minerva chuckled, then promptly stopped as she realized that what she had just suggested might actually have tremendous therapeutic value.

"You know what we need to do next?" she said.

"What?"

"Test it on a second subject. You'll do nicely."

"Hey!"

7

“T HANK YOU FOR COMING TONIGHT,” said Satori as a small group of people materialized into virtual existence near him.

“Oh thank you,” one of them replied. “I’ve been consuming your rhetorics for a long time. I’m curious to hear what you have to say about the recent discovery.” Satori nodded kindly but then noticed others materializing as well.

“Lovely meeting space,” said the new arrival, looking around and admiring the vista.

“Thank you,” said Satori. They stood on an expansive circular area of flattened bare red earth, shaped into a shallow cone, like an amphitheater with a central stage. It was large enough to accommodate a few hundred guests, enough for the expected gathering. If more than anticipated arrived, Satori could easily expand the space at a moment’s notice. Although the amphitheater was cleared to make space for the visitors, there were dense trees carpeted across the landscape beyond the perimeter. A broad sky with a similarly red tint stretched overhead, with two crescent moons high above one horizon and a third gibbous moon low above the opposite horizon. Below the two crescent moons, an orange sun descended slowly toward distant mountains, providing optimal illumination. The temperature was optimal. The humidity was optimal.

As people appeared, Satori briefly greeted them and then moved on. People mingled, waiting. Eventually Satori decided it was an adequate showing and he moved to the center of the circle. As he spoke, he eloquently walked around, facing all directions periodically, indicating that there was no front or back to the amphitheater.

"Welcome my friends," said Satori. His voice reached the farthest parts of the amphitheater, initially with the same architectural precision that had enabled bare-voiced Greeks to echo throughout ancient stone amphitheaters, but further facilitated by virtualized augmentation wherever necessary.

"First, thank you for accommodating my antiquated method of speech. I could speak directly into your minds in this place of course, but this," he opened his arms indicating both the physicality of the space and his own outmoded style of public speaking, "is perhaps more encompassing of the group dynamic, I think. If you were to hear my voice in your head, or even just my thoughts manifesting in your mind, you would not hear me as a group—a family, I hope, soon. So, I will speak like this, and you will hear me all together. And together, we will explore the possibilities of the Caelunisian Neuralium.

"Word reached our inner worlds here in the Center quite recently, concerning the discovery of this marvelous creature, and I do use the word creature on purpose. It is not just an animal, or an organism. The Neuralium is a *creature*", he enunciated, "for it was surely created. Created for us!" The audience mumbled and nodded in agreement.

"The Neuralium is a gift from god. We all know it...we all *know it!*" More agreement from the crowd. "The EOUSP has plagued us since before many of us existed. Now I admit, I didn't actually spend my long life consumed with the EOUSP." Satori paced around the small circular area in the center of the amphitheater, glancing at various attendees, engaging with them charismatically. "I have spent my life pursuing the other great mystery of existence: our minds. I always assumed someone else would solve the conundrum of the EOUSP before I would, but now I'm not so sure. Many have worn the Neuralium's configuration at this point, but only I have shaped that experience into a conversation with the divine. Who here has worn the Neuralium network?" Satori declared with curiosity. Many hands went up. "And who HAS NOT?!" he yelled with excitement, roiling up the crowd. Many more hands went up, along with cheering, and the energy steadfastly rose.

"Well, you're all leaving here with that experience tonight," he said. "I have led a few sessions at this point, but you all here, tonight, are still amongst the first to experience the Neuralium in my prescribed fashion." He opened his arms expansively, indicating the current space. "But, my method of use is not so cavalier as you may have seen elsewhere since the Neuralium's arrival on our shores. It is a hallowed gift. It is a CREATURE created as our greatest gift in a million years! It is not a trifle, nor a recreation." The last word positively dribbled out of Satori's mouth with contempt. "It is not frivolous. The Neuralium. IS. HOLY! Through the Neuralium we gain not just a vision of our personal ending, but a vision of the great ending, the ending of all things, the ending of everything. No, we get something more profound than that. We get a vision of ourselves outlasting... withstanding." This last statement started a stir among the crowd. Satori sensed it but before he could speak, he was interrupted.

"I've heard it does no such thing," said someone sitting in the middle, neither fervently close to the center, nor reservedly far back. "I've heard it reveals nothing but despair, and yet, I hear everyone is excited by it anyway. I wish to try it, and I am curious about your approach, which is why I haven't tried it up until now, but I didn't come here expecting any real answers. Do you believe it offers a way out?" Satori nodded understandingly, and paced patiently back and forth. He smiled knowingly, with the bottomless confidence of having refined his religious message. Gone were his earlier apprehensions when deliberating his options with Rihon. God had shown him his path in the form of the Neuralium and he had embraced it.

"The Neuralium will show you no answers, my friend. "Nothing of the sort. But it shines a light on the problem posed by the EOUSP, the challenge of all creation. It shines it so brightly, so piercingly, that you come through the other side understanding another way to survive.

"You're not suggesting anything so quaint as extra-physical phenomena, are you?" groaned another person. "You aren't going to start talking about miracles, are you?"

"No no," said Satori with a congenial chuckle. "God works through the tangible media of creation. No one has suggested otherwise since time immemorial." He waved to new people still appearing and taking seats. "I'm so glad to have newcomers here tonight. The word must be spread. The Neuralium's gift, meant for us, no accident that it is, must be spread. And no, I am not suggesting that the Neuralium shows us an extra-physical path. I am saying that such a path already exists within each of us. Our pain has lasted so long over this last remaining unknown, and I will show you how the Neuralium can light another path, one too dark to have been seen before." He paused for intentional effect. "Who's ready?!" he declared joyously. The crowd hollered its collective excitement.

"Okay, he said, is there anyone who does not have access to the Neuralium already? It is available through this space, if anyone hasn't accessed it yet." The crowd underwent a moment of mild disarray as people explored the interfaces and external modules available to their brains, wherever those brains resided elsewhere on the planet. Many had their own modules, physical, alongside their brain orbs. And the rest took up Satori's offer to attach to the various emulations of the Neuralium's network available through the virtuality.

"This is a guided voyage," said Satori. "Within this place," he gestured again to the general surroundings, "I will take charge of our individual connections. But while we each have own module, I will synchronize the interfacing process for everyone as a group. We will voyage together."

"Everyone settled in?" he said, as he attempted to concentrate on moderating several hundred separate interfaces simultaneously. "It can be an intense experience but I will be guiding us through it together. Ok everybody, let's have a conversation with god, shall we? Here we go," he said softly and reassuringly.

8

DEIMOS STRODE CONFIDENTLY INTO THE CHAMBER, all eyes turning toward him as he arrived. The room was enormous, loosely elliptical in floor plan, surrounded by ornate curved walls, fluted and ribbed, with half columns spaced evenly around, supporting an absurdly high ceiling, capped with a dome. Vivid light illuminated the room, but without piercing sources. Rather, light glowed heavily off the round ceiling, like a sky. Deimos strutted down a central aisle and joined a few hundred others at a large elliptical table, annular in shape, with most of its interior area cut away, revealing a wide open space. He didn't sit immediately. Behind the table on all sides, the rest of the room provided seating for thousands of spectators, mostly filled to capacity already. More crucially however, nearly invisible from view, the room was perfused with millions of imperceptibly small vision sensors embedded in the walls and suspended in the air throughout the volume. These sensors triangulated the scene, building a moment to moment model with a precision near that of the wavelengths of light the sensors detected, and integrated the scene through data networks in the walls, then the floor, then the very ground itself, and ultimately into the planet-spanning filamental data network. In this way, a near-perfect recreation of the scene played out in the planet's largest virtuality, extending the audience beyond the few thousand attending in person, to whatever portion of the planet's 250 billion inhabitants cared to observe. Such a carrying capacity would have been uncomfortable if everyone corporealized at the same time, but the vast majority of the population lived in the spacious virtual offerings at any given moment.

"Fashionably late as always, I see," said the assembly moderator, a regal woman seated at the center of the longer curve of the elliptical annulus forming the table. Deimos smiled, looking around the room, waving to the crowd.

"I was speaking at another event," he replied, grinning. Several people at the table rolled their eyes, but across the planet, billions laughed along with Deimos. He took his seat.

"Well, now that we can start," said the moderator, "today's session has a fairly routine agenda, I believe. First up, there is the matter of the new solar array. Ghuleraie, would you like to present it?"

"Thank you," said another person at the table. As he spoke, anyone sitting far away in the large chamber—or just sitting far away at the large central table for that matter—could bring the speaker into central focus by narrowing their visual focal length at will. Distance wasn't much of a barrier. He continued. "The new virtuality is growing rapidly, as are its energy requirements. A new orbital solar power array has been arranged for its power needs. The next—"

"We have more pressing matters to address," Deimos declared.

The moderator attempted to speak. "Deimos, it's not—"

"That's right," said Deimos. "We must take seriously the threat from research on the planet of Caelunis."

"Deimos, we will get to that."

"No, said Deimos, this is a more pressing matter." A sizable minority of the audience filling out the room cheered their support, while a smattering of the dignitaries at the table also nodded stoically. The moderator looked around in frustration.

"We have an agenda for this meeting, and the subject you wish to address was added to that agenda, at your specific request I might add."

"Excellent, let's discuss it now, in that case." Deimos stood again, having barely sat down.

The moderator spoke harshly. "You have been granted a seat at this table due to your having garnered the necessary votes of support, but you are a new member of this council and I advise you to learn its protocols and procedures."

"In fact," said Deimos, "I have garnered a plurality of the vote, have I not?" Many people sitting at the table vocally grumbled at this pronouncement, while at the same time, a small but raucous group within the room erupted in support.

The moderator almost visibly rested her forehead in her palm, but stopped short at the last moment. "A plurality doesn't mean very much here Deimos. This assembly is extremely diverse. We represent over 300 stellar systems of the Center, with several trillion individuals. Your plurality, as you remind us, is modest at best. We will get to your issue today, I promise."

"More support than anyone else sitting here, you say," said Deimos. "Thank you for conceding the point. Tell you what?" he said casually, "I would like to make a motion right here and now that we rearrange the agenda to put the Caelunis emergency at the top of the schedule."

"There is no emergency," said someone else.

"Only I can call for a vote to amend the agenda," said the moderator.

Deimos just smiled. "So do it." The moderator looked around the room, and at the attendees at the table, and realized it would cause more trouble not to call for the vote. For fear of looking oppressive, she conceded.

"Fine. The motion is to move the Caelunis issue, item 28-3-85-2, to the top of the agenda. Would anyone like to second the motion?—*Not you*, Deimos. You requested it. As I said, you need to honor protocol. You can't second your own motion for Earth's sake."

"Second the motion," said a small chorus sitting at the table. The moderator sighed.

"All in favor?" she said, practically deflated. The vote was tallied mentally and immediately available to everyone present. The moderator hesitated as the tally materialized in her mind, along with everyone else's. "Ummm, okay," she said, "That was a bit unexpected, but the motion has passed. Deimos, the floor is yours, I guess, but try to keep it brief, would you? Your usual bluster is unnecessary in these chambers. We're all here to get work done."

Deimos literally hopped up and slid over the table to the central area inside the annulus, and then proceeded to parade around in the enclosed area while he spoke.

"Deimos!" declared the moderator, but he ignored her.

"To summarize," he began, "Word has recently arrived from some dreary planet called Caelunis in the Lueur system, a fairly remote and uninteresting locale if I may say so. There in the wild lands, a rather eccentric researcher appears to have found an organism that, when consumed as some sort of drug—"

"That's not remotely accurate," objected someone at the table, but Deimos simply continued talking.

"As if there could be anything less important than the intellectual obsessions of a reclusive scientist concerning the goings on of some weird creature from an alien swamp—"

"Forest," the same person interjected.

"thousands of light years away," Deimos finished. He snickered and his minor support within the audience laughed along with him.

"If a few weirdos want to hide in the middle of nowhere and poke and prod squishy alien bugs, I don't really care," said Deimos. Laughs rippled through a few audience members, who were shushed by those around them in annoyance. "But we have now learned of this Neuralium bug, which I maintain is a completely unimportant pursuit when our needs at home require urgent consideration."

"Like the new solar array?" said the person Deimos had forcefully supplanted at the beginning of the meeting.

"Precisely, my socially concerned associate!" declared Deimos. "While, what's her name, one Minerva I believe," he drizzled the name, garnering another curl of chuckles from scattered audience members, "is out there playing with her laboratory and other toys, we have real work to do here.

"But my friends, it is far more serious than that. This bug has been determined by this Minerva and her jolly band of scientists—"

"I believe she works alone," someone said.

"Even worse!" said Deimos. "Who is overseeing this work? Who is approving it? Who is ensuring it is conducted properly, or should be conducted at all?! As I was saying, this bug's brain gives people an experience of the EOUSP!" This was not a surprise to anyone, as the news of Minerva's research had recently pervaded the Center's numerous stellar systems but the significance of the discovery was positively gravitational and the room reacted with a certain verve to Deimos's restating it out loud. "This is not good news, I say! No, not at all. This is serious. These scientists out there are playing with powers that could affect us all."

"You have been voicing your concerns about the EOUSP for hundreds of thousands of years Deimos," said someone new at the table. "Why don't you just leave it alone already?" Deimos's demeanor became increasingly severe, decreasingly jovial. He walked around in tight circles inside the interior space of the large annular table, clearly agitated.

"This issue cannot be left alone," he said. "It has long been theorized that if any solution were ever found to the EOUSP, it would destabilize the entire universe!" Several people at the table and throughout the audience—

and across the planet—vocally groaned their annoyance, but simultaneously a few others roared their support.

"Enough!" declared the moderator, not to Deimos but to the crowd. "This assembly will not be interrupted in this manner."

Deimos continued. "As theorized, our universe is but one in an infinite cycle: A singularity spawns the unfurling of a universe. The universe evolves and then it dies. From its ashes, a new singularity forms. And on and on." He paused for effect. "BUT, each universe must be born anew! Granted its own fresh start, its own *self-determination*! It shall not—must not—be contaminated with the detritus of the prior universe! Nothing can be permitted to survive to the next. It would be sacrilege."

"Your theory borders on myth," said someone at the table. "Dare I say you almost sound religious. Perhaps you should trade notes with this recent prophet, Satori." A large swathe of the room laughed out loud.

Deimos continued. "Even if you disregard the intrinsic moral argument of granting each subsequent universe its own separation from all that came before, there is another argument, even more serious in fact."

"We know your theory, Deimos," said the moderator. "But that's what it is. A theory."

Deimos talked on. "If an act of survival, be it of matter, energy, or information, should bleed off the whole from one universe to the next, then it diminishes the constant energy of the entire system," said Deimos. "The next universe will be that much smaller, weaker. Over time, over *incomprehensible* time, each universe begetting the next, the whole system will run down as individuals from each universe hold themselves off to the side to survive its demise. Each universe will dwindle relative to its prior, and then one day, it will simply end. The end of everything. An end infinitely more horrific than the EOUSP or the end of our meager single universe. No, the end of all things!

"And I will say one last thing. We don't know how much energy it takes to start another universe. It might *require* the current balance. It is possible the universal cycle can only initiate with the totality of energy available. Which means there won't even be a long fading out of universes getting smaller. Instead our selfish attempt to survive the end of our universe could trigger an immediate collapse of the system. The very next universe might fail to spark. The whole thing could simply end, just like that!"

The room paused for a brief moment.

"Your theories are already known, Deimos," said the moderator, "and I can see it causes you great consternation—"

"Don't you dare patronize me," Deimos hissed.

"Your theories lie outside the closure of physics, so long ago solved now," continued the moderator. "There are things we can know, and there are things we cannot know. We have the model of our reality, our physics, our world. What you are speculating on is questions that cannot be established by empirical methods. What you have, Deimos, is your faith. And the rest of humanity should not be subjected to your beliefs. There are other models of the universe's placement within some greater system, and there are yet other models by which it is an invalid phrasing to even contemplate an otherness with respect to the universe. You preferred cyclic universe theory, and the related energy dissipation theory, is but one on offer. There are many others."

"We can't take the chance," said Deimos. "This researcher out there on Caelunis is playing games with the future of existence itself. Do you all hear me on this?!" His supporters in the background hollered, and those at the table, few as they were, nodded and vocalized their support.

The moderator sighed. "We have several more issues to discuss today."

"We haven't voted on a course of action yet," said Deimos.

"That will require far more than the plurality it took to get you a seat at this table, which I'll point out you seem rather averse to actually sit at. Would you please return to your seat?!" she said with startling seniority. Even Deimos was somewhat rocked backward by her tone. In an attempt to succeed in his next move, he chose to rejoin the formality of the assembly and returned to his seat.

"I request a vote," he said. "As described in the agenda item, I request that this assembly formally reprimand the Caelunis scientists, especially this Minerva character who seems to be spearheading the investigation."

"It's too late," protested someone at the table. "She has published the entire Neuralium connectome. What would you have us do, even if we agreed with you, which the vast majority of us do not?"

"There is time yet to salvage this disaster," replied Deimos. "My understanding is that this bug's brain merely imposes on a wearer a vague hope of a solution, but offers no particular insight. We may have gotten lucky here. If we declare—and enforce—a prohibition of related research to prevent it from advancing any further, we can yet prevail and save the entire universe from these murderous miscreants."

"Objection!" declared someone at the table. "Characterizing this honest researcher, who has shared her research openly, without a hint of deception or ill intent, as a murderer, is open slander, and likely to inspire radical vigilantism."

"Agreed," said the moderator. "Deimos, you will moderate your tone in this chamber." She sighed. "I will call for the vote," she continued, "but I remind you that even if passed, this would be a mere formality. Caelunis is not entirely remote, but not near the Center either, at 14,000 light years away. No action we take here will have any consequence out there, neither in practical terms, due to the distance, nor in terms of actual political force for the simple reason that we don't operate that way. The Center has no jurisdiction over the entirety of the galaxy. It takes thousands, even tens of thousands of years to convey instructions—I won't even dignify your request with the phrasing of conveying 'orders'—to remote stellar systems. They are free to govern themselves as they see fit. No one has ever conceived of a better way to structure a galactic society. The concept doesn't even make sense Deimos! That said, I call for a vote. All those in favor of issuing an advisory statement—"

"—A reprimand of the current research and a formal prohibition of further research," corrected Deimos.

"That is, admittedly, how you phrased your agenda item when you wrote it. All those in favor issuing a..." the moderator sighed, "This is highly irregular. A reprimand against this Minerva and a prohibition against continued investigation into EOUSP-related neural configurations, please issue your votes now."

Votes rolled in and were tallied, again in a direct mental accumulation available to all simultaneously. The room was silent for a moment as everyone absorbed the result.

"The vote has failed to pass Deimos," said the moderator. "I won't speculate on everyone else's reasons, but as I said, this assembly lacks both the formal authority and the practical means, at a delay of 14,000 years, to do anything like what you have requested.

"Okay, moving on. Item two on the agenda folks," the moderator chuckled lightly, "the solar power array for the new virtuality. Shall we?"

9

LYSANDRA READ AND REREAD THE ANNOUNCEMENT A FEW TIMES TO MAKE sure she believed it. A mere 145 years after she and Ceolbur had discovered a network configuration that evoked the EOUSP quale, a cosmic blink of time, something new had been discovered pertaining to the same subject matter.

"Ceolbur, have you seen this?" She reached out through Ailuros's planet-infusing, fibrous data network. Neither of them was corporealized at the moment and although their brain orbs sat directly next to one another, buried in the bunker deep within the bedrock below the cliff on which their home resided, they were experientially and socially farther apart than voyagers on opposite sides of the galaxy. Lysandra had been in a virtual world of one sort and Ceolbur had been in an entirely different world, a completely different existence. They may as well have resided in two different universes.

Ceolbur responded from far off reality. "Have I seen what?"

"Some bioresearcher named Minerva has discovered an organism on Caelunis—never heard of that planet, I admit—whose connectome, when scanned, emulated, and incorporated, sparks a EOUSP quale! Some life form she has named a Caelunisian Vertipodae Neuralium."

"Really? Show me." Their abstraction of existence then extended beyond mere interplay of words as Lysandra directly shared the report in a shared mental space. Ceolbur consumed its content rapidly, also taking note of a large data block included with the report.

"They've provided the entire connectome with the report," said Ceolbur.

"Yes, anyone can replicate this organism now," said Lysandra. "Doubtlessly, people all over this part of the galaxy are experimenting with it already. We have to see what this is like immediately."

"Agreed," Ceolbur responded, "I'll join you soon."

"I'll wait—impatiently! Don't take too long."

When Ceolbur eventually corporealized in their house, Lysandra was anxiously studying the connectome.

"I've been trying to understand the integration while I wait for you," she said. This Minerva, never heard of her, seems to suggest interfacing the Neuralium in some pretty complicated ways. I'm not sure how she came up with it."

"Intuition," said Ceolbur.

"I don't believe in intuition. I believe in method. She found these particular interfaces between the module and the brain somehow."

"Intuition," teased Ceolbur with a smile. "We can ask how she came up with it later." They went to their preferred surroundings, outside, under a resplendent sky dome.

"What held you up?" Lysandra asked somewhat listlessly.

"Well, actually, I was getting to know some people who experiment with merging of minds. I've always found the topic interesting."

"Like you and I do?" asked Lysandra.

"No, nothing sensual. Well, actually, perhaps. I'm not sure, but not *necessarily* that." He squinted at his own realized uncertainty. "It's more about joining together in cognitive and creative aspects, forming a cohesive thinking system."

"Ah. Interesting. I didn't know you were interested in that. You'll have to show me sometime."

They relaxed into their neural interfacing chairs, becoming inseparable, somewhat indistinguishable even, from the furniture—which itself aesthetically grew from the garden's ground as if it belonged there. Lysandra tried to relax, tried to slow down. The integration would go more smoothly that way. But she was too excited. Ceolbur took her hand.

"You're practically buzzing, Lysandra."

"Right. Thanks." She concentrated on the feel of his hand in hers and settled down a little. She breathed and counted for a moment.

"Okay," she said, "first thing's first, let's emulate the connectome." She proceeded to unpack the enormous data block included with the report. There were billions of neurons involved, each one described by a complicated array of parameters that governed its distinct action potential processing function. Then, there were many more synapses than neurons, trillions, each carefully parameterized with various excitatory and inhibitory behaviors, modulating and mediating behaviors, habituation behaviors. There were uptake inhibitors and reuptake inhibitors, and reuptake inhibitor inhibitors!

None of this data was represented in physiological terms of course: molecules, proteins, hormones. The chemical traits had been abstracted away, leaving behind pure mathematical functions of signal-propagating cause-and-effect. That was where consciousness and qualia lay, in the interplay of information flowing through itself in myriad ways.

The data block also included descriptions of the broader environment in which the network operated. In the organism's biological domain, these features consisted of biochemical agents that would bathe, permeate, and then alter the firing behavior of the neurons or the propagation behavior of the synapses, but again, that had all been abstracted away by the information-theoretic brain emulation. This process had been solved a million years ago. Ancient obsessions over some elan vital of biochemistry had been washed away by the recognition that these chemical agents and interactions were simply altering how neurons fired action potentials between one another. It all came down to the sputtering, twitching, vibrating, transmission of signals within networks.

"How could we have ever come up with this crazy design?" said Lysandra as she looked over the topological properties of the organism's brain, the particular ways in which its neurons were connected and grouped together.

Why did a particular signal propagation have a particular *feel*? Why was red red and pain painful? Why was any given experience the result of an associated network topology and firing behavior? "In the space of all possible neural configurations," continued Lysandra, "how could we have ever stumbled across this dizzying arrangement? No wonder it had to evolve on an alien planet thousands of light years from humanity's origin before we could find it."

"You've never found a way to design qualia," said Ceolbur as sensitively as possible, knowing it was a sore point.

"No one has," responded Lysandra. "The sheer size of this search space! Look how many neurons are involved in just this one region," she said.

"A daunting vexation," Ceolbur replied. "It's quite obvious," he continued, "now seeing this network configuration, that it would have taken forever to trip across it in a nearly flat search space. With no steady slope to follow up toward this peak it is essentially a random sampling process to find and test various configurations. No wonder we never found it before."

"You know what, though," said Lysandra. "I can see how it relates to our previous discovery. See these regions here? These neurons have a connection topology similar to our previous network. This network isn't just another EOUSP network. It's in the same class as our prior network. They're related somehow!"

"Well that makes sense," said Ceolbur. "That's why they evoke comparable experiences. Both give similar perceptions, the EOUSP in some fashion."

"Yeah, I suppose that makes sense," muttered Lysandra as she continued to study the data in front of her.

She had trailed off. "So," said Ceolbur, "we may as well try it."

Lysandra considered their options. "Before we attempt to integrate it with our previous module, let's simply see what Minerva has found. Let's try this network, alone, first, to see what she discovered on Caelunis. Then we can try combining it with our network next."

"Sounds good to me," said Ceolbur. They proceeded to build and test the emulation based on the report, feeding test stimuli to various afferents of the network and observing how the module reacted. When they were convinced the emulation was operating correctly, they were ready.

"Ceolbur, I always do these things first. You should do this one first."

"We aren't testing a new design this time," he responded. "Minerva and her colleagues on Caelunis vetted this network ages ago. By now, it has reached thousands of worlds."

"Okay. And?"

"Well," he continued, "we don't need one of us to oversee its usage by the other, so why don't we try it together?"

"Awe, a wonderful idea," declared Lysandra. "Let's do that." They were already situated in the interfacing chairs, so all they had to do was duplicate the emulation so they would each have a separate module, and then connect the emulations to their chairs, their skulls, their brains—their minds.

"All settled in?" asked Lysandra, as a giggle of excitement washed over her.

"See you on the inside," said Ceolbur. Lysandra opened the connection to the Neuralium emulation and was almost immediately bowled over by its evoked quale, not only of the EOUSP but of a strange sensation of hope, or as Minerva as phrased it in the report, a quale of 'the feeling of believing in the existence of a solution, even while any truth of a solution remains likely totally irrational and unrealistic.' She sat with the sensation for a while, wordless, almost breathless.

"Are you getting this Ceolbur?" she said with quiet awe.

"Yes," he responded, equally affected. After a pause, he continued. "It's a remarkable sensation. I can see why it has sparked so much interest." They sat in their chairs under the bare sky, soaking up the quale for a while, but they both realized the obvious implication.

"Enough of this," said Lysandra. "Let's combine it with our previous network."

Night had descended over Lysandra and Ceolbur's longitude of Ailuros by the time they regrouped from a break. With little distraction left to delay them, they headed outside. Roofs were for the needy, namely those in need of a roof. And they didn't. The open sky was far more enriching.

They settled into their neural interfacing chairs and stared momentarily at the night sky above them.

"You get unusually quiet when you stare at the stars, Ceolbur."

"I suppose I was mildly lost in the moment," he replied peacefully.

"Well, I'm considering various ways to combine our previous network with the Neuralium," said Lysandra. "There are some curious similarities and I think I can align those regions pretty easily, but some of it doesn't combine so easily. Can you look for a way to combine region 88-75-25 of our network with 724-81 of the Neuralium?" Ceolbur nodded and got to work on the task while Lysandra continued working on a different part.

"Remember," said Lysandra, "the goal isn't to produce two separate modules that are simultaneously integrated with a human brain. The goal is to unify our previous network with the Neuralium's so as to produce a single new network, a merger of the two."

"Right," said Ceolbur as he concentrated on the work, eager to help Lysandra with her life's passion. This went on for a while, with each of them attempting to combine their assigned subnetworks. Eventually, they were ready.

"Okay," said Ceolbur, "let's see how it goes. You're first." Ceolbur pulled up the controls for assisting and overseeing Lysandra's connection while Lysandra readied herself to wear the new network. She found herself helpless to a certain giddiness however. How might this differ? The previous network gave a visceral sense of the EOUSP itself, like never before experienced, and the Neuralium gave a strangely ameliorating sense of hope, albeit with no practical indication that such hope was justified. What would the combination do?

"Send me in," said Lysandra. Ceolbur steadily dialed up the module's propagation power, but as often occurred with neural configurations, he was frustrated to watch as the module's internal networking rapidly rose to an internally consistent level of activity, an attractor in the space of firing patterns. Lysandra soon found herself subjected to the full onslaught of the network's processing, its computation, and ultimately its ethereal metaphysical abstractions. But Ceolbur didn't hear any vocal expression, just a change in Lysandra's artificial respiration, an ancient and now pointless instinct, merely included in body forms for its sensations and associated experiences. Lysandra was clearly in a heightened state. Ceolbur watched her vitals and waited.

"Ceolbur," came the soft voice of Lysandra in some strange daze.

"You doing all right or do I need to wipe your memory again?" He was only half-joking.

"Ceolbur, there's a solution."

"You don't mean..." He trailed off.

"This quale. It reveals that there's a solution."

"What?! Doesn't the Neuralium already do that?"

"No. The Neuralium grants a hope for a solution, but it doesn't clarify that there actually is one. This quale is different. I now know there is actually a solution." It took Ceolbur a fraction of a moment to fully understand the impact of Lysandra's statement. In that moment, his brain, both human and extended, sputtered trillions of action potentials. Those neural spikes congealed into millions of mathematical computations, hundreds of cognitive thoughts, tens of perceptions and remembrances and psychological states—and one conscious realization. The EOUSP had a solution.

He was incredulous however. "Sorry to sound doubtful, but are you sure?"

"I am absolutely certain. I simply know it. I can feel the truth of it."

Ceolbur scoffed at the incompleteness of her statement. "So? What's the solution already?" Lysandra didn't respond, clearly lost in thought. "Why are you holding back the greatest discovery ever made? For Earth's sake Lysandra, what's the solution to the EOUSP?"

She eventually responded. "I don't know."

10

"THE MESSAGE STOPPED TRANSMITTING," said Kaimea with pained disappointment.

"The recent extragalactic communication?" said Quinlan, a colleague elsewhere on Nyveron. "It stopped completely?"

"Totally gone. We've achieved partial success decoding the message. Would you like to join me to work on it one more time?"

"Of course."

A little later, Kaimea and Quinlan convened in Kaimea's preferred workspace for such studies. They were standing on an infinite, perfectly flat, almost glass-like surface. Around them, floating in the air, there were countless visualizations and representations of pieces and sections and segments of the alien message. Analyses of one sort hovered over here, and of another sort over there. At a thought's notice, they could directly access any of these various analyses and cognitively comprehend them more directly than by visual portrayal, bringing the semantic connections and meanings to the forefront of their attention. But as they shifted their attention between various components of the analysis, they could *hang* the other pieces in space around them in this manner, for rapid retrieval whenever connections revealed themselves.

"To think, this is only the twelfth communicating species we have ever discovered," Quinlan said, as they stared helplessly at the data in various abstractions, conversions, interpretations.

"And to think," responded Kaimea, "that we've never had so much as a single back and forth with any of them. We've only been at this for a million years. The nearest communications were received soon after the Exodus and came from four million light years away. Our responses, which we sent a million years ago, won't reach them for another three million years."

"It *is* an odd activity to engage in, to be sure," said Quinlan. "This one is much farther away of course, 300 million light years. We will never communicate with them at this distance, not even once."

Kaimea sighed. "So, here we are. The most recent message from sentient beings in a new galaxy has suddenly stopped transmitting. And to make matters worse, we've only translated a small portion of the message. I fear this may be the end."

Quinlan simply continued to scrutinize the message. "Well, it never hurts to start at the beginning and go over it again. It isn't like we haven't learned anything about the message. We understand about thirty percent of it, right?"

"Well that depends on what you mean." clarified Kaimea, "It's clearly divided into three sections, around sixty quadrillion bits total. First a much smaller section, about one percent of the total, here," she indicated a chunk hanging in the air, rich with symbols and translation and meaning. "But then there are two remaining larger sections, about ten percent and ninety percent of the total, each. Both of the larger sections contain what appears to be raw data of some sort, not linguistic or symbolic communication, but we basically have no clue what they contain. We've made no progress at all on those two sections. They are essentially random data. Quadrillions of random bits. Only that first small section, about one percent of the total, has clear markers of linguistic content."

"Meaning we think it it conveys an actual message," clarified Quinlan.

At Kaimea's directed thought, that section expanded to fill the space around them in enormity. Its sections were spread out, its structure, as far as understood, was displayed as clearly as possible. "Right," said Kaimea. "And we have decoded about thirty percent of that, just that tiny piece—which isn't as much as we would hope for under the circumstances."

"Because they've stopped transmitting?"

"Yes!" exclaimed Kaimea. "What hope is there now? They've stopped transmitting the message after a thousand years—"

"934," Quinlan interjected.

"Okay, 934 years. Sure, it would impossible for them to coincidentally align to Earth years, much less powers of ten of Earth years," said Kaimea. "So 934. And after all this time, we can't translate it yet."

"But, in all fairness," said Quinlan, "we've been at this point for a long time. It hardly matters that they've stopped transmitting now. In the past 934 years we have received precisely 512 cycles of the message—oh that's interesting. An obviously suspicious number for being a power of two. I didn't realize that when you called me earlier."

"Yeah, that *is* strange, isn't it?" said Kaimea.

Quinlan continued. "It clearly repeats on purpose so that any listener can first latch onto the signal at any point in time and be assured of eventually getting the entire message. We have everything we will get to help us translate it. We have the entire message. 512 identical instances of it, in fact."

"It doesn't make any sense," said Kaimea. "Surely they would design the message to be remarkably straightforward to comprehend. What else is the point of such a massive endeavor, transmitting a message not only into interstellar space, but across 300 million light years to a completely different galaxy?"

"Okay," said Quinlan. "Let's go over it again. Maybe something will jump out at us, even though we have, as I said, been at this state of decipherment for most of 1000 years."

"Well," said Kaimea, "beyond the basic structure of containing a small part, about one percent, and two larger parts, about ten and ninety each, and beyond knowing that the larger parts are some sort of abstract data blocks and that the smaller part is linguistic, which is to say an actual message, we also know that it has the usual signatures we would expect of a message organized to facilitate aliens—"

"That's us," clarified Quinlan.

"Right, to assist utterly alien beings in learning and translating the message."

"Yes," said Quinlan. "I haven't looked at it in centuries, I admit. Let's see. So for example, it begins with very simple patterns, which we had no trouble translating into basic mathematical and arithmetical concepts. From there it steadily gained complexity building upon itself in what can only be interpreted as a deliberate, self-starting system of comprehension and communication."

"And," said Kaimea, "we have determined that their language is primarily logographic, single symbols representing entire words or ideas."

Quinlan completed the thought. "Of which we have translated about thirty percent before our efforts..." Quinlan trailed off.

"...simply stopped producing results," finished Kaimea. "We're completely stuck. We haven't made any progress in 900 years. And now the message is simply gone." Kaimea visibly sighed. "Why would they stop transmitting when their message is clearly indecipherable?"

Quinlan responded, "Perhaps their civilization died out, or perhaps the transmitter was destroyed by, well, anything. It transmitted faithfully for nearly a thousand years. Maybe it just reached a point of system failure."

"After precisely 512 cycles?" said Kaimea. "That's very suspicious. 512 is such a meaningful number, precisely two to the ninth power. Besides, they would design it to last longer than 934 years if they intended the message to be received. That's a pretty short lifetime for a cosmological project of this sort. It's just luck we detected and received it during such a short window of time. If it *is* a system failure, they would have repaired it or replaced it, and it wouldn't have been exactly 512 in the event of a random failure either."

"So total civilization collapse then," repeated Quinlan, "thereby preventing them from restoring and maintaining the transmitter."

"But then why exactly 512 cycles?" said Kaimea. "It makes no sense. And wouldn't they deploy a transmitter of that sort to be completely automated? It should almost certainly be overseen by a powerful de novo capable of all aspects of its maintenance and self-repair for—well—forever. Well, for the lifetime of whatever star is powering it at any rate. It ought to last a billion years! Augh! This is so frustrating. I dare say there is something fundamentally indecipherable about it."

"Why would they do that?" asked Quinlan with disbelief, as he continued to scrutinize the data splayed before them.

Kaimea continued. "I can't think of any reason to go to so much trouble just to send a thirty percent translatable message, along with quadrillions of bits of useless data. It just doesn't make any sense."

"This is really frustrating you, isn't it?" said Quinlan. "You're still hoping to find a solution to the EOUSP in messages from another sentient species, aren't you?"

"It stands to reason," she replied. "By the time anyone in another galaxy is transmitting enormous messages for long spans of time to other galaxies, they are necessarily very advanced. We have never found another way to solve the EOUSP, but maybe someone else has. We just have to solve it."

"We've been mulling over the EOUSP for a million years," offered Quinlan. "Maybe it can't be solved."

"I can't accept that." Kaimea sighed.

Quinlan studied Kaimea's frustration, then the data suspended in the air, then Kaimea again. "I don't see you at social functions very often. Is this all you've been doing for 1000 years?"

"No, of course not. I love Nyveron. I get up into the mountains and out on the plains for long stretches. And of course there's the network—whole worlds as my disposal."

"I meant time spent with other people, Kaimea. Even though we are remote relative to the rest of the galaxy, we still have a robust population here. Why don't you spend more time with, well, anyone?"

Kaimea looked away. "I have friends, Quinlan. I just don't go to the big parties."

"Hmmm," Quinlan replied thoughtfully. "There's a whole galaxy out there, you know."

They both looked at the data again. "Well, keep at it," he said. "Something may yet reveal itself to you. And you're always welcome to join the rest of us if you want to step away from it for a while."

"MmHmm," she replied, already distracted in thought, staring once again at the message she had already studied for so long. "Perhaps."

11

"HAVE YOU ATTENDED ONE OF VELLION'S PERFORMANCES BEFORE?" asked the woman standing before them.

"This will be her first time," said Ceolbur, Lysandra at his side, "but I've been a fan of Vellion for a long time."

"Welcome," the woman said to Lysandra.

"Thank you." Lysandra looked past the woman to see farther in.

"Tonight's performance will be for a limited audience. Take a seat anywhere you like." Lysandra and Ceolbur explored the setting. They had traveled to another part of Ailuros, to the home of Vellion, a renowned performance artist. They were in an intimately sized room, dimly lit, with columns interspersed, holding up a low flat roof. The columns disrupted lines of sight such that it was difficult to judge the size of the room, but the acoustics of murmuring voices coming from the interior suggested it didn't extend very far. Lysandra gazed into the obstructed room. The floor was peppered with small luminescent purple circles which responded to nearby footfalls by becoming brighter and then oscillating gently. The columns has similarly colored vine-like tracings curling and branching up them.

"I can't believe I haven't seen one of Vellion's performances before," said Lysandra. "We've lived here for so long."

"I'm surprised as well," mirrored Ceolbur. "I would have thought the nature of his act appealed to your curiosities about the possibilities of existence and experience."

"Perhaps I have become too withdrawn into my own work," said Lysandra. "I spend so much time exploring and designing networks that I miss opportunities for new insights."

"I've tried to say that to you before. I'm glad to hear you say it yourself for once." This made Lysandra feel even worse.

"I'm disappointing you," she said.

"No," he said. "I'm just glad you're considering it now." Ceolbur surveyed the room, looking for a place to settle down for the show. "Come. Let's sit over there." Ceolbur indicated a bench ahead of them. Lysandra began to make sense of the room. They moved farther in and realized that the ceiling directly above them would illuminate gently with glittering white and aqua scintillations, but only directly above them in some reactive fashion. As they moved inward, the layout became more apparent. The initially myriad columns were revealed to actually be radially arranged around a central stage, which was also surrounded by concentric rows of benches. The benches had been lost among the dim lighting and the confusing columns from where they had initially entered. As they approached the bench that Ceolbur had chosen, a group of people politely cut them off.

"Are you Lysandra?" The speaker, a tall man with deliberately attractive features, practically gushed at her.

"Yes? Ummm, maybe?"

"You recently published the EOUSP solution! You're huge!"

"Oh, uh, am I?"

"Are you unaware of the impact your work is already having?" Everyone in the group nodded.

"I don't think it has reached very far yet," Lysandra said.

"Well it has pervaded the local systems, and I can tell you, it's spreading like wildfire. You're going to be a celebrity."

Lysandra was practically at a loss for words. "Really?"

"What you've accomplished is simply incredible." The group all nodded and mmhmmed in agreement.

"Well, thank you. That means a lot to me."

"Enjoy the show," the man said, gleaming at their exchange. They parted with the group and continued to the bench they had their eyes on, near the front. Other people filtered in, with the usual variations in body type but with general uniformity to maintain a societal cohesion. In virtual locales, these constraints tended to loosen up significantly, but here, everyone presented as moderately human.

"Zarael!" declared Ceolbur. A man approached them, apparently alone.

"Ceolbur, nice to see you here. I didn't know you were coming."

"Sit with us," said Ceolbur. Zarael sat on the other side of Ceolbur.

"So you're Lysandra," Zarael said, leaning forward slightly to see around Ceolbur. "Your name is getting around. That's quite a neural configuration you've put together."

"I couldn't have done it without Ceolbur. We're a team."

"It's nice of her to say that," said Ceolbur, "but it's all her, honestly." Zarael looked back and forth trying to assess who to offend first with his followup.

"Well, I know you Ceolbur, and if you say you didn't contribute anything to it, then I believe you. HA!" Zarael literally slapped Ceolbur on the back and laughed boisterously.

"Not quite what I meant," said Ceolbur, "But okay."

The lighting suddenly became darker, then over the central stage it became brighter. Everyone quieted down.

"This will be good," said Zarael.

"Have you seen it yet?" asked Ceolbur.

"Nope, I have no idea what to expect. But I've seen his work before."

A vaporous cloud rapidly emerged from the apparently porous ceiling over the stage and quickly solidified into a person—a man, Lysandra believed, it was hard to tell as he was remarkably androgynous, surely by intent. Lysandra was wondering why the man had required this additional vaporous material from the ceiling to corporealize instead of invisibly relying on material from the air, but quickly ascertained the answer as the man very suddenly divided in two, mitosis-like, stepping out of his singular body in opposite directions. Then, almost as quickly, they divided again, this time stepping forward and backward, and there were now four identical people arranged in a square, all facing the same direction. Lysandra now understood. There wasn't nearly enough raw material in the air to corporealize this many solid bodies in rapid succession, so additional material had quickly flooded the stage to kick off the performance.

"Welcome," said the four people in perfect unison. It was an odd auditory perception. Their voices were identical so the only indication of their multiplicity was the interfering sound waves arriving at Lysandra's ears from four separate mouths at four separate distances from four separate locations on the stage. As they continued to speak, they each rotated to face outward to the viewers, who were arranged all the way around the stage with no notion of a front. "Welcome," the man—the men—repeated. "I am Vellion. Tonight, we explore ourselves, or ourself. Our definition, our boundary, the us and the not us. We explore our limitations, our possibilities. The possible and the...impossible?" His intonation rose, still four in unison.

The four figures rotated back to a single facing direction as they finished this last word, and as they finished speaking, all four people then quickly stepped to the center of the stage, two forward at an angle and two back and angle, and in so doing perfectly recombined in space as a single person. The merger of their bodies was accomplished as smoothly as if they had been built of pure light, yet they were solid. Their material bodies had simply blended together quickly enough to achieve the intended effect. Lysandra couldn't help but wonder if this single person had four times the mass of a normal person, or if the four people a moment ago had had one fourth the mass of a normal person. There was no way to know for sure based on the circumstances, although as she dwelled on this momentarily, she realized the necessity of the preceding vapor implied additional mass, suggesting an answer to her curiosity.

"Please be aware," said Vellion, "that tonight's performance will involve neural interfacing. You may have heard of the great cosmological artist Rihon's recent installation Contemplating Oblivion?" There was nodding and hushed agreement throughout the crowd. Lysandra was equally aware and fascinated. "Well, in similar fashion, tonight will involve your direct participation, so I thank you in advance."

Lysandra felt Ceolbur take her hand. This action was difficult to attend to however, as she also felt the performer's mind pressing into her own. She had the peculiar experience of simultaneously continuing to see the stage from her vantage point on the bench, but also seeing the audience through the performer's eyes. He was managing to keep these two perceptions in balance for the audience, which Lysandra respected as no mean feat since competing visual presentations had a natural tendency to undergo visual dominance, wherein one view won the battle for conscious awareness and the other was essentially blinded away, but Vellion was maintaining an overlapping view somehow, such was his artistic and technical skill.

Then she felt him rapidly divide again, as he had done moments ago, but this time, she was riding along with his visual perception. Vellion danced and otherwise gesticulated in performative ways. Throughout his physical act he was also driving the audience's psychological perception. Sometimes Lysandra was viewing through her own eyes, sometimes one of the branches of the performer on stage, and sometimes multiple branches simultaneously with a rather dizzying visual overlay. As he shifted her perspective rapidly, she experienced no vertigo, much less nausea. Nausea was amongst the most dismal qualia that evolution had ever stumbled upon and the vast majority of people had forcibly ejected it from their neural functionality eons ago.

Over the course of the performance, Vellion's act became increasingly ornate in order to push the boundaries of possibility. His branches would trade body parts, simply removing them, handing them to each other, and reattaching them. They would pop their own heads right off their necks, and then plant them back down on another branch's neck in coordinated unison, sometimes planting them backwards on their necks for comedic flair, which delighted the audience.

Briefly, when unified as one again, he reached directly into the side of his own head as if his skull were a mere gelatinous film, removed his brain orb, the same small metal sphere everyone had in their head, and then melodramatically pondered his brain held aloft in his fingertips with a contemplative expression. For the briefest moment, Lysandra wondered how he had done this, since the brain orb needed a physical connection to the body, but she then realized he must have *very* rapidly reorganized his central nervous wiring so as to reconnect his spinal cord to the brain, no longer through the neck, but now through the shoulder, the arm and ultimately the hand holding the brain. As he once again projected his point of view into her mind, she felt herself in his position, looking at his brain in his hand, outside his body. The unspoken question, the *art*, was, *where was his metaphysical self now located?* Was he located where his view into the world seemed to place him, always inside his now empty head from where he visually viewed the world, or was he now located at the nexus of his neurological and psychological processing, his brain, which now resided nowhere near his head and not even inside his body? It was a question without an answer. The audience was merely supposed to wonder.

Then, as if to deliberately betray Lysandra's prior intuition, he tossed the little metal orb, his brain, up in the air and then caught it again, in so doing breaking the physical connection Lysandra thought she had made sense of. At this point, it was no longer a mere acrobatic act. It had become a magic show of some sort. How had he physically disconnected from this brain, tossing it aloft, and yet caught it so precisely when it fell back?

Ok, this guy has my attention now, she wordlessly thought to Ceolbur, who smiled back at her, gleeful at her enjoyment and bafflement.

Furthermore, Vellion was heightening the question of self location. She felt the next contemplation being pressed into her mind: should he—should she, along with him—expect to be *feeling* the movement of being tossed in the air as the brain flew up and fell down? Or should he not feel it because his body remained stationary, aside from the light toss of his arm? Because of course he didn't feel that strong upward flight, since his body and nerve-endings were steadfastly still. This, of course, was the entire point.

Vellion then branched again, and the multiple branches had the gall to *juggle their respective brains between each other!* Yet how were they doing this with no physical connection between their brains and whichever body each brain was now in charge of—was entirely unclear.

More acts and tricks followed. In one act, Vellion would subject his various branches to differing, and even competing, sensory experiences, such as viewing a red object, a large dodecahedron held in the palm of his hand, with one branch and a green one with another branch. He then reintegrated and felt the simultaneous concurrent memories, again dragging the audience along for the psychological ride. If he flitted between the two memories quickly, he could create a *remembrance experience* of seeing a yellow geometric object as the red and green memories competed for his present attention. Lysandra was, of course, familiar with the interplay of multiple memory streams associated with branching and reintegration. Most people had significant practice with this process, but this artist was an expert at holding multiple integrated memories teetering at the edge of awareness at the same time, either flitting back and forth so fast that they blurred, or achieving the near-impossible feat of remembering both in overlap. This was extraordinarily difficult to do and most people could not do it well—and he was sharing his skill with the audience by enabling them to feel his perception.

He then pushed it even further. Standing still, with no physical action involved, he then concentrated on remembering the red dodecahedron and the confabulated yellow memory that had never actually occurred! The yellow experience had been the simultaneous—or perhaps the rapidly oscillating—red and green memories, but he now had a *memory of reflecting on those branches* and the memory itself was of seeing yellow. As he now oscillated between recalling the earlier memory of gazing at a red object and recalling this slightly later yellow memory—*that never actually occurred*—he was able to confabulate a new memory, this time combining red and yellow into orange! But there had never been a yellow perception to begin with, not a physical one at any rate, so to use it as an element in blending sensations into a new one was that much more astonishing. The audience audibly gasped as they all felt this experience together.

Vellion continued to perform acts of this sort throughout the performance. And eventually he wound down.

"Thank you everyone," he wrapped up, "I truly appreciate you joining me this evening. I hope that even as old as we all are, I have shown you something new tonight." With that, he decorporealized and the same hazy smoke drifted back up into the ceiling and vanished.

"Wow," said Ceolbur.

"No kidding," said Zarael, still sitting on the other side of Ceolbur from Lysandra. "I've seen him perform before, but that was spectacular."

"The way he held multiple branch memories concurrently," said Lysandra. "I've never had a knack for that. I always have to remember one branch's memories or the other's at any moment."

Zarael responded, "Say, Vellion mentioned Rihon at the beginning. Have you ever seen his work?"

"No," say Lysandra. "He tends to live and produce his art near the Center. We don't venture that way very often."

"It is...urban," Zarael admitted. "But I mention it because Rihon is arranging another piece and I think you two should go. I'll be there for sure."

"Thank you," said Ceolbur. "I think we can make that happen."

"Yes," said Lysandra. "Nice to meet you, and thank you for mentioning that. I agree with Ceolbur. We should attend Rihon's next installation. But for now, home, Ceolbur. Yes?" He nodded and they returned to their secluded house on the cliff, to the view of their mountain.

12

*E*NLIGHTENMENT *BECKONS*, READ THE PLACARD. The words were many stories tall and hung suspended in the air far above the ground. They appeared like glittering gold and seemed to rotate to face any given person within the virtual space, as if that person was the only person there. But that was not the case. There were nearly a million people scattered throughout the space. Gravity had been suspended in order to fit people within three dimensional space more efficiently. Each attendee could simply fly to whatever location they chose—within a confined set of options, namely on the perimeter of a huge invisible cylindrical wall, somewhat like a coliseum but much taller. No one was behind anyone else. People continued to wink into presence and proceed to find a location from where to watch the event. Satori had considered constructing a more abstract space, in which each person could figuratively sit directly in front of him for a more personal experience, but he felt it was important to create a sense of expansive enormity. He wanted everyone to spatially appreciate that they were part of a tremendous group, a new family.

Satori paced in the center of the arena, of sorts. Although he would be distant and tiny to most of the attendees, they could readily adjust their visual focal length at will, to focus on Satori if that suited them.

When he felt enough people had gathered, he stopped, looked outward, and spoke. "Welcome!" His voice boomed artificially throughout the space. Everyone quieted down.

"Welcome," he repeated and paused. "Welcome to this gathering of Lysandrism, or so I'm trying to name our new family, although I'm embarrassed to admit that people keep calling our little enclave the Satorians. I'm not sure I can refer to myself in the third person. I'm far too modest to take such credit." He smiled and chuckled, eliciting a correspondingly corny reaction from the crowd. "I am but a humble messenger in these exciting times." He paused for effect.

"We here have something in common. Actually—wait a minute, hold on," he feigned awkwardness. "Who's attended one of our meditations before?" Rather than count nearly a million hands lost in the crowd, he simply cognitively received the answer as everyone contributed their individual response. "813,490!" he declared. And how many of you are new today? ... "428,223. Wow! Can you all feel that energy everyone? Over a million people in one place, with one godly goal? And that's just here, today, in this pleasant little space. Our new family is expanding and discovering the same truth in over 300 star systems as we speak, each a new House of Lysandra, led in many cases by one of my branches I humbly submit, but in other cases by newcomers to our cause, newcomers to enduring *hope!* We have over ten billion adherents and the word is literally spreading at the speed of light across the galaxy.

"But I am merely the deliverer of this message to you. It is Lysandra who is our true savior. She brilliantly combined the Neuralium, which we utilized in our earlier explorations of the EOUSP quale, with her own passionate work, producing the next iteration of the quale. She is delivered to us directly by God! I'm telling you that here today." The crowd murmured with energy.

"Lysandra's latest configuration only washed up on our shores recently. Who here has worn the network, known the quale?" People energetically contributed their answers. "139,317. Oh boy! This is going to be a special day. So many will feel it for the first time. Enlightenment lies with our reach! We are close, I can feel it. Lysandra will deliver us from a million years of EOUSP darkness." He paused and walked back and forth for a moment, then stopped and faced outward again. "WHO WANTS TO TRY IT?!" He hollered. The crowd didn't bother politely contributing votes to this question. They simply yelled and stomped with excitement.

"Just to be clear," said Satori, "This is not just for fun. No triviality." Others are wearing Lysandra's network and feeling the quale as some sort of play thing! Sacrilege, I say! With me as your guide, we will achieve something far more substantial than those addicts, those distraction-seeking, bored, shallow fools. I will guide you through the true *voyage* of it, the journey of consciousness that starts here, plain, naked, without the quale, as we sit without the network attached. I will help you interpret it, understand the feelings it grants to you, feelings no one has ever known before now. For us, here, today, this is not a novelty. THIS IS HOW WE KNOW GOD!"

13

K AIMEA COULD BARELY CONTAIN HER EXCITEMENT. She was once again in the virtual workspace where she preferred to work on her studies of extragalactic messages, notably the most recent message, from the twelfth extragalactic species to ever make contact. However, little attention had been paid to the message in recent centuries. 1868 Earth years had passed since the message first arrived, and 934 years later the transmission had stopped, which was precisely 934 years *ago* in fact. In all that time, humanity's efforts to decode the message, primarily led by Kaimea no less, had made no further advances after the first few decades of flourishing progress. But now...

Kaimea paced back a forth in the workspace, its glass floor reflectively stretching to infinity, its lack of planetary curvature offering no horizon. It simply faded into a mist at a far off distance. Sections of the message, signal analysis and linguistic analysis of the message, visualizations and interpretations of the message, all hung in the air in the workspace. The visual portrayal was the merest surface-level of offering however. At an intentional thought, she could pull any visual element to the forefront of her awareness and the corresponding web of information pertaining to that element—the semantic network of accumulated *knowledge*, thus far—would become the focus of her attention, the locus of her expertise. She would then *know* it, not just see it. Or she could stand back, figuratively speaking, and see the entire landscape of knowledge all at once, albeit in a broader fashion. *I wish I could hold an overarching deep expertise of all these pieces at once*, she thought, frustrated by the fact that the scope of information available outpaced the capacity of a single brain. Human knowledge had worked this way since the first human was struck by the notion to scratch a mark in a cave wall to remember something for later—the storing of memories outside the brain. Despite the vast expansion of capabilities offered by fortification, the totality of knowledge had grown alongside that tremendous project.

Dwelling on this circumstance, she pondered, *I wonder if the de novos can hold all of this knowledge at once.* A pang of envy coursed through her.

Others began to arrive in the workspace. Quinlan arrived, with whom she had deliberated when the message suddenly vanished after 934 years of steady transmission. Eventually, over fifty people arrived—or appeared—in the workspace.

"Thank you for coming everyone," began Kaimea.

"Of course. It has been an exciting day," said another attendee.

"Absolutely!" said Kaimea. "As you all surely know by now, we had a major change in the most recently discovered extragalactic transmission yesterday. After transmitting for 934 years, and then stopping for 934 years, it has suddenly begun again." She scanned the crowd. "But this time, the message is completely different."

"Some people haven't had a chance to look at this at all yet," someone asked. "What do we know so far?"

Kaimea continued. "Many of us have been working continuously since the message resumed. It bears all the statistical and informational properties of the linguistic section of the first message, so we have every reason to suspect it is essentially the same sort of content, probably linguistic prose for the most part."

"Where do we stand on deciphering the new message?"

"We've already translated several new symbols from the first message using the new message as a key. Obviously, we only have a tiny portion of the new message, as it only just resumed transmission yesterday. The first message, which transmitted for 934 years, repeated itself precisely 512 times before it vanished. If the new message is of comparable size and is transmitted at the same bitrate, which it is, then logic dictates it will take one to two years for us to receive the full second message, just as with the first message. However, I have formulated a theory in the last few hours that the second message will turn out to be much smaller. In fact, I predict it will be approximately one percent the size of the first message, aligning in size with only the linguistic portion of the first message, not the two huge data blocks, and therefore I predict that this second message might repeat one hundred times more frequently. If I'm correct, we will have the complete second message within a matter of days."

A rumble of murmurs ran through the group. "What is your reasoning for this theory, Kaimea?" someone asked.

Kaimea stood against the backdrop of data analyses suspended in the air behind her, with her colleagues spread around in front of her. "We have been plagued by an absolute conundrum concerning the message this species sent us. Concerning their civilization, the people, who sent it. Why did they only transmit for 934 years and then suddenly terminate the transmission? Why did they transmit it a coincidence-defying 512 times, a perfect power of two, which would be immediately recognized by even the most rudimentary recipient civilization? Why does the message seem impenetrable to all attempts at decipherment beyond partial success, just thirty percent? Why are the two larger data blocks, representing ten and ninety percent of the message, totally obfuscated beyond any recognition? And now, new questions. Why did they resume transmission 934 years later? *Precisely* 934 years later, the exact duration for which they transmitted the first message? I have devised a theory."

Her audience waited, rapt. "Let's assume they wish to convey something of phenomenal value to us. The canonical secrets of the universe."

Audible groans swept over the group. Quinlan spoke. "We all sympathize with your passionate hope to find the solution to the EOUSP amongst the stars, your hope that it will simply land in our lap from afar. But eleven species have reached us already and nothing of the sort has ever been received. We have reveled in eleven alien cultures of art and philosophy and science and culture. But none of them has shined any light on the EOUSP, Kaimea."

"Perhaps it has nothing to do with the EOUSP," she replied. "But something important. Just bear with me. What if we discovered something of profound importance? It could be about the EOUSP or about something else. What if we wanted to communicate it to others like us, other far advanced civilizations that have achieved total proficiency over the material resources of existence? But, what if our discovery, whatever it might be in this hypothetical scenario, required the greatest responsibility and maturity? It couldn't be shared with younger species and civilizations." She paused.

"And?" prodded someone.

"How could we communicate such information to others of sufficient advancement but without inadvertently conveying it to those we deemed unready?" She paused again, but no one spoke, expecting her to continue. "I think a good test of a civilization's readiness would be its ability to maintain cohesion and stability over long periods of time, that is, to avoid collapse, in effect. So, design the message so that it must be received over a very long span of time in order to be understood. Transmit part of the message for a while, then pause for a while, then transmit the other part of the message for a while. Then pause for a while again. Finally, repeat the process, likely forever. I'm guessing that the missing key will not only unlock the remaining seventy percent of the message block, but also the impenetrable data blocks."

The group contemplated this to themselves and then started exchanging quiet thoughts amongst pairs and triplets. Eventually, "That's a highly speculative theory, Kaimea," said Quinlan.

"I agree," she replied, "but since I'm theorizing this new message will cycle in a few days, we'll know soon enough."

A few days later, the group convened once again to confirm the first piece of Kaimea's theory.

"Six days and the message began to repeat," someone in attendance said as they all gathered. "Nicely done Kaimea."

"I bet the second message will terminate after 512 cycles," she said, "but that hypothesis will take a little longer to test." She laughed lightly and everyone else followed suit. "Combining the completed first message—the linguistic section—and the second message has been fairly straightforward. As we would expect, the final completed message is intentionally designed for clarity and comprehension, so decoding it at this point has not been dreadfully challenging. However, while the message is decoded now, it is not necessarily fully translated."

Quinlan clarified this distinction. "We have all the symbols in their proper place in the message, along with some associated diagrammatic and visual data, which is rather interesting. We have a basic star map of their civilization for example. At the time of the transmission, they had just finished reaching the farther edge of their galaxy. And we have imagery of their planet of origin, which looks like a lovely place. And they included other images and diagrams that suggest that much like us, they are interested in matters of mind, cogitation, science if there is anything left to discover, culture, art—things of that nature. We have encountered similar priorities from most of the other eleven extragalactic contacts as well, of course. However, while the images have been fascinating, the symbols pertaining to the text remain challenging. As I said, we now have all the symbols decoded—we know what the symbols look like and where they go in the message, this is what we only had thirty percent of before, and now we have the rest of it—but we are still determining the *meanings* of all the symbols."

"So, we have a full decryption of the linguistic section, but we still can't read it," said a person near the front. "Why would they design a message that still can't be understood even after we apply their own decryption key to it?"

"I don't know," said Kaimea. "Perhaps they're still hiding something until a third message arrives with another key. I have no idea. That said, Quinlan, would you like to discuss some of the newest discoveries?"

Quinlan stepped up. "Thank you Kaimea. We have known for a long time that the translated thirty percent of the linguistic portion of the first message contains cosmological and astronomical content. There are clear references to cosmological evolution such as the universe's singularity origin, the coalescence of the first galaxies, the stellar main sequence by which stars arise, generate heavier elements, and then enter various stages of demise, things of that nature."

Another researcher spoke up. "They can't possibly think they're teaching us anything new about cosmology. We weren't even able to decode the sections we already did without knowledge of branches of math that we only discovered after the closure of cosmological science. Anyone at this level of advancement already has a clear understanding of the evolution of the universe, both from the past, and modeled into the future."

"Agreed," Quinlan said, "They are presenting cosmology for some other reason. They aren't trying to teach it to us. Kaimea will speak to recent discoveries that shed some light on that mystery in a moment. Curiously, in their logographic language, we had already found, in the earlier partial decoding from the first message, symbols that don't seem to say much other than remark on rather obvious traits of cosmology, such as cosmic expansion, long time spans, and the eventual dissolution of useful energy, aka heat death. This was all rather vague until the clarification provided by the second message. Kaimea, would you like to continue? You ran the initial calculations that combined the new message with the old one, thereby completing the decoding entirely, leaving us only with questions of translation now."

Kaimea stepped back to the center. "As Quinlan said, our level of understanding for the last 2000 years has been quite simplistic, seemingly deliberately so. It was for this reason that I theorized the message had been deliberately obscured—encrypted in effect—and I have given my theory as to why the aliens might do that: to prevent less stable and therefore potentially less responsible civilizations from gaining whatever wisdom they wished to impart in their message."

"Seems rather pretentious," someone said.

"Not if they are in possession of some nugget of tremendous knowledge, but which also carries tremendous risks or danger," said Kaimea. "Whatever their motive, that has been my operating theory and the more complete decoding and ongoing translation bolsters this theory. These symbols here," behind Kaimea one of the suspended visuals of analysis came into larger focus, showing hieroglyphic symbols from the message, "were among those we found in the first message but could not translate. But with the decryption via the second message, we now know what they mean. Take this one for example." She gleamed with joy. "This is clearly a reference to darkness.

"Now this symbol," a different symbol overtook the central visualization hanging in the air over Kaimea, "is rather interesting. We already knew it meant cold, but in other parts of the first message, that meaning didn't seem to make any sense in context. We now know why. It is often combined with a modifier symbol over it. See? We now know that this modifier is a temporal marker, in effect converting a noun to a verb, since verbs occur over a span of time. It no longer means cold in this context. It means 'becoming cold'.

"And it gets better than that!" Kaimea began to get excited as her presentation unfolded. Yet another symbol came into central focus. "We found another modifier. There are a host of symbols", a table of multiple symbols now enlarged to emphasis, "that represent tangible concepts, but all have this same modifier over them. This one is similar to the darkness symbol, this one is similar to depth, this one is similar to cold, this one is similar to entropy or running out of energy. And this last symbol represents the number one but has both the temporal modifier and this other modifier. See? So temporally, it now represents a numerical sequence descending to one, but it also has this other modifier. See?"

"What's your theory?"

"I think this is a sentiment modifier!" declared Kaimea. "They are expressing emotions associated with their more tangible concepts. So to go over them again, not darkness, but the sentiment or feeling of darkness. Not depth, but the feeling of depth. Not cold but the feeling of cold. Not entropy, but the feeling of running out of energy. And this last symbol, not a numerical sequence descending to one, but the feeling of becoming the last of something. We don't even have a word for that ourselves, the feeling of becoming the last of something. Like, ummm, the loneliest loneliness you can possibly imagine...And there's more!"

"There is?" anonymously from the back of the audience.

"Absolutely!" she said. "Most importantly, this symbol!" Yet another completely obscure hieroglyph centered into view. "Here, in the first message, we have known for a long time that it means zero, but now we see it in this position with both modifiers, just like the number one. So it means a numerical descent down to zero, but also with a sentiment modifier!" Kaimea practically yelled this final statement. "Don't you see what this means?!"

"What is the sentiment of becoming zero," someone asked. Kaimea just smiled, waiting for realization to collide with her colleagues. "You're talking about death aren't you?" the same person continued. "But there can be no sentiment of death. You can't feel anything about becoming dead because you're dead at that point."

"Okay, fair enough," said Kaimea, "But what if it doesn't *quite* mean death. After all, it doesn't just mean dying in the context of others surviving. It was a reference to this numerical descent down to zero. So it doesn't just mean *a* death. It means the *last* death. Don't you get it?" She looked at the faces looking back at her, not necessarily with unknowing, but with incredulity at Kaimea's line of reasoning and ultimate conclusion. "Everyone!" she declared. "They're talking about the EOUSP! The most pressing issue of our civilization is also the most pressing issue of their civilization." First, the group was utterly silent. Then they took on a decent fervor of reaction and discussion.

"There might be other interpretations," someone said. "Perhaps it means something entirely different. The more tangible elements, I think we all agree about. They clearly want to convey cosmology and astronomy to us. But what about the rest of it? The linguistic section, even fully decoded now, is full of long stretches of untranslated symbols. We have the symbols now, but their meaning, especially to a completely alien species, is not yet clear. There could be entire libraries of literature in there. Why have they left the linguistic section so incomplete after providing us with the key? What more are they waiting for?"

Another person spoke up. "I'd rather focus on figuring that out than on speculating as to the most abstract interpretation of the message. Let's continue to focus on the first section, slow as the progress may be. We need to figure out what they're actually telling us." Kaimea deflated at this reception of her idea.

"Okay, sure," she mustered.

"So what about the two data blocks?" someone asked. "We haven't made much progress on that either."

"Bit of a mixed bag I'm afraid," said Kaimea. "The larger of the two data blocks, representing almost ninety percent of the entire message, remains utterly inscrutable. But the recent message included what can only be described as a straight up decryption key for the smaller data block, the ten percent block."

At that, multiple people tried to speak at once. The winner repeated himself. "So, wait, we now have the full decryption of the smaller data block? That's a huge step forward."

"Except that I have absolutely no idea what the decrypted data actually is," said Kaimea. "It's as if the decryption key rehashed the entire data block into a different data block, essentially blending the bits into a new set of bits, but it is just as meaningless to me now as it was before."

"Then why do you think that was a decryption key in first place, and why do you think it was intended to be applied to the smaller data block in that particular fashion?"

Kaimea brought several symbols into view. These are the decoded, and successfully translated, glyphs pertaining to the newly provided key in the second message. There is no need for speculation or ambiguous interpretation here. The translation of this passage of the linguistic section is clear now. The key is provided and it is intended for application to the smaller data block, and the exact mathematical method of applying the key so as to convert the data block into its decrypted format is all perfectly clear. The only remaining mystery is what the converted data block means or contains. I haven't a clue."

"It's not quite as random as it was before, though," said someone who hadn't spoken before. At his own discretion, despite not being the speaker's position where Kaimea stood, several forms of analysis of the converted smaller data block expanded into view in the air above the group. "Look at this. The original data block has no meaningful statistical features at all. It's as random a sequence of bits as one could imagine."

"Which we would expect if it was encrypted," pointed out Kaimea.

"Sure, but what you have decrypted now has structure," the previous speaker continued. The analysis of the data block meandered in the air, revealing various scrutiny of the data. "It naturally segments itself into numerous discrete chunks now, each with varying statistical distributions.

See? And most of these segments now have uneven power distributions. It's full of patterns. "

"And yet, I can't figure out what it actually is," said Kaimea.

"So, it's decrypted, but we don't understand it," said one person.

"Or the decryption is flawed or incomplete," said another person, "thereby revealing some degree of structure, as we see here, but not properly revealing its specific details."

"I don't know what to make of it," said Kaimea with open disappointment. "But obviously, I would love for everyone else to look at it as well. Perhaps you will see something I've missed."

"What could it be?" someone asked.

"Perhaps it's the totality of their cultural output for the last million years," someone said. It could be a categorically organized archive of everything they've ever created."

"Why specifically that?" someone asked.

"If they are in dire dread of their own extinction, as Kaimea theorizes, then wouldn't they want to send their art and creations out to others to appreciate? Isn't that what we would do?"

"But the EOUSP is bigger than extinction," said another person. "The EOUSP isn't about this one species or civilization dying out. It's about everyone and everything dying out everywhere. In a full EOUSP interpretation there is no one left to send anything to. And, if we are speculating as to the meaning of the decrypted smaller data block, then what does that leave for the much larger data block to hold?" The group stared helplessly at the data for a while.

"Well, anyway," concluded Kaimea, "this is where we currently stand. If anyone is looking for me for the next thousand years, you can probably find me right here." She laughed uncomfortably.

"There's a big party later to celebrate the transmission resuming," someone said. "You would be the guest of honor, of course. Your predictions about this latest message have assured your fame."

"Ah," said Kaimea, throwing Quinlan a desperate look. "I'll think about it." *I'll think about it?!* she thought to herself angrily. *What the hell? Just say yes! What's the matter with you?*

"I will personally see to it that she attends," said Quinlan as he gave Kaimea the softest and most reassuring smile he could.

She squirmed, then gave in, and smiled awkwardly. "I would be honored," she finally said.

14

THE ASSEMBLY MODERATOR LOOKED DEIMOS OVER. Deimos was barely holding himself together, and a large crowd supporting him wouldn't calm down to let anyone else speak.

"In this space, all voices are heard," declared the moderator, trying to quell several forms of anger, first that of Deimos and his cadre, and then reactive anger from others who wished Deimos would calm down and let others speak. "If everyone will participate sociably, we can proceed."

Deimos stood up from his seat at the grand annular table in the same assembly hall from where he had made his previous pronouncements, 21,000 years ago. The chamber was completely full, both the dignitaries sitting at the table and in the audience seating filling the room. Spread over the planet, billions were observing through the data network. "I demand formal sanction against the researchers Kaimea and Lysandra. Their work must be forbidden!" repeated Deimos for the third time.

"All options are on the table. All courses of action are on the table. Please allow others to speak as well." The moderator gestured to their spacious surroundings, the very political core of galactic civilization. "Many of you have transited in from other major municipalities of the Center. We represent 300 worlds in tight proximity, and furthermore, we represent the legacy of humanity, for we are located near its origin, near Sol, near Earth. We must conduct ourselves in a manner dignified of our surroundings. Orsiel, I believe you were going to speak next." The moderator shot a sharp look at Deimos to keep quiet.

"Thank you moderator. Deimos has been offering his proclamations, as well as recording his thoughts in his well known rhetorics, for a very long time now. Not once has he produced any evidence that his theory is correct." This sent Deimos's supporters again into an immediate uproar.

"Please!" said the moderator. "If we are forced to defer this deliberation until a later time, no progress will be made at all. Deimos? Where's your evidence?"

"The EOUSP is the most dangerous idea in the universe," he said, ignoring her request. "First that pretentious artist gets everyone riled about that the EOUSP. Then some eccentric biologist on a muddy planet in the middle of nowhere finds some alien bug that gets everyone thinking all manner of dangerous thoughts. And now some reckless quale-diver is trying to actually *solve* the damn thing! This can't be allowed to continue. We have good reason to believe any survival of the end of the universe would break the cyclic multiverse's infinite rhythm of birth and death. Matter, energy, and information—entropy—are tightly intertwined—"

Orsiel cut him off. "Deimos, we hardly need a physics lesson from you."

Deimos continued. "The universe contains a precise quantity of these three concepts, matter, energy, and information. Many have theorized for millennia now that the cyclical multiverse depends on a perfect harmony of these three concepts, recycled as the very fabric of each subsequent universe. If any amount of the matter-energy-information triad were to be held aside—"

"Yes, yes," someone said. "So prove it already, Deimos."

Deimos continued forcefully. "Your ignorance is irrelevant. The EOUSP is the most dangerous idea we have ever encountered, and if a solution were ever found, it could spell the end of everything!"

Deimos's supporters hollered in support and could not be quelled for some time. The moderator repeatedly attempted to restore order, but it took some time to achieve this.

"That's all very grandiose of you Deimos," spoke up another person in attendance, but all you have is your theories. I wouldn't even call them that. You are conjecturing—"

"How dare you!" declared Deimos.

"—conjecturing, I said, and you would have us institute prohibitions by force the likes of which humanity hasn't seen since the times of the Exodus, following the initial fortification of our biology—and the earliest de novo creations too, I humbly acknowledge—when we began our spread from

Earth across the galaxy. Frankly, we're just too damn old for that sort of nonsense now. What you ask for is incongruent with our entire societal structure."

"Be that as it may," said Deimos. "In this case, due to the severity, nay the criticality, of the situation, stronger methods are required."

Orsiel huffed out loud. "Society will not reorganize itself to suit your whim on a moment's notice. Have you even considered how your request—"

"—Demand, not request, as I wholly admit. I am demanding this!"

"How would your demand even be actualized?" continued Orsiel. "This Lysandra lives on Ailuros, in the Zareasman system. And Kaimea operates from an observatory above Nyveron, in orbit of Eilunedra, on the outer rim of the galaxy. Their communities are both well outside the influence, much less any notion of control, of the Center. How would you propose we enact any sort of authority over them, 9000 and 14,000 light years away respectively. The galaxy is just too big."

"You aren't listening to me," said Deimos. "It doesn't matter if it's difficult. It simply must be done. We must stage an irrefutable moratorium, and Lysandra must be brought under supervision to ensure she never continues her work." This brought gasps from the crowd.

"You would have us imprison her?"

"To save the very fabric of existence itself? Are you kidding? Of course I would." The congregation then descended into side discussions, mutterings, whisperings.

The moderator spoke in calm but firm tones. "May we all continue to consider Deimos's argument and request. If a call to action is decided upon, we will do so accordingly. This assembly may yet decide to take some course of action on this issue. For now, I say we let this meeting end, so as to consider other important topics that require addressing."

"This isn't working," said a woman in a dark red outfit, lounging in an ornate chair. Deimos looked around the room, his strongest supporters looking to him for guidance. She continued, "political action will never get in front of this issue before Kaimea and Lysandra cause real trouble."

"Yes," said Deimos, "I'm starting to agree."

"Kaimea is a side issue," said another woman. "If there is information to be found in extragalactic communications, someone will find it even if Kaimea is stopped. We really can't do anything about that. We will just have to hope that leads to a dead end. But Lysandra is different. She appears to possess a nearly unique skill at network configuration design, quale-diving as they call it. If we can stop her, we may impede such research practically forever."

"We may have to take more assertive action," said a man standing by a window, looking out instead of back toward the group. Deimos scanned the faces, their expressions, to read their reaction to this statement. He saw agreement.

Is this what I'm becoming? he thought. He truly preferred the diplomatic solution, the rule of law, but he also questioned its ability to handle a risk of this severity and urgency. This was about the future of existence itself, not some trifling political disagreement.

"Give me another solution," he said. The group contemplated briefly.

"We don't actually need to kill her," the first woman said pensively, with incredible curtness. Several people grimaced at the overt declaration. "Her potential to complete this network she's working on, it hinges on her admittedly impressive skill. If no one else can do it, well then, all we need to do is bring her down to the level of the rest of us, a mere tinkerer, not a tremendous researcher potentially capable of achieving something no one else can."

"What do you suggest?" asked Deimos.

"Couldn't we somehow, oh, neurologically stunt her? Just a little. Just render her skill a bit more—ordinary."

"Oh come one," said a new speaker from the sidelines. "Brain orbs have been impenetrable since the origin of fortification."

"Perhaps there's a way," the woman continued.

"In a million years it's never been done," said Deimos. "Encryption has always been a step ahead of decryption. Whenever a new technology enables decryption of current encryption techniques, that same technology enables the next generation of encryption as well. The bottom line is that it's easier to scramble data than to unscramble it. It's built into math itself."

The man by the window spoke. "That's right. The only person who could access or alter her neural functionality through subterfuge or force is Lysandra herself, because the keys are on the inside. It has always been that way." The group thought briefly until Deimos admitted the conclusion this discussion had led to.

He spoke slowly and with deliberation. "We're talking about the fate of the universe here. The fate of all subsequent universes in fact. We will have to consider all options." He sighed heavily. *I guess this is what I'm becoming, after all.*

15

"HAVE YOU SEEN WHAT'S HAPPENING IN THE CENTER?" asked Ceólbur as he found Lysándra near a modest stone fountain, surrounded by people vying for her attention. He pushed his way through the small crowd as she drew him near from a distance with an inviting wave. They had converged at this rather grand social gathering on Ailuros, an opportunity for people from all over the planet to meet outside the various virtualities otherwise on offer through the planetary myceliumesque network that pervaded every clump of soil above the mantle. The venue was a sprawling, eclectically connected distribution of gardens and arboretums, loosely delineated by small streams with numerous foot bridges to facilitate meandering self-reflection. But tonight this assemblage of oases was taken over with the abounding party.

"Ceólbur, thank goodness you're here. I've never been so popular in a million years." She smiled politely at the people hearing her say this, not wanting to necessarily offend her admirers.

"Well, you're quickly becoming the most famous person in the galaxy."

"Oh don't be ridic—you don't think so, do you?" she said with a bit of a lilt in her voice. "I wonder if our branchlings at Rihon's grand unveiling will be this popular. Of course, they won't arrive for another few thousand years." She drifted slightly sideways and kicked a foot to the side to catch herself.

"Are you entirely stable right now?"

Lysándra smiled at him as she positively leaned against one person in the tight group, a woman who seemed all too pleased to be of any assistance to her. "Someone might have offered me a neural module a while ago," she said a bit dizzily, "aaand I might still be wearing it."

Ceólbur blinked. "Why would you do something like that?"

"I was feeling overwhelmed by the attention and a very nice—although rather strange—person said it might help me overcome my social...I forget the word he used now. Or was he a she? I think his body was switching back and forth while we were speaking. I've seen that before on occasion. This module is making me see strange things though. In addition to helping me loosen up a bit—"

"I'll say," said Ceólbur.

"In addition," she continued, "I keep hallucinating quick flashes of some sort of visual percept, but the visions don't linger long enough for me to make sense of them. I think it's a side effect or error of the module though. He clearly intended for it to help me relax at this party, aaand I think it's working."

"So you're wearing random neural modules from strangers now. And by your own description, it might be so sloppily constructed that it's invoking potentially harmful neurological signals in your visual processing."

"Harmful? It's a hallucination. Relax. Besides, what's the worst that could happen? It kills me?" The group around them laughed. "So then I revert a couple hours. So what? I made an etching before the party. I'll be fine."

"Well that's definitely the new module talking. That's not the Lysándra I know."

"Lots of people are comfortable with reverting a little bit in the event of an accident. What's a little bit of memory loss to a million-year-old." She guffawed in a self-impressed tone and the groupies laughed again.

"Isn't she wonderful?" someone said.

"Yes, and lots of people *aren't* comfortable losing even a fraction of a second," said Ceólbur, "regardless of a having an auxiliary brain pattern etched away, precisely because they are overly attached to their current stream of consciousness—as illogical as I've always found that reasoning to be. And you have always struck me as rather reserved about metaphysical identity issues. You don't branch very often for example, and when you do, you try to reunify as soon as possible." Ceólbur glanced around at the crowd still lingering and hoping for Lysándra's attention. His glances drew the attention of the crowd.

"Hey! You're Ceólbur, right?" said someone who joined the group a moment ago. "Lysándra's quale-diving partner?"

"Yes, and Lysándra looks rather out of sorts. I'm going to take her somewhere else."

The person ignored his statement and continued. "You were there the first time she experienced the EOUSP quale, then."

"Better than that," broke in someone else. "He was the second person to ever experience it. He knows its consciousness better than anyone—well except Lysándra perhaps."

"Here, try this," said one of the people present, a handsome young-looking man—not that anything resembling true age was remotely informed by appearances. He produced a palm full of small confections, each swirling with endlessly animated colors. Everyone within reach, Lysándra included, confidently took one and promptly plopped it in their mouth.

"Oh that's marvelous," she said. "An utterly new flavor, I would say."

"Yes, I experiment with taste and flavor qualia, always seeking new chemistry, new molecular arrangements. It's the same taste buds and associated neural structures—"

"Some of us have diversified our sensory abilities in that regard," a person pointed out.

"Fair enough, but the point is, even with existing sensory systems, we can still experience entirely new flavors." As this person continued speaking, Ceólbur took one himself, with reservation. "Isn't it weird to imagine that this flavor we're all now experiencing was always there, always available to us, but until I created this molecular cocktail, its conscious quale had never before been known? Isn't that just incredible?"

"It makes me wonder about the serendipity of flavors that *do* exist," Lysándra remarked. "For example, what if the cacao tree had never evolved on Earth? But for that evolutionary quirk, we might never have had chocolate! My dears! Imagine it. No chocolate! I cry for it."

"One shudders at the notion," said the person offering the confections. "I couldn't bear it."

"And yet," completed Lysándra, "surely there are many, perhaps infinite, flavors out there as wonderful as chocolate that have never been discovered, never been experienced."

The confectioner pondered. "We should lament their absence just as much as chocolate even though we have no notion of them at all." The otherwise boisterous group became vaguely melancholic for the briefest moment.

"Oh well!" declared Lysándra, bringing everyone to laughter.

"Lysándra, we really need to talk about what's going on in the Center. Not everyone is fawning over your new neural configuration."

"Really?" she said. "Who doesn't want to know the solution to the question to end all questions to end all questions to end—wait, did I say that part already?"

"Curious choice of words." Ceólbur twisted the corner of his mouth. "Some people think the quale really will end all subsequent questions. Some people think it will end everything."

"What's this guy talking about?" asked another person as the crowd drew in. More people had accumulated around them as Ceólbur's own minor recognition spread throughout the party.

"Ceólbur is always looking out for me," said Lysándra with a laugh. She extended a straight-elbowed arm and index finger to make flirting contact with Ceólbur's shoulder. "Isn't he just splendid?" She gleamed at the people seemingly hanging on her every interaction with Ceólbur. "Wait! Did anyone else just see that?" she said, frowning, as her eyes suddenly darted around the air momentarily. "Oh, now it's gone. Never mind."

"Can you please disable that module Lysándra? These threats from the Center are serious."

"Hmph." A moment later Lysándra's demeanor changed noticeably as Ceólbur observed her shift away from the tight crowd in all directions, clearly now feeling herself boxed in. "Ooookay," she said, "I'm not sure I like this better, to be honest. Maybe I shouldn't have disabled it. Ummm, excuse me everyone. *Excuuuse* me!" She started pushing her way through, grabbing Ceólbur's wrist with a vice grip as she moved past him. He dutifully followed as she marched them to a short brick wall dividing two zones of the garden, a quieter place somewhat removed from the energy of the party. They settled against the wall, with Lysándra looking around, taking the scene in. Ceólbur focused his attention on her.

"I've never had this kind of attention," she said. "This EOUSP quale is really gaining traction."

"And as I said, not entirely good traction. Have you ever heard of this Deimos person in the Center?"

"The Center? I haven't ventured toward Earth in thousands of years. I don't pay too much attention to the goings on in that region. Earth reminds me of old memories. Reminds me of him. You know who I mean. Reminds me that he hasn't been here this whole time, seeing all of this." Lysándra continued to look past Ceólbur. The party was enormous. People had transited in from all over Ailuros to celebrate the new year. She continued, "It's curious that celebrating planetary orbits remains a popular marker of the passage of time, and yet every society does so on a different cadence depending on the planet in question. Why are we so willingly arbitrary?" she mused out loud.

"The passage of time reminds us of the EOUSP," remarked Ceólbur. "It isn't too critical what that passage of time is, so the local year suffices on any given planet, but marking time in some fashion is still valuable to us."

"But that's weird, don't you think? If we dread the EOUSP, why do we conscientiously track its inevitable arrival someday?" Lysándra continued to look past Ceólbur, absorbing the crowd.

"You're enjoying all of this, aren't you?" he said.

"I disabled the module as you asked. And I was happy to get some space when I did that."

"Yes, you didn't like feeling crowded in, but you still enjoy being popular."

"Hmmm, that's interesting," she responded, as she held out her hand and a full wine glass almost instantly materialized in her poised fingertips. "I wonder if I do. But Ceólbur, that's not why I'm doing this work, not for some sort of cheap fame. I just genuinely think we found something important and I want to make sure everyone benefits from it." She took a sip and then continued to observe the scene, clearly more interested in the party than their conversation.

"Say it more directly," said Ceólbur. "Say why you're really doing this."

"I just did."

"No. Say it Lysándra." She looked at him directly for the first time, turned the corner of her mouth, weighed the option he was putting to her.

"It hurts to say it out loud."

"You already did a moment ago, but you didn't connect the two. Lysándra, admit why you're doing this already."

"What do you want from me? This whole project is just about one long lost love from a million years ago? That makes me sound crazy, Ceólbur. This is so much bigger than one person."

"It doesn't have to be bigger than that for you, but you should admit it to yourself."

"Look Ceólbur, it can be both at the same time. Solving the EOUSP is for everyone, not just me."

"It won't bring him back," said Ceólbur.

"Quite the opposite," she said. "It exacerbates it."

Ceólbur raised an eyebrow. "What do you mean?"

"See, without a solution to the EOUSP, he only missed out on the partial eternity of this one piddly little universe. Dying twenty years before fortification cost him this life, this galaxy, such as it is. But it *is* finite in some sense, right?"

"I see," said Ceólbur. "But if you solve the EOUSP, humanity may survive infinitely longer, and therefore his loss is that much more tragic."

"Precisely." They paused. "But I have to complete it anyway. It's like my gift to him...or..."

"A penance?" Ceólbur asked.

"Hmmm, perhaps."

"But it wasn't your fault. He just died. Everyone died back then."

"I didn't," she retorted. "Anyone who made it to fortification didn't, for the most part."

"You can't do this to yourself Lysándra. It isn't your fault that you lived a few more years than he did. You don't owe him anything."

"Then it's just a gift Ceólbur. It doesn't have to be more complicated than that. It's just something I'm doing. Call it in his honor...or whatever. I don't care what you call it. Humanity needs it and I might be the only person who can do it."

"Oh wow. This party really is going to your head. You think you're the only person in the galaxy who can finish the quale? Get over yourself Lysándra." Lysándra looked around, anywhere except at Ceólbur.

"We're going to have to be careful from now on," said Ceólbur. "This Deimos fellow is dangerous. I think maybe we should slow down about any further developments."

"Oh come on!" She faced him again. "We aren't done yet Ceólbur. The quale is incomplete. I can feel it. The network can be improved. I *know* it!"

"And what if this Deimos doesn't want you—us—to complete it? He isn't alone. People in the Center are listening to him. He even has a seat at the Assembly! He's influential Lysándra!"

Lysándra sighed heavily. "Ceólbur, I can't stop. This is huge. We've found something profound. Aren't you excited about it too? Can't you *feel* it? Oh that's an interesting observation, the quale of the excitement of the impending solution to the EOUSP. That's a good one." She sipped from her glass. "I need you to help me finish it Ceólbur. Who cares if I'm doing it for him or for me or for you...or for all of humanity?"

"I don't know if I want to finish it. At least not until I know if we're safe. Even if we do refine the network and the quale further, maybe we should keep those refinements to ourselves, at least for a while."

Lysándra visibly grimaced at that suggestion. Then a fraction of a second later, her entire semblance shifted as if she'd become a completely different person. She stood straighter as her shoulders perked back, she tossed her hair, a silly smile gripped her face, and a glassy gaze completely disconnected her from Ceólbur. "I'm going back to the party," she said with a glittering grin, and before Ceólbur could even register that she had reactivated the recent module, she had already glided away.

16

"**S**HALL WE BEGIN?**"** said Satóri in a raised voice to get above the rest of the crowd. The crowd, previously milling about, chatting, slowly took on structure as the attendees found seats in the meeting space, a grand circular hall of ornate marble and other beatific stone, topped with a tremendous dome. Although circular in design, the seating layout only wrapped three quarters of the circumference such that a given speaker could centralize the group's attention in one direction against the sidewall. The entire building, with its capacity for the expected hundreds in attendance, had been grown from scratch the previous day, of course.

Satóri continued. "We chose this, the planet of Ylorin, for this conclave, not so much because it is where we first offered our message to the people, true though that is, but more because this place is reasonably centrally positioned within our nascent galactic dispersal. The various heads of Lysandrism have spread in equal directions from Ylorin, and likewise can converge here for this meeting fairly easily, minimizing the transit time for the farthest out of you here today."

"While we get settled, I'm curious, how many Satori branchlings do we have?" Various methods of direct neural communication ensued. "About half then," he said, "Our message is now being carried across the galaxy by hundreds of non-Satori branches. That's just wonderful. Just wonderful." The crowd converged to a certain harmony and Satóri continued.

"Ok ok everyone. I call to order this, the first Conclave of Lysandra. Everyone, please gather so we may begin. Since we are meeting today on planet Ylorin, from where we first shared our message with humanity," he said, referring to the ancestral Satori's inaugural sermon from the red-earth virtuality, "and consequently since I am the *conscious elder* here," his having accumulated more conscious time than anyone else present since everyone else had entered various periods of stasis during their transits to remote stellar systems to set up new Houses of Lysandra, "I will serve as a loose Mediator of Ceremonies, but of course we are a collective, so speak up as you may."

"As a first order of business, since many of you have transited here from farther out and have consequently lost considerable conscious time, I will begin with a brief status update. Lysandrism currently counts 1053 worlds among its flock." The crowd applauded. "Yes yes," Satóri said, smiling. "In addition, you have each reported your memberships and I am pleased to inform us all that in total, the Lysandran House now raises the consciousness of over thirty billion members, both fortified and de novos alike!" The crowd applauded vigorously. "Furthermore, as I ascertained while awaiting our final arrivals, approximately half of our house leaders are non-Satori branches. That is just wonderful. The gift from Lysandra is truly spreading across the galaxy at the speed of light now." He exaggerated of course, but the metaphor landed nonetheless.

"The purpose of this conclave, and any subsequent such gatherings, is to maintain cohesion of our faith and decide matters of policy and practice going forward." This sent discomforting murmurs through the crowd.

"Such cohesion may be difficult to achieve," said another Satori branching as he stood up.

"Satòri, leader of our house on the world of Arendiad. Welcome. What do you mean?"

The speaker continued. "I and other leaders amongst our recent thousand, as you graciously point out, have been discussing shared concerns for centuries now, mostly amongst our tight-knit Pleiades stellar neighbors—with whom we have enjoyed proximate and therefore frequent communication. And we are unconvinced of Lysandra's continued role in developing the EOUSP quale." This sent quite the ruckus through the crowd.

"You can't be serious?" was one response that rose above the clamor.

"Quite. There are thirty-four Pleiadean worlds, with as many separate houses, and our unusually close cosmic distribution has facilitated unity of our faith and expectations. We have been discussing this for quite a while in fact."

"Is this true?" said the mediator, addressing the larger group. Nearly thirty people immediately stood up, a mix of Satori branchlings and non-Satori individuals. A few stragglers eventually stood up as well with slightly less enthusiasm, bringing the total to thirty-four.

One of the new standers spoke. "Satòri from Arendiad is correct. We have been discussing this for a while and are in fairly uniform agreement."

"What is the nature of your objection to Lysandra?" said another Satori in the crowd. "She is practically our savior."

"No she isn't." The first detractor moved from his position in the seats to the central point where the mediator was standing. "She is lucky, that's all. She stumbled onto the EOUSP quale. By her own admission, her initial discovery indicated practically nothing of import, just a vague sense of the EOUSP, notably with no indication of an actual solution whatsoever. She then had the sheer—and mere, I dare say—serendipity to combine her early network with that of the Neuralium, which she played absolutely no role in discovering whatsoever, thereby refining the quale and ultimately revealing that a EOUSP solution does in fact exist."

"That's not fair," said someone, but the detractor ignored the interruption.

"If anything, this discoverer of the Neuralium, a biologist named Minerva," was the first to realize hope in an actual *solution* to the EOUSP. That was the gift of the Neuralium, and as we all know, our entire faith as we sit here today, was not predicated on Lysandra's original discovery, but rather on Minerva's!" This frank realization sent the crowd into near mayhem.

A non-Satori attendee stood and spoke. "I am the first non-Satori prophet of Lysandrism, having built our seventeenth House on the world of Montanoth. The House I lead precedes the first Pleiadean House by 400 years, mind you." The Pleiadean who had been speaking scowled at this superficial claim of authority as the speaker continued. "The earliest days of our faith were, admittedly, structured around the Neuralium, but we were little more than a mystery cult at that time, gathering around whatever dim light we could find in the cosmic darkness. We weren't actually *godly* at that time. We were merely reveling in the new state of consciousness brought on by the Neuralium. It was Lysandra's later combination of the first two networks, and her resulting discovery of an actual *solution to the EOUSP* that crystallized our earlier clan into an actual *religion of god*. We are Lysandrans, not Minervans! No disrespect to Minerva and her marvelous gift to us all."

Yet another Pleiadean Satori spoke up. "The truth is, Lysandra had been fairly shy from the public eye. Frankly, she just doesn't make a very good prophet. It has always been difficult to rally newcomers to her personage because she is practically invisible."

"She's 9000 light years away!" came a voice practically lost in the large crowd. The speaker stood up. "Discounting our earlier days during which we practiced exclusively with the Neuralium, word only reached us in the Center of Lysandra's discovery about that long ago. Which is to say she is, as we speak, probably only just learning of the rise of Lysandrism right about now. As we stand here arguing, I'll point out. She hasn't had an opportunity to make herself more publicly available to her followers."

"Our followers follow Satori," someone said, "Frankly, a lot of the public calls us Satorians, not Lysandrans."

The mediator literally slapped his forehead at this statement. "That is absolutely last thing we have ever wanted."

"You have no priority here," someone said. "You have no more say in what we are called, or what we ultimately do, than anyone else here."

"I wasn't claiming any primacy over our shared Satori tree. We are all equally the ancient Satori who first preached on the red earth millennia ago, gathered our nascent flock, and demonstrated to the people that the Neuralium was more than a recreational escape. All I said was that we should each be aghast that anyone would call our house Satorianism. Lysandra was sent to us by *god*, people! Who are we to demand even more from her at this point? Her continued role is god's decision, not ours. Perhaps her gift to humanity was complete with her previous work. Perhaps she has done all she was sent to do."

"I'm afraid that's not good enough," said a Pleiadean representative, once again.

"Explain," said the mediator.

"Her work continues as we speak. She is surely trying to refine the network and clarify the quale right now."

"You say that like it's a bad thing. We're all eager—desperate even—for the completion of the quale. Our worship currently utilizes the quale she gifted to humanity to help us understand god's plan for the preservation of consciousness beyond the duration of the universe, but our understanding remains incomplete. While we now know there is a solution to the EOUSP, we do not actually know what that solution is yet. We don't even know if the solution is feasible yet! It could involve something that, although barely within the boundaries of physical feasibility, nevertheless lies outside the reach of practical application. What if we have to fold a billion galaxies on top of each other to do it? We don't know yet. We *need* the final quale. The fact that Lysandra continues her work is a *good* thing!"

"Yes, but she works outside the faith. She may be the figure of our worship, but she is nevertheless a heretic."

"NO SHE ISN'T!" shouted several voices simultaneously. One person continued ahead of the rest. "You speak blasphemy! She would have to actually denounce the faith to commit heresy. You're being ridiculous. As we all just admitted, she is barely even aware of her thirty billion fervent followers. She hasn't even been offered a chance to embrace her role in god's plan. If anything, it's *our* job to bring that light to her. Maybe that's what god sent *us* to do. Not just share it with everyone else but bring god's chosen one to the light since, as you say, she doesn't even know the gravity of what she has accomplished."

The detractor was unmoved however. "The simple fact of the matter is that the quale must be completed *within* our house. Call us Lysandrans, call us Minervans, heck call us Satorians, I don't care. We must complete the quale before anyone else. The one thing we all agree on here is that the EOUSP quale is the purest, most enlightening, most *godly* thing in the entire universe—dare I say in the entirety of reality itself. It *must* become the domain of our faith. Every person across the galaxy who first experiences the quale should—*must*—do so from within the guidance of Satorian oversight. Otherwise, it will be played with, like a trinket. It will be party entertainment. We all know that."

"What are you suggesting?"

Several Pleiadeans looked at one another across the room. "We have to tell them," said one.

"Tell us what?"

The Pleiadean who had first spoken and who had said the most throughout this debate spoke quietly but forcefully. "Lysandra cannot be permitted to finish the quale without our oversight, much less without first agreeing to join our house, her house of course. And if she refuses..." There was no need to verbally complete his thought. In the brief silence that followed, one could have heard the footsteps of an angel dancing on the head of a pin. And a moment later, nothing short of seismic pandemonium consumed the hallowed chamber, inadvertently amplified to a deafening roar by the perfect dome overhead.

17

*"The network reveals the quale. The quale reveals the path.
The path reveals the way. The way reveals...the truth?"*
—*The Ontoscendians*

T HE AILUROS NEW YEAR'S PARTY WAS OVER. Lysándra had transited back to her home on the cliff and steadily slid down a psychological and emotional ramp into a state of post-party recovery. Staring at the night sky, she turned the events of the evening over in her mind. The strangers, the attention, the sudden celebrity, which was a new conscious sensation in and of itself for her. She had never been famous in a million years. While an ancient life should have afforded her, and anyone else, numerous opportunities to gain attention, there were also *many* more people to thin such prospects out, and they were distributed by light years—and actual years. Hers had been a quiet million years, steadily, ceaselessly exploring the infinite space of neural configurations, steadily, ceaselessly feeling the shape of innumerable conscious perceptions.

She watched a meteor streak across the sky, her visual percept of its movement through her visual field leaving a wake of conscious awareness of its velocity, mass, inertia, and likely material composition, as well as its reverse-projected path backward through the sky informing her of its history. Her brain subconsciously calculated the likely path it had taken through the solar system and she became immediately aware of its likely origin in the second asteroid belt beyond one of the farther planets. Without intentional contemplation, she simply *knew* these facts about the meteor as it flew by, disintegrated, and flashed away.

What about the strange neural module? she suddenly remembered silently. *That person was so peculiar.* Feeling socially awkward and longing for Ceólbur's company to navigate the situation, she had gently observed a few conversations from the outer fringes until all of a sudden, she had been identified by a variety of strangers. Rapidly, she had found herself the center of a mild swarm with a flurry of questions hurled at her. Then, this one person, with an oddly vacant look to his eyes who both stared her down in one moment and looked past her head another, had seized her palm in his and offered a nonvocal, mental message of offering a neural module to her, transferrable through their connected palms. She had initially hesitated with obvious good prudence, but the pressing crowd of fawning admirers and the stranger's promise that it would help her relax had pushed her to make a hasty decision. After all, she had made a recent etching. It wasn't her most likely course of action but ultimately, under the highly unusual circumstances, she had accepted it. The man had then almost immediately drifted away so fast she barely noticed his exit, and then she had been left to her fans until Ceólbur showed up.

With the exuberance of the party no longer a distraction she recalled the extraneous effects of the module, mostly flashes of hallucinatory imagery. The most likely explanation was simply a glitching artifact from a rather poorly designed neural module. A sloppy or imprecise design was likely to cause transient random visual qualia. Yes, she told herself. By far the most likely explanation was that the module had been cheaply designed. Ceólbur's concern had been reasonable.

But still, she was curious.

She was already outside, gazing upward and occasionally outward over the cliff, so she relaxed into a network-interfacing chair, which mushroomed out of the ground as she approached. She settled in and pulled up the module in her mind for investigation.

Seems routine enough, she concluded after giving it a once over. She quickly etched an auxiliary pattern of her current neurological state into secure storage so she could be restored with minimal memory loss in the event that the module killed her this time around, but having already tried it at the party, she felt reasonably safe about the experiment. Then, with a bit of scrutiny, she identified the portions of the neural configuration that seemed most likely to evoke the social lubrication it had inspired and excised them from the configuration. She wanted to maintain lucidity for this experiment. All she wanted to do was recreate the visual phenomena, the hallucinations. When she was ready, she activated the module.

As at the party, the only immediate and long-lasting effect would have been the emotional traits, the social relaxation, and she had disabled those traits. The visual glitches had been sporadic, and therefore nothing much happened for a while. But she waited patiently, happy to gaze at the stars in the meantime.

A glitch flashed into her vision but vanished too quickly for her to access it attentively. *Hmmm.* She made an adjustment to her own visual processing to enable continuous recording, not of her external surroundings, and not even of her retinal visual receptions, but of her own internal visual perceptions. She waited patiently. Another meteor sliced a razor-thin thread across the sky which rapidly dissipated away. A few minutes passed. Then another glitch. She promptly disabled the module and retrieved the recording.

There you are. I gotcha! An image became available to her. *Huh, that's interesting.* It seemed to be nothing more than a simple textual message. A short phrase had appeared in her vision and then vanished very quickly. All it said was 'Seek the Ontoscendians'. *What the heck is that?* she thought. Before pursuing it, she tried the module for a longer time, gathering additional glitch recordings, but they all revealed the same hallucination, the same terse message.

Lysándra queried the strange term on Ailuros's data network but found nothing. She tried variations on the term and still found nothing of seeming relevance. The likely etymology was fairly obvious, two recognizable roots, but as for any historical usage or reference, it all came up empty. *Shoot!* She pondered her options, but ultimately couldn't find any useful information about the Ontoscendians, whatever they were.

"Have you ever heard the term Ontoscendians?" asked Lysándra, as she and Ceólbur were wrapping up a quiet evening a few days later.

"Doesn't sound familiar," said Ceólbur with some thought. "I don't believe I've ever encountered it. Where did you hear it?" The sun was half concealed by their mountain in the distance, sending deep orange rays across the forest toward them, luminous rays that scintillated with black patches as the alien leaves fluttered in the treetops. The mountain itself was in pure silhouette except for a thin orange stripe painted across its top edge where it met the sky.

They headed inside, preparing to descend to the bunker, etch their recent brain states for retrieval in the event of any catastrophe, and decorporealize entirely.

"It was essentially whispered in my ear recently. I have no idea what it is."

"Hmmm." Ceólbur approached Lysándra, looked her in the eyes briefly, and then hugged her, trying to ignore his feelings of frustration. It didn't work.

Lysándra embraced him back and sighed over his shoulder. "I'm surprised I can't find any reference to it in the Ailuros data network."

"Have you tried the archives? Older data isn't necessarily maintained with immediate and full indexing."

"That hadn't occurred to me. I assumed it was a current reference. Good idea."

Ceólbur timed his inhales to her exhales so their abdomens fit together and attended to the sensation of the musculature of Lysándra's back, running his fingers along the bumps of her vertebrae. He was clinging to her in more ways than one. At the realization, he pulled back so they could see one another. He met her eyes, feeling both love and irritation. She wasn't listening to his concerns and he knew it. She was in real danger and just wouldn't listen. This time, it was he who sighed.

"What?" said Lysándra, looking directly into his eyes.

"Nothing." They fully separated. "Check the archives. See you soon." He smiled, half-so, and gazed out the high window-wall just in time to see the final sliver of piercing sun vanish behind the mountain with a conclusive flare. Then he rapidly dissipated into nothing as his body and brain orb were reduced to atom-level constituents, leaving Lysándra to likely do the same a moment later.

The archives could be accessed from anywhere via the Ailuros's planet-wide data network, but they could be accessed more quickly and efficiently from one of a few localized regions closest to one of the archive's various storage locations. So she decorporealized briefly, just long enough to transit through the network to one such region about a quarter of the planet's total longitude and a sixth of its latitude away. She recorporealized on an open, flat, sandy beach. Not dry sand, but rather a nearly level, wet tidal flat. Powerful surf endlessly curled up and self-obliterated against one boundary of the beach while high dunes far inland walled off the other boundary, leaving a wide tidal zone in between. Off these dunes, an almost permanent gale blew mesmerizing sheets of dry sand that swept down onto the mudflat and then raced furiously along the length of the beach at ankle height, weaving powerful, sandy rivulets that frantically veered, merged and separated, somewhat dizzyingly, from as far up the beach as Lysándra could see to equally far down the beach past her.

Upwind of Lysándra, she saw some people on the beach, and downwind, she saw others. But although they looked fairly ordinary, these two groups in either direction could not have been more different from one another if one had tried to imagine so. For this area was The Gate. It was, as it happened, also the location of one copy of the archive's storage. Upwind, Lysándra was seeing reality as it truly was. The people she saw were corporeal, physically there, either walking toward her on the physical beach, toward The Gate, or away from her, back to the physical reality of Ailuros. But downwind, the people she saw were, to varying degrees, noncorporeal presentations. Those walking away from her were venturing farther into Ailuros's largest virtuality. Those walking toward her were venturing outward toward reality.

She proceeded in the downwind direction, into The Gate. The wind blew from behind her so that she had to resist being swept along the beach faster than she intended. With each step she took, her sensory receptions—the sights of the wind-swept sand and the exploding surf, the sounds of the wind resonantly whistling and the waves crashing, the tactility of the air pushing against her back and the sand grains stinging her ankles, even the smell of the salty air and of organic seaweed—all blended into the perfectly synchronized virtuality that mirrored the ocean and the wind and the beach with flawless precision. At some point along her walk, she was no longer receiving any physical sensory receptions. She was only receiving comparable perceptions of the virtual variety. Likewise, she herself had steadily and fully decorporealized. She was now just as much in the virtuality as if she had simply entered it by the more traditional means of decorporealizing. There was no way to know precisely where The Gate began and ended. One just had to go far enough along the beach to no longer be within the transition zone.

As she passed through the transition zone of The Gate, new structures had slowly emerged ahead of her, invisible from the corporeal end of The Gate, transparent while transitioning, and fully resolved once through it.

Where from the physical end she had seen nothing downwind but the long stretch of bare beach, she now saw ahead of her tremendous architectures. One would initially be confused by the fact that, while some of these huge edifices were inland from the beach in reasonable fashion, others perplexingly appeared to be embedded in the distant mudflat or even in the ocean, seemingly flooded and brutalized by the unforgiving waves. But this was not the case. As she continued to walk away from The Gate, the beach itself faded away entirely, revealing all these buildings to reside in much more pleasant—and wind-free—surroundings by the time she reached them.

One such building was the archive. To call it a building was inadequate however. Was a planet a mere stone? The archive, humanity's legacy of knowledge, was hallowed ground in a million-year-old, galaxy-spanning civilization, and it was rendered appropriately regal. Under a polka-dotted sky, she now faced a towering structure that was under no requirement to conform to limitations of mass, support, strength, or even continuity. Some sections were disconnected not only from other parts, but from the ground. A confusing flourish of countless pinnacles erupted skyward, reaching practically out of sight. They curved and bent in ways that physical architecture could not have supported, and they moved and changed shape continuously, again out of mere virtual capability. Baroque detail swam dynamically across the surface of the stone construction, making the outline against the sky ooze as if alive. Through an array of flying buttresses, which were of course merely ornamental, she approached the entrance, a set of doors that would have accommodated an Ailurosian whale if such a creature had been inclined to visit.

The sound upon entering through the doors of swimming stained glass was deep and echoing—tangibly emotional. Again defying physics, the interior opened into a space that made no sense when the building was viewed from outside. There were no shelves, and certainly nothing resembling books or display screens or anything so archaic. The archive merely offered efficient access to its copious data stores, in addition to a shared culture in which people could quietly absorb information. Throughout the interior, Lysándra saw people in various forms of information engagement, some solitary and others in groups.

Lysándra settled into a quiet nook with rays of light shining past it from high vertical windows. She established a neural connection to the archive and began her search. Keyword searching was unlikely to work, as the archive consisted of many *folds*, compressed and almost unsearchable. They had to be unfolded first—one at a time. And so, with the assistance of some automation, she proceeded with the task.

And after a concerted effort, she actually found it! *Thank goodness!* she thought. She mentally opened the unfolded record and settled in for a languid consumption what would surely be a lengthy and detailed account of the glorious Ontoscendians:

Record query: Ontoscendians
Record label: Ontoscendian (pl. Ontoscendians)
Record etymology: Ontological transcendants
Record age: 802,325 years
Record location: Records of this age are not stored in the Ailuros archives. Please refer to the Thalassia archives instead.

Lysándra blinked and stared in disbelief, both at the age of the record and its startling terseness. 800,000 years. And five measly lines of summary. She was well aware that the archives on the next planet out from Zareasman, Thalassia, had older and more thorough archives, but hadn't initially anticipated she would need to go to such lengths. She considered her next move. She could have requested that the record be sent to her, but she could just easily transit there instead, and she always liked an opportunity to get off-world. She wasted no time in doing so.

Upon arriving on Thalassia, Lysândra headed directly to the archive without even corporealizing on a dais. Thalassia's largest virtuality was slightly different in look and feel from Ailuros's, more agrarian with very little urban infrastructure. The archives here were represented as a vast forest of enormous, timeless trees—of an unEarthly style. Sitting in eerily quiet glades on soft moss or woven-vine furniture, visitors would retrieve archive records in a variety of visual or other modalities and absorb ancient knowledge with the sound of alien birds flitting through the undergrowth and the sights of alien clouds drifting across gaps in the canopy overhead.

Knowing precisely where in the archive to look this time, Lysândra promptly pulled up the correct fold, unfolded it into decompressed form, and consumed the Ontoscendian record. She spread the record out in the air in front of her. There was remarkably little to it, in fact, but thankfully more than the pitiful Ailurosian archive had provided.

Record query: Ontoscendians
Record label: Ontoscendian (pl. Ontoscendians)

> *Record etymology: Ontological transcendants*
> *Record age: 802,325 years*
> *Record: Discovered during an archeological excavation initiated from the planet Fringalis in the Thorigon system, 22,000 light years from Earth.*

Lysândra let out a long low whistle of amazement. While 22,000 light years from the Center was still remote in Lysândra's own time, it was wholly untamed frontier 800,000 years ago. She continued to read.

> *The excavation explored the nearby system of Siremala, including its planet Cianthara. Cianthara's civilization was completely destroyed by an undetected coronal mass ejection, sterilizing the entire planet. In that historical period, there were no nearby worlds with transit stations to which the inhabitants of Cianthara could have escaped. Consequently, the entire population perished. Not a single person is believed to have transited off Cianthara or escaped by physical travel.*
>
> *The archeologists named the civilization the Ontoscendians since the original inhabitants' own name has been completely lost. This name reflects archeological discoveries of remnants of research into the nature of being, the extent of conscious potential, and neural network design with associated qualia exploration, all combined with numerous references to their having seemingly solved the End-Of-Universe-Survival-Problem, aka, ontological transcendents. However, the discoveries pertaining to End-Of-Universe survival are presumed to be either apocryphal or an error in the archeological analysis.*

What?! Lysândra gasped. Had the Ontoscendians not only solved the EOUSP, but done so via their advanced neural configuration designs, implying their solution was some sort of quale, perhaps the same one she had been building this entire time?! The only thing Lysândra needed was the location of the star Siremala and its planet, Cianthara.

> *No more information is available on the Ontoscendians at the time of this record. This record has been marked as incomplete and open for future entries if and when such information becomes available.*

That was it. Lysândra huffed out loud at the absence of an actual location for Thorigon or Siremala, then frowned and considered her options. Perhaps she could reach out to the archeologists who had performed the excavation or written the record. They could very well still be alive of course. After all, she was considerably older than the archeological excavation. But to her unending vexation, the record curiously included no such identifications. *Augh!* How could that be?

Lysândra poured over every component of the record again, and then a third time. She had overlooked nothing. The record could provide her with no additional information. She proceeded to search the remaining archives for the new references, the names of the stars and planets described, but she found nothing. The archive was simply incomplete on such ancient and far-flung societies. They had been lost for good.

She closed the entire record from her sight in disgust and lay back on the moss in the warmth of a ray of sunlight, watching purple clouds wisp across a pink sky. Now what?

18

L YSÀNDRA'S FIRST CONSCIOUS PERCEPTION WAS OF CORPOREALIZING ON THE glowing white transit station dais on the planet of Ermozara, in orbit of the star Vimrei. Before her, a sprawling atrium held similar transit stations distributed along five adjacent sides of an octagonal perimeter wall, with the two walls adjoining these five left blank and the last wall, eighth, left absent, leading into a hallway. Above her, the broad ceiling consisted of a uniformly luminous, low-curvature dome. In a relatively sparse fashion, people were walking through the atrium between the transit stations and the hallway.

She stepped off the dais and accessed the planetary travel records, looking for information about Ceòlbur's arrival. This inquiry revealed that his transit stream lagged behind hers slightly, simply due to random data shuffling in some intermediate transit router. Checking the local date, Lysàndra realized that her own transit time had achieved an efficiency of approximately ninety-five percent. One hundred percent would have implied traveling in a gravitationally straight line at the speed of light. One hundred percent efficiency could only be achieved without the use of intermediate routing and associated delays, which was nearly impossible over longer interstellar distances.

Ceòlbur's transit would almost certainly be nearly identical to hers. Nevertheless, after a 9000 year trip, his data had apparently lost a few days here and there in routing stations along the way. Lysàndra left the transit facility to explore the planet until Ceòlbur's arrival.

She exited the transit complex into a lush city, run through with elegant varieties of life. Apparently, Ermozara was a planet on which life had never evolved beyond mono-cellularity, as was the norm throughout the galaxy, but upon its colonization, Ermozara had subsequently been thoroughly populated with a variety of species from other galactic locales.

The city was spacious, as eternal-aged beings had no patience for discomfort or crowding. A row of buildings stretched away from her. These buildings completely lacked for straight edges, corners, or anything even resembling industrial efficiency. Woven into their curved architecture were extensive plant-like lifeforms, but unEarthly in appearance: vines, trunks, and surfaces that resembled leaves except for their continual movement. Blues, cyans, and aquas dominated the alien flora as the vines stretched right up, around, and even through the buildings. Presumably, the same vines and trunks grew through the interior spaces concealed from view as well.

As was the trend with Rihon, his latest art unveiling was a huge deal. A substantial portion of the system's cultural capacity across multiple planets, moons and orbital stations seemed to be overtaken with the big event. Everywhere Lysàndra went, she found people discussing it and banners and other media of a visual, interactive, and neural-engaging sort, raising awareness of it. Even the mycelial data network's larger virtualities, many of which were veritable planets in expanse themselves, were publicizing the event. And yet, Rihon had been as classically secretive as ever about his debut. No one had the slightest idea what the new art installation actually was. But everyone agreed that the creator of Contemplating Oblivion, which was still in operation and continually hosting a steady tide of visitors, was overdue for a major spectacle. That former masterpiece was 27,000 years old after all. Rihon was so overdue, in fact, that people would have wondered if he had faded away, except that invitations to this current event had gone out right on the heels of Minerva's discovery, millennia ago. Clearly he had begun planning new work on a grand composition almost immediately.

She lazily explored and enjoyed Ermozara's offerings until Ceòlbur arrived a few days later. She then met him at the transit nexus and they continued to explore the planet together for a few weeks until the opening gala of Rihon's composition.

The day of the unveiling, nothing else on the entire planet was deemed of much importance. It was all anyone could talk about. The population of the Vimrei system had bloomed from its usual fifty billion to well in excess of 500 billion. Although the grand opening would only accommodate a tiny fraction of the new visitors, people would subsequently pour in to see the installation, day by day, for years to come.

The day before the big event, Lysàndra received a peculiar card at her residence. It possessed the appearance and fragility of gold leaf, although did not tear at handling. No writing or other embellishment adorned it, but it came alive in her hand, gently folding, rolling, and undulating in the cup of her palm. Just as she became confused by what else it could do, or what else she was expected to do with it, it vaporized into gold dust that flew up off her hand and—maintaining its dust-like texture, no longer shiny leaf— formed a life-sized, three-dimensional bust of Rihon in the air before her, who was unmistakably recognizable, given his fame. Still lacking any color other than pure gold, the dust-textured head engaged with her directly, tracking her movements and gaze.

"My dearest Lysàndra," the bust said in a graceful tone and deep voice, moving fluidly as it spoke, "I would like to most cordially invite you and your colleague, Ceòlbur, to be my guests at the opening gala of my latest creation. Upon your arrival, please identify yourself at the entry and you will be guided to the VIP section. I very much look forward to meeting you in person." The figure smiled, turned and nodded directly to Ceòlbur as well, and then disintegrated away entirely.

"Wow," said Ceòlbur. "Half a trillion attendees and you get a personal invitation. I wonder why he singled you out like that."

"The timing is a little odd, I'll admit," Lysàndra responded, looking out the window over the cityscape spread before them. "Rihon announced this artwork right after the biologist Minerva's discovery of the Neuralium reached the Center, so if I expected this piece to reflect any event or person in particular, it would be her research, not ours. It hadn't previously crossed my mind that it would necessarily have anything to do with either of us. Perhaps that was silly however."

"You continually underestimate the impact of your network," said Ceòl- bur. "Maybe you could consider waking up to the reality of it now?"

The Vimrei system comprised five planets, three populated, with forty- three moons of notable size between them. Rihon had converted an entire asteroid into a thin shell surrounding the moon Regenium in orbit of Krasavitia, completely shielding it from view. This shell was a remarkable structure in and of itself. Despite antiquated notions of surrounding stars within a solid shell to absorb their solar energy, it was, in practicality, impossible to do this since, even if the shell rotated so as to keep the equatorial region from falling into the star, the poles of the shell would merely spin in place and therefore have no defense against the star's gravity. Consequently, the best way to construct such a shell was from a cloud of satellites that orbited the star—or in Regenium's case, orbited the moon—along a variety of axes, with each satellite extending an expansive sheet facing in toward the star—or moon. In this way, a sufficiently dense cloud of satellites residing in a range of orbital altitudes could completely enclose a star—or moon. As such, Rihon had acquired the entire moon of Regenium 18,000 years ago and begun constructing such a shell. It seemed ostentatious, even for Rihon, to go to such efforts just to cloak a moon from view while he secretly constructed some ornate art piece on its surface, but this was Rihon after all. It was unwise to under-estimate his flair for the dramatic.

When the formal time of the official event had arrived, they made their way to the grand gala. As per Rihon's design, Regenium was accessed by first transiting to one of several orbital stations that resided at orbits above the shell, and then subsequently transiting down to the lunar surface to experience the art installation. Lysàndra and Ceòlbur joined the millions of other gala attendees in steadily accessing substellar transit stations on Ermozara and then transiting to these orbital stations around Regenium—as others did the same from all over the solar system. There, they corporealized on adjacent daises and found themselves in the extravagant setting of the orbital station. No detail had been spared. They were on the slate-blue non-repeating tiled surface of an entirely artificial sphere, a planetoid of sorts. This was the orbital station. At standing height, the horizon was only a few hundred feet distant. Lysàndra quickly calculated that she could probably walk around its circumference in about an hour, which a little more calculation determined would offer just under 300,000 people a modest crowding of space to mingle in, not too bad for a fancy gala of this sort. The forty or so total orbital stations around Regenium would then provide a capacity of a little over ten million gala attendees for Rihon's grand unveiling. The total visitor influx to the Ermozara system for this inauguration would surely take a long time to slowly visit the installation after the opening night.

Transit daises were scattered seemingly haphazard across the blue gray surface. At widely spaced intervals, solitary columns twice as wide as a person was tall, glowing evenly so as to illuminate the surroundings, extended several stories up and supported an outer glass sphere that contained the entire planetoid like a green house. The outer sphere had no seams, and other than its refractory and reflective properties was otherwise difficult to discern, as it revealed the night sky above, splashed with stars and slashed through by the Milky Way. People were engaged in the usual chit chat, awaiting the arrival of Rihon, as more guests transited in. Practically as soon as they stepped off their daises, Lysàndra and Ceòlbur were greeted by a primly dressed woman.

"Welcome Lysàndra and Ceòlbur. I am Ananda, Rihon's assistant. May I offer you anything? Food? Drink?"

"Wine," said Lysàndra, desiring her vice of choice.

"This station has the usual amenities. Help yourself." At a thought, a full glass materialized in Lysàndra's fingers.

"Thank you," she said. Ananda looked at Ceòlbur.

"Oh, no thank you," he replied.

"If you will follow me please," she said, "Rihon is waiting for you." Lysàndra and Ceòlbur gave each other a look and then followed Ananda to a one of the glowing columns, which then opened to reveal an inner cylindrical chamber. They entered and the floor promptly descended into the interior of the planetoid. Moments later they settled into a large open space, almost unpopulated, unlike the surface. The room stretched across the entire interior of the planetoid. The usual furnishings of comfort were distributed across another tiled slate-blue floor. Lounging chairs, low tables, fountains, plants, and a variety of games of various sorts: such items seemed simply strewn across the near-endless floor. Distant glass walls and a transparent ceiling revealed the dizzying, triangularly arranged beams and girders holding the entire spherical structure together as far as they could see in all directions. While the ceiling of this interior was transparent, they could not see the surface with its attendees above them, as the view was totally obscured by the meshwork of beams composing the planetoid's skeleton.

"Welcome," came a sonorous voice. Across the cavernous room they saw a tall and imposing man approaching them, unmistakably the famous Rihon. An entourage of Rihon's acquaintances sprinkled throughout the room turned their heads to see what had caught Rihon's attention. Rihon walked up, clad in slightly shimmering garb, with hair that seemed to float lightly around his head. "As I'm sure you know, I am Rihon. It is an honor to meet you—*you both*," he quickly clarified.

"*You're* honored?" said Lysàndra, sputtering on her wine slightly. "Until we received your invitation earlier today, we had no idea you knew we were even here. We are but two among millions attending tonight."

"Nothing could be further from the truth. You are not two among millions. You are two separated from millions. Separated from trillions in fact. What you have accomplished—" Rihon trailed off in awe. "There is another though. Someone I want you to meet." He turned to look across the gaping room, searching the retinue of VIPs for one in particular. "Minèrva!" He called out, desperate for even his impressive voice to carry the distance. Far across the room, Lysàndra resolved one person out of the gathering, so far away that no features were immediately distinguishable. "Why don't we meet her half way," Rihon joked. The three headed toward the woman while she approached them as well. They met in the middle, where Lysàndra now recognized the preferred corporealization of the famous biologist whose prior work had set her own research on such a profound path. "Lysàndra, Ceòlbur, I would like to introduce you to Minèrva. Minèrva, these are—"

"Yes yes," Minèrva cut in. "What a marvel to meet you. Your extension of the Neuralium is simply astonishing. I never had such high hopes when I first discovered it."

"To the contrary," said Lysàndra, "I—we—never would have made it far past our feeble first steps without having your discovery to propel it to the next stage."

"Yeah yeah, you're both modest. We get it," said Rihon. "You do realize that your discoveries—first yours Minèrva, and then yours Lysàndra—have become the dominant recreational drugs in the Center."

Minèrva snorted and literally jerked with laughter. "I bet she *doesn't* know that yet, and what a wonderful way to drop such news on her." A drink appeared in Minèrva's hand, ornate and decorated beyond recognition, churning with animated color and peculiar living textures. She thigh-bumped Rihon and flashed him a sparkly smile. Lysàndra noticed Rihon return the smile.

"Ummm," said Lysàndra, "Obviously, people on Ailuros and in the adjacent systems have been known to use the Neuralium in similar ways. And I suppose I was aware of comparable usage of the network I published after combining the two."

"It has gone much further here," said Rihon.

"That's an understatement!" said Minèrva. "It's the primary practice of the—" she giggled, "the Cult of Lysàndra, they call it."

Lysàndra literally shook her head with surprise. Ceòlbur spoke first. "You can't be serious."

"It was the Cult of Minèrva first," said Rihon. "The Neuralium was the basis of a small enlightenment-seeking sect. Started by someone I know, in fact. Satori is his name."

"That was cute for a while," said Minèrva, "but nothing like what happened when your updated network arrived. It's a full blown religion now." Minèrva framed an imaginary placard in the air with her hands and spoke melodramatically, "Lysandrism!"

"I...don't know what to say," said Lysàndra.

"Do you not realize how big this thing is?" said Rihon. "Boy are you in for a surprise later today."

"What do you mean?" said Lysàndra. Rihon chuckled. "What do you think this is all about?" He opened his arms, indicating the entire space in which they stood. "Wow, Ailuros is really out there."

"I've been more concerned with this Deimos fellow than whatever some Satori cultist is coming up with," said Ceòlbur. "I haven't found the news about him the least bit quaint." Minèrva's coy demeanor diminished instantly at that remark as she suddenly looked grave.

"Yeah," Minèrva said. "Deimos is no joke."

Rihon just rolled his eyes however. "Don't worry about that kook. There are always people like him. He's been protesting my work since before either of you landed on the scene. He didn't like Contemplating Oblivion for my merely shining a light on the EOUSP and that was before you two contributed anything to the discussion. Just ignore him."

"He is a disturbing element," said Minèrva. "He has a large following. I guess I haven't quite figured him out yet."

"Forget him," declared Rihon.

"This isn't putting me at ease," said Ceòlbur. "Lysàndra, I keep telling you to take this seriously."

Lysàndra huffed. "Rihon's right. Someone always steps up to fill the complaining niche. This Deimos is just another noise-maker."

"Enough," said Rihon. "Tell us, what's the next step, you two? We need a more complete quale." The three weren't sure if he meant Lysàndra and Minèrva or Lysàndra and Ceòlbur.

"Lysàndra is hard at work," said Ceòlbur. "But I wish she wouldn't pursue it quite so insistently, or at least I wish you would agree not to publish whatever you develop as a result."

"Any new leads?" asked Minèrva, her brief moment of unease vanishing. "New ideas for what to do next?"

"Oh, I'm not sure," said Lysàndra. "It's a pretty dark art, trying to refine networks of this sort."

"Keeping it to yourself, eh?" said Rihon, who had clearly misunderstood her vagueness for deception. "Can't blame you. I can relate. Look where we're standing, just outside the event horizon of End—" he cut himself short. "Almost gave it away." He winked.

"You call the satellite shell an event horizon?" asked Ceòlbur.

Minèrva rolled her eyes. "We should count ourselves lucky he doesn't call it Rihon's Event Horizon Spec-tac-u-LAR." She waved jazz hands in the air as she said this and laughed.

Rihon rolled backward with a laugh. "Well, that's what it is. The horizon beyond which information, even knowledge, of the innards is unknown."

"Not after today, of course," said Lysàndra.

"Yeees," said Rihon, squinting pensively. "I'll have to call it something else after today, won't I?" He glanced past them at other VIPs arriving. "Is that...? I think it is. If you'll excuse me, I believe I have hosting duties to attend to." He set off back the way they had come, toward the column-supporting elevator.

Minèrva looked Lysàndra and Ceòlbur up and down. "I've been separated from my branchling for so long I can't imagine we have anything in common now," she said, changing the topic so abruptly Lysàndra felt the discombobulating quale of a double-take.

"Caelunis is slightly farther out than Ailuros," admitted Lysàndra. "But it hardly matters how far we travel. It's like yesterday to us."

"Yes, well, but I've been here, in the Center for a little while, for one thing. But also, my branchling has been conscious and aware this entire time, including while I was in transit. She accumulated 14,000 years of experience while I was traveling here."

"Fair point," said Ceòlbur. "I suppose the same is true of us, slightly shorter, but yes. Do you intend to return?"

"I don't know." She gave Rihon a look across the long room. "Even though I would leave a branch behind here if I returned, obviously, I'm not sure the branch heading home would be happy to leave all this behind now." Her facial expression displayed a rapid cascade of inner thoughts. "Caelunis is pretty remote. I think it would make more sense to move inward instead of returning outward again. I should message my branchling on Caelunis and recommend she consider *stasis-transiting* back here, if she is so inclined. Why even leave a branch of ourselves there when she comes here, which is what I did of course. She should move her entire self here instead of leaving a part of herself out there indefinitely."

"Stasis-transiting is an uncommon practice at interstellar distances," said Ceòlbur. "Leaving the remaining branch in stasis while you transit and only reviving it in the unlikely event of a transit failure, but otherwise destroying it upon receipt of successful transit. Interstellar distances and delays of awaiting the receipt from the destination just don't make it very practical."

"I know," said Minèrva wistfully, "but now that I'm here, I realize I don't want to be on Caelunis any longer. I think my branchling would feel the same way if she were here. Well, actually, I know she would, because here I am, feeling it." She laughed uncomfortably.

"Odd thing is," said Lysàndra, "we couldn't even leave local etchings on Ermozara when we transited to this station today."

"No security of transit at all?" said Minèrva. "That's rather shocking."

"Well," said Ceòlbur. "we were etched for the brief duration we were in transit from Ermozara of course, to insure against any immediate transit failure, but Lysàndra's correct that they then cleared the etching buffer for other visitors coming here today instead of stashing it for longer term security. I guess there's way more transit traffic in the system today than usual—what with this event—and they didn't properly prepare for it."

"In effect," said Lysàndra, "not only did we transit from Ermozara without branching—and why would we if we are only in the Vimrei system for this event itself—but we also *stasis-transited* in a roundabout way, with our etchings on Ermozara now erased to make room for other travelers. So, as we stand here, at this gala, we're actually the only instantiations in the entire system of ourselves that came all the way to the Center from Ailuros for Rihon's big event."

"Wow, lots of folks are coming here for the gala," said Minèrva. "Several million just today, and billions for the entire event, which will last years, I suppose. Makes sense. I've been here on the station for a few weeks while Rihon finalizes the unveiling. But he won't let me through the, uh, event horizon," she groaned, "so I have no idea what's in store down there."

"How did that happen, if I may ask?" said Lysàndra. "A lone scientist, studying on an outlying, uninhabited planet for thousands of years, suddenly connects with a gregarious iconoclast like him? Seems an odd match, if I may say."

Minèrva smirked at Lysàndra with a look she couldn't quite translate. "To the contrary, I think I was on Caelunis far too long. This, "she gestured their surroundings, "feels more like me. He feels more like home, I suppose. Most of us don't make a big deal out of whether we're fortified humans or de novos—it hardly matters in most respects—but he wears his underlying nature quite openly. It's almost like he wants people to know his art isn't quite human." She paused thoughtfully. "Oh I don't know. Perhaps it's all just a marketing ploy with him, playing off people's fascination with his nonhumanness to draw bigger crowds."

"Hmmm," said Ceòlbur, "so, is there no more work to do on the Neuralium?" He glanced around the room as he said this.

"Oh we had that little bugger solved ages ago," said Minèrva. "Every atom in the damn thing has long been known. And I—and my assistants, they're just minimal de novos, not much to talk to—observed its behavior in its natural habitat for thousands of years. Heck, by the time we were done studying it, it was starting to evolve into something else. Nothing lasts very long on Caelunis. The genetics—not based on nucleic acids at all, mind you —mutate quickly there. Species barely last five or ten thousand years on Caelunis."

"Seems like a place that could support research forever, in that case," said Lysàndra.

"Well, if my branchling is happy, good for her, but I'm certainly not going back. Ha! Saaay, you two should join us later."

"For what?" asked Lysàndra. Minèrva just exhaled loudly with a snicker and started moving away. "Just for some fun." She looked them up and down one last time. "See you on the surface."

"We'll see you there," said Ceòlbur. With that, Minèrva headed back to one of the other small groups in the room, leaving them all alone.

19

"CEÒLBUR." MINÈRVA APPROACHED LYSÀNDRA AND CEÒLBUR AGAIN. They had been navigating the VIP space rather awkwardly since their abandonment when they heard Minèrva call out to them.

"Yes? How are you enjoying this leisure time before the unveiling?" said Ceòlbur.

"Oh I'm fine. Since I've been here several weeks, I've gotten to know Rihon's construction team. Several of the people you see here are his assistants. They've worked with him on the construction of his various creations for centuries, millennia in some cases."

"And you have no idea what they've created down below on the moon?" asked Ceòlbur.

"Not the foggiest clue. How exciting!" A pause ensued.

"What did you want?" said Lysàndra. "I meant, how can we help—that sounds formal. Uh, why did you call us?"

"Right," said Minèrva. "Well, this pre-unveiling gala, of sorts, will go on for several hours. Rihon isn't sending anyone down to the surface until later, so we have some time to kill, aaand," she sidled a bit with pursed lips of anticipation, "I thought you might want to join us for a little fun," she said directly to Ceòlbur.

Ceòlbur squinted with suspicion. "Say more."

"Have you ever participated in a hive?" she said devilishly.

"The concept has been around forever," he replied, "But I haven't. I might have tried something a long time ago, but not since I met Lysàndra, I suppose."

Lysàndra winced. "I never said you couldn't."

"I didn't mean that. I just, we haven't, is all."

"But—" Lysàndra sputtered looking for words.

Minèrva's eyes darted back and forth between the two. "You can join too, of course," she said. "I just didn't get that sort of a read off you earlier. Was I wrong?"

"I suppose not," Lysàndra said. She looked around the room.

"She's quite linear," said Ceòlbur.

"Hey! I'm the most famous quale-diver in the galaxy," she retorted.

"Yes, but you aren't even particularly comfortable with branch-transiting. I mean here we are at this very moment. Tell me you haven't been worrying about how you'll reunify this experience with your branchling when we get back?"

"I wouldn't say 'worrying'. I guess it isn't the most comfortable concept for me."

Ceòlbur kissed her right there in front of Minèrva reassuringly. "You're right. You are the most famous quale-diver in the galaxy. Your buzz is the nature of consciousness, not so much the nature of identity. You are the best person anywhere—ever, I would surmise—at finding new configurations and new qualia. You don't have to be fascinated with absolutely everything else on top of that."

"Hmph." Lysàndra sighed. "I'm sorry, you should go with Minèrva," she said.

"You sure you don't want to come?" asked Ceòlbur.

"No, you're right. It's okay." Lysàndra looked more desperately around the room. She caught Rihon's eye as he chatted with another group and Rihon promptly enthusiastically waved her over.

"See?" said Minèrva. "Rihon needs his guest of honor. Ceòlbur come with me. I'll look after him, I promise." Ceòlbur watched a complicated expression flash across Lysàndra's face, but she gave her final blessing anyway and took off in the direction of Rihon.

"Come on," said Minèrva. "This'll be fun."

Ceòlbur followed Minèrva to a small group of people standing in a circle without speaking. They were obviously communicating in a more direct fashion. In its more intimate applications, this could be a rather sexual activity. Was that what Minèrva had invited him to, he wondered. Was this hive actually an orgy? It didn't have to be, he was fully aware, but it also could be, depending on the circumstances, and Minèrva had thus far provided no salient details.

As they approached, the circle widened to make space for two more without anyone looking up. Minèrva had simply engaged in the mental connection before they reached the circle. Minèrva took Ceòlbur's hand and guided him into the circle. He looked around to see who was there. The circle comprised twelve people in addition to the two of them, a decent mix of the sexes, with a handful of androgynous ambiguity, which was demographically unremarkable. Everyone didn't necessarily have their eyes closed, but those with their eyes open had the blank stare one would expect of a heavy day dream or trance, indicating that they weren't attending to their external visual stimuli. Unlike Minèrva's kind gesture, the rest of the circle wasn't holding hands. They were simply present, as if in a group meditation.

Welcome Ceòlbur, came a voice in his head. This wasn't the hive. This was simply his entry into nonverbal communication with someone in the group. In an indescribable way, he knew the voice came from a man across the circle from him.

Thank you inviting me, Ceòlbur responded.

We waited for you, as you requested, Minèrva. Is everyone ready? the same person expressed. This statement reached everyone in the circle in a way no more peculiar than speaking out loud would have seemed. If anything, the speaker's prior direct communication of welcome to Ceòlbur had been the more peculiar expression since there was no obvious way to accomplish such private communication by voice amongst a crowd. A chorus of nonverbal *yeses* and *let's goes* and *I'm readies* rang out in the nondescript place where such communications transpired.

Ceòlbur felt an otherness lingering on the periphery of his thoughts. It took the shape of sociability, a sense of other people, other minds present somewhere on the edge, somewhere in the dark space beyond his moment-to-moment focus. He pointed his attention at that sensation of others, moving himself toward it. He felt clumsy however. Hiving was a skill, much like many meditative practices that involved looking inward and seeing things that were usually left to instinct and the subconscious. And as with any skill, it took practice, which Ceòlbur sorely lacked in this domain. He concentrated on the sensation of others at the border of his mind. It was a more direct connection than merely hearing verbalizations. That was easy. That simpler feat was accomplished by piping another person's vocalizations directly into one's auditory cortex, literally emulating the superior temporal gyrus response to speech interactions. Hiving was a much deeper connection. If Ceòlbur could manage it, the boundary between his mind and the others would blur, all the while the neurological boundaries between their brains would, of course, remain as steadfast as ever. He concentrated on his perception of others in the misty borderlands of his mind.

He felt his hand being squeezed. *I can see you trying to reach us*, came Minèrva's voice in the conventional nonvocal-yet-vocal communication. *Come toward us*, she said. He knew she couldn't come get him. The journey that needed to be traversed was within the boundaries of his own mind. No one could retrieve him or pull him over in the same way that no one could forcibly violate another's mind. Modern brains had been designed with such security measures ever since the Great Fortification. He would have to find his own way to the outskirts of his mind. He sighed. Concentrating on his own inner monologue was precisely the wrong thing to do. That was the core of his self, the very center at the farthest radius from his boundary.

Relax, said Minèrva. *Follow the thread that leads to the group. You can do it.*

Ceòlbur had a brief sensation of out-of-body. He smiled knowing that the associated lightweight sensation, the sensation of his head floating away from his body, the sensation of his limbs stretching and retreating away from his torso, was one of Lysàndra's favorite qualia. He enjoyed it too, and he presumed it was the right direction to head in here as well. As he drifted away from his bodily association, he felt himself drifting toward the perception of others. That feeling grew stronger. He began to feel something between thoughts and voices, not quite either, or perhaps an amalgamation of the two. He could tell what the others were thinking, but it was a jumble. There were eleven other people after all and the whole point was to not take turns, but rather to find a resonance that pervaded the whole. His arrival actually stirred the resonance up, messing things up a bit, like dropping a pebble into otherwise smooth waves across the surface of water. He could feel that he had disturbed the harmony of the others, but he sensed no resentment. To the contrary, the group immediately reacted with practiced coordination, recomposing the harmony until again a sense of resonance took hold—but this time he was on the inside. He had successfully integrated his unique timbre into an eleven-part orchestra, growing it to twelve parts, and now their symphony could continue unabated.

Individuality was simultaneously preserved and inconsequential while in the hive. He felt no risk to, much less assault on, his personhood. He felt no fear. He felt his willing control over his participation, his ability to with-draw at a moment's notice as easily as an orchestra member could get up and walk off the stage any time he or she chose to do so—albeit with a comparable sense of disruption and offensiveness.

He briefly sought out Minèrva's pattern. It might take multiple forms. He might catch a glimpse of her own internal monologue for example. But most people didn't have much of a monologue when hiving. They had abandoned it to venture to their own boundary, just as he had. Her pattern could take other forms. Each person contributed their own personality, their quirks, their strengths, their weaknesses. This was their personal timbre. He could feel her loneliness on Caelunis. He could feel her desire for her branchling to rejoin her. He could feel her adoration of and attraction to Rihon.

Nice of you to join us, she said. He could feel the smile behind her face as if it were his own, the stretch of the cheek muscles and at the corners of his mouth, the brightness in her own eyes as if in his own eyes.

Everyone ready to play a game? This thought did not arrive as an auditory voice. It was a pure realization on Ceòlbur's part of a comparable thought expressed in someone else's mind. He could sense which timbre it was, but had no idea who in the standing circle it was. He dared not open his eyes for fear he would lose his connection, so he just went with it. A chorus of *yeses* rang up from the group. *I will paint an initial scene. Each of you then contribute. Go beyond imagery. Use all the senses, then go beyond your senses. Fill the scene's feelings, not just its appearance. Let's see what we come up with.* Ceòlbur saw a mental image form. It felt like the intentionality of imagining an image in his own mind, except that he hadn't originated it. An open field. Rolling hills. A mesa with and a razor-sharp top. Details were absent however. The color was flat, textures were minimal. Ceòlbur frowned momentarily but then realized this was intentional. The initiator had set up a rudimentary canvas for the rest of the hive to work on. As he observed, the scene began to fill in around him as the other participants joined in.

It was more than a scene however. He felt the presence of others viewing it with him. He felt his perspective shifting from one location to another as his mind haphazardly flitted from one mind to another. He took a breath and seized control of his mind's leaps from mind to mind. He settled down inside one of the other minds observing the scene, not his own. He could now attend to that mind with greater focus. A thought raced through his head, not his own, and the field suddenly differentiated into billions of tufts of grass. The other person had done this, but he had ridden their creative process along. Then yellow and purple wildflowers erupted across the landscape like a floral wildfire. The thought of that felt more peripheral though, as he realized that the flowers had been added by someone other than the mind he had settled into. He still wasn't doing this right, he realized. He should be able to feel everyone's minds simultaneously. He pulled himself out of the mind he was observing from the inside and tried to feel the entire hive simultaneously. This was a practiced and honed skill however and he was clumsy.

How are you doing? he felt Minèrva ask. No, not ask. Minèrva was simply wondering it in a nonvocal fashion. It certainly hadn't been a direct inquiry to him. Before he could directly respond, he already felt her reaction. *That's good,* she was thinking. What did that mean? But then he made sense of it. He had formulated his response to her question, not as a sequence of words, but simply as his own reaction to her thought, his response of *I'm okay, trying to get the hang of it,* to which she had promptly felt her own internal response, *that's good,* which he had then felt. This was going to be tricky, he realized.

He tried to stay outside a single hive member's mind and feel everyone at once. Someone was thinking about the mesa. Then, without notice, the sides of the mesa, previously featureless, vibrated and settled into the flutes of hexagonal basalt columns rising up the mesa's walls. The detail was incredible. Right down to the last microscopic crystal embedded in the rock. He could see and feel the totality of the mesa. Someone else, perhaps multiple participants, were focusing tremendous attention on the finest details of the mesa's geology.

He felt a discombobulation. The resonance of the group had suddenly flailed. He then observed as the sky first turned blue, then orange, then blue again, and then orange yet again. Two people were clashing over their intended contribution to the scene. As the hive began to work more intimately for him he sensed the aesthetic preference of the two minds out there in the mental mist. He could actually feel both preferences at once. The resonance quickly returned as the two minds found their cohesion and rapidly settled into a rhythm. They hummed briefly with concordance, came to a mutual preference, not a winning and a losing, not even a compromise, but a decision that neither could have made alone, a decision made by some harmonized being that only existed as their merger, and then the sky became sunset watermelon to perfect mutual satisfaction.

He suddenly felt something lofty and magnificent. Someone in the group had had a spark of inspiration. Just as he was realizing what that realization was, it manifested faster than he could process it as, suddenly, the most complex blanket of clouds he had ever beheld materialized out of the air, high in the sky, at about half coverage, showing the fuchsia sky through. The clouds, volumetric, shadow-pocked and dense, smoldered with energy and pure light. Everyone piled on the inspiration and the clouds oozed and flowed and accumulated depth and texture beyond anything he had ever beheld.

Add something, he heard—felt—as Minèrva gently invited him in. He wasn't sure this sort of creativity was his strength and the others were expanding the scene faster than he could come up with an idea of his own, but as he watched a small flock of birds dart past his bodiless point of view into the scene—did he remember feeling someone create them a moment ago, he wasn't sure—he made an attempt. At an intentional thought, he invoked a small tree in the midst of the grass. It pushed the tufts and the wildflowers outward, burst upward, expanded its trunk, and settled into an initial form. He quickly ordained it with basic branches and leaves, but was unsure what to do next. He felt the hive quickly draw its attention to the tree. Ideas exploded, thrived, morphed, and died faster than he could follow them. A coordinated preference was designed and refined, all of this happened almost instantly, and the tree immediately erupted with four-petaled bright lavender blooms that continuously color-cycled through variations of lavender and purple and blue hues, with similarly colored glitter continually raining off them to the ground, rapidly turning the grass beneath the tree the same color with scintillating glittery dust. He felt the hive compliment him, another pure thought: *Nice tree*, accompanied again by the sensation of genuine compassion and smiling. He felt he could barely take credit, as the fanciful blooms, the product of the hive, were far more glorious than the brute trunks and bare leaves he had initiated, but he felt nothing but warmth and appreciation from the hive.

And then he found the true essence of the hive for the first time. He could feel multiple ideas surfacing from all members, but crucially, he had completely lost the ability to differentiate which ideas were his own and which were someone else's. The savannah suddenly peppered with hundreds of instances of his tree, each of the same fantastical species but also as diverse as any natural conglomeration—but had that been his idea? He realized the question wasn't even valid. That was the entire point. He could feel twelve emotional perspectives, but also a quadratic combination of pairs and trios and quartets of those emotions intermingled, the feelings of people who did not exist except as a union of two or more other people.

This went on for a while, the scene becoming increasingly ornate and eventually discarding conventional notions of gravity, biological form, and even routine weather. Deep canyons split across the landscape. Strange sheets of rain swept across the land like long curtains, arriving from one horizon and departing over the other. Marbled planets, some spherical and some octahedral, expanded into view, hanging luminous and enormous, low in the sky. Inverted mountains balanced in the distance, teetering on their upside-down snowy peaks, with the snow and rocky debris steadily falling away, downward, onto the shadowed field below. Thousands of peculiar animal-like creatures lurched, rolled, bounced, and flew back and forth over the land. All the while, his sense as an observer or participant faded into the background as he felt and became something else, something expanded and multi-variate.

When the hive was done, everyone reveled in the scene while and the initiator complimented everyone. He then explained that no effort would be made to save the creation. It would be destroyed when the hive dissolved. All that would remain was their personal memories of it, perhaps fragmentary, perhaps crystalline, depending on each person's skill at splicing hive memorabilia off to take home—which of course Ceòlbur was not practiced at. He expected that he would remember this like a dream later. It might feel visceral, the imagery might linger somewhat, but the emotional qualities of the scene would be the more indelible memento—the visual details would likely fade.

He sensed a pause as everyone surfed their emulated endorphins.

So, who wants to fuck? he suddenly felt. This was immediately followed by a rowdy response of humor and jubilation, and he felt the hive rapidly assume a very different sort of energy and intimacy. He quickly withdrew to his own mind.

Thanks for joining us, he felt Minèrva's mind express. At this point, they were sufficiently synchronized that even the semblance of vocal communication had vanished between them. He was simply experiencing her appreciative sentiment in the same way she was feeling it to herself. He returned all the way back to his own center, felt himself as a solitary person, saw the ruckus beginning to ensue just outside the boundary of his mind where the others were building energy for their next activity, and then he opened his eyes. He knew he could maintain his connection like this, if he wanted, eyes open. He noticed others in the circle with their eyes open, with glassy stares of unawareness, but he used this opportunity to disengage from the symphony, then from the orchestra, then from the stage entirely. Just before he fully disconnected, he felt Minèrva squeeze his hand once again and then release her grip. He was out.

20

RIHON STEPPED UP ONTO A STAGE. They had departed the VIP interior of the orbital station and ascended to return to the public event on the surface of the planetoid. Rihon's presence was being projected onto numerous replica stages on the planetoid so that all guests could see him speak. Likewise, the same projection was shared in similar fashion across the multiple planetoids orbiting the moon. In this way, all of the millions of people in attendance could observe Rihon's speech firsthand.

He paced patiently back and forth for a while, building anticipation. When he finally spoke, he did so without stopping or turning to face the crowd, almost looking at his feet as he strode.

"Thank you for coming," he began in a quiet voice, as if he were lost in his own thoughts instead of engaging with legions of fans. "I am truly honored that you have made your way here today. I know that some of you began your voyage thousands of years ago from the far reaches of the galaxy, and your commitment is not lost on me." He was still pacing back and forth. "I began this project almost immediately after learning of the Caelusian Neuralium. The first time I wore its neural configuration..." He trailed off, stopped pacing, and turned to face the crowd. "The first time I wore the Neuralium, something profound changed within me. I hardly need to describe it to you. Surely almost every person here has felt the same thing, felt its effects. I cannot improve on the words of the venerable researcher who discovered the Neuralium, Minèrva, the first person in the galaxy who felt it, who knew it." He paused long enough for the silence to settle upon the crowd, and then he hollered. "HOPE!" The crowd roared. "Although we know it will be billions of years, potentially longer, until the seemingly inevitable befalls us, the fate of the universe has nevertheless felt known and inescapable for a million years now, since the Closure, since the Fortification, since the Exodus. We have known the future all this time and yet we have found no way to survive it." He spoke more quickly and with greater energy. "Not only will humanity most assuredly die, but so will all living things. All *conscious* things! Mind itself will die. All our accomplishments, all the accomplishments of other beings whom we have made contact with in other galaxies. It will all end! We have found no way out, and yet, Minèrva gave us hope. And that hope has revitalized humanity in our current era. *Minèrva has woken us up!*" Applause and cheering.

He grinned wickedly. "Would you like to meet her?" he said. Another uproarious response boomed from the crowd. He beckoned off stage and Minèrva gingerly walked up, clearly nervous under the gaze of millions of observers. Rihon took her hand and held it straight up, standing next to her. He would have offered her a chance to speak, but she had admitted in advance she couldn't imagine doing so and he had politely honored her preference. "Minèrva," he said. "Thank you...stand there would you. Let the wonderful people see you while I continue." She stood awkwardly just slightly off center while Rihon mustered his second act.

"But as you all know," he said. "It didn't end there." To Rihon's surprise the crowd spontaneously started chanting Ly-san-dra in repetition. Rihon easily spoke over the hoard. "Yes yes. The greatest quale-diver to have ever lived discovered a tremendous neural configuration the likes of which humanity has never experienced. A quale of the EOUSP!" The crowd cheered. "We didn't know such a thing was possible at the time. But the quale remained mysterious even to Lysàndra. Neither she nor anyone else could refine it beyond its initial EOUSP evocation. But it was real. It was substantial, and we all knew it. And then...and THEN! Lysàndra had the unique brilliance—unique among all of us from across the galaxy—to combine her network with the Neuralium, a feat no one else had managed to do. And that brings us to today." He paused, looked pensively upwards, away from the crowd, toward the glass ceiling above them, toward the stars. "We now know. We KNOW! We know there is a solution to the EOUSP! Existence. Mind. Consciousness. Love. Endearing love my beautiful people. These things will live on longer than the UNIVERSE ITSELF!" he screamed. At that, the crowd simply lost its ability to control itself. Standing before every stage on every planetoid, the millions of attendees roared with borderline hysteria.

Rihon waited patiently and then repeated himself. "Would you like to meet her?" The response was immediate. He beckoned again and this time Lysàndra felt herself being practically pulled up on the stage by Rihon's charisma. She trepidatiously ascended the few steps onto the stage, saw Minèrva laugh uncomfortably as she empathized with her own plight, and then proceeded to Rihon's side. He whispered in her ear, "Turn toward your fans, would you?" She looked back toward the steps and met Ceòlbur's supportive expression at the side of the stage, and then faced outward, unsure where to look. She looked over the people in front of her, to the near horizon, a bumpy line of heads packed together in the distance, curving from left to right around the short radius of the planetoid. She saw the crowd cheer and start chanting her name again. In this moment, for the first time, she began to understand what is was that she had done. This was what Rihon had meant earlier when he attempted to convey to her the significance of her work. Until now, she had simply failed to comprehend the enormity of her circumstances. She became aware that Rihon was applauding her at her side. She looked to him, unsure what to do other than stand there. He saved her by guiding her to a location next to Minèrva. She took her place and watched Rihon from behind as he continued speaking.

"On the moon of Regenium below us, I have constructed a monument in honor of these two incredible researchers' achievements. These inventors, these creators. Our saviors." All of this felt very overblown to Lysàndra as she reflected on the fact that no one knew whether the solution to the EOUSP was even remotely feasible. All of this might be for nought, and in a moment of sober reflection, anyone ought to be able to admit that fact, and yet, she saw no sign of such acknowledgment from the raucous crowd. "I would like to present to you my latest composition, Enduring Oblivion! THANK YOU EVERYONE!" The crowd underwent one final frenzy and Rihon led Minèrva and Lysàndra off the stage. Ananda quickly went up on stage and addressed the crowd with not nearly so much flare.

"Thank you Rihon for this incredible creation," she said. "The surface below will accommodate all attendees. Please move to the transit stations and we will reconvene on the lunar surface. And enjoy!"

Ananda exited the stage and joined Lysàndra, Minèrva, Ceòlbur, and Rihon.

"I'm quite excited to see what you all think of it," said Rihon. "Shall we?" He indicated a transit dais near the base of the stage. Ananda went first so she could assist with pedestrian traffic as people arrived. Then Minèrva went. Then Ceòlbur. "See you down there," Rihon said, gesturing her to the dais, invitation style. Lysàndra stepped up onto the glowing dais. Her vision went dark, the sound of the crowd faded to silence, her proprioceptive sensations of her body thinned to nothing. Then she felt her consciousness dwindling, not like falling asleep and not like fainting, but yet another way for her consciousness to drop away. As with any loss of consciousness, she didn't feel the moment when it ended. And then she immediately felt a wobbly sense of recovery on a new dais—standard and identical to all other transit daises with its glowing circular floor under her feet. But she now stood in new surroundings.

Lysàndra had been offered the opportunity to be among the first visitors from the orbiting planetoids, so she saw only a few people standing around, taking the scene in. Stepping off the dais, she found herself on the lunar surface. The entire surface of the moon had been reworked into a completely engineered structure, totally lacking in divot or bump, crevice or ridge. No semblance of unworked regolith, craters, fissures, canyons, or volcanos remained. The natural regolith, apparently four discrete and homogeneous colors—pure gray, apricot, vermillion, and peridot—maintained a slightly dusty and soft texture beneath her feet, marbled with ribbons and swirls without blending or muddying the distinct colors. Rather, the vibrancy of the four colors was maintained along sharp delineations of meandering borders. Upon close inspection, Lysàndra ascertained that the boundaries were actually fractals. Wherever she looked closely, she realized that instead of sharp lines of separation, they were actually fine waves, swirls and spirals that doubled back on themselves along the boundary between two adjacent colors.

While the ground had been reworked perfectly flat, it had interspersed discrete height changes spreading far and wide across the landscape, an infinite expanse of terraces, with any adjacent height change always the exact same rise, about the height of a standard step. Some of these terraces, rose, step by step, as high as two or three stories, always via a series of perfect terraced steps. The marbled color variance wrapped from any horizontal surface up the adjacent vertical risers in a smooth continuation, and then wrapped again onto the next level of terracing. However, she noticed that as the terraces gained height, the marbled colors became somewhat washed out, whiter than they were at lower terrace levels.

"Look up," she heard from Minèrva's soft voice, as if awe-struck. Nearby, she saw Minèrva gazing upwards. Lysàndra did as instructed. The sky was black, but densely salted with trillions of scintillating stars, far brighter and more crowded than the natural sky would have presented. The stars were so luminous and numerous that they produced a bright moonlight-like illumination of the surface, by which she had easily appreciated the colorful landscape. As she watched closely, she noticed very long, but subtle, dark silver straight line segments slowly slipping this way and that across the sky, like incredibly long pieces of wire. She eventually realized that the lines were not individual, but rather, organized into sets of four, meeting at right angles, bordering huge squares that were sliding slowly across the sky in completely random directions. Some of these dark-silver-edged squares were consistently in front of others. Any one square moved in a perfectly contiguous arc rising from one horizon, lazily crossing the sky, then setting beyond the opposite horizon over the course of a few minutes. After a moment's reflection, she realized that she was seeing the individual satellite shields from the underside, completely blocking the interior and exterior from one another. The edges of the shields clearly suffered slight refractive imperfections that betrayed their square profiles. The uncountable speckles of stars, on the other hand, did not move. The inner surface of the satellite shields were huge displays and their projected star fields moved across their fields in perfect synchrony to keep their displayed images absolutely immobile.

"Wow," said Lysàndra. "That's so beautiful."

"Look over there," said Minèrva pointing. Lysàndra followed and saw objects other than stars in the artificial sky. Imaginary planets came to her awareness, in some cases huge, simulating what the moon would see if in orbit of a host of planets other than its one true host planet, Krasavitia, which was completely blocked from view. Bright nebulae of reds and blues, wispy, slowly waved back and forth. Occasional meteors lanced across the display decoratively.

More people rapidly accumulated on the surface via the multiple transit daises and diffused across the landscape. Ceòlbur was standing nearby as well. He came to stand by her while she quickly calculated that, given the apparent curvature of the moon and its implied surface area, and the apparent density of attendees from where she could see, the crowd had just about completed the final transits from the planetoids to the moon.

Everyone stood around, oooing and aahing, but otherwise wondering if this was it, an elaborate planetarium of sorts. But of course, Rihon had much more prepared for them. As the last person transited down, the next stage of the performance began to take shape. Without notice, the images of planets and nebulas faded away, leaving only the starscape. Then, the points of light began to rearrange into groupings while filaments as thin as spider webs emerged, connecting the stars within the groups and between the groups. Pulses of light began to fire along the lengths of filaments, action potentials propagating from one node to another. It was immediately obvious to Lysàndra that this was a depiction of neural activity, but whose? The pulses moving along the filaments increased in speed and frequency until they were no longer visible as the filaments simply quivered with activity. The groupings then took on throbbing patterns, indicating periods of heightened or lessened activity from one group to another. Still, it wasn't immediately clear what sort of neural activity this was, or whose activity it was.

Right as Lysàndra had the significant realization that she was watching the activation of the neural configuration she herself had made galaxy-famous, she began to feel its psychological effects. But that was impossible. A network module could only interact with one person at a time. For Rihon's previous work, Contemplating Oblivion, everyone felt the art work's effects, but only because everyone was passively receiving one person's experience, the primary observer standing at the vertex of the platform where the inlaid rays in the floor met. She had heard of the renowned Satori's mass meditations using the Neuralium—and apparently he had begun using her revised network as well for his religious purposes, the same network they were now observing—but in those cases, each person had to use their own module, and in effect had to have a somewhat private experience even though they were doing so in a shared environment. But Lysàndra could immediately tell Rihon had accomplished something different here, something new.

As the EOUSP quale was evoked by the artwork's implementation of her published neural configuration, she felt it soak into her bones. All the previous components of the quale were there: a spiritual sense of the EOUSP, as per her first network, and also a sense of hope for a solution, as per the Neuralium, and finally a powerful recognition of the fact that a solution existed, per her second network. As she felt this perception saturating her sense of experience, and as she watched its activity fluttering above her, she became keenly aware of a sense of collective experience. Ceòlbur took hold of her hand and she knew he felt the same thing. She wasn't just feeling her own experience of the EOUSP quale, like in Satori's demonstrations. And she wasn't just a member of a passive audience feeling someone else's experience, like in Contemplating Oblivion. In this case, everyone on the moon was feeling the same thing at the same time. The artwork was engaging with her. And it was engaging with Ceòlbur. She could feel his presence through the network. To say nothing of feeling millions of other people too.

"It achieves a resonance with everyone present," she heard Rihon quietly say as he stood nearby. "It harmonizes all participants into a single, uniform synchrony of neural firing and conscious experience."

"So we aren't just feeling some primary observer, as with your last piece?" she said.

"No. It creates a unique harmony among those present at a given time. We are experiencing the quale as a single multimillion-person entity that is no more one of us than another. It is all of us at once. And tomorrow when other people attend, it will be that population's collective experience instead of ours. Enduring Oblivion is different every time you visit because its sensation depends not only on your glorious network of the EOUSP, but also on the reactions of everyone else who happens to be in attendance at the same time. Millions of people will be here at any given moment. They will be constantly coming and going all the time, for years, for centuries, perhaps for millennia. The quale will live in a persistent state, unending, for as long as anyone is present on the surface, but it will also continually change every time someone arrives or departs."

Lysàndra's eyes were hot with tears. She had never felt the EOUSP quale like this before. It was vastly more powerful than her previous experiences testing it.

"You can feel its magnified effect, can't you?" said Rihon. "Of course, I have none of your skill at refining the revelation of the quale itself. I have not improved on your perception of the solution one iota beyond your own accomplishment, but I have managed to bring the observers into a synchronized neural firing pattern and perceptual shared experience, and thereby amplified its apparent emotional impact, which I was surprised by when I first chanced upon it."

"It's brilliant," said Lysàndra. "It's simply brilliant." She tore her gaze away from the sky and looked round. Everyone was staring upwards, trance-like, and almost everyone was on the brink of tears. She had never seen anything like it.

"How did you do this?" she said. "How did you accomplish this?" She received no response, but intuited that Rihon was smiling with appreciation.

"This is fucking amazing," she heard Minèrva murmur to herself nearby. "The Neuralium is nothing compared to this, and that's saying a lot. The Neuralium is incredible. But this...is so far beyond that."

"Our greatest strength is our unity," said Rihon. "We may be alone in the darkness, but at least we're alone together."

It was right about the time that Lysàndra was observing a peculiar expression on Ceòlbur's face as he gazed upward that things started going wrong. She detected a tingling feature of the quale that shouldn't have been there, but it was subtle enough that she was quickly distracted by Ceòlbur's expression, so she briefly forgot about it. He had a forlorn look, verging on sorrow. She approached him and looked upwards in tandem.

"Want to tell me what you're thinking?" she asked, taking his hand in her own.

"I can feel everyone. Can't you?"

"Yes. Rihon was explaining it to me a moment ago. He really does create incredible things, doesn't he?"

"I don't even care about the quale in this...this piece," he said. "I just want to feel all the people. We're all so connected."

"MmHmm," said Lysàndra. "You've made similar comments in the past. I think there's something here that resonates with you. You should explore that." She continued to watch and noticed, again, that the quale had taken on discomforting sensations. She frowned. Yes, something felt needle-like about the quale, something sharp. As she observed the view overhead, she tried to make sense of how things now looked different. The animation of the network's neural activity, distributed across the satellite shields, shifted in erroneous ways at the overlapping boundaries between adjacent displays, some sort of synchronization problem between the satellites, it seemed. And since the network being displayed was in direct correspondence to the network they were all wearing, this disruption was apparent in her sense of the quale as well. Something was very wrong.

The visual scene decayed further as the quale itself also degraded in quality. The view now seemed to have holes in it, and then she suddenly realized she was seeing true sky in gaps between the satellites, the natural starscape behind the shield. *What is going on?!* She thought. The satellites seemed to have lost their coordinated orbital dance. She looked at Rihon nearby and realized he was just as confused as she was. Ananda was standing with him and they were clearly furiously working in some shared mental space of technical oversight and project management that she was not keyed into. She watched them as they traded rapid desperate discussion she couldn't quite make out. Then she saw them turn on their heels and practically run through the loose crowd in some unknown direction, she presumed toward a control center of some sort from where they could more effectively troubleshoot the circumstances. The crowd was in an obvious state of disarray. Everyone was muttering their befuddlement with neighbors. Repeated declarations rang out over the surface declaring mass confusion.

Then, to everyone's horror, Lysàndra saw one satellite clip another. A rain of sparks erupted from the point of contact, and each of the two satellites was sent into rapid, opposing spins. A moment later, each of those two satellites similarly impacted other satellites with substantially greater eruptions of sparks. This cascade spread quickly until the entire sky was an utter chaos of fragmented satellite pieces flying completely haphazard, colliding with ever greater frequency and breaking into ever smaller pieces. By now, the network's psychological effects had fully collapsed and disconnected from everyone's brains.

As if to taunt Lysàndra's doubt that it could get worse, she felt a deep vibration in the ground from somewhere over the horizon, followed soon after by a corresponding low pitched rumble. Everyone immediately comprehended what had happened. A wave of screaming swept over the crowd and everyone was instantly running in all directions at once. She felt and then heard another rumble from over the horizon in another direction. She watched with calm, shocked awe as people mobbed toward the transit daises, and for the first time she noticed that they weren't glowing! The transit stations were all nonfunctional. That made no sense. Surely they weren't powered by the shield satellites. This shouldn't be happening! As if the mob couldn't have become more panicked than its initial flight, the global failure of all the transit stations by which they could have escaped surely accomplished this feat. Millions of people were now in a state of sheer terror.

Ordinarily, people might have partially accepted such a state of affairs with relative gentility, secure in the knowledge that recent etchings could be used to revive them with little more than a few hours of memory loss. But the exacerbating problem was that there were no such etchings stored at various transit stations around the solar system. There hadn't been sufficient storage allocated in advance of the gala to ensure such etchings were possible for a high-attendance event of this scale, and transit failures were so rare at distances within a solar system—unlike interstellar transits, which were slightly riskier—that people generally didn't worry about it too much. Of these crucial facts, millions of people were now keenly aware in the present moment—their current branches were on the cusp of total loss.

Some had accumulated long stretches of experience and memories since their last etchings and this had impressed a grave sense of identity on them should they now be lost. Lysàndra realized this was true of herself, in fact. She and Ceòlbur had not etched since their interstellar arrival. There just hadn't been a practical need. As Lysàndra watched this all play out with an oddly serene state of perplexity, she felt Minèrva and Ceòlbur simultaneously grab her respective arms, trying to tug her away.

"Where are we going?" she yelled at them above the din of everyone screaming and clattering satellite fragments exploding against the lunar surface. More pieces continued to crash all around them. People, their bodies, and more importantly the metal orb brains in their heads, were being obliterated by the destruction.

"We have to get near a dais in case they start operating again," yelled Ceòlbur.

"But they aren't working at all," Lysàndra yelled back. "Where did Rihon and Ananda go? They might be somewhere safe, an underground control center perhaps."

"Good idea. They went that way," yelled Minèrva, pointing. The trio took off, dodging around other people running in a crazed frenzy in all directions. A large chunk of a satellite practically erupted as it concussively smashed into the lunar surface to their right, throwing them wildly into the air and dispersing them far from one another. By the time she had arced back to the surface, landing safely from a fall that would have crushed an antiquated human's bones to shards, she didn't have any idea where Minèrva and Ceòlbur were. She bounded up a series of terraced steps nearby, trying to get to higher ground from which to search for them.

And that was the last conscious thought she had. Lysàndra was simply gone. Body, brain, mind and person. No more.

21

"**J**UST WHAT THE COSMIC HELL IS GOING ON UP THERE?!**"** Rihon practically yelled. He and Ananda had just burst out of an elevator into a subterranean set of rooms deep within Regenium. A handful of operators accompanied by several simple de novos were scattered through the rooms, working at control panels that were meant to interface with the shield satellites, the transit stations, and pretty much the entire infrastructure of the moon.

"We're still analyzing it now," replied an operator as he worked at a control panel. "The satellites' orbit-maintenance routines appear to have failed completely."

"That much is obvious," said Rihon.

"What about the transit daises?" said Ananda. "Why can't anyone up there escape? I tried sending the elevator back to the surface so people could at least come down here, but the system is claiming the elevator has nowhere to go. The surface structure the elevator ascends to was destroyed in the few seconds we descended here."

"Which means we're all trapped down here," said Rihon.

"I'm not sure what's wrong with the transit stations," an assistant said. "Their power modulators are offline. I haven't been able to bring any back online yet."

"People are dying up there!" Rihon said. "Many of them don't have etchings on the other planets in the system. This is so spectacularly rare, no one would even plan for it."

"Sir," said an obedient de novo, "This goes beyond rare. There can only be one explanation for the satellites and the transit stations failing simultaneously. They are completely unrelated and disconnected systems. They share absolutely nothing. No infrastructure, no data communications. They don't even rely on the same power sources. They are totally separate systems."

"Which means," said Rihon, understanding the assistant's point, but he couldn't bring himself to finish the statement out loud.

Ananda completed the thought. "This was deliberate. It was sabotage."

"More than that," said the same assistant. "A perpetrator would not need to disable the transit stations to intentionally destroy the satellites, which means the satellites were not the target. Destroying your creation, destroying the satellites, was merely the means to the true end, the actual goal of this attack."

"You can't be serious," said Rihon, understanding the implication.

"The goal was clearly to kill everyone on the surface," the assistant finished.

Rihon squinted and frowned thoughtfully. "No, not everyone," he said. "The goal was to kill someone, but not everyone."

"Why do you say that?" said Ananda.

"Because even if many of the attendees didn't produce recent etchings right before transiting here, they nevertheless have *relatively* recent etchings—or simply have other concurrent branchlings—somewhere else. Despite the horror transpiring at this very moment, the fact is, most of these people will still only lose a moderate period of time. Of course, people are strongly attached to their moment-to-moment sense of self. The fear of one's impending demise, even with knowledge of an etching mere seconds old, still inspires a dreadful sense of panic. Such a reaction is intrinsic to our conscious awareness of the immediate present. But when the etching is later revived, any such person will have lost essentially no time at all. Their identity—their memories, personality, experiences—may be practically unaltered depending on the age of the etching."

The assistant considered Rihon's statement and asked, "Why would someone orchestrate a sophisticated act of violence just for the wicked glee of inspiring the brief panic right before everyone dies—only to have everyone revive a few hours later anyway? Even if someone wanted to create a million *memories* of that panic, for unbelievably sadistic reasons, those memories will be erased when everyone is subsequently killed. A few minutes from now, there will be no memories of the horrors on the surface at all."

"Perhaps whoever did this was trying to erase someone's recent memory," said Ananda. "Perhaps someone up there possesses knowledge that would be harmful to whoever has done this?"

"But this attack had to be planned far in advance," said Rihon. "No, the point of what is happening here can't be the relatively brief loss most people on the surface will undergo."

"Then what was the point of this?!" asked Ananda, exasperated.

Rihon contemplated his forming theory. "Because you're right," he said to the assistant who had spoken previously. "The goal probably *was* to kill someone, just not everyone."

"But how?" said Ananda. "Presumably everyone has etchings and branchlings somewhere else, probably scattered throughout the galaxy." Rihon didn't immediately respond, knowing Ananda was moments away from finishing her own thought. "You can't be serious," she said. "That would mean whoever did this had to coordinate another simultaneous attack hundreds, potentially thousands of light years away. It would take millennia to plan and synchronize an attack of that nature."

"MmHmm," said Rihon thoughtfully. "And we're trapped down here, unable to do anything about it. Unable to even issue a warning to the other locus of this attack."

"A warning would be impossible!" declared Ananda. "Even if we knew where to issue a warning—"

"We do know," said Rihon.

"What?" Ananda said. "In any case, a simultaneous attack must already be underway, whereas our warning would only be issued now, centuries too late."

"Or millennia too late, as you point out," said Rihon. "You're right. We couldn't warn them if we tried, which we can't."

"Who could possibly be the target of an attack like that?" Ananda said. "You? Even if your art is contentious, does anyone want to kill you over it?"

"It isn't me," Rihon said knowingly. "I wasn't the target of this attack, but I know who was."

22

U KONSTRA: A NEUTRON STAR ON THE SURFACE OF WHICH LIFE SOMEHOW evolved under crushing gravity and disintegrating radiation.

Ukonstra didn't exist.

Well, sort of.

Lysăndra and Ceŏlbur oozed around one another, their nearly-two-dimensional forms sliding in contact like thin sheets.

"Are we swimming or exploring today?" asked Lysăndra, her blobulous form gently swirling around. The immense gravity of Ukonstra would not permit her body, such as it was, to develop much height, so she existed as a nearly two-dimensional amoeba-like being, as did most of the diverse fauna of Ukonstra.

"Oh swimming, I think," said Ceŏlbur, "Unless you were thinking of exploring the western mountains. We haven't been there yet." Lysăndra gazed over toward the imposing and ascendent mountains, mere blips on the surface of the gravitationous star, or stupendous peaks if that was the totality of one's world. Lysăndra and Ceŏlbur had never slid up them or viewed outward from their meager—or vertiginous—heights, gazing over the far horizon of the photonically scaturient star.

"Swimming it is," said Lysăndra. "The sea is warm today. The shaerdile and brodelai will be schooling actively and we can swim amongst them."

They seeped across the landscape, which gleamed a blinding violet-tinted white. If not for their endemic adaptation to living directly on the surface of the star, the temperature and illumination would have simply demolished them in an instant. The sea was a nearby region where the neutrons bonded somewhat weakly, giving one the ability to swim, in a fashion, in the shallows. Lysăndra and Ceŏlbur slid in and then slid sensuously over and under one another, while various aquatic species flowed around and over and under them.

It was around this time that the very nature of reality began to glitch problematically. The rendering of physics and various sensory stimuli—tactility and vision mainly—faltered and sputtered. This was spectacularly perplexing for Lysăndra and Ceŏlbur given their experiential immersion, their forgoing of their true memories and true selves. As far as the were concerned, Ukonstra was their home, their *reality*, and their protozoan bodies were, well, *their* bodies. This discombobulation of a seeming failure of fundamental physics didn't last long however, since as soon as their interface to the virtuality showed signs of error, they were promptly disconnected.

Lysăndra spontaneously corporealized in the central room of the house. With her sense of self fully restored she frowned at the spectacularly rare occurrence, looked up at the glass ceiling overhead, and sighed. Ceŏlbur walked in from another room.

"What happened?" he asked.

"I'm not sure yet. Let's take a look." They accessed the network and investigated the situation, poking and prodding countless parameters that governed their interface to the planetary data network, its infinite nearly-invisible strands permeating their home, the cliff it sat on, and the rest of the planet's crust.

"The entire house is losing connectivity," said Ceŏlbur. "And it's going fast. We've lost ten percent of our connection matrix."

"Something's eating the data lines," said Lysăndra.

"Literally?"

"Well," continued Lysăndra, "I don't know if a living organism is actually ingesting them, but they are being physically degraded. I'm pulling a sample up now." A tiny section of the wall of the house was put under microscopic investigation and both Lysăndra and Ceŏlbur gasped.

"Is that some sort of secondary network?" said Ceŏlbur.

"I think so. The wall is infiltrated with some other web of tendrils. I've never seen anything like this."

"And they're attacking the data network," said Ceŏlbur. "See that?"

"I do," said Lysăndra. "What in the world is going on?"

"I'm not able to contact anyone," said Ceŏlbur. "All my communiques are failing somewhere just beyond the house. I think the entire cliff is being invaded by this stuff."

"Ceŏlbur, what happens when this stuff gets into us, our bodies, our brains? Decorporealizing isn't going to do any good if this—thing—is eating the entire cliff."

"Oh no," said Ceŏlbur. "Our transit dais is dead, and I can't grow another one. It isn't working."

"And with the corrupted data transmissions," said Lysăndra, "we can't get out over the physical network either."

"We might have to actually make a run for it," said Ceŏlbur.

Lysăndra took a moment to respond as she ran some calculations. "I don't think we can outrun this. We'll catch it as our feet hit the ground. The whole cliff is going quickly. The bunker is infected, see that? There's no hope of decorporealizing and waiting this out, whatever it is."

"So we'll fly out without touching the ground," said Ceŏlbur. "Let's go, right now!" But instead Lysăndra grew a chair from the floor and sat down. "What are you doing?!" yelled Ceŏlbur. "We have to go now!"

"Look," she responded. "It's too late." Ceŏlbur looked at the data Lysăndra was studying. It was a sample taken from her own body. "I'm already infected with this stuff. My body is useless. If I go anywhere, I might even spread it to another part of the planet. I wonder if this is going to eat all of Ailuros." She watched with a certain calm as Ceŏlbur paced back and forth frantically, having realized he was similarly infected. "Even if it hasn't gotten into our brains yet," she said, "we have nowhere to store them. There's no way out. This thing is moving really fast."

"Our connection to Ukonstra died from here," said Ceŏlbur. "It's centralized in our house. It doesn't appear to be elsewhere on the planet, just here."

"It might spread from here," said Lysăndra.

"But it still originated right here," said Ceŏlbur. "What does that mean?" They considered the circumstances as the foreign data-mycelia rapidly dissolved the original mycelia all around them, and the data networks within them.

"I suppose it means this was deliberate and it targeted us specifically," said Lysăndra. "How else could it begin right under our home?" She looked at Ceŏlbur and he stopped pacing long enough to look back, horrified. "Ceŏlbur, we've been murdered." They looked at each other, the inevitability settling upon them.

Her thoughts became scrambled, her vision became grainy, her hearing took on noisy gritty sounds, her skin tingled. As her sight dimmed, she barely saw the faint and blurry form of Ceŏlbur's body give way, collapsing to the ground. And then she was gone too.

23

"LYSÂNDRA, WHERE ARE YOU?"

"I'm still at the archive. Is everything all right?"

"Hold on, I'm coming to you." A moment later, Ceôlbur appeared, standing on the archive's virtual but perfectly natural grass, near Lysândra.

"A large portion of Ailuros has gone down," he said. "Apparently, nothing is getting through in either direction from the rest of the planet. Lysândra, it includes our home with our branchlings, assuming they haven't gone somewhere else on Ailuros at the moment."

"Geez. Okay," she responded, taking it in. "I'm surprised you're even on Thalassia. I thought you would be there. I'm glad you aren't."

"I decided to catch up with you here to see what you had found in the archive."

"I did find some more information on the Ontoscendians, but it was still rather sparse. I'm not sure what to do next. But, what's going on on Ailuros? We're more than an hour away, so we're only just now receiving these apparent communications errors regarding some sort of failure that occurred that long ago there."

"This is crazy," said Ceôlbur. "I've never heard of something like this happening before. An area the size of a continent becoming unresponsive to all communication?" They continued to study the news coming in while attempting to send messages to their branchlings. "We won't know the success or failure of these communication attempts for two hours or so," he said.

"Look at this," said Lysândra. "It's a physical problem of some sort. The data network is being…attacked or…eaten?…by a similar sort of predatory network of a similar structure. You don't suppose this is natural do you?" Ceôlbur studied the same data for a while. "I've never heard of a planet whose natural lifeforms could harm our data network infrastructure. And we've been on Ailuros for hundreds of thousands of years already. Why would this happen now?"

"Everyone is trying to figure this out," Ceôlbur said. "Look at this, they were able to follow along as this…this…problem occurred, but they couldn't counteract it quickly enough to stop it until it had covered a tenth of the planet. I hope they get communications up soon."

But Lysândra had a sinking feeling. "Ceôlbur, look at how destructive this stuff is. They've already deconstructed its makeup. Look at it. This is going to affect way more than the data networks."

"But," Ceôlbur protested, "it only affects industrial molecular types. See? What's your point? It isn't eating the rock or the Ailurosian plant-life."

"No," agreed Lysândra, "but it will probably attack all forms of infrastructure built on the same physical and material components as the data network."

"Buildings?"

"Ceôlbur!" she declared. "That's not my point." She watched Ceôlbur looking back at her. "It's going to affect people!" Ceôlbur frowned pensively, absorbing this statement for a moment.

"So their bodies will disintegrate. They can just restore from an etching." But the moment the words escaped his lips, he already realized the error in his reasoning. "Oh no Lysândra! You can't be serious."

"Just look at it," she responded, literally gesticulating in the air as she simultaneously rendered the reporting visually in front of them. "Within the affected area, ten percent of the surface of Ailuros, not one molecule based on our construction materials is going to survive."

"So it doesn't even matter if they have etchings," said Ceôlbur.

"No," said Lysândra. "Their most recent branchlings outside the affected area will be the milestones of their revision."

"But, that's us," Ceôlbur responded. "I only just transited here. It's highly unlikely my branchling transited anywhere else after I did, and I can vouch that your branchling hadn't transited anywhere since you departed here either."

"Then yeah," Lysândra said. "As you said, it's us. We're what's left of them."

Lysândra watched Ceôlbur turning the implications over, a rapid flurry of expressions crossing his face. "We have branchlings in the Center, attending Rihon's grand art exhibit, I suppose," Ceôlbur said. "They could have carried ourselves forward in the worst case."

"Hardly matters," muttered Lysândra. They left 9000 years ago. Admittedly from their perspective, they have accumulated relatively little experience and memory since they were in transit most of that time. But you and I have been here, conscious the entire time. If we weren't on Thalassia right now, the deaths of our Ailurosian branches would lose 9000 years of history."

"Fair point," said Ceôlbur. "A genuine death in most respects."

Lysândra looking mournfully around. The ultrareal sky was beatific and peaceful. One would never have imagined the horrors unfolding on the next planet in toward Zareasman.

"I hope they didn't suffer," she said.

24

SATŎRI CONSUMED THE INFORMATION COMING OUT ABOUT THE ATTACK WITH the same sense of shock that was now sweeping outward across the galaxy at the speed of news, the speed of light. He took a moment to be aware that he was experiencing a rare quale, eviscerating shock. At his side sat one of his oldest branchlings as they engaged in a tight mental connection requiring no outward speech. His branchling sensed his awareness of his own shock and reacted with an awareness of that awareness. Satŏri *felt* that from his branchling and became aware at yet another level of abstraction. But the pair didn't dwell on this cascade much further. There were other matters to focus on. He simply couldn't believe that the famous Rihon's greatest creation since Contemplating Oblivion had been deliberately destroyed on its opening night.

Much less that doing so murderously ravaged millions of people, his branchling thought in response.

At least some of whom lacked any recent etchings or branchlings, Satŏri thought back. *The scale of loss is unfathomable.* Satŏri felt tears arriving. *Summed over the total attendance, thousands of years of conscious experience and memory formation were wiped away.*

Probably over a million years worth, his branchling concluded. They shuddered in unison at the simultaneously realized notion that anyone in attendance might have completely lacked an etching or branchling, total information theoretic death, without even a partial survival by some other branch or revivable etching.

Yes, I agree, Satŏri said—thought. *I can't even imagine such a thing.*

And yet, replied his branchling, *it's likely there were at least a few such victims among the vast numbers in attendance.*

Satŏri had attended as well, and he had died in similar fashion.

He was not the Satori who died there, of course. And like many others, the visiting Satori had lacked an etching from before transiting to the gala from elsewhere within the Vimrei system, and had similarly perished. No, as he sat here now, he was the branchling who had remained behind, or was that the one sitting next to him? Whose thought had that been?

It was you, the other expressed with a kind smile.

Could this attack have been one of the factions of Lysandrism? they suddenly wondered simultaneously.

It also could have been a follower of Deimos, expressed his branchling.

Or it could have been orchestrated by Deimos himself, Satŏri finished.

Rihon watched as the moderator introduced the session to the assembly. "We are here today to initiate a preliminary investigation into the recent tragic event that occurred on Regenium. This moon was obtained as the sole property of Rihon, acclaimed cosmological artist, who, let the record be known, is all but ubiquitously recognized and requires no further introduction. Rihon acquired Regenium approximately 18,000 years ago for his recent creation, a piece named Enduring Oblivion." Rihon shifted a bit as these opening remarks were laid out in cold factual terms. In the room, along with himself and an oversight panel, there were many others in attendance, including a pair of branchlings of the venerable Satori, whose religious leadership had earned himself significant notoriety. Nearby, Deimos glowered under the panel's suspicious glares, although he was in no way under official investigation, just the judgment of public opinion.

The moderator continued. "The sequence of events is already established, but for the record, within the first few minutes of the public unveiling of this art piece, the totality of satellites orbiting Regenium underwent a system-wide failure of their orbital maintenance routines. Uncharacteristically, at the exact same time, every transit station on the lunar surface also failed. This combination of events led to the unimaginable travesty that no one in attendance was able to escape as the satellites crashed into the lunar surface, resulting in a near total loss of life. Survivors include Rihon himself and his primary assistant Ananda, in addition to approximately five percent of those trapped on the surface." Rihon winced as he glanced over at Minèrva, who had, against all odds, escaped the calamity unscathed.

"Now, the question is, how did this happen, and given the apparent likelihood that this was intentional, who was behind it?" All eyes swept toward Deimos, who stood defiant against the storm.

"Rihon, please convey to the panel the details of your investigation so far, given that you were in the control center at the time of this purported attack." Rihon then proceeded to lay out a series of low-level details about the satellite control routines and the transit station installations. Although signs of sabotage were discovered in the associated control structures, there was no apparent way to trace the subversive alterations to any source.

"This is a vague and troubling situation," said the moderator. "We seem to have very little information to go on at the moment, although of course the investigation will continue with absolute authority and unrelenting diligence. An act of such unmitigated violence will not go unpunished." The moderator then turned her attention to Deimos.

"Deimos, you can understand why suspicion has been directed toward you. You have made no secret of your objection to Rihon's work in the past. In fact, you have openly condemned his portrayal of the EOUSP." Rihon rapidly contemplated these words, turning over in his mind his near certainty that neither he, nor his artistic creation had been the target of the attack, but rather that Lysandra had been the true target. Little did he know that precisely one other person—well, two—had come to the same conclusion entirely independently.

"But you overlook the fact that no one knew the subject of Rihon's latest work until moments before the unveiling," said Deimos. "There was no particular reason for me—or anyone else for that matter—to expect it to involve the EOUSP. While this was admittedly Rihon's largest creation since Contemplating Oblivion so long ago, he has nevertheless produced a copious portfolio of smaller pieces in the intervening millennia, many of which had nothing to do with the EOUSP. So how could anyone with ill intent toward Rihon's EOUSP artwork have known in advance to target this particular creation?" Murmurs of acknowledgement burbled through the crowd.

"Perhaps the perpetrator had someone working on the inside from the very beginning," said another member of the committee. "One of Rihon's construction crew. They could have been placed thousands of years ago."

"I have no way to defend myself against unsubstantiated conjecture," replied Deimos. "That is pure speculation."

This investigation will go nowhere, Satŏri conveyed mentally to his fellow branchling as they watched the discussion. *These perfunctory inquiries will go on for decades, perhaps centuries.*

His other responded. *Agreed. Any evidence will fade out before it can be discovered.* They jointly considered their options. *Whoever committed this act planned far in advance.*

Satŏri nodded. *Whoever did this was precise. This attack was surely planned with great care, no mistakes, and a long lead time.*

His branchling continued. *Solving this will require methods that the committee is too hamstrung by bureaucracy to manage.* They sighed in unison as the meeting droned on.

They don't even have a correct understanding of this assault, thought Satŏri.

The response: *They think Rihon was the target, but it was our beloved Lysandra. How will they ever solve this crime when they misunderstand that underlying fact?*

The pair sat in silence momentarily until one of them spoke-thought again. Was it Satŏri or his branchling? Did it matter? Was it even a valid question? *There's only one way to handle this.*

The other one, whoever that was, nodded. *We're going to have to send a spy into Deimos's community in order to protect Lysandra.*

We're the only ones who can protect her now. Lysandra will never be safe—

—as long as Deimos is left unrestricted.

Even Rihon conveys no indication of understanding—

—that neither he nor his great creation were the target of this attack. They glanced toward Rihon in a single coordinated motion, tilting their heads in synchrony, blinking as one. *Poor Rihon, sitting there thinking this was committed against him. We should contact him with our thoughts on this matter. Perhaps we can bring him some comfort.*

But we will keep our plan to ourselves.

Agreed. In fact, given the frangible nature of our branches of late—

—we can't even trust other Satori branches with our plan.

For Lysandra, the venerated.

For Lysandra, the inviolable.

25

LYSÂNDRA CONSIDERED THE OPTIONS SPREAD BEFORE HER. To her left, a quale of the heat of a warm mug combined with the weight of tired arms and the texture of soft velvet. To her right, the kinesthetic flow of a physical skill briefly becoming effortless, coupled with the moment of realization when the punchline of a joke resolves into clarity. And centered before her, musical frisson shivering up her spine, one of the most emotionally consuming sensations she had ever beheld, combined with the scent of cardamom and the texture of cool glass beneath fingertips. She selected the option to her left and played it into the central area. Around this center were seated Ceôlbur and three other friends. The quale she played took its place atop the pile, thereby replacing the quale that anyone perceived when attending to the pile.

"Ugh, good play," said Tria, a woman to her left, who proceeded to consider her own turn. With Lysândra's turn over, she gazed outward, away from the game, toward the nearby shoreline where gentle waves rolled endlessly in. She and Ceôlbur lived on Thalassia now and the group sat in the shade of Thalassa's yellow trees, near a glittering beach that slid into warm aquamarine water. Sand filtered between her toes.

"You quale-divers are so good at this game," said Priello, sitting opposite her, laughing to conceal his hopelessness regarding the game. "It's practically unfair." Broken shadows swayed across their playing area through the leaves fluttering above them.

Lysândra smiled in appreciation. "Well, I'm not very good as your crazy metaphysical identity games," she responded. "The last time we let you choose the game, I got stuck without a sense of spatiotemporal adhesion for a month. It took Ceôlbur a week to convince me I wasn't popping into existence every five seconds with a lifetime of artificial memory implantations."

Everyone laughed. "That was hilarious," said Faimee, next after Tria in the circle. "You kept calling us your 'solipsistic phantasms'. You didn't think any of us were real." They laughed harder as Lysândra fake-pouted with self-deprecation.

"Well, I think she has us beat this time," said Tria. "I've got nothing to work with here." Tria threw her entire metaphorical hand in the air and her collection of qualia abstractly dissolved in a fizzle of epiphenomenal mist.

"Hold on," said Ceôlbur. "There's two more tricks left in this round. Tria may be out, but I'm not quite finished yet."

"Me neither," declared Faimee, who was up next. But instead of playing her hand she studied Lysândra's face quizzically, which had adopted a distracted expression. "Lysândra, your hand's dipping. I can feel your qualia. Everything all right?"

"Yes." Lysândra pondered momentarily. "I just got an alert though."

"Anything serious?" asked Ceôlbur, always at the ready with concern.

"No, nothing like that. I have a standing alert against all data feeds, looking for anything pertaining to the EOUSP. There's news from Nyveron."

"What's Nyveron?" asked Priello.

"A planet in orbit of Eilunedra, on the outer rim," Lysândra responded. "Wow, this is incredible. Check this out everyone." The news appeared in the air above the center of the table where the qualia from the game figuratively resided, and everyone studied it together.

"Extragalactic species twelve," said Priello.

"We detected their initial signal a little under 2000 years ago," said Lysândra, "relativistically speaking of course. The signal was detected on Nyveron much earlier, obviously."

"As I recall," said Tria, whose skin and hair scintillated under the red Zareasman sun that dappled through the loose tree cover, "they transmitted for a while and then suddenly stopped, leaving the message mostly uninterpretable. It was quite vexing when it first vanished."

"But look," said Priello. "It has resumed now." The group silently consumed the news briefly: the second message, its terse content relative to the original message, its application as a key to unlock the remainder of the linguistic portion of the message. And the remaining mystery of what the logographic symbols actually meant.

"*Look at this!*" Lysândra practically yelled. "The aliens solved the EU-SOP!" The group studied the report.

Ceôlbur frowned. "Maaaybe. The lead researcher, Kaimea, is making that claim, but most of her colleagues don't agree with her. See?" The rest of group continued to discuss the implications, but Lysândra became lost in the report as she noticed something familiar and was pulled deeper into the well of absorbing fascination.

"Lysândra!" she heard for the third time, yanking her back.

"What?" she replied.

"We were discussing the newly revealed portion of the message that discusses their galactic exodus.

"Never mind that," she responded. "Look at the section of the report concerning the smaller data block." The group focused on the relevant portion but just gave Lysândra a shared look of confusion.

"What do you see here Lysândra?" asked Tria. "They still don't know what it contains."

"This data! It looks like a neural configuration!" Lysândra squealed. At least two of her friends audibly scoffed.

"An alien network?" said Ceôlbur. "I see no mention of that in the report."

"Yeah," said Faimee. "Surely, quale-divers on Nyveron would have tried wearing the network already, if that's what it was."

"I agree," said Lysândra, "but the data isn't quite right. The patterns indicate general similarities to networks of interconnected neural processing units, but there are sweeping errors throughout the data as well. It's all a little bit off, frankly. I think it's mistranslated somehow. They've completely misunderstood what they have on their hands."

"Wouldn't they detect the same error you're seeing now?" asked Priello.

"They aren't neural researchers," said Lysândra. "They're astronomers. I think they just didn't realize the precise nature of this data. The errors are concealing the meaning of the data. They're probably just flummoxed at the seemingly useless data they have."

Priello tilted his head, frowning. "But other quale-divers on Nyveron would have caught the error."

"I don't know," said Lysândra. "They would have to see these very subtle statistical errors I'm noticing to even think of looking at it a different way. This data block needs to be decrypted differently to fix the error. I think everyone on Nyveron just missed the mistake."

"But you can see the difference?" said Tria.

"Our Lysândra is special," laughed Priello. Everyone nodded.

"Wait!" Ceôlbur protested. "You aren't seriously considering—"

"Yes! I have to go there! I have to meet this astronomer, Kaimea, whoever she is, and learn how she attempted to translate the data blocks. Maybe I can help her fix it."

"Lysândra!" Ceôlbur declared. "17,000 light years? It'll take you forever to get there and back."

"34,000 years to be precise. I better start packing," she said teasingly.

"This is crazy," said Ceôlbur. "Are you sure you don't have the information you need in the report?"

"I don't think I can do any better than they did decrypting the message on my own. I don't know much about the standard techniques for studying extragalactic messages. But the astronomers on Nyveron are the best in the galaxy at this stuff. That's why they congregate out there on the rim. I need to get to them. We might be able to help each other. They might be our best hope of properly interpreting this message and getting this—oh my goodness—this *alien* neural configuration. Can you even imagine it?!"

Faimee spoke. "There are probably a million expert astronomers in the Zareasman system. Maybe ten million. Couldn't you ask them for help?" Lysândra considered this, wondering why she hadn't even thought of such an obvious idea. Eventually, she sorted it out and replied, somewhat surprised at her own realization.

"I want to meet the astronomers who have been spear-heading the research on a potentially alien neural configuration for the last 2000 years, especially if it might have applications to the network Ceôlbur and I have been building. For Earth's Sake, what if it's the *same* network?! That would be incredible. I want to go to the *source!*"

"I know that," said Ceôlbur. "I'm just pointing out that by the time you reunify, you will have gained another 34,000 years. What's the point?"

"Well, only one of us is going to gain all that additional time. The one who travels to Nyveron and back will only accumulate the time spent there, working on the message. It should be a blink to that branch. Then we'll reunify and we'll have that gained knowledge combined with what we currently know, and then who knows? Maybe it'll make all the difference and we'll improve the network. Don't you see how important this is?"

Ceôlbur shook his head, agitated. "Lysândra, I understand this is important to you, but why can't you focus on what's here and let the rest of the galaxy take care of itself? Look at what happened on Ailuros? This project isn't just a risk you take for yourself. You're endangering others."

Lysândra literally huffed out loud. "The actions of crazed terrorists are *not* my fault." Their friends watched somewhat uncomfortably as the interaction unfolded before them.

"But we could, at least, isolate ourselves as long as we're putting a target on our backs. We should leave. We should go to some unpopulated star."

"Do you really want to be that alone? We have a life here."

"No, I don't want to live in the middle of nowhere. I want you to stop pursuing this until the threat is dealt with and it's safe to continue. It's reckless to stay here as long as we're going to continue to attract attention from murderous psychopaths. We should leave."

"You two can't go!" protested Tria. "Right guys?" The others nodded. The conversation lulled briefly and the sensation of sand gently prickling her ankles in the breeze centralized in Lysândra's attention.

"Well, I think it's crazy," Ceôlbur continued, "but ultimately, it won't affect us here too much, short of potentially bringing more bad attention our way. It's beautiful how passionate you are about this, but I think it's dangerous. So, head off across the galaxy if you must. We'll continue here pretty much the same, regardless."

Lysândra's brows scrunched as she felt the pain of the discussion, but she didn't know what else to do about it, so she left it at that. She just *had* to know what this other person had discovered. Call it an obsession. At that thought she realized it *was* an obsession. And at *that* thought she second-guessed whether she was on the right side of the issue. And at *that* thought she doubled-down—with herself—about her resolve to plow forward regardless of any other factors. Nothing was going to stand in her way—a notion that immediately brought her back to the obsession thing, which she pushed out of her mind as quickly as possible.

She wanted a glass of wine—and so one appeared. But then she wasn't thirsty and so dismissed it just as quickly.

"Who's hungry?" declared Priello with a smile and a bit of a flourish.

"I could eat," said Faimee.

A few days later, Lysândra made a new etching and transmitted it toward an interstellar transit hub 1000 light years away. It would take several hops to reach the incredibly distant Eilunedra stellar system and its nestled planet of Nyveron. Lysândra was on her way to meet the mysterious Kaimea —and Lysändra never left Thalassia.

26

9OOO YEARS HAD PASSED SINCE THE AILUROSIAN ANNIHILATION. The population of the Zareasman system—populaces on the other planets, moons, and orbital stations—had rebuilt and moved on long ago. Lysändra and Ceôlbur had equally long ago resettled on Thalassia even though Ailuros had been repaired within scant days of the disaster, modulo unrecoverable information losses, most critically brain orbs and etchings, which had to be reset to their most recent milestones from elsewhere on Ailuros, or in the stellar system—or the galaxy, as necessary. Lysändra had found no additional clues to the location of Cianthara and the Ontoscendians in the archive. She was stuck. Maybe she would hear back from her branchling on Nyveron one day. Maybe not.

"More news from the Center," said Ceôlbur, one day, as he perused the steady stream of galactic goings on flowing in from all directions, but heavily concentrated in the direction of the Center, where humanity—and cultural activity—was the most populous. Lysändra turned to look at Ceôlbur.

"What's the news?" she said. She looked out from their new house, grown right up out of the sand, backed away from the surf a bit, facing the the setting sun. This home had an open, cabana-like design. Walls could render from the air as needed, or present as as borderless windows, or be dismissed entirely, vaporizing away. An armada of diminutive, insentient de novos constantly shooed away the alien versions of insects and other fauna, weeded out flora that cropped up inappropriately, and ceaselessly moved sand from where it was to where it ought to be. Sturdy bedrock offered them a deep and stable brain bunker, tightly interwoven into Thalassa's myceliumesque data network—along with the rest of the house of course.

"You remember that Deimos fellow who was so critical of your earlier work?" asked Ceôlbur.

"Yes. I remember him," said Lysändra. "As I recall, he was also openly critical of the researcher who discovered the Neuralium on which we based our subsequent design. Minerva, I believe. I wonder if our branches ever met her at Rihon's unveiling."

"That's what this news is about," said Ceôlbur.

"I wonder why our branches haven't returned yet," mused Lysändra. "They must have chosen to stay a while because this is about the time they should have returned to reunify, assuming they wished to do so, I suppose."

"Lysändra!" Ceôlbur said urgently. He stood and marched over to Lysändra where she was gazing out from a balcony above the house's suspended roof, looking over the ocean. The open sky gaped above them. The alien equivalent of leaves rustled around the perimeter of the roof with a wind-blown, glass-like sound, like brittle shards delicately and melodically clattering against one another in light tonal resonances.

"What?" she said, sensing his urgency and looking toward him.

"The entire event, Rihon's next great art piece. It was destroyed." Lysändra huffed in amazement and then tapped into the news feed herself without asking Ceôlbur for indirect clarification.

"Something called Enduring Oblivion," she said. "An entire moon apparently, the surface completely obliterated on its opening night! What?!" she declared as she read. "Millions killed. Ceôlbur look at this. Etchings were unavailable prior to the event. You don't suppose this is why we haven't heard from our branchlings yet."

"I think we're dead," Ceôlbur replied. "I mean they're dead, at any rate."

"Wait a minute," said Lysändra. "We've received a direct communique on the data stream from the Center. The timing is almost identical to this news, only minutes behind."

"Who is it from?"

"You won't believe this. It's from the artist."

"Rihon? *The* Rihon? He contacted you directly?"

"His communication clearly addresses us both, in fact. He says he met our branchlings in person. He enjoyed meeting us. He would like to extend an invitation for us to join him again." Lysändra looked at Ceôlbur. "That's nice of him. He says—oh—we were his guests of honor, it turns out."

"Really?"

"Enduring Oblivion appears to have been heavily influenced by our work on the quale. Apparently it was built directly on our neural configuration. We were central to the festivities apparently! Oh, and this is curious. So was Minerva, the researcher who discovered the Neuralium."

"And?" said Ceôlbur, sensing there was more.

"He—" Lysändra cut off.

"What?"

"He...extends his condolences on the loss of our branchlings. You were right. They perished in the disaster." Lysändra looked away from the message momentarily and caught Ceôlbur's gaze. They froze briefly.

"Ceôlbur, there's a little bit more in the message."

"Yeah?"

"He emphasizes an oddity of the accident, namely that the transit stations failed simultaneously with the satellite failures." Ceôlbur didn't respond and Lysändra presumed he was studying the news alongside her.

"As a result, they don't think this was an accident," said Ceôlbur, reading over the news feed. "How could anyone do something like this on purpose?" He paused. "What does that have to do with Rihon's message to you?"

"You're not going to like this. Rihon theorizes that you and I—well, he emphasizes me, but I've always stated that our work is mutual—"

"Lysändra! That isn't the point right now. What did he say?" Ceôlbur had already connected the dots at this point however.

"Rihon theorizes that I was the target of the attack. His message is, in fact, a warning that we may be targeted here, on Ailuros. He admits that this message will almost certainly arrive far too late. 9000 years late, I suppose."

"Wait," said Ceôlbur as the math forced itself into his awareness. "The Ailurosian Annihilation occurred at practically the same time as Rihon's unveiling, relativistically speaking."

"Precisely," said Lysändra. "Rihon believes there was a coordinated two-prong attack—on you and me. Out of everyone in the galaxy, these two events were coordinated to inflict the most harm against anyone attending the unveiling from Ailuros. I suppose there must have been others, but out of the entire galaxy, only a tiny fraction of the attendees would have been from our little galactic hamlet. In fact, not all of Ailuros was destroyed. Our home on the cliff was the epicenter of that event."

"And how many of those people would have been Rihon's guests of honor?" said Ceôlbur. "How many would have produced the research that was the subject matter of Rihon's art piece?" Again, they stood in silence as the full realization settled on them.

"You know what?" said Lysändra.

"I do, in fact," said Ceôlbur, thinking along with Lysändra. "It was pure luck we were on Thalassia when Ailuros was attacked. If anyone had ventured a guess where we'd be at that time, so as to plan such an attack—"

Lysändra completed the thought. "They would have guessed we would be on Ailuros at that time."

"Or you," said Ceôlbur. "I doubt they came after me. But you—"

"Stop saying that, please."

"This no time for humility, Lysändra. You have to take this seriously. Ailuros was destroyed to get to just one person, you."

"That's unfathomable," said Lysändra. "I can't...that's just..." Ceôlbur moved toward her, but she moved away as he approached. "All that destruction and loss. There were people without recent etchings on Ailuros. All because of me?"

"I've been telling you to take these threats seriously."

"*You're blaming me?!*" she practically yelled.

"No. Of course not. I'm trying to keep you safe!"

"I had no idea anyone would try something like this!"

"Of course not. That's not what I meant. But, to be honest, even if you continue to work on this, I don't think you should necessarily publish any advances, at least not immediately."

"Just let the terrorists win, huh?"

"I would call it being cautious," he retorted, but he could tell what was coming next, and before he could say anything further, Lysändra had completely decorporealized, lost into the virtuality somewhere. Ceôlbur practically shook where he stood as he fumed at her departure. So typical of her, to just run away in the middle of an argument. The worst part was his final thought before he gave up on the matter for the time being. *She isn't going to slow down one bit as a result of this. In fact, she'll probably work harder than ever on completing the quale now.*

Ceôlbur turned back to the first thing Lysändra noted from Rihon's message, an invitation to come to the Center—for the second time, by any reasonable logic—to meet Rihon, or meet him again, as it were. That was sounding more appealing by the minute now.

27

LYSÄNDRA LOOKED AROUND AT THE CROWD. There were easily a million people in her vicinity, a virtuality running on an orbital station in a solar orbit around Zareasman. She had snuck into a Satorian ceremony, disguised to avoid the inconveniences of celebrity, to see what this religion centered on herself was all about. An infinite expanse of white light extended in all directions, rendering her sense of scale and distance worthless.

She looked around at the serene attendees. *Why am I even here?* she asked herself, and then she remembered and answered herself in such a stark experience of self-conversation that she momentarily had a visceral sense of housing multiple persons in her ancient mind.

Because you want to see what Satori and his Lysandrans are doing with your work, formed the response in her mind.

Yes, but why do I care about that?

Because you're egotistical.

No I'm not! But she dwelled on the response a moment. Was that the only reason she was here? To bask in her own fame? *No, that's not entirely it,* she retorted, literally to herself. *I feel like the EOUSP quale is my responsibility and I want to make sure it is being utilized responsibly.*

No, you're just the biggest narcissist in the galaxy. Where was this doubt coming from, Lysändra thought with increasing aggravation? *Ceölbur was right when he accused you of enjoying your fame.*

The EOUSP quale is the most important discovery in an age, in an era. It's bigger than me. It's more important than me.

Shush, came the combative voice with profoundly anthropomorphic verisimilitude. *He's about to speak.* Lysändra hpmhed at her self and attended to the local Satôri, floating above her in the center.

"Welcome," boomed Satôri's voice throughout the space. "Please take a position of comfort. Thank you for coming today. It has been a while since we held a service and I thought it might be nice to arrange another gathering. I'm so thrilled to see all of you here. In a few moments, I will guide us through the primary ritual of Lysandrism, the Rite of Hope, our communal sharing of the EOUSP quale, gifted to us by our venerable liberator, Lysändra. Let me take a brief moment to also recognize Lysändra's comrade—" Lysändra tingled at the expectation that Ceölbur would receive his due credit "—the infamous researcher, Minerva, without whose own contributions, Lysändra's work would have been unfathomably more challenging." Lysändra cringed. No wonder Ceölbur was always upset with her.

She zoned out as Satôri droned on. Instead of remaining fixated on his voice, she found herself distracted with people-watching the crowd around her. Everyone was watching Satôri with rapt attention and odd smiles of contentment—no, it was serenity she realized. Elsewhere, people looked literally entranced with pure tranquility. Was this what she had done for the galaxy? That didn't seem like a bad direction for events to be tilting toward. And yet, she had always found situations like this, the masses falling into an aligned conscious state, drawn in and threaded through like separate fibers pulled and twisted into a linear yarn, to be off-putting somehow. It was the willing sacrifice of independent thought that annoyed her so much. No one here was doing anything except letting Satôri do the thinking for them, and they seemed utterly happy about that choice. But she knew that they would argue they had chosen such alignment of free accord, or even that their massive union was the entire point of the exercise, the abandonment of the ego and the embrace of the community.

Ceölbur sounded like this whenever he expressed his curiosity about coordinated mental experiences that Lysändra had never found appealing. This religious ceremony felt almost identical as far as Lysändra could tell, albeit with less direct neural connections consolidating the people into a single entity. And yet, as she watched these million people coalescing into a single state of thought, guided by Satôri as if he were an entrancing locus in attentional attractor space, they seemed almost the same as Ceölbur's hive curiosities. Whatever it was, she didn't like it. She never had. If anyone in the galaxy was her perfect likeness, it was someone who realized—or even shared—this almost aggressive individuality, nonconformity. Or just plain selfishness as her inner voice had seemed to imply. Was she good or bad? Right or wrong? And would she ever feel *that* sort of alignment with another person?

"Well then," said Satôri, somehow seizing Lysändra's attention momentarily. "Are we all ready to begin?" The ethereal hollow echo of a million voices calmly agreeing reverberated throughout the luminous space, which seemed to unnaturally amplify the crowd's voices in the same way it had amplified Satôri's speech.

Lysändra felt Satôri guiding her state of consciousness into the EOUSP network, her network, the one she had given him, given everyone. But she expected this to feel different from the numerous times she had experienced the network on her own. She was curious what it was like to experience it Satôri's way.

But she didn't get the chance. Just as the experience of the EOUSP quale started to flood her mind with awe and trepidation, and just as the further inspiring quale of a solution lingered slightly beyond reach, she was interrupted.

Alert Lysändra, an urgent communique has arrived. The alert wasn't so much a literal sequence of words, either written or spoken. The alert simply arrived in her mind as a direct injection of information.

She pushed Satôri's guided trip to the periphery of her attention momentarily, letting the EOUSP quale fade off to the side, and attended to the alert. She looked at it over and over. How could this be correct?

> *I believe you are seeking information concerning the Ontoscendians. I'm sorry I couldn't help sooner, but here are the galactic coordinates. I hope this helps your research.*

She consumed the message multiple times in near shock at its content. How could anyone have known to send this to her? She had discussed the Ontoscendian lead with no one except Ceölbur. The only other person who knew anything about her discovery of the Ontoscendians was the odd stranger who had initially pointed her in that direction long ago with the glitching neural configuration and its minimalist hallucination. She could only presume this tip came from the same person, and it was just as anonymous as it had been the first time.

But why first tell me to find the Ontoscendians and then wait another 10,000 years to reveal their actual location to me? she thought to herself. She mulled it over and eventually came to the simple conclusion that her secret benefactor must have not initially known the location either, and had only just found Cianthara more recently, and was now divulging that additional information to her. The whole thing would have felt like some sort of trap, except that the archive record had been legitimate. Provenance confirmation had come up clean. The Ontoscendians were real, and appeared to have solved the EOUSP, and had then been lost in a planet-wide catastrophe that left no survivors. All of that was accurate archival information.

Ceölbur wouldn't be happy about this. He would try to talk her out of it, in fact. The simple fact was that she could transit a branch to Cianthara without Ceölbur even knowing. Heck, even the branchling that remained in the Zareasman system after she dispatched to Cianthara wouldn't know the results of such a quest for 48,000 years at a bare minimum. Her branchling currently on route to Nyveron would likely return to Thalassia around the time this branchling was just arriving at Cianthara. With that realization, she decided to avoid overthinking the matter. It was obvious what she had to do, regardless of whether anyone else would approve.

Within the day, she had prepared a new etching and sent it on the first leg of what turned out to be a complex trip route. Not too surprisingly, Cianthara—and its entire stellar system of Siremala in fact—hadn't been populated for hundreds of thousands of years. Siremala had become a wildly unstable star, not worth attempting to populate. As such, there was no interstellar transit station there to receive her transit signal. She would have to transit to the closest stellar system, Verkennaros, and then travel the final leg, thirty-seven light-years, by matter-travel, at perhaps a tenth the speed of light if she was lucky, one percent if she wasn't. It would depend on the efficiency of the laser that would propel her to Cianthara from Verkennaros. The very concept was practically unheard of except at the galactic frontier where humanity was still crossing the farthest reaches and filling in its expansion at every star along the way with transit stations, but Lysändra had never ventured farther from the Center than Zareasman. There was very little exploration in this region. This would be a true adventure for her.

She wished Ceölbur could have come with her. Or more specifically, she wished Ceölbur was the kind of person who could have—would have—come with her. How could she be the most famous person in the galaxy, and have a partner she was sharing her life with, and still feel so utterly alone?

28

RIHON STOOD ON THE PLATFORM OF THE ORBITAL STATION, exposed to the vacuum of space. The shadow of a wall on the left side of the platform cut right across his body, plunging one foot into unimaginable cold while subjecting the other to searing solar heat, but his body felt none of it. The soles of his feet bonded to the station's outer surface via Van der Waals forces as he paced back and forth, looking outward at his next creation, still in final stages of construction. Half the sphere of the cosmos was laid out above him, the Milky Way slashing through the middle, the local sun, Oudara, off to one side, a piercing light blue disk against a black background.

Nearby, Minèrva stood on the same platform. Her form was striking, similarly anchored to the platform to avoid spilling away into space, likewise half illuminated by Oudara's blue tinge and half utterly lost in shadow. She was facing away from Rihon, also gazing upward at the incomplete stages of his project.

"It's much bigger than a moon," she remarked. "Nothing like your previous creation."

"No. It actually stretches the full solar orbit at this distance. It will be the largest piece I have ever constructed. It is, in fact, ready to be experienced now. That's why I asked you here today."

Minèrva looked out to the space ahead of her at the various elements of the art piece. She didn't really understand them yet. Beginning at the edge of the platform on which she and Rihon stood, there was some sort of illuminated track or ribbon weaving off into space, roughly along the station's orbital path around Oudara. It was difficult to determine whether the track had any material form or whether it was pure light. If it was material, it was so sheer as to confuse the senses in that regard. This trail, or whatever it was, petered out merely due to distance, but clearly led to some sort of gravitational anomaly suspended in the same solar orbit, far off in the distance—a good portion of the orbit away in fact. The anomaly itself was not visible at this distance, but she could see how it bent and twisted the stars behind it in obvious gravitational fashion. Other than that, she couldn't make the next elements of the construction out.

"This track fully circumnavigates the sun?" she asked.

"Yes. It isn't a rigid structure, as you can see. It only maintains its shape by active orbital maintenance, pushing and pulling various segments of the track to maintain a clean orbit."

"And that object out there, bending the starlight. That's something you created?"

"It's the first stop—Oh, Ceõlbur just arrived." They greeted Ceõlbur as he emerged through a sheet of light from the interior of the station, which housed, among other things, several interstellar transit platforms. "Welcome Ceõlbur. It's so wonderful to meet you."

Ceõlbur walked out onto the platform, exposed to space, and marveled at the aesthetics of Rihon's design of the station and this exterior area. "Nice to meet you too, although I suppose we've met before, in a sense."

Without missing a beat, Minèrva jumped in. "Yes, so true. It was a pleasure to meet you last time as well. I'm so sorry about what happened."

"You're Minèrva, yes?"

"Yes. We spent a little time together last time, right before, well, just before."

"We did?" Ceõlbur noticed the odd wisp of light leading away from the platform off into space.

"Yes, and if you will permit me, you must accept my invitation to a somewhat similar event again."

"She wants to take you hiving," said Rihon. "Your counterpart found it tantalizing."

Ceõlbur's gaze followed the track out to the gravitational anomaly. "I'm familiar with the concept, but haven't tried it much. Maybe a bit here and there."

"Neither had your branchling," said Minèrva.

"Is that part of the artwork?" Ceõlbur asked, indicating the anomaly.

"Yep," beamed Rihon.

"It must be a good portion of this station's orbital distance away. How far is it?"

"There are only a few stops in the entire orbit. Lysandra chose not to come?" he asked, clearly disappointed.

"She both revels in her celebrity status and finds it uncomfortable at the same time. I think she wasn't sure how to meet you, now knowing that your entire previous artwork was more or less inspired by her." Rihon noticed an odd expression cross Ceõlbur's face, suggesting that perhaps there were other reasons she hadn't come along as well. Tension between Lysandra and Ceõlbur, if he was reading the expression correctly.

"Well, I hope I get the opportunity some day," said Rihon. "She was as incredible in person as her research—your research—had led me to expect."

"MmHmm" responded Ceõlbur. "It really is quite difficult dealing with what happened. We didn't realize until we saw the news, and your personal note indicating your theory that the two events were related, much less that Lysandra was the direct target of such a horrific conspiracy. We, she and I, we aren't the galactic celebrity types, much less the targets of massive murderous plots. I'm not sure how to keep her safe. She seems determined to continue her work."

"I see," said Rihon. "I am less certain myself now."

"Really?" said Minèrva. "After all the work you've put into the topic?"

"Hopefully you will understand better after you see this latest piece."

"Well then," said Minèrva. "When will you unveil this one?"

"Not for a while yet, but you two should try it. You'll be my first external testers, as I have been much more guarded about internal help this time. I'm sure someone was working from the inside to sabotage Enduring Oblivion, so this time I have employed almost entirely insentient de novos."

"That borders on paranoia," said Minèrva.

"I'm de novo myself," said Rihon. "I admit I find these simpler types... discomforting. They are explicit shadows of what I could have been if I hadn't been granted the necessary network of richer inner consciousness and self-determination. What does that make me? What does that make the difference between us? The shape of that difference. Its properties...But they won't betray me so they're all I work with now."

"I used similar assistants with my research on Caelunis. I understand your motivation."

"So do you have a name for it yet?" asked Ceõlbur, once again indicating the light trail leading off around the sun.

"I do." Rihon turned to face outward, gazing at his own creation. "Behold Accepting Oblivion."

"Accepting?" said Ceõlbur.

"Yes, quite," said Rihon wistfully. He trailed off. Minèrva cocked her head, looking at him with curiosity. "Don't worry about me, Minèrva. You've been around me long enough to know I'm up to something. You'll see soon enough."

"Hmmm," she said, narrowing her eyes. "I can't wait to see it."

Minèrva found herself with Rihon and Ceõlbur inside the station in a lounge area where people could gather before or after seeing—or better yet, experiencing—Accepting Oblivion. Some of Rihon's entourage were there as well, mostly his artist friends, none as famous as he, but some noteworthy nevertheless. A few were less artists than philosophers and varying popular renowned public speakers. Most were lovers in one capacity or another.

"Shall we?" said Rihon. Minèrva took Ceõlbur's hand and Rihon's hand in her own. She winked at Ceõlbur, then knowing he was watching, deeply kissed Rihon.

"See you inside," she said, looking back at Ceõlbur as she spoke.

"What do I do?" asked Ceõlbur. Minèrva just smiled at him devilishly and closed her eyes. She could only assume Ceõlbur had followed suit and done the same. She felt around in her mind, grasping the early sensations of the hive, its warmth starting to glow on the horizon of her attention. In the throng, she found the stand-out, the sensation of apprehension, and approached it.

Hello Ceõlbur.

Minèrva, hello. So, my branchling did this with you last time?

Something similar. It's different every time. Tonight's crowd is a bit rowdier than the group I introduced your counterpart to. This will be... interesting.

I don't know how to do this, he expressed to her.

He didn't know either, she responded. Minèrva proceeded to guide Ceõlbur toward the personas amassed around them. She was impressed at his ability to comfort himself with it, once again for the first time. He was a natural. But he was in for a ride. She congratulated him when he had successfully left his egocentric self behind and joined the hive in the nebulous space where none of them resided individually. Then she turned her attention to the rest of the group, letting Ceõlbur observe.

Okay everyone, came a thought from the organizer, not really a voice, just the comprehension of an intention from elsewhere in the rapidly congealing ubermind. *Toss a memory into the center. Any memory will do.* Minèrva thought for a moment and focused on an ancient memory, hundreds of thousands of years old. Flying in long sweeping arcs around a gas giant with countless thin rings, hundreds of concentric threads spooled around the planet. She rode the magnetic fields, feeling them push and pull her along the field lines. Eddies in the gas giant's clouds spun themselves into thousands of knots below her. Orange, red, purple. The double suns around which the planet orbited, one yellow, one white, shined brightly on the planet's clouds, bringing them to vivid, swirling brilliance as she continued to feel the inertial sensations of riding the magnetic paths around the planet. She felt the emotional warmth of the memory too, the exaltation it inspired in her, the awe of the giant's size and of the gaping cosmos surrounding her. The emotions were the valuable part of the memory of course. She offered this memory into a central mind area, where other memories were collecting from the group, beginning to intermingle like variously colored paint poured into a cauldron.

The observer mentally intimated again. *Now we create a single unified experience from the elements before us. Visual properties, auditory, tactile, semantic, but especially the less tangible, the evocative, the emotional. Use whatever you want from any memory available in the pot, ignore whatever you don't find appealing. We each paint with our own brush, but we work from the same palette and on a single canvas. Let's create something spectacular.*

Minèrva went to work, observing how quickly the rest fell into the rhythm of the activity. She glanced at Ceõlbur's mental pattern and confirmed that he was contributing as well. She was stunned by his contributed memory of watching helplessly from Thalassia as a significant portion of Ailuros was all but destroyed. She felt his anguish at the death of his own branchling on Ailuros, all the more tragic by his later discovery of the near-simultaneous death of his other branchling on Regenium at Enduring Oblivion. She felt his further suffering at realizing that his deepest partner had been the target of these coordinated attacks, and that she had similarly doubly perished. She felt his heavy guilt that so many others on Ailuros had suffered similar fates as the malevolent mycelia data network consumed a tenth of the surface of Ailuros before an immune response could be successfully implemented and released into the original network to fight back—all because of this obsession Lysandra had recklessly pursued, and which he had tolerated, and even assisted. When Minèrva saw that he was participating in the hive activity, molding the amalgamated memory, she eventually turned back to her own contribution, but avoided using Ceõlbur's memory as a color of her own palette. It pained her greatly. She would leave it to others to use it if they saw fit to do so.

As the hive coalesced, she could no longer discern her own choices and actions regarding the overall activity. She could see the memory in the middle amalgamating from the contributions but could no longer keep track of which parts she was adding and which others were adding. The memory continued to evolve and gain complexity, yet it was unclear precisely what she was doing. Of course, she realized in a moment of lucidity, there was no she anymore. This made her wonder who was having this realization in the first place. Wasn't *that* person Minèrva? And then it hit her. She wasn't sure it was Minèrva who was contemplating her degree of individual contribution in the first place. It might be someone else, or some combination of the others, or everyone feeling the same uncertainty at the same time. The hive had successfully integrated. And yet she was still there, free to rise up and look down separately at the group at a moment's notice if she chose to do so, but why would she want to do that? It felt so good, so harmonious, so loving.

After a while, the jointly constructed memory felt complete and the group observed and felt and experienced it together for a while—and felt each other feeling it, and felt it as this new being that only existed while the hive existed. Minèrva remembered Ceõlbur and grasped a bit of singularness to ponder his circumstances. He had done well, but how would he fare as the hive got wilder over the course of the evening?

The organizer put his figurative hands into the middle of the hive and pushed everyone apart a little bit to prepare for the next game. Minèrva felt this action impose a little more individuality and pondered with anticipation.

All right, expressed the organizer, as the slate was wiped clean and the previous memory activity faded away entirely. *Next activity. Everyone ready to get a little rowdier? One person in the middle. Minèrva, you're up!* Minèrva felt herself tingle all over—a reaction she knew everyone else was immediately sympathetically experiencing along with her—and figuratively stepped forward.

Rihon, Minèrva, and Ceõlbur returned once again to the station and exited through the light wall to the exterior platform, leaving nothing to separate them from the infinity of existence.

"Whenever I'm exposed to space like this I feel like I will drift away and be lost forever," said Ceõlbur. "Not in a frightening way of course, just a sense of vertigo, I suppose."

"You'll be secure the entire time," said Rihon. "Here's how it works. You walk to the edge of the platform and stand right at the beginning of the track. When you are ready, step onto the track. You will partially decorporealize and ride the track to a series of displays, many of which are interactive. They will challenge you, challenge your beliefs, your values. You will end up back here, hopefully forever transformed."

"What do you mean by 'partially decorporealize'?" asked Minèrva.

"I think you and I are past the point of ambiguous trust," said Rihon, chuckling.

"But what about the general public?" asked Minèrva. "What about Ceõlbur here?"

Rihon just smiled. "Perhaps it requires a certain leap of faith to cross a chasm that one has never before had the courage to face."

"Geez sweetie," said Minèrva. To her surprise, Ceõlbur promptly walked right up to the edge of the platform, his toes literally hanging off, with nothing but the universe below them. The wispy track, mostly translucent, shimmered before him. And then, before Minèrva could voice any further objection, he stepped out into the shimmering nothing, placing a foot on what appeared to be nothing more than a tenuous ribbon of light. Minèrva saw his body rapidly dissolve, but noticed that his orb brain did not entirely dissipate into some sort of virtual space. Instead, the orb's structure seemed to briefly smear across the width of the luminescent trail, a slight brightening across the expanse of the ribbon, as the totality of his neural configuration was reformed to the light beam. And then she saw the bright belt that was Ceõlbur, now converted to light and integrated into the trail, practically vanish away along the light track at dizzying speed.

Rihon turned to Minèrva. "He will complete the solar orbit, stopping at a few waypoints, in a few hours." He gazed somewhat distractedly at the starscape and the blinding nearby sun. "You're next."

"Fine," she said. She walked up and stepped directly off the edge without even a moment's hesitation, unwilling to let Rihon see any further apprehension on her part.

She immediately realized why Rihon had utilized a partial decorporealization. Full decorporealization would have involved etching her brain state into a static configuration and transmitting it, as a static pattern, to some other location at the speed of light. She would have then recorporealized at some new destination, with no sense of the passage of time in between—and no experience during the transit either. But this was entirely different. She could feel herself sliding along the orbital path at *almost* the speed of light. There was very little frame of reference for her astonishing movement. Oudara to her left was shifting this way and that slightly as the trail's path meandered a bit in its orbit. The stars were, of course, too far way for her to appreciate any notable parallax except over the full duration of the artwork as she eventually crossed to the other side of her orbit around Oudara, but from moment to moment, even moving as fast as she was, she could not discern such alterations in the stars.

However, she was not merely exposed to the vista of space during the ride. Rather, the ribbon, which of course was tightly integrated with her neural processes, was exposing her to a barrage of sensory experiences, taking her on a tour of sorts. Of a simpler variety, she saw—or felt—visual and auditory imagery and sounds of humanity's darkest historical moments. Wars, greed, exploitation, short-sightedness, selfishness. Rihon had collected media from a million years of history, even including elements from prior to the Great Fortification and the Galactic Exodus that followed. There were selections from history she had not given a moment's thought to in hundreds of thousands of years. She also noticed a very clear depiction of the destruction of Regenium during the unveiling of Enduring Oblivion. In addition to mere visual and auditory stimuli, she felt emotion and memory records pressed into her mind, the neural recordings of individuals from across time following the technological availability of such recording methods. This entire experience seemed focused on the worst elements of humanity across time.

It didn't last long though. She could see that she was rushing to the first stop, the gravitational anomaly that had initially been so far off. She was soon upon it. It rushed up, filling her view, and she felt herself come to a halt. The historical images and related elements of the ride ceased and she was faced with the anomaly. It had all the characteristics of a small black hole. There was an utterly black core, and endless contortions of the stellar background around its edges. Although there was nothing more to look at, this object had its own neurological component, not unlike the similar element from Rihon's earlier artwork, Contemplating Oblivion. In that triad work, one of the three elements had been a dark vortex that pressed its infinite void into the viewer's mind. This gravitational anomaly was similar. She felt the enormity of it, the singularity at the center, consuming and destroying everything. A neural impression appeared in her mind, guiding her to the intended interpretation. This gaping blackness represented the death knell of humanity, and of everything else too, in fact. It was a visual manifestation of the EOUSP, the infinite ending of all things.

She was soon whipped away, sliding nearly as fast as light along the trail again. This leg of the ride exposed her to a completely different set of historical images, sounds, and emotional and memorial evocations. The totality of humanity's art and music and poetry poured into her. Direct emotional sensations of awe and wonder and embrace and love settled over her with tangible density. Was she merely reveling in such fantastic beauty and accomplishment, or was she being crushed by it? It was hard to tell the difference. The neurological antecedents of overwhelming tears burned through her mind despite her current lack of any associated physiology with which to cry, given that she was no more than a beam of light at the moment.

She arrived at the next stop. Here, floating in orbit around the sun, she perceived a planet-sized white sphere. At first it did nothing. It pressed no neural sensation into her mind, nor did it seem to suggest she should react to it a certain way. But then, slowly, she felt herself slide along the track at a leisurely pace right through the sphere's exterior. Once side, she saw pure white in all directions of course, somehow self-illuminated—or perhaps Oudara was making the sphere glow uniformly. This view of white in all directions resolved into other scenes however. At first, there were scenes of rather busy, but warming, social harmony. Groups of people engaged in joint activities of joy, but more critically, of coordinated good. These scenes drifted away and were replaced with scenes of oneness, solitude, but not loneliness. Scenes of meditative calm. These scenes drifted away and new scenes arrived. Minimalist, almost empty, almost devoid of structure or content. She stared at the imagery and realized that it resolved itself more clearly if she stopped trying. As she did this, she realized some sort of subtle neural configuration was being pushed in. Clarity, acceptance, an abandonment of regret, mistakes. She realized Rihon was trying to depict enlightenment, if not necessarily full blown Nirvana. Not the true experience of it, which of course he could not very easily impart externally to the viewer, but he was reminding the viewer of the concept, the goal—the process of pursuing it. The scenery changed one final time. The white sphere became a cosmic planetarium—initially not too dissimilar from the view outside the sphere in fact—but faded in some sense. All the depictions of galaxies and stars steadily dwindled until she was inside a pure black nothingness. This would have been confusing except that during this same period of the presentation, as the galaxies and stars withdrew and shrank away, Lysandra's EOUSP quale was incorporated into Minèrva's experience and she felt its now widely recognized sensation of surviving cosmic death, the very same cosmic death she was witnessing as the depiction of stars and galaxies faded to black. Rihon's message was clear. To survive the EOUSP would be tantamount to achieving Nirvana. Wasn't that what the crazy cult leader Satori had been saying too? It struck her as a little odd that Rihon would find common cause with such a crackpot, but she remembered Rihon and Satori actually knew each other. Rihon had told her about meeting Satori a few times. Perhaps he was more spiritual than Minèrva had given him credit for.

She slowly slid along the track, breaking through the outer wall of the white sphere, reentering the natural cosmos. She then quickly accelerated and zipped along to the next stop. There was no additional experience to this leg of the ride, just a gentle neural nudge to reflect on the artwork so far.

The next stop brought her to the most peculiar sight of all. Suspended in outer space, she perceived a literal measuring scale. It was classical in appearance, golden, lit brightly by the sun, taking on an odd green hue as the blue sun illuminated the gold. Its form was ancient and conventional. A central pillar stood—on nothing of course, floating in space—with a fulcrum suspended across its top and a long arm stretching out in two directions. From the ends of the arms hung chains that held two shallow plates. Compared to her own sense of scale, it was obvious that the bizarre object was at least the size of a medium-size asteroid, or a small moon. It utterly towered over her. On one dish, she saw a jumbled pile of the first images she had witnessed, dark and violent and malevolent. On the other she saw a similar pile of the other set of objects, history's artwork and representations of accomplishments. The scale teetered back and forth. Each time it passed the equality point, where the arm was horizontal, a sphere would briefly flash into view above the scale, as large as the scale itself. When teetering toward the negative side the sphere would be pure black and gravitationally anomalous, like the first stop along the track. When teetering back the other way toward the positive side, the same sphere would briefly appear, but this time white, like the next stop along the track. In either case, the sphere would disappear again as the scale swung through the balance point to the other extreme. It did this, back and forth, indefinitely. The implication was obvious. Rihon hadn't been the remotest bit subtle. Did humanity deserve enlightenment, he was asking the viewer? Did humanity deserve the solution to the EOUSP? Rihon obviously wasn't sure himself anymore. *How could he*, she thought, *after what happened to his previous creation, after its subversion as a tool of both mass murder and singular assassination at the same time.*

Minèrva realized that before she could proceed, she was expected to cast a vote at these scales. Clever. Over extended time, as millions, and then billions, and then perhaps trillions of visitors experienced Accepting Oblivion, it would steadily accumulate an election of humanity's opinion on this question. She contributed her vote and immediately felt herself slide once more along the trail, ultimately completing the orbit and returning to the orbital station, corporealizing at another platform on the backside of the station, with a similar light wall that would grant her reentry to the station's interior. Rihon and Ceõlbur were standing on the platform talking when she felt herself regain mass and inertia and felt her feet confidently bond with molecular adhesion to the station's surface. Ceõlbur had, of course, only just corporealized a moment before her. She walked up to them.

"I'm not going to ask what you thought, and certainly not how it made you feel," said Rihon. "I just need to know if it's ready for the public yet." Minèrva looked at Ceõlbur and he nodded back.

"It's perfect, my darling," she said. "You've outdone yourself. You should unveil it immediately."

29

IN ONE SENSE, 17,000 YEARS HAD TRANSPIRED BY THE TIME LYSÃNDRA FELT herself corporealize on a glowing dais on Nyveron. Her pattern had been in transit, hopping from one interstellar transit hub to another, across 17,000 light years, to the very edge of the galaxy, teetering at the brink of the chasm that stretched into the intergalactic void—veritable nothingness.

In another sense, absolutely no time had passed at all. Moments ago, by her recollection—and her feelings—she recorded an etching of herself. She didn't even feel her departure of course, since that was performed on the static etching, at which point she was nothing more than a data record devoid of dynamic neural processing or any associated conscious experience. She remembered bidding farewell to Ceôlbur before making the etching. She recalled his fairly uninvested interest in her voyage since he and Lysãndra would simply continue their life together immediately after making the etching. As far as he was concerned, she had never left.

She stepped off the dais and was quite astonished to find herself face to face with someone who had arrived to meet her.

"Hello?" Lysãndra said apprehensively to the stranger, who was paying her more heed than she expected upon her unannounced arrival. Lysãndra glanced around her surroundings. There were multiple daises scattered within a large room. A clear domed ceiling revealed a teal sky, greener than she was used to, with slightly blue-tinted, icy clouds situated high above.

She looked past the woman who was facing her a little too closely. The room had soft, diffuse light that accentuated the glowing daises. The floor was a reflective stone, like polished marble.

"You're Lysãndra, right?" said the woman draped in glittered pink hair that calmly and endlessly shifted through various hues of reds. Her gaze then disassociated briefly as Lysãndra realized she was attending to some internal communication. Perhaps she was accessing the interstellar transit records to confirm the arrival for this particular dais.

"Yeees," said Lysãndra a little uneasily.

"Oh that's just splendid." The woman continued to look at Lysãndra, then blinked a little awkwardly and stepped forward even closer. Although your transit was quite direct, considering the total distance and number of hops—ninety-four percent in fact—I did receive notification of your impending arrival a little sooner, which is reasonable considering that such trivial communiques are vastly smaller than whole brain patterns. Right?"

"Of course." Lysãndra squinted suspiciously as she pieced it together. "You must be Kaimea." she said.

"Yes! Absolutely. What a pleasure to meet you." Kaimea's hair rapidly cycled through a range of purples, magentas and reds, then settled down to its slow but continual shifting of reds.

"Truly, the honor is mine," said Lysãndra, "I have traveled a long way to meet you."

"Oh gosh, you have no idea," said Kaimea. "Even out here on the galactic edge, everyone knows who you are, the great quale-diver." Lysãndra rolled her eyes but Kaimea didn't notice. "Heck, you have you own religion. I can't wait to discuss absolutely everything with you."

"Yeah, religion. I heard about that too."

"Come come. No time for this nonsense. We have *work* to do. Come with me!" Kaimea practically pulled Lysãndra and they departed from the transit nexus.

"You have to tell me all about your work," said Kaimea. "It isn't my specialty, I'm afraid. Of course, amongst Nyveron's inhabitants there are plenty who do the sort of thing you do, fiddling around with neural configurations and such, but I haven't yet become an expert myself. I am just fascinated though." They briefly walked through an enclosed interior, elegantly lit, with architectural ribs and other curves supporting curved walls and more domed ceilings that revealed the teal sky. They exited to a lavish exterior. Purple grass and magenta shrubs spread off to the horizon. Finger-sized spherical plant-like organisms, varying in color between hot pink and vermillion, each sphere attached to the ground by a thin stalk about knee high, waved around gently, leaning toward them as they walked past. Lysãndra and Kaimea followed a cleared walkway for a while farther, not necessarily going anywhere in particular.

"The entire planet only has a few million people," Kaimea continued. "We've considered growing our population, but it isn't a coincidence that it's rather thin here, being out here on the rim of the galaxy. We don't tend to build up dense societies here. People of such a shared inclination tend to aggregate in places like this. There's no other habitable planet here, not even much in the way of large orbital stations. A few smaller ones perhaps, mostly to soak up solar energy. Nope, it's just our comfy purple planet out here on the rim."

"MmHmm. I like it. I always try to find natural spaces myself."

"Absolutely, right? You'll just love it here then."

"Where are we headed?" asked Lysãndra.

"I didn't even ask," said Kaimea, "Did you have a specific plan for your arrival, since you weren't expecting me to greet you?"

"My plan was to seek you out, to be honest."

"Excellent, well in that case, I thought I'd get your settled in. And later, we can look at the message together."

"Sounds like a plan," said Lysãndra smiling, hungry to get down to work, but also enamored with Kaimea's friendliness.

"Absolutely." Kaimea's eyes twinkled at the attention. "Are you planning to live primarily in the virtualities or did you want a physical abode of some sort?"

"I've always enjoyed having a little physicality, especially with expansive views. I'm sure Nyveron's virtualities are incomparable, but I like—"

"No need to justify it," said Kaimea. "I absolutely understand. I feel the same way, in fact. I'll show you my own home while you're here. Since Nyveron is rather sparsely populated, people can get a lot of space if they choose. We can find you a place easily."

"So what's it like," Kaimea continued, "being so famous? I must confess, I garnered a small amount of notoriety here for my work on the message, but nothing like what you've encountered."

"Someone tried to kill me for it, so there's that," said Lysãndra, somewhat dead-pan. "They succeeded in killing my branchling in fact, along with millions of others." Lysãndra avoided eye contact. "I just want to complete the work."

"I see. I'm sorry to hear that. It must be heavy to think that someone's issue with you became a problem for others." Kaimea paused. "I hope no one was truly lost, no etching, no branchling."

"MmHmm," mumbled Lysãndra uneasily.

"I wonder how people are receiving news of the alien message," said Kaimea, deliberately changing the subject.

"I guess you wouldn't know, out here," responded Lysãndra, "but I can venture a guess."

"I suppose news of the message will have reached the Center a while back," said Kaimea, "but any news of how it has been received won't get back here for a little while longer."

"Since you have determined the message relates to the EOUSP in some fashion—"

"I'm convinced they solved it!" said Kaimea energetically. Her hair color-cycled furiously for a moment.

"That's why I'm here," said Lysãndra. "You don't have to convince me." Lysãndra smiled disarmingly at Kaimea, who pursed her lips in response, calming down.

"It took some convincing to get my colleagues to agree to my interpretation of the message. A lot of people here think I've jumped to a conclusion."

"Well, my guess is that the same people who came after me, namely someone named Deimos, will be none too pleased about your own discovery." At this, Lysãndra noticed Kaimea's hair go pure white as her cheerful demeanor shrunk away.

"Deimos?"

"You know him?" Lysãndra asked. Kaimea literally grumbled and then glared into the distance.

"He's the reason I first came out here. He didn't approve of my theory that the solution to the EOUSP would be found in extragalactic messages. He harassed me so much that I essentially fled out here to the rim...but it turned out to be the best place to do this work anyway. The observatory can see more of the sky from here."

"That Deimos fellow seems like trouble," said Lysãndra. "But he isn't the only one."

"What do you mean?"

"That religion you mentioned. It's a surprisingly diverse pool of beliefs. Some factions worship me as a literal messiah," Lysãndra sighed momentarily, "while others protest that my work should only continue within their religion, whatever the hell that means. I've even heard rumors some of them want me to stop, similar to Deimos. I'm not sure if they're dangerous. I guess being their literal saint doesn't get me the necessary grace if I don't first convert."

"Good grief. Well maybe you and I can crack this thing together then." Lysãndra smiled and Kaimea gleamed.

"I'd like that," said Lysãndra.

"Absolutely," beamed Kaimea. "So, I'll show you my home first and then we'll figure out what your long term plan is." Kaimea mentally indicated planetary coordinates to Lysãndra, smiled, and then decorporealized. Lysãndra looked around once more and then followed suit.

They recorporealized in a wide field. Kaimea took in the sight of her home savannah with the waist-high fuchsia grass covered in silver spherical seeds, and the lavender cone-rooted alien trees with their flat disks that would periodically snap upwards around the alien birds, dusting them with pollen. She looked over and saw Lysãndra delighting in the scenery as well.

"It's quite remote, isn't it," said Lysãndra.

"Yeah, no one for several days journey in any direction. I love it."

"Lonely?" Lysãndra tried to imagine enjoying her similarly remote domicile without Ceólbur.

Kaimea looked at the ground. "Oh, I dunno. I love my work. And I love it out here. Just look." She brightened as she swept the view with her arms.

"I feel the same way. I live in similar circumstances, although there is one other person."

"Oh," said Kaimea.

"Not sure what we are these days actually."

"Oh," in a very different tone. They took the view in for another drawn out moment, what with time taking on a different dimension from their ancient forms prior to fortification.

Kaimea pointed upwards, but it was daytime and there where no stars to see. "Let's go see the observatory," she said. She led Lysãndra to a structure in the middle of the field, her home. It consisted of myriad transparent surfaces, windows and skylights in effect, each with an organic and asymmetrical polygonal perimeter—pentagons, hexagons and similar—and each surface bowed outward slightly as if inflated by internal pressure. These sections fit together in eclectic ways along their edges to form eight bulbous rooms that intersected like soap bubbles. Through these fully transparent window walls, Lysãndra could glimpse the usual adornments of residence. As they approached, one such ground-level section disintegrated in a drizzle of geometric shards that rapidly shrank and vanished. They entered.

"I love your style," said Lysãndra, looking around.

"Thank you." They relaxed for a while, discussing all manner of curious subjects. Wine was involved, at Lysãndra's insistence. Eventually, Kaimea asked "Want to see the observatory?"

"Most definitely," said Lysãndra enthusiastically.

They decorporealized once again and transited straight up to the observatory orbiting Nyveron. There was nowhere to corporealize but the observatory had sufficient network processing to operationalize a modest population along with a nice little virtual presence that effectively granted the observatory itself as a sense of embodiment to any visitors. Kaimea settled into the familiar sensation of feeling the observatory as her own self, as her body. She *became* an astronomical observatory. Lysãndra had the same experience of course. Kaimea could sense that they were briefly vying for control of the observatory's experiential interfaces, which were implicitly shared by all concurrent residents. Kaimea and Lysãndra were, in effect, two separate minds feeling—and controlling—a single body, with the associated discombobulations until they found their unified footing.

"I suppose I didn't ask if you were okay with this," said Kaimea. "You're such an experienced quale-diver that I assumed you were familiar with this sort of shared experience."

"Actually, I don't engage in shared experiences much. My closest companion would be more familiar with it, I admit."

Kaimea's thoughts rapidly rippled through a series of states at the mention of this companion but she quickly moved on. "Do you mind continuing?" Kaimea suddenly realized that while she was appreciating sharing the observatory in a bodily fashion with Lysãndra, an almost intimate experience despite their total lack of physically sensing one another, she hadn't actually asked Lysãndra's feelings on the matter. It wasn't all that uncommon a practice. Heck, she and Quinlan had run the observatory in tandem several times. It just felt different to her because it was Lysãndra, which she then rationalized to herself objectively made no sense.

"I don't mind." Kaimea imagined she could see and almost feel Lysãndra's gentle smile, but of course there was no explicit indication of this. "Show me what this observatory does." Kaimea felt Lysãndra relinquish her mental grip on the various controls, riding along in effect. At Kaimea's will, the observatory powered up various external illumination that enabled them to see the enormous curved dish stretching out in all directions from their central location. Kaimea switched their perspective to a location on the edge of the dish and they looked across it with the far edge practically dissolving at such a distance into the spattered stars beyond. Suspended above the dish at its focal point, they could see a separate structure, seemingly disconnected from the dish. It housed the signal receivers located at the dish's focal point. The dish itself was currently configured for longer wavelengths, radio frequencies, and had the structure of an open lattice. Kaimea reconfigured it and they watched as every hole in the dish rapidly shrank and disappeared. Now configured for much shorter optical wavelengths, the dish appeared as the most perfect curved mirror either of them had ever seen, and still utterly beyond comprehension in terms of sheer diameter.

"Pretty neat, huh?" said Kaimea.

"It's phenomenal," replied Lysãndra. "That's the solar wind we're feeling, right?"

"Yep. Eilunedra, the sun, right over there. And there's Nyveron below us." Kaimea turned their perspective and they looked down on the planet. Dark blue oceans, almost black, swallowed up a sizable area but most of the surface was covered by indiscernible life, revealed only as marblings of color. Browns and tans of sand and soil, purples and reds of plant-like life. The icy-blue clouds she had previously seen from the underside were equally visible from above, dolloped across the planet like gentle puffs.

"How long have you lived here?" Lysãndra asked.

"I hate to admit it, but after my interactions with Deimos, I came here and have never bothered returning to the Center. I prefer it out here."

"So, hundreds of thousands of years," speculated Lysãndra. Kaimea didn't respond, but she momentarily released her emotional response into the observatory's network, knowing that Lysãndra would implicitly experience an empathetic response: nondescript wistfulness.

"I see," said Lysãndra, who now knew that Kaimea truly was lonely, even if she didn't admit it, even to herself. They paused and took in the sight. "It is a remarkable observatory. Let's go look at the message, shall we?" she finished. Kaimea hadn't disabled the emotional connection, and so she then felt Kaimea's glee at the suggestion.

Kaimea closed the observatory's visitation routines, only brought online for the benefit of their brief presence, and they transited back to the surface.

Upon returning to Nyveron, Lysãndra and Kaimea had little reason to further delay the point of Lysãndra's visit. Kaimea having described her preferred workspace, they went straight there without even bothering to corporealize upon their planetary return. They soon found themselves in Kaimea's preferred workspace, with its infinite glass floor and myriad samples and analyses of the message splayed out in the air. Lysãndra quickly adapted to the workspace's mode of interaction, discovering how she could narrow in on any element of the research she chose, either merely bringing it to the forefront of her attention or also visually expanding it in the workspace for others to share.

"So, over here we have the first message," said Kaimea. "It transmitted for 934 years, presenting 512 repeating cycles of the message. It contained three parts. Here you can see the smallest part, which we quickly interpreted as linguistic, which is to say we considered it an actual message of sorts. And here are the other two parts of that message, which appear to be data blocks of some sort. We were able to decode a small portion of the linguistic section and determine that at least some of it discussed the EOUSP, as you know."

Lysãndra nodded, following attentively. Although she had learned all of this summary overview from the published report, it helped to have the original researcher carve a straight path through it.

"Now over here, you can see the second message. Note that there was a 934 year gap during which all transmission ceased. The second message is very small compared to the first and turned out to be a key for decrypting a considerable amount of the first message. I am of the strong opinion that the further decryption implies that the the inhabitants of this other galaxy actually solved the EOUSP." Kaimea was visibly excited as she said this.

"That really is incredible," said Lysãndra. "I read it in your report but it is thrilling to see it here."

"Right? Absolutely," said Kaimea, laughing.

"Does everyone agree with your interpretation of the message? When I read the report, it seemed as if actually interpreting the glyphs might involve a bit of...creativity."

Kaimea frowned. "Yeah, there are definitely other theories floating around. The biggest question is whether they are claiming to have solved it, or whether they are asking for a solution."

"Ah." Lysãndra sighed. "That's a big difference."

"But I think they solved it!" said Kaimea.

Lysãndra chuckled. "Okay, let's go with that for now. So, keep going."

"Well, I'm afraid that's where I am actually. The second message provided a key, but we're still working on understanding the full message, and I'm afraid we haven't made much progress on the two data blocks yet."

"I have a theory about that," said Lysãndra with a friendly smirk.

"Yeah? Oh this is great. I'm so glad you're here. We've been stuck for a long time."

"I believe the data blocks are neural configurations. I think the aliens are quale-divers."

"Oh wow." Kaimea practically smacked her own forehead. "That's why you came here the moment our report about the message reached you. You think the alien message relates closely to your own work. Oh that's just brilliant." They stared at the data momentarily. "But why did you come all the way here? Even if I failed to recognize the data blocks as neural configurations, why didn't you just use them on your own on Thalassia?"

"I tried. Somehow, the way you applied the key to the data blocks resulted in corrupted conversions. I came here to have you show me how you attempted to use the key to convert the data blocks. I'm hoping we can find another way, or at least an alteration of the way you first did it."

"Shoot, so you think I messed it up, huh? That would explain why it seemed broken after I decrypted it. That's embarrassing."

"Don't worry about that. You did a good enough job for me to recognize its importance, its relevance. Let's just fix it."

"Absolutely," said Kaimea, twinkling. "So, here are the two data blocks from the first message and here's the second message, which I attempted to apply as a decryption key." They scrutinized the analyses for a while but after trying a few quick ideas, eventually concluded the work would not immediately fall into place.

"Looks like I'll be here awhile," said Lysãndra, smiling at the realization as she glanced at Kaimea.

"Well, that doesn't sound so bad," Kaimea replied.

30

24,000 LIGHT YEARS IN A GRAVITATIONALLY STRAIGHT LINE, a quarter the diameter of the Milky Way. 25,000 years of actual transit time, traveling hop by hop in the straightest possible line between intermediate locales. Lysăndra had arrived in the stellar system of Verkennaros, a star with no rocky planets, but supporting a couple dismal gas giants that could be used for raw materials to build orbital stations in either planetary or solar orbits. She had arrived at one such station. Of course, she had experienced no passage of time. The intervening 25,000 years had felt less durational than an ordinary fading of consciousness and immediate reawakening. She stepped off the dais and found herself in a small dark room. The glow of her dais, the only transit station in the room, was practically the only source of light, save a few fixtures in the corners of a low flat ceiling that pressed down on her.

Moments ago, millennia ago, she had familiarized herself with the transit route she would take to reach Cianthara from Thalassia. The home world of the Ontoscendians, in orbit of the star Siremala, hadn't been inhabited for hundreds of thousands of years, and as such, there was no transit station there. Consequently, she had targeted the star Verkennaros, the closest stellar system, thirty-seven light years from Siremala.

No one was here to greet here however. She exited the transit room into a claustrophobic hallway and began to explore the station, hoping to find someone. After a while of twisting and turning through metal corridors that lacked even simple windows by which to glimpse the exterior, she eventually turned into a room that differed in encouraging ways. It was better lit, with a higher ceiling and a large curved window that showed the exterior shape of the station, its metal chassis blinding in the nearby light of Verkennaros, which lay somewhere off the right, out of view. She was taking in this view, noting the constellations she had never seen before, an entire skyscape of stars she had never seen before, when another person corporealized on the other side of the room.

"Sorry, so sorry," said the man. "So so sorry. We get so few visitors. You would think it would be a tremendous event that would garner equally tremendous celebration, but to the contrary, I'm afraid we completely lost track of the advance notification of your impending arrival." The man looked out the window with a distracted expression and lost his train of thought.

"Hello," said Lysăndra. "Nice view of the station from here."

"I...I haven't corporealized in a very long time. As I was saying, we received notice of your arrival, but that was a few hundred years ago, frankly. I corporealized to meet you as quickly as I could when I was alerted to your arrival on the station." He recomposed himself and walked across the room, quickly closing the gap between them. "I'm Eero. Wow, *the* Lysăndra. This is amazing. Even out here, your accomplishments have been known for a very long time. It is a pleasure to meet you."

Lysăndra sized Eero up for a moment, glanced back out the window, then back again. "So I'm *the* Lysăndra, huh?"

"Surely most of the populated portion of the galaxy has received your work by now, except perhaps the farthest reaches. We first received the publications pertaining to the Neuralium, which were quite exciting of course, and then later we received your work as well. Integrating the Neuralium into your own network designs, huh? Very exciting stuff. Very exciting indeed."

"I see. And where exactly am I? It was unclear how many targets might be the eventual destination of my transit signal."

"That makes sense," said Eero thoughtfully. "Truth be told, the stations that were here when you set out could have been gone entirely by the time you arrived, and likewise new ones not even conceived at the beginning of your trip could have been fully constructed before you arrived. This station is younger than your trip for example."

"Quite," said Lysăndra.

"You are on Orbital Station Linnea, in a close orbit of Verkennaros. We are able to access ample solar power at this distance."

"That's good to hear. I'm going to need to matter-travel for the next leg of my journey. I presumed lased solar would be the best option."

"Wow, yes, very exciting," said Eero. "I'm sure we can set you right up."

"So what is this station like?" Lysăndra asked.

"Virtual only. While you have discovered that there is a modest habitable space here, just enough to operationalize the station, all habitation is virtual."

"Population?"

"Oh, about 80 million, but we have so much power, being in such a close orbit of Verkennaros, that our virtuality provides a planet's worth of living space. It's quite lovely. It has been running for about 10,000 years now."

"Splendid," said Lysăndra. She looked out the window at the unknown stars. "Just the one station then?"

"No, there are several stations around Verkennaros and a few around each of the gas giants. Including this one, there are eight total, supporting a population of 400 million."

"Sounds like a good layout." Lysăndra contemplated her situation. "I will likely want to depart as soon as possible. I'm sorry to be rude if you were expecting a more protracted visit."

"I assumed as much. To have come all this way, you had to be on a mission of some sort. It only stands to reason you would be rather goal-driven as a result. Why don't you enjoy our offerings while I arrange matter-travel for you. What is your destination?"

"Siremala. Cianthara specifically."

Eero frowned with confusion. "Ah, I see. Well, it's an odd place to want to go, but quite near, so it shouldn't be too difficult. We should be able to provide you with a coherent beam not only for your departure, but for the necessary braking maneuver upon your arrival. And your ship will be able to carry sufficient configurators to build and grow any material resources you need for your time on Cianthara, including an interstellar transit station you can use for your return leg, so as to avoid the need for any further matter-travel."

"That seems like a sensible mission design. Thank you for your assistance." She paused. "Why in all this time has no one ever ventured to Cianthara? Here you are in a system with no planets at all, and Cianthara is so close by."

"For the reason I was initially surprised you wanted to go there in the first place. Siremala is no longer a stable star. It is highly variable and pulsating. It just isn't worth the trouble, frankly. There would be no point in attempting to establish a society, or even an outpost, of any sort there. I'm not sure what you are hoping to find on Cianthara, to be honest."

"I see. Well thank you again."

Lysăndra found herself to be too distracted with her mission to be able to enjoy much of anything else, and so was relieved when Eero notified her that resources had been secured to grow a lased beam ship for her. They regrouped in the same control room as before.

"I hope you have enjoyed your brief visit," Eero said. "Now regarding your ship, did you wish to run a virtuality so as to travel in a dynamic state?"

"You're asking if I want to be conscious for the trip?"

"Yes, but it will require a slightly larger ship, more resources, things of that nature. That adds mass, which will slow your travel somewhat."

"Ah, I see. In that case no. I would prefer to get to Cianthara as quickly as possibly even if that means traveling in an etched state."

"No problem." Lysăndra watched as Eero made final configuration adjustments and grew the ship from raw materials. The ship itself was minuscule. It contained the necessary material resources to store her etched brain pattern and to grow an initial swarm of configurators, which would in turn build and grow anything she needed, including a brain orb and body. The core of the ship, discounting the sails, would fit in the mass and volume of a large grain of sand. Once launched, it would briefly be guided away from the orbital station. At a safe distance, it would unfurl an enormous mirrored sail, circular around the tiny core. The sail was only atoms-thick but as wide as a small asteroid. Linnea station would then direct lased light onto the sail, and would continue to do so throughout her journey. Depending on the efficiency of the trip, she would reach between one and ten percent the speed of light. Part way through the trip, her ship would deploy a second sail ahead of her ship that would reflect the lased beam back onto the front-facing side of the primary sail, acting as a brake and slowing her ship down at Cianthara. Likewise, the solar wind coming off her destination star, Siremala, would slow the ship down as well. Her ship would then rework the material of the sail, first into an aerobrake for slashing through

Cianthara's upper atmosphere a few times, and then again as a heat shield to punch through the lower layers of the atmosphere, and then finally a third time as a parachute for her eventual arrival on Cianthara. It could even become an aerofoil for flying over the planet instead of plummeting to the ground, if she saw any point in doing so upon arrival.

"Ready to go?" asked Eero. "Everything is set."

"Thank you again for assisting me."

"Oh thank you. It was a pleasure to meet the creator of the EOUSP quale."

"MmHmm," she responded uncomfortably. Lysăndra made an etching and promptly went into stasis, losing consciousness, having no need or desire to leave a conscious branch on Linnea station.

...And then, without so much as a moment of experienced transitional time, she instantly felt herself regaining consciousness again, corporealizing, but now she was on a new world thirty-seven light years away—and a thousand years later.

But little did Lysăndra know, she had a stowaway.

31

LYSÃNDRA STOOD ON THE LANDING OF HER NYVERON HOME, now several years old, watching a flock of cloud-like creatures float past. Each was a relatively distinct blob of fluff, with a nondescript physical boundary and no clear anatomical features. As they floated—or flew—together, the would gently repel or bounce off one another, maintaining their individuality, and yet they floated with coordinated movement.

Suddenly, with surprising speed, the flock rapidly converged into a single larger form and its surface appearance altered somewhat, gaining a rigidity that had been lacking in the individuals. A moment later some other creature she hadn't seen before, with sharp wings and a gaping maw, arrived from above in a murderous dive, turning up short at the last instant, clearly determined to avoid colliding with the flock's defensive form. It had missed its chance to dive *through* one of the defenseless individual's cloudy form and scoop up a meal carved out of the cross-section of its own shape intersected with its intended prey's ellipsoid. The hungry predator swooped off almost at quickly as it had arrived, as if embarrassed that Lysãndra had witnessed its failure, and the flock soon reverted to its individualized state, floating to some destination with mild intentionality.

Lysãndra had obtained a parcel of land from where she couldn't see any other artificial structures. In a temperate climate where canyons and ancient dried out fjords sliced across color-banded geologic strata, she had grown this simple house, just enough to accommodate a view, a neural interfacing chair for network experimentation, and basic furnishings worth keeping semipermanent even when she was absent or decorporealized. There wasn't much point in adding persistent furnishings beyond that minimalism. Whenever she needed more space and a fancier presence, say when anyone visited, she could rapidly grow additional structures as needed and then dissolve them after her guests departed.

Lysãndra reflected on the progress thus far as she watched the cloud flock drift away. She had met Quinlan and the other researchers, who were all quite enamored to meet her in return. She and Kaimea toiled over the message for months, slowly teasing out additional symbols from the linguistic message. The key from the second message had decrypted the symbols, but determining their meaning had been left to a correlational and pattern-matching exercise. While Kaimea was correct in her suspicion that the message now contained all the information necessary to translate it, the work seemed almost irrationally convoluted and difficult, as if they were missing some key element of understanding. The message had been cleverly designed in such a manner that mere statistical inferencing was almost completely incapable of success, while richer, conscious-led, *intuition*-led analysis could slowly tease apart the ways in which the symbols carried meaning, but even this second process was remarkably tedious. It was as if the aliens wanted its recipients to have to apply their own conscious attention to the message in order to comprehend it, and yet it was needlessly difficult even from that perspective. They were misunderstanding something. Lysãndra was sure of it.

"I found a new symbol," said Lysãndra one day, as they were working together. Kaimea, standing nearby on the glass floor, came over.

"I know that one," said Kaimea. "It has vexed me for ages."

"See how it's constructed from smaller pieces?" said Lysãndra. "If you take them apart and rotate them in various ways—"

"Ah, you're actually rotating the symbol in three dimensions," said Kaimea, "as if it is a physical object. And, oh, you're even rotating the subcomponents of the symbol that you pulled apart to reveal the surfaces that were concealed from view as they were pressed against one another to form the main symbol, like a stack of blocks, sort of. But how are you inferring what the pieces should look like on the concealed surfaces as they rotate into view?"

"They look like these other symbols from another angle. See? Each reveals a hidden portion of the other."

"That's crazy! Ok, so you think the larger symbol means…" Kaimea squinted with thought. Lysãndra waited. "Based on the sentence around it, I'd say something about time. Ummm, future or forward or later. Perhaps tomorrow? Something like that."

"I thought it might mean next cycle," said Lysãndra.

"A cycle could be a day or a year," said Kaimea.

"I think it's a galactic orbit, perhaps their home world completing an orbit of the center of their galaxy. See how the very next symbol is the symbol for galaxy?"

"Aaah, that fits with this other symbol because the units are in some long measurement relative to light."

"Like a light year," said Lysãndra.

"Yeah, except that while light itself is a constant, a light year requires knowing what a year is."

"So," said Lysãndra, "this is measuring light-somethings, something long, like a year."

"Yeesh, said Kaimea. "This is taking forever."

"I found something else though," said Lysãndra. "Same symbol. Look here in the second message, the short one, the decryption key."

"Oh yeah, it's there too."

"But in this case the symbols are being used to create a complex mathematical formula for decrypting the message, right?"

"Of course," said Kaimea. "So?"

"I think you can't use the same key the same way on the three parts of the message. This symbol is a reference to some sort of time cycle, right? Well the message cycles too. First, it repeats 512 times per presentation, and second, the entire sequence—the first message, then a pause, then the second message, then another pause, and so on—that cycle repeats too, arguably forever I suppose."

Kaimea struggled to understand. "Okay, but how does it tell us how to apply the key in different ways?"

"I think 512 is the important part," said Lysãndra. "512 represents incrementing from one iteration of the message to another."

"Sooo," said Kaimea thoughtfully, "what if 512 represents a way to permute or increment from each section of the message to the next section?"

"Precisely!" said Lysãndra.

"How?"

"I figured I'd just multiply the entire key by 512 before applying it to the second piece of the message, the smaller data block."

Kaimea frowned. "So that's why it didn't work for me previously. I didn't permute the key by 512 before applying it to the second portion of the message, so I decrypted the second portion incorrectly. That's incredibly frustrating. I guess it's worth a shot." It took essentially no time for Lysãndra to complete the calculation, first altering the key from the second message, and then reapplying it to the first data block. She scrutinized the resulting data. Kaimea just looked on in confusion. "I suppose it has richer structure now, but it clearly doesn't contain the same kinds of symbols in the first part of the message. What do you think?" asked Kaimea.

"I'm going to study this or a while," said Lysãndra, already half-entranced by the new representation of the data laid bare before her.

"Fabulous. I'll leave you to it," said Kaimea. She leaned in and kissed Lysãndra's cheek and then instantly vanished before Lysãndra could even turn her head in shock.

"Kaimea. Kaimea! Meet me at my home."

Lysãndra was standing at her balcony when Kaimea corporealized nearby. They stood at the edge, the architectural style seemingly hewn from a rocky cliffside as naturally as if it had formed by erosion. They gazed over the desert landscape, with its canyons zig-zagging across, the result of the planet having literally cleaved apart in some ancient seismic spasm. Needlelike spires rose from the desert floor to dizzying heights. By all appearances they seemed too thin and fragile to survive and yet somehow there they were. They were alive and therefore self-repairing, flexible, and resilient. Their sharp tips, above the height from where Lysãndra and Kaimea stood, continuously bent and curled and wrapped around in random ways, catching something from the air that Lysãndra couldn't make out at her distance. The sky, just on the green side of blue, stretched high overhead with icy crystalline clouds, turquoise, plopped here and there.

"Hello," said Kaimea. "Just enjoying the view?" A large and dense flock of flying animals, individually unresolvable but collectively majestic in form and movement, twisted and spun in peculiar flight from one side of the sky, across the landscape, eventually to the other side.

"Well, actually, I completed the translation of the smaller data block. It's ready."

"Oh my goodness! And it was a neural configuration, right?"

"Most certainly. It is very clean now that the key has been properly applied." Lysãndra gave Kaimea an inviting look, "And we're going to try it tonight."

"An alien neural configuration," said Kaimea, with amazement.

"Not just that. Alien conscious experiences, alien qualia, whatever that may consist of. I can't even imagine, but we'll know soon enough."

"The prior eleven extragalactic species never conveyed this sort of thing in their communications," said Kaimea. "We have no idea what the conscious states of those other alien species are like."

"Well, we're going to get a glimpse of this one," said Lysãndra. "I've been adapting the fine details at the edge of the aliens' network so it will interface with our fortified and de novo brains."

"Our brains are hardly compatible with prefortified humans as it is," said Kaimea. "The idea that you could further adapt an alien brain seems even harder."

"Actually, I found it easier to adapt to our contemporary brain structures than it would have been to adapt to an unmodified human brain. The neural configuration in the smaller data block implies that the aliens' brains are more similar to our modernized neural structures than to old-fashioned humans."

"I wonder if that means they went through a similar technological evolution," wondered Kaimea.

"Almost certainly," said Lysãndra. "No doubt, any technologically capable species would eventually supersede its biological evolution with the advantages of deliberately crafted augmentations."

"Augmentations that eventually lead to complete replacements. Fortification," said Kaimea.

"And the fact that I was able to adapt the alien network to our fortified brains, now a million years evolved in intentional and technological ways beyond our natural origins, suggests that all technological species undergo this process, fortification, along a relatively confined route."

"That seems so unlikely," said Kaimea.

"Well, the truth of it is, we still don't understand the connection between the physical and the metaphysical. We have no idea why certain networks inspire certain qualia. This discovery would seem to suggest there is a fairly narrow set of solutions to challenges of this sort."

"I can't believe you figured this out," said Kaimea. "Is it safe?"

"I always make an etching before trying a new network. If the experience goes badly, I have two options. I can erase the memory of the time-period during which I wore the new network before it transfers to long term memory, or in the worst case, I can simply revert to the etching. I would like your assistance."

"Absolutely! How so? I'm not an experienced quale-diver."

"You've taught me so much about the message and how you study the symbols." Lysãndra smiled at Kaimea. "It's my turn to teach you my craft. Let's go try it out." Two interfacing chairs grew out of the floor of the balcony and they each settled into one, the chairs gently molding to their bodies along the contact surfaces and tightly integrating with the backs of their heads so as to achieve a high-bandwidth interface with their brain orbs.

"Okay," said Lysãndra. "First, I'll pull up the control interface. You'll be in charge."

"I will?"

"You will oversee my neural functions, my sympathetic nervous functions, things like that. You need to watch for seizures, habituations, attractors that spiral either down toward zero or up toward infinity, any other signaling-processing problems. You need to monitor brainwaves at a variety of frequencies so as to detect if the amplitude—the strength—of any such waves rises into a dangerous zone. Here, just absorb this." At a thought, Lysãndra presented a bulk of comprehension and understanding, which Kaimea directly accessed. She rapidly acquired a high-level, if somewhat vague, overview of the task for which she would be in charge and then spent a few minutes digging into the details of each piece of knowledge the memory bulk had granted to her. Pretty soon, she was an expert at the task and eventually notified Lysãndra that she was ready.

"Okay, let's see what this alien neural configuration does," said Lysãndra.

Lysãndra settled into the chair even deeper, relaxing, almost melting.

"This might be a strange sensation," Lysãndra said. "It's literally the first alien neural configuration ever worn by a human. In all my million years doing this, I've never encountered some of the network structures and organizational properties this network utilizes." She hesitated and became concerned. "Kaimea, what if it doesn't work at all? What if the network won't even interface with a human brain, or what if its neurological behaviors simply don't invoke any qualia. Our brains engage in all sorts of inner signal processing of which we have no conscious awareness. What if it just doesn't work?"

They pondered her question briefly. "Well," said Kaimea, "What else are we going to do at this point, right?"

"I just don't want to let everyone down," Lysãndra said. "So many people are already benefiting from the network in its current form, the merger of the Neuralium and my initial discovery. Everyone is hoping I can improve it."

"I'm just glad you're here to help me figure it out," said Kaimea reassuringly. "I'm going to open the interface now. Let's give it a try."

"Yeah, of course." Lysãndra recanted her reservations and drove out the apprehension. "Right, Kaimea. Do it."

Kaimea activated the network. Lysãndra immediately realized her concern had been premature.

"It's definitely working," she said, "although I'm still getting used to it. Might take a moment."

"What's it feel like?"

"Are the beta waves synced between my brain and the module? I'm not sure it's quite right yet." She waited for a response.

"Oh I see it now. They are slightly out of phase. How could you tell that from the inside?"

"Lots of practice. Out-of-phaseness between brain waves in my brain and in an external module has a quale in and of itself. I learned to recognize it long ago."

"Hold on, I think I can adjust it." Lysãndra waited.

"Yes, that's better," Lysãndra said right on top of Kaimea saying, "I think I got it."

Lysãndra soaked up the sensation. It didn't have much of an emotional timbre, she noticed. She suspected that wasn't because the aliens were emotionless beings, but rather that this particular sensation, whatever it was supposed to convey, was not emotional in nature. It felt almost technical, like instructions, but nothing so prosaic as rote commands or actions to be taken. It felt like...she tried to make the determination...

"Okay," said Lysãndra, "I think I know what's going on here. It's definitely unusual."

"Do you feel the solution to the EOUSP?"

"I feel nothing pertaining to the EOUSP at all."

"What?! That's the whole point of this."

"I'm getting two sensations at once here. Can you pull up the first section of the message for me? I have a hunch. I want to see the symbols from the linguistic section." Kaimea presented the first section, spread out in a vast virtual space where they could both see it together.

"Oh wow!" she immediately declared. "I can read it. I can read all of it Kaimea! Whoa! This is incredible."

"What? Seriously? Ugh, more layers of encryption from these aliens. What is it with them anyway?"

"I'm telling you, the entire linguistic section is simply laid bare to me now. It's like I'm fluent in their logography. This section here," she brought a smaller piece into central focus, "where you barely translated any symbols at all. It's a description of their own exodus, the tale of their spread across their galaxy."

"Oh good grief!" said Kaimea. Stop it. Get out. It's my turn." Kaimea laughed, but also sort of meant it. "What else?"

"Here's another section," said Lysãndra.

"A bunch of math we've never made any sense of," said Kaimea.

"Yep, but I've got it now. It's several theorems, one of the remaining areas of inquiry after the closure of physics. There is nothing left for us to learn about the workings of the physical world, but in the realm of abstractions, of math, we are always discovering new things. Math goes on forever. They have about 700 theorem solutions here. I wonder if any of them are new to us. Who knows what answers are buried here. It isn't really my field to know such details. It'll take a while to go over all of these."

"Oh you're just killing me now," said Kaimea. "I'm serious. It's my turn."

"Wait," said Lysãndra with a sudden change in her tone. "I said there were two sensations associated with the quale. What is this? Hold on. There's something else." Lysãndra went silent for a moment. Kaimea couldn't easily see what Lysãndra was attending to as she watched the control interface, but it didn't seem to be the linguistic portion anymore.

"Okay, this is good," Lysãndra said. "I'm quite certain this network and its quale are also the way by which to access the larger network and its associated quale, the really large data block I mean."

"So," said Kaimea, "you're saying this smaller network, from the smaller data block, decrypts or unlocks the larger data block? The other block is nine times larger than this one. You're saying it's another neural configuration? It must be a much more complex network, and presumably a more complex quale."

"Which makes sense if the second network is the EOUSP quale," said Lysãndra. "We expect it to be vast and complex. However, from what I'm getting here, I wouldn't characterize it as a decryption key necessarily. I would say this quale, the one I'm getting right now, is more like a psychological state of readiness...a willingness sort of...I can't find the right word. In order to access the experience that will be granted by the larger network, we must know how to put our minds into the necessary receptive state. This quale helps us do that part."

"Sounds like meditation," said Kaimea. "Meditation and enlightenment aren't the same thing, but one is a significant part of the path to the other."

"An apt analogy," said Lysãndra, still allowing herself to calmly consume the ongoing experience.

After a while, Kaimea spoke again, impatiently. "So can I try it already?!"

After Kaimea wore the smaller network and became only the second person in the galaxy to feel an alien conscious quale—and implicitly *know* a sentient alien state of mind—and after she spent a considerable amount of time pouring thorough historical records in the linguistic section that had vexed and eluded her for 35,000 years—they decided to try the larger network.

"Who should go first?" asked Kaimea. Lysãndra thought about it for a moment. Here it was, the moment of truth. Her millennia of pursuing an incomplete neural configuration with its imprecise revelation of a partial EOUSP quale was all behind her. The alien message was clear—at least to Kaimea, and she agreed with Kaimea's interpretation. The aliens didn't claim to have some vague sense of the EOUSP quale. They claimed to have *solved* it. Moments from now, Lysãndra could very well hold in her mind the solution to the greatest mystery in the universe: how consciousness and life—how culture, art and music, and almost infinite stories rendered from almost infinite imaginations—how the ultracolor, shockingly vivid, surreality of trillions of dreams across trillions of slumbers—how all of this grandeur could survive the ultimate universal annihilation instead of inevitably fading and dying—and vanishing. Here she was, on the cusp of obtaining that answer. The answer.

And she flinched. "I think you should go first," Lysãndra said. She heard herself say the words and couldn't believe it.

"Why?" said Kaimea with surprise.

Objectively, Lysãndra found a simple way to rationalize it, but it wasn't the real reason.

"You know," Lysãndra continued, "Despite all this ridiculous fame I have garnered, the truth is, you have been pursuing the solution to the EOUSP far longer than I have. You intentionally pursued it in a different way, hoping to find it amongst the stars, hoping someone else out there had already solved it, and in the end, you were right all along. Here it is. I, on the other hand, wasn't searching for it this whole time. I clumsily stumbled across it, and much more recently than you too, and while I admit I became committed to its completion as soon as I realized what I had found, that doesn't change the fact that this passion, this drive, has been with you practically from your beginning. I'm stepping into your realm here. This is yours. It always was, Kaimea. You should go first."

"Wow," said Kaimea with brimming tears. "After Deimos practically chased me out of the galaxy I never thought anyone would understand how I felt. I hadn't even thought to see it that way. I thought it was yours from the moment I learned of your work."

"So?" said Lysãndra.

"Is that really it? I mean, even if you want to let me have it, don't you also want it as badly as I do? You seem apprehensive."

Lysãndra sighed. "Kaimea, we don't know everything about each other yet."

"Do you want to tell me?"

Lysãndra felt a comfort with Kaimea that she and Ceôlbur hadn't had in recent millennia. She absolutely wanted to tell her. "I lost someone," she said. "Before the Great Fortification."

"Whoa."

"I've spent a million years regretting that he missed out on, well, everything. A twenty year gap meant the difference between death and eternity for him. That's what separated him from the rest of us. A stupid twenty year missed opportunity."

"And you regret it? You blame yourself?"

"Oh, not in practical terms. It's not like it was directly my fault, but all of us, I mean society, civilization. We could have fought harder to figure out fortification sooner. Billions could have been saved."

"You can't burden yourself with that, and it was so long ago, and it was no one person's fault, certainly not those who had so little influence? Were you famous or powerful or influential in some way? Could you have expedited the development of fortification and your...friend's?"

"He was more than that."

"—your partner's salvation? Could you have done anything about it?"

"No no. Objectively, of course it isn't my fault. I just..." Lysãndra trailed off. They sat there a moment.

Kaimea asked "And somehow, his loss gives you reservation about experiencing the EOUSP quale? I don't understand the connection." Lysãndra didn't respond, unsure of how to explain her reasoning in the moment. "I would be honored to go first," Kaimea continued. "But only to give you a moment to think on it. I think you should do it too, all other issues aside."

"I understand," Lysãndra said. She dwelled for one more moment, and then said, "Let's get you hooked up." Lysãndra took the controller role and Kaimea settled in. Lysãndra spent a few minutes looking over the parts of the module network that would connect directly to parts of Kaimea's brain, where signals would sweep back and forth, like waves sloshing in a pond.

"Okay, this is a little tricky," said Lysãndra. "We're going to use both alien networks at the same time. You need access to the network we already wore, with its quale we already experienced, in order to know—or feel—how to most effectively experience the second network. That's how it unlocks the second network."

"The meditation analogy again," said Kaimea, "I will use the experience evoked by the first network to access the experience evoked by the second network."

"That's the basic idea. I'm guessing it will make sense when you're there. The conscious experience of the first network should—I'm hoping—guide you right into the second experience, hopefully without much effort on your part. That's kinda the whole thing with consciousness. You don't have to *try* to experience a red quale when you look at a red thing. It just happens. But, following our analogy, the sensation of enlightenment for example, it might be harder than a simpler quale. We just don't know yet."

"It might be more like a sensation of oneness or ego-dissolution or just ordinary out-of-bodyness," said Kaimea. "None of those experiences necessarily come easily. People spend their entire lives trying to achieve those experiences."

"Right. Such states of consciousness don't seem to simply fall into place like the qualia triggered by external stimuli. These other states are triggered by getting our internal, recurrent, isolated networks to fall into local attractors of firing behavior, and without an obvious external trigger. It comes down to *thinking* ourselves into the right frame of mind. In lieu of direct external sensorial triggers, like looking at a surface of a particular color, we have to use other interventions. Back when we were biological, we would sloppily flood our brains with chemicals that would alter our network firing patterns and our resulting conscious experiences. Ever since fortification, we skip over the chemical imprecision and directly prod our networks into firing patterns that have long been established to produce these conscious states we find so tantalizing. But in this case—"

"In this case," said Kaimea, wanting to show that she understood Lysãndra's quale-diving expertise, "we will use the smaller network and its state of mind to access the second network's state of mind."

"A reasonable description," said Lysãndra.

Lysãndra activated the first module and Kaimea quickly settled into its sensations. She didn't focus on the intrinsic fluency in the alien language that she now felt so naturally with the network activated. Rather, she focused on the other evocation, a feeling of readiness and anticipation of some other state just out sight, just out of reach, but a preparedness nonetheless for that next state.

"Ready for the next network?" Lysãndra asked.

"Ready enough."

Lysãndra activated the second network, flooding Kaimea with trillions of signal propagations from only the second sentient alien neural module to ever be tried by a human. Lysãndra watched the brain activity intently, both Kaimea's and the module. It elicited a rich set of neurological behaviors. The module buzzed with numerous independent regions. It contained nearly as many neurons as an entire human brain, including the massive brain expansions humans had undergone after fortifying. The module poured its processing into Kaimea's brain, and Kaimea's brain poured her own processing back across the interface into the module, and so on. It quickly became impossible for Lysãndra to ascertain any meaningful distinction between the module's functions and Kaimea's. It had simply become part of her. She carefully looked over the details while waiting for Kaimea to say something, anything, to report on what was happening.

Suddenly aware that she was waiting for some response from Kaimea, she carefully confirmed that Kaimea's signals still seemed safe, but by all appearances, Kaimea's brain functions seemed to be operating within acceptable parameters. Lysãndra felt the heat of relief wash over her and continued to wait.

"Iii'm not sure what to make of this," said Kaimea. "It's confusing, and very...busy. It's a...colorful quale. Not literally of course."

"Hmmm," said Lysãndra with concern. "I expected it to be more explicit than that."

"It definitely feels like the EOUSP quale again. There's no question about that. And it also feels like the solution, or like it implies the existence of a solution."

"We already knew that," said Lysãndra, further concerned.

"It goes beyond that, I'll admit. It doesn't just feel like the promise of a solution. It feels like..." Kaimea trailed off at a loss for words. "I think you should just try it for yourself," she finally said.

"Does it feel spiritual? Most people react quite strongly to it."

"Oh yes, don't misunderstand my failure to describe it. It has all the powerful effects we've come to expect from your EOUSP quale. It feels really good in that respect, I suppose. I was just hoping that the actual solution would be more," Kaimea sighed, "tangible, I suppose."

"I'll see if I can make sense of it," said Lysãndra. She detached Kaimea and they switched roles.

"Do you need me to oversee it for you?" asked Kaimea. "I'm sure you can do it yourself of course."

"I prefer to have someone else at the controls when trying out new networks. Obviously we can attach and detach, enable and disable, modules on our own, but for experimentation like this, it's nice to have someone else watching over things."

"Okay, hold on." Lysãndra waited while Kaimea studied the interface between Lysãndra and the module. After a short duration, "Okay, I think it's ready. Here goes the first network."

Lysãndra felt the first network enter her conscious awareness, with its implicit invitation to attach the second network and feel her way through its various sensations. Seeing nothing of concern, she indicated to Kaimea to continue, so Kaimea enabled the second network. Lysãndra quickly understood what Kaimea had meant, the tremendous torrent of activity roaring through the module and then the surge of activation sweeping back and forth across the connection between her brain and the module.

Lysãndra felt it immediately, but it was tumultuous and wild, difficult to make sense of. As Kaimea had indicated, recognizable notions of the EOUSP quale permeated the experience. She could feel the awe and enormity and infinitude of the universe, and also its finitude and ultimate demise. She could feel the anguish of sextillions—or septillions—of conscious minds scattered throughout the whole universe, mostly located in galaxies so remote that their stars would never shine on human eyes, all those minds slowly snuffing out in the eternal frigid black of the dying everything. This was most definitely a EOUSP quale, a very powerful one at that. But it remained chaotic and needly. The network didn't seem to perfectly coordinate with her brain.

She tried to relax and let the first network's evoked quale do the work for her. It gave her nondescript, intuitive instincts that shined a light on the path through the raucous sensations and perceptions flaring up in her mind. As she did this, the chaos settled down a bit, only partially, and she felt the next layer. Again confirming Kaimea's description, Lysãndra could now perceive the notion of a solution, although it felt turbulent, like the earlier sensations this network had evoked. It was more than the hope of a solution, more than the Neuralium. It was...she dwelled on the feeling, trying to ignore the prickly aspects of it, focusing on its deeper essence, bringing it to the forefront...it was the reality of a solution, not merely the hope of it. But she already knew that. Her recent network had already confirmed that a solution existed. She became frustrated. Was this all she would get, just confirmation of what she already knew?

Lysãndra lingered on the feeling of the EOUSP solution, trying to find the edges, the shape, the texture of it in qualia-space. She forced herself to once again lean on the first network's quale for guidance. The first network's role was so thin, so nebulous, that if she looked directly at it, the capability it granted her simply slid away. But if she defocused, if she let it literally pull her along, she felt herself heading in a new direction within the EOUSP quale's enormous space and complexity. Yes, there it was, something new up ahead. The solution was real. The solution was visceral. She hung onto it, waiting for it to clarify.

And then it hit her. It hit her like physicality. She felt it in her chest like a true weight.

The solution to the EOUSP was most definitely feasible, practical, achievable.

She gasped.

"Everything okay?" she heard Kaimea say with a voice that sounded like it had drifted across a foggy lake from out of sight.

She didn't want to respond, she didn't want to lose her grasp, but she muttered a quiet "yes," and turned back inward.

This was it. This was why she had traveled 17,000 light years. Until this moment she, and the countless others who had worn her latest network, had experienced and confirmed the *existence* of a solution, but no one could discern whether the solution was even remotely *practical*. It could have required folding ten-dimensional space in on itself with the power of a thousand black holes. Or it could have required scooping up the mass of a million galaxies and compressing them into a singularity. Or it could have required building an entirely new network with an entirely new quale but with absolutely no indication whatsoever how to discover or design the required network. It could have been real, yet utterly unachievable.

But no. Now, as it lingered before her, it was as clear as a vacuum. She could not have been more confident now of the veracity of the truth. And that truth was that there was, somewhere out there, an entirely reasonable way to survive the end of the universe.

She let herself move on. She wanted to stay there, but she needed the rest of it. The aliens had promised the actual solution. She could see—figuratively—another shore to sail to in the huge space of this quale. This alien network had created the most complex experience she had ever felt. There it was, a little farther ahead. The solution. She sailed toward it. Or to be more specific, she once again let the intuitive quale of the first network pull her across the map.

The solution was right in front of her, but it danced around with phantasmagorical edges. She turned it over in her figurative hands, looking at it in different ways, but as Kaimea had indicated, it lacked 'tangibility'—Kaimea's words. It wouldn't stand still for Lysãndra. It wouldn't solidify. This entire experience had been jagged from her moment of entry, and it was worse here than anywhere earlier.

"Something's wrong," she said.

"I know," said Kaimea. "I couldn't get a hold of it. I could sense it. It was all around me, but I couldn't figure out what it was actually telling me."

"I can't either," said Lysãndra. "The quale has been choppy from the start. Something is very wrong." She continued to work at it, going back and forth between genuine effort on her part and letting the intuition of the first network show it to her. Neither approach worked.

"Why doesn't it work?" asked Kaimea.

A theory formed in Lysãndra's mind. A dismal and depressing theory. "My best guess is that the aliens' brains are insufficiently compatible with ours for us to comprehend their experience of the solution. That would explain both why it has felt so noisy throughout, and why at the end it fails to coalesce into a clear answer."

"So humans can't understand the solution to the EOUSP?" said Kaimea, her voice literally cracking on the brink of grief. So much of her life poured into this project. Was this how it would end?

"Not necessarily," said Lysãndra. "We just can't understand it through the minds and brains of this particular alien species. I think this is as far as the aliens can take us, but that doesn't mean it is inaccessible to humans. We will just have to find a more human-accessible version of the quale." Lysãndra just about collapsed in on herself. How would she ever do that? How would she further refine the network at this point?

She disconnected the module without even bothering to let Kaimea do it from her external controls. They looked at each other, the only two people in the galaxy holding the knowledge they now knew. Lysãndra smiled softly at the sight of Kaimea's hair slowly meandering through a random sequence of mauves, plums, and crimsons. Then she stood, walked to the edge of the balcony, leaned against it, and watched Nyveron spread before her.

Kaimea followed, stood next to her, and tentatively put her hand on Lysãndra's hand on the railing, which Lysãndra didn't withdraw. "Now what do we do?" Kaimea asked.

32

S ATÒRI STOOD ON THE EXIT PLATFORM OF ACCEPTING OBLIVION, surround-ed by hundreds of other recent visitors. Most of the crowd stood rather idle, quietly contemplating Rihon's latest creation or discussing it with others on the platform, perhaps groups that had come together or perhaps strangers they had just met and bonded with over the shared experience. He had attended with a group as well, his own followers.

"Thank you for recommending we do this Satòri," said someone nearby. "When you invited your entire house to see Rihon's work, I wasn't sure we should go. I have found your interpretation of our faith to be the most revelatory and have not been too keen on the perspectives of outsiders, such as Rihon. But I see why you wanted to see this, and why you wanted us to see it as well."

Satòri nodded solemnly, still enraptured by his own takeaway, still trying to make sense of something simmering deep within him. Accepting Oblivion had made an impression on him, but he hadn't quite determined how it blended with his own beliefs yet.

"I've met Rihon before," said Satòri. "He and I have shared a similar awe for a long time."

The man responded. "But you still believe that Lysandrism must evolve away from your confused branchlings, leading their own congregations in the wrong direction, yes?"

Satòri quietly nodded again, deep in contemplation, but not bothered by the expressions of this loyal member of his house and follower of his teachings.

The man continued. "Lysandra's research must be pulled within the fold of our faith. It cannot be entrusted to anyone else, not even Lysandra herself, since she does not understand the full *spiritual* implications of her own work. You have explained this clearly, and I agree. Only we—in fact, only our house in particular—truly understand the godly implications of her work. She is, as you have put it, both a saint and a heretic at the same time."

Satòri winced. He had continually failed to reveal to Lysandra, the most crucial agent of god to ever live, the significance of her own work. She was not merely a human making happenstance discoveries. She was blessed. How had god chosen her when she forsake the spiritual importance of solving the EOUSP? She treated it like everyone else, as a curiosity. A passion, yes, but nevertheless she had expressed nothing but blindness to the fact that she was a manifestation of the divine—and worse, she had expressed no interest in joining, or even interacting with, her own spiritual followers.

His thoughts were again interrupted by his disciple.

"But now, having seen the long arc of the EOUSP quale through Rihon's eyes, I feel something different." This piqued Satòri's attention, for he too was feeling something different. Did this person have the same revelation he had?

"Go on, my friend, please. I wish to hear your thoughts."

"Oh thank you. I think now, maybe, perhaps..." trailing off with nervousness.

"Speak your mind. We aren't here to judge one another's reactions, only to discuss them. Frankly, my thoughts are mixed at the moment as well."

"Well, yes, the EOUSP quale must be not be completed outside the faith. That much is clear. But, forgive me for saying this, perhaps it should not be completed *within* the faith either. Rihon's message resonates deeply with me." Satòri felt himself literally jolt as he heard this person speaking his own reaction back to him. "Do you think that, just maybe, Rihon is whispered to by god as well? Perhaps like Lysandra, he doesn't even realize he is working for god, but he is nonetheless."

Satòri glanced toward his uneasy follower. "And you think god's message to Rihon is that the EOUSP quale must not be completed at all?"

"Well, at least not now. As Rihon shows so clearly, maybe we just don't deserve it yet."

"You know what?" Satòri put his hand on his pupil's shoulder. He saw the man shrink with nervousness in anticipation of a reprimand. "I was thinking precisely the same thing." Satòri smiled his usual disarming smile and saw the man melt with relief before him. "I think perhaps we only heard half the message before, the need to prevent Lysandra from completing her work if we refuses to join our house. But now I think we are simply intended to prevent her work from being completed, period. Perhaps that is why god sent Rihon to us, to correct our lost way and set us on the right path."

"What will we do now?'

"There is another person, one who wields significant political influence, who has seen this necessary outcome for a long time. We must join forces with him." Satòri could see the man trying to think it through.

"You don't mean the rather bombastic semi-political figure, Deimos, do you?"

"None other," declared Satòri with satisfaction now that he had come to a concrete realization. "The very same."

"But, he is just about the most ungodly person I can think of. He's horrible."

"He's just another tool in god's hand, as am I, as was Minerva, as is Lysandra...and as is Rihon apparently. I will dispatch someone, perhaps a branchling of myself—perhaps you, my friend!—someone from our house to collaborate with Deimos. He will appreciate this union, I am sure of it. Lysandrism has become one of the greatest forces in the galaxy. Even divided as we currently stand, we can rally vast armies to our cause, to our *shared* cause. He will see that we are in alignment. Yes, he will agree to this partnership, I am sure of it."

33

LYSÃNDRA REGAINED CONSCIOUSNESS AFTER A 17,000 YEAR TRIP FROM Nyveron back to Thalassia, a mere blink from her perspective of course. Her consciousness had faded out on a transit dais on Nyveron as she gazed fondly at Kaimea who stood there waving goodbye, looking rather forlorn, and then she had instantly reemerged on a dais on Thalassia. She had considered branching, leaving a version of herself on Nyveron, but she was not yet committed to a long life stranded on the outer rim of the galaxy—even just one branch of herself. Of course, there was one very tempting reason to stay, which she only properly realized as she watched her vision of Kaimea's saddened expression fade away under her evaporating consciousness. Her final thought as she drifted off was one of panicked dread. *Have I made a mistake?!*

It was with that very thought resurfacing in her mind that she corporealized on Thalassia. She wavered momentarily with regret, hesitating on the dais under a dwindling evening sky, purple on one horizon where Zareasman had recently set, nearly black overhead with the brighter stars twinkling through. The air was cool, the marblesque stone of the dais underfoot hard and polished. Numerous interstellar daises were intermittently dispersed in the vicinity, with corresponding pedestrian traffic. There was neither roof nor walls, but weather was kept at bay by atmospheric manipulators. No one corporealized in the rain here.

She immediately came face to face with herself, in essence the very same branchling who had etched her and sent her on her way millennia ago.

"Welcome back!" said Lysãndra as Lysãndra took notice of her. "I received notice of your impending arrival about a hundred years ago and a further update a few days ago. No surprise that the terse status messages dodged through the interstellar data network more efficiently than your etching." They stood a moment, absorbing the time that had transpired between them. "So, were you successful on Nyveron? What did you learn? You have to tell me everything. Oh my goodness! Just everything!" Lysãndra laughed with delight.

Lysãndra forcefully pushed her thoughts of Kaimea aside at the sight of her excited branchling—it was too late now anyway, 17,000 years too late! She stepped off the dais and approached Lysãndra, an occurrence that might be plain and common for many people, but which was rare and discombobulating for her. Lysãndra could see a similar expression of unease on Lysãndra's face. "Partially successful," she said. "We'll both know everything soon enough, of course."

"Yes of course," Lysãndra responded. "We should reunify as soon as possible, later this evening at home perhaps."

Lysãndra tilted her head with consideration. "I'm surprised you didn't reunify my etching as it arrived without letting the dais corporealize me. Why even perpetuate my branch any further after I had been in stasis for a 17,000 year transit?"

"Well, we've never been the most comfortable branchers, you and I. I thought it best to grant you the autonomy of expressing your preference regarding reunification."

"Mmm, yes, sensible—and considerate. Thank you. I suppose I could have indicated my willingness in the transit directives, but no matter. I'm not—we're not—the most experienced travelers."

"Do you wish to reunify immediately," said Lysãndra, "before any further divergence is accumulated? I feel no urgency, so it's up to you."

"No urgency from me," said Lysãndra. "Later tonight will be fine. Is Ceôlbur here? I suppose 34,000 years on his part to ten measly years on mine will be—difficult—to integrate."

"Yes, he's still here in the system, but not on Thalassia at the moment. Come on, let's get out of here." They ventured home. After so much time it was no longer located in the same place of course, in the equatorial region by the warm ocean. Lysãndra led her to a completely different part of the planet, deep in a verdant, temperate forest, backed against a cliff, near the base of an exalted waterfall.

"Why not at the top?" asked Lysãndra a bit mournfully, scanning up the sheer wall of rock. "We always favored the grand, open views from high altitudes."

"The top of the cliff is above the tree line. It blows a gale up there far too frequently, no good for permanent residence without some weather modification, which would be..." She searched for words.

"Rude to the environment," Lysãndra finished, laughing, realizing the irony that some regions did precisely that, such as the off-planet transit station.

"Exactly." Lysàndra laughed in response. "But I agree with you. I go up there regularly for the view."

They entered the abode, carved into the base of the cliff, with the alien forest growing right up to the vertical rock that stretched practically out of sight overhead. The home consisted of an eclectic web of rooms that sprawled deep into the rock. In lieu of windows, obviously impossible, corner-to-corner display walls in most rooms offered real-time, depth-representational views of random locales spread across the planet. With a bit of corporealization synchronization, she discovered that she could walk through such walls to emerge in those remote locations elsewhere on Thalassia with no deviation in synchrony.

"So where's Ceôlbur?" Lysãndra wandered through the home, exploring its offerings. There were no explicit light sources. The interior simply existed in a state of illumination coming off the display walls.

"Ceulbur," Lysàndra corrected. "He's currently at some social gathering. His interests have diversified of late. He's on Joteiche Station. It didn't exist when you left, 34,000 years ago, of course, but it's one of the larger solar orbital stations now, in virtual extent I mean. It's exclusively virtual in fact."

"Diversified interests?"

"Yes, he has taken a keen interest in merged cognition and consciousness, hiving as it's often called. I can't say I've ever understood the appeal myself, but he finds something rewarding in the experience apparently. I guess something has been missing for him.

"I see."

"Lysãndra, there are things you need to know. Much has happened."

"I'm sure," said Lysãndra. "It's been ages. Should we just reunify now? Perhaps that would be more straightforward than discussing it."

Lysàndra made a concerned expression.

"What?" asked Lysãndra.

"Our branchling died and so did Ceulbur's. When we visited Rihon's art installation, Enduring Oblivion, it was attacked. It was a massive disaster.

Rihon believes we—well, our branchling—was the primary target of the attack, but many others perished as well."

Lysãndra stared blankly as this news registered. It had only reached Nyveron after she departed. "That's...incredible. I mean horrible. I mean..."

"It actually happened at the exact same time that Ailuros was attacked, which also targeted us, it turns out. It was a synchronized act of horrific violence coordinated across 9000 light years, planned far in advance."

"Why in the world would anyone do that to us?" Of course, she already knew the answer, and Lysàndra knew she knew, so she didn't respond.

"What does that have to do with Ceulbur's new interest?"

"Oh, it's just that Ceulbur learned that his branchling had tried this hiving business while at the festivities for Rihon's event, and that sparked his curiosity here. And then he attended Rihon's next unveiling and apparently took part in similar experiences again, so he tells me, and has returned and reunified with those experiences. And now he seems rather taken with the concept."

"I see," said Lysãndra, still absorbing the news. "We should just reunifiy. This is a lot to integrate. I think we just need to consolidate and pick up from there."

"Probably best that way," said Lysàndra, obviously sorry to have broken such heavy news to her own branchling. "Shall we?"

"Any time," said Lysãndra. Neural interfacing chairs partially mushroomed and partially materialized in place, an odd combination. They sat down and Lysãndra felt her body gently bonding to the surface, her head similarly fixing to the headrest behind her.

"This is generally more easily accomplished in stasis, I suppose," said Lysàndra.

"We can do it that way," said Lysãndra. "See you on the other side." Lysãndra initiated her own stasis, bringing her entire neural functioning to a halt, losing consciousness far in advance of the completion of the process of course. Next to her, Lysàndra did the same thing. Soon after, both of their bodies decorporealized entirely.

And then moments later Lysendra awoke, corporealizing in the front room of the house, with a wide view of the forest outside the window, the only window possible in the house, the dark understory dappled under what little sunlight could penetrate the canopy. Dark shadows oozed between the trunks and merged into blackness at a distance. As she attended to her episodic memories—memories of past personal experiences—she could now recall a combined set of experiences. She could remember making an etching of herself, sending it off into the interstellar network toward Nyveron, and promptly returning home on Thalassia the same day. That memory was 34,000 years old, of course. But she could also remember making an etching on Thalassia and suddenly corporealizing on Nyveron a moment later, which felt no more discomforting than jumping into or out of a virtuality—or teleporting either virtually or via the mycelia network elsewhere on the planet. That memory was only a few years old, spanning only the duration she had been on Nyveron. And finally, she could remember decorporealizing for the last time on Nyveron and summarily recorporealizing on Thalassia, which felt like it had occurred only an hour ago, since it had.

But she could also recall 34,000 years of intervening memories of having lived on Thalassia, culminating in going to the interstellar transit station to meet her impending arrival an hour earlier. And most curiously, she could recall events on Nyveron and events on Thalassia that had occurred at the same time, but she had no way of *knowing* that was the case without checking her memories against a calendar. She couldn't *feel* their concurrency in any particular way. To the contrary, the concurrent memories from her Thalassia branch felt 17,000 years old while the concurrent memories from her Nyveron branch felt like they had spanned the most recent ten years of her life, which of course they had.

The strangest sensation was of her memories *prior* to the branching. There was only one remembrance of any such memory, say of witnessing the Ailurosian Annihilation from Thalassia, a mere millennium before she departed for Nyveron. Was that memory a thousand years old, or 35,000? Any given recollection of that memory felt one way or the other depending on whether she centered her perspective on her Nyveron or her Thalassia timelines.

And now, Lysendra went forward with her newly gained knowledge from the alien message. The EOUSP solution was feasible, some genuinely achievable feat, but what that solution actually was remained vexingly unknown. Her work was not done yet.

Lysendra and Ceulbur settled in for the latest iteration of the EOUSP quale. Her having already worked out the details of how to interface with it during her time on Nyveron, there was no need for one of them to oversee the other while wearing the network, so they wore it together, simultaneously.

"I'm not going to simply *tell* you what I discovered," said Lysendra. "I want you to *feel* it directly and realize the implications as a surprise." She smiled lovingly at Ceulbur, who gave her a playfully suspicious look in response. They settled into their adjacent neural interfacing chairs and held hands.

"I take it from your phrasing," said Ceulbur, "that the network is not yet complete, that the quale does not yet fully reveal the EOUSP solution."

"I'm afraid not, but I made progress. Hopefully, I can find a way to further improve it, although I'm rather out of ideas." She didn't mention her branchling who had, with any luck, just about arrived at Cianthara at this time to seek out the ancient and dead Ontoscendian civilization. Ceulbur knew nothing of that.

"Let's see what you've got here," said Ceulbur.

"You sound apprehensive."

"Not about the network or the quale. I trust you of course. Whatever work you've done on it is top notch, I'm sure."

"What's bothering you then?"

"Let me wear network first. Maybe it will change my perspective."

"Ok." This time it was Lysendra's turn to sound apprehensive. They relaxed, activated their respective modules, and let the EOUSP quale perfuse through their minds, at first decorating their conscious sensations, peppering around the edges, but steadily taking over until their entire awareness was saturated with EOUSP awe, as well as a venerated sense of its solution. But this time, there was a new layer, as Lysendra had recently discovered. The solution now felt acutely achievable, not just some abstraction beyond the reach of practicality. Ceulbur felt for the first time the undeniable reality that all the accomplishments of history, all the productive output of humanity, all the experiences and memories and knowledge and wisdom and emotions could carry on after the last iota of usable energy had drained from the universe and the last particle of the last black hole had evaporated away.

Ceulbur opened his eyes and watched the forest sway gently outside.

"Okay," he said, after a pause. "So the solution is...possible."

"Yes," Lysendra responded.

"That's a profound step forward," Ceulbur said. "This really does change things. The solution isn't just an abstract palliative for EOUSP angst and suffering. There really is some way to do something about it."

"Yeah, it's real," Lysendra continued to respond, anxious for his reaction.

Ceulbur furrowed his brow with heavy contemplation. "I suppose you want to publish this new network."

"Of course. Why wouldn't we?"

Ceulbur sighed. "This will bring even greater threats against us, that's why. How will you ever fend off the full might of those who would kill an entire moon and sterilize half a planet just to get to you?"

Lysendra withdrew her hand from his and stood from the chair, which promptly shrank into the floor until every trace of its former presence was erased. "This doesn't belong to us Ceulbur. We have to give it to everyone."

"Perhaps the opposite is true. Perhaps we're responsible for it, responsible for the consequences, the harm it could cause." Ceulbur stood from his chair as well.

"That would be a *good* thing," said Lysendra. "Imagine the effect of giving everyone the realization that all of this—" she spread her arms metaphorically "—can go on. How can that possibly be bad?"

Ceulbur shook his head. "We can't know that. There's no way to foresee the outcome of profound, society-altering changes like this. What if some people wish to keep it for themselves and prevent others from accessing it? What if we're unleashing those who are currently only coming after us to go after everyone else? You could be putting a target on everyone. Think about it, those trying to stop you would have to stop everyone if you release this network? For Earth's sake Lysendra, this could start a galactic war!"

"Or it could save us all. I can't believe you're against this." Ceulbur could see Lysendra practically in tears. "Why aren't you with me?"

"Because you're going to get yourself killed!" he declared. "This Deimos fellow. Don't you see how dangerous he is? You act like this is all just for fun. Some sects of that crazy Lysandrism cult are against this too. Can you imagine how dangerous they could be?"

Lysendra was practically shaking before him. "This is bigger than us. We've discovered something incredible here, and it isn't our decision whether everyone everywhere gets to know it, or gets to choose what to do with it. Each person has the right to make that choice for themselves."

Ceulbur scoffed. "So you're going to publicize it. You've decided."

"Oh I don't know...I hadn't thought not to until now...of course I thought I would...maybe?...yeah, probably...I guess."

Ceulbur gazed out the window again. The forest felt dark, the shadows eerie. "The new network is incredible Lysendra. I'm not denying that, but this is reckless. We shouldn't publish these results. We should just continue to work on it privately, if at all. But you don't seem inclined to listen to me, so I just hope you know what you're doing."

"So do I."

34

Upon Lysăndra's initial corporealization on Cianthara, she had found herself standing in an ecosystem unseen for hundreds of millennia, rich with novel lifeforms, but she saw nothing resembling architecture or a civilization. Of course, she had come down completely at random. There was an entire planet to explore. Within a few days she had grown and deployed aerial surveyors that climbed to stratospheric heights and then glided around the planet indefinitely, solar-powered, sending back planetary scans across all wavelengths.

After a few weeks stationed where she had first arrived in the equatorial region, receiving remote reports from the surveyors, she had a decent understanding of Cianthara's continents and bodies of water. She had also discovered what surviving ruins there were to be found after 800,000 years and had quickly ascertained where the major urban centers resided— nowhere near her initial location it turned out. The Ontoscendians had lived here for tens of thousands of years and had built a significant civilization, replete with sprawling cultural centers. Having no idea which urban region to start with, she had simply chosen the one that seemed the largest. She grew a body readily capable of long distance flight and then set off. This trip also gave her an opportunity to witness the planet beneath her with her own eyes instead of through scans from the surveyors, although the survey data could be consumed practically firsthand anyway.

The planet lacked hemisphere-spanning oceans, but tremendous seas slid beneath her, azure waves with white foam along their leading edges, huge flocks of orange, flighted lifeforms strafing the water so closely they were drenched in spray. When over land, she swept above open plains that stretched a full day's flight, layered with glaring silver grasses that shimmered like tinsel in the sunlight of Siremala. Wind-blown waves swept back and forth across these silver carpets while herds of spindly-legged creatures, gleaming white with piercing blue spots and stripes, a hundred times larger than a human, seemingly tumbled across the landscape with a gait that was difficult to comprehend. The whole herd would look up in unison at her as she glided overhead, but took no other interest in her. The plains gave way to tawny deserts, separated into broad geometric sections, each delineated by blue rivers shored with silver and black plant life that contrasted sharply against the sand. Then the forests. What passed for alien trees appeared from her altitude to be a single blanket of shiny charcoal hue. While it was still heavily pocked and broken, showing that a lush tropics thrived beneath the uppermost layers, the canopy itself, a speckled sheet of mid to dark grays, gave no impression of individual trees—or whatever they were. It was simply a continuous ashen coverage. Occasionally, however, she would pass over a gaping hole where one such tree-thing had fallen over. Into these vertical caverns she could gain a slightly improved understanding of the forest layers. Interior gray sheets of similar sub-canopy coverage layered upon layer downward somewhere toward the forest floor, which itself was utterly lost in darkness. Due to Siremala's inclination, no light ever shined all the way into these holes and she had no idea what was at ground level.

Eventually, she reached her destination. A temperate ecology of scattered trees, always with their pewter, and occasionally black, solar sheets, held aloft on cork-screwed red trunks. These trees were dotted individually across a flat landscape otherwise covered in more of Cianthara's representative silver grass, but clear signs of architecture were everywhere to be found. Mounds, entirely grown over and heavily eroded, but unambiguously artificial in shape, were scattered in all directions. There were also sheer vertical buildings, decrepit, but long-lasting given the advanced materials and techniques employed following Earth Exodus, fully overgrown with red and orange vines splayed with gray solar sheeting. She landed on high ground from where she could oversee an exploration, the shiny grass crinkling under her feet, and then grew and deployed a huge swarm of tiny flying assistants that dispersed and permeated every crevice of the city. Where genuine excavation was required, larger and more capable earth-movers were rapidly grown, put to work tunneling as needed, and then dissolved back into the environment upon completion.

After a year on Cianthara, Lysăndra had a comprehensive understanding of this particular city. During that time, she had dispatched similar swarms of explorers to the other major city ruins around the planet, and within the second year, she had a similarly comprehensive understanding of every major urban center Cianthara had to offer. She had considered branching to oversee this effort from multiple positions simultaneously, but she had never been particularly comfortable with branching, unlike many other people, including Ceôlbur to some extent. She preferred to maintain her linearity whenever possible. She had often wondered if this was a weakness on her part, but had never made a concerted effort to overcome it.

And so, her work continued. She learned as much as she could about the Ontoscendians. As the previous archeological expedition from Fringalis had determined, the Ontoscendians exhibited a pervasive obsession with the EOUSP. It seemed to be the defining pursuit of their culture. And as with the prior expedition, she found numerous references to their advanced work with neural configurations. They appeared, by all rights, to be thorough brain engineers and quale-divers. But she could find no particular artifacts or records tying these two passions together. Was there any connection between the EOUSP and quale exploration for the Ontoscendians? Perhaps the Ontoscendians had solved the EOUSP in some entirely different way.

As the second year wrapped up, she began to lose hope. Her work had been thorough, and while she had learned much about the Ontoscendians' interest in the EOUSP, she could find no indication that they had solved it, much less how.

But then, one day, that all changed.

What do we have here? she thought, noticing yet another report coming in from a rather distant city. *More EOUSP research, I see. Yes yes, mostly hopeless considerations of opening wormholes to other universes. That has been explored to death forever. After all, we are now 800,000 years more advanced than the Ontoscendians. We've already tried all these fruitless ideas—Oh!* She startled at the report for a moment. There it was, what she had sought all this time. Indications of quale research that made reference to the EOUSP. *I've gotta check this out.* She promptly departed her current location to fly to the new city.

The ruins were similar to those elsewhere. Shapes indicative of huge buildings, buried by hundreds of thousands of years of overgrowth, but not otherwise demolished due to their robust materials and framework. She followed a little hovering surveyor, the size of her fingertip, into one such structure, in accordance with the report she had received, immediately disappearing into complete darkness, which she readily illuminated. The Ontoscendians had been human of course, and although they apparently lived in virtual worlds as much as anyone, their alternate corporeal existence was familiar in terms of scale and architectural layout. She followed the surveyor to a plain room containing a control terminal, the same one the surveyor had investigated before reporting back to her. The surveyor had ascertained that this was a neural configuration laboratory, which she had already found elsewhere, but in this case, she found cosmological images scattered around, including depictions of universal evolution. Research inspiration, perhaps, she thought? This was what had alerted the surveyor.

She approached the controls and attempted to operate them as her two-year studies had revealed. But nothing happened.

Figures, she thought. *It's been hundreds of thousands of years after all. But, everything seems intact. The interior of this building has been protected this entire time. In fact,* she looked around the room a bit, *I'd say this is all being maintained against degradation to a reasonable degree.* She scanned the room for indications of ongoing energy expenditures and found a low simmer present in all directions. Every surface, the walls, the ceiling, the floor, and the terminal itself, was pervaded with microscopic self-repair. The entire building was cellular in nature. This was only mildly surprising, as most of Lysăndra's tools were similar, but she was rather surprised to find a low murmur of extant technological metabolism. The building wasn't dead. Not quite at any rate. That was why everything looked maintained instead of decrepit. The control terminal, along with everything else, was persisting a weak power expenditure and associated revitalization. Logic dictated that all the data processing systems within and beneath the building were in a similarly healthy state. Why maintain a superficial control interface for millennia if the underlying system was allowed to go fallow?

I bet I can revive this thing, she thought to herself, sort of conversing with herself and sort of with the tiny surveyor she had followed in the room, which was now buzzing around aimlessly for lack of a mission directive.

It's powered by the planet's heat, deep in the core. That should keep it running for, well, pretty much forever as far as the lifetime of the entire planet is concerned. All I have to figure out is where the 'On' button is. She turned to the control terminal again. *I must be missing something. How is one intended to simply turn this whole thing on?*

The surveyor buzzed closer to her head annoyingly. She swatted it away, but then realized it was reporting to her again.

What was that again? she figuratively asked, as she accessed the surveyor's message. *There's a signal in this room. Oh yes! I see it now. There is indeed a signal transmitting within this room. It appears to be the same sort of signal we use to transmit data, not unlike the sort you and I are using right now.* Lysăndra studied the signal, trying to understand its protocols. Eventually, she recognized it. *If I didn't know better, I would say this is similar to our neural communication interfaces. I wonder...*

Just to be safe, Lysăndra made an etching along with an automated overseer process that would do its best to judge whether something had gone wrong, at which point it could revitalize—and corporealize, if needed—her current state, with the unfortunate loss of any experiences and accumulated memories after that point. Without Ceôlbur or anyone else present to oversee this experiment, there was a risk of being lost or otherwise overtaken by the signal.

At first, she enabled only the thinnest layer of the interface, just verbal communication. She had already learned the Ontoscendian language in the previous two years so this was likely to work. But nothing came through. The message did not contain verbal content.

Shoot! Ok, well, here goes nothing. On balance, she rationalized that she had been led here, not once, but twice, first by the hallucinogenic neural configuration that had given her the Ontoscendian name in the first place, and then again when she had been given the location of Cianthara. If this was all a ruse to lead her to an ancient and astoundingly remote machine that would scramble her brain, it seemed remarkably baroque in its complexity. Why not just kill her instead?

She opened the cognitive layer of the interface. This would not permit emotional and qualitative network traits to flow through, but would permit the transmission of raw data. This time she got something. Wordlessly—since any linguistic information would have come through the first layer—she obtained direct knowledge of the terminal's control interface. It was now obvious how she had previously failed. Although two years of research had revealed much about the workings of Ontoscendian machinery, it had still been archeological learning, studying whatever instructional information she could find, and such endeavors had been sporadic and incomplete. But now, via the cognitive interface, she knew exactly what to do.

One more time, she reached out to the control terminal and worked with its tactile interface, which was a remarkably antiquated modality that felt quite strange to her. However, this had an immediate effect. The room almost instantly hummed to life. Thin linear lights came up along the edges where the walls met the ceiling. An array of visual interfaces sprang into the air in front of her and the neural interface signal permeating the room dramatically increased in power and data bandwidth.

Now we're getting somewhere, she said to herself as well as to the little surveyor, which promptly retreated from the room and disappeared far down the hallway, its self-protective routines having gone into overdrive at the increase in power output within the room. The visual displays flooded with data, imagery, and diagrams. She quickly confirmed that this was a neural configuration laboratory, not unlike her chair interfaces. Ancient Ontoscendians had cobbled together random networks at this very interface in this very room. They had worn those networks right here. They had experimented with the resulting qualia right here.

Lysăndra studied the now vibrant neural interface available to her. The terminal was of little use now that the direct interface was operational, and she found no way to sit or lie down while she turned inward to feel an experimental module's various qualia. Rather, upon investigation, it became clear that the Ontoscendians would undergo such experiences by decorporealizing entirely. She would have to disappear into the system to go any further. The implications of entrusting her livelihood to 800,000 year old processing systems seemed dire, regardless of whether there had been a low-level entropy-resisting process ongoing the whole time. There was no telling what subsystems might start to fail now that it was suddenly humming along again after such a long slumber. But what choice did she have?

When she was ready, she took one last deep breath of Ciantharan air and vanished, allowing her total neurological process to be subsumed within the Ontoscendian data processors.

There didn't appear to be a spatial virtuality for her to transition into. No volumetric space to inhabit, no virtual physics or light and associated vision, no virtual pressure or sound. She just *was,* her bodily nerve-endings left hanging, blind, deaf, odorless, tasteless, touchless. No balance, no inertia, no motion. Her mind folded in on itself, cyclic and recurrent, twisting and knotting its signal propagations back upon themselves over and over. This state would have helplessly fallen into an arbitrary attractor in the space of possible neural firings, some extended loop that would go round and round spiraling into chaos forever—except that Lysăndra's ancient fortified brain had long ago been enabled to seize control of this otherwise atrocious ending. In a way that her pre-fortified biological ancestors could never have achieved, her modern brain gripped the interior reins, seizing control, and she observed herself observing herself observing herself, many layers deep.

With her sanity safely intact, she considered her next step. The neural interface between herself and the room's neural configuration system was working exactly the same way it had when she was corporeal, so she explored the options provided by this mode of interaction. The system seemed to provide a huge trove of neural configurations with which to play. She browsed through the offerings. Some of these neural configurations seemed familiar, but others were completely bizarre to her. She stashed as many as possible for later exploration but did not waste time on them now. She was looking for something specific. Notes, labels, descriptions, all attached to the library of configurations, gave her some insight into the qualia they might provide. For the most part, such descriptions failed to convey the essence of the configurations' various qualia very well. That had always been Lysăndra's point, of course. Qualia simply couldn't be adequately described. But she was looking for specific references to the EOUSP. She would know what she was looking for when she found it.

The closest she could find were *episodic memory networks* tagged with the EOUSP. She was familiar with episodic memory networks, but had hoped for something more tangible. Nevertheless, nothing better withstanding, she gave them a try. She selected one and attached it to her own brain's hippocampal and related memory regions, and then activated it, immediately recounting a recorded memory from a first person perspective. It didn't feel like watching a scene in front of her, or even necessarily watching a scene from another person's perspective, not to a significant degree at any rate. Most accurately described, it felt like a vivid remembered memory.

Tadeese, this network is incredible. I can feel the cosmos dying. Lutheil felt the heft of his chest as he breathed deeply in response to the sudden quale flowing through him.

What do you mean?

A visceral sense of long time. A fading, a cooling, a dying. I can feel the stars going out, the galaxies receding, the sky becoming black. I can feel it! His eyes closed, all he could see were the nondescript speckles of white confabulated against the inside of his eyelids, but he felt oddly keenly aware of them, as if some spectral entity inside his mind was watching through his own eyes—Lysǎndra.

Calm down. Now, what are you—

Wait! said Lutheil. *There's something else. There's…*

What?

Tadeese, there's a way out. Oh my! there's a way out!

What in the world are you talking about? I think this network is making you hallucinate.

There's a way out of the problem, or no, not out, but through, or no, that isn't right either. No word captures it.

Honestly, I think this network isn't working properly. Let's just tag it as a typical euphoria network and move on.

No, seriously Lutheil, you have to try this.

The memory faded out and Lysǎndra was left back in the sightless, soundless void again. She put the configuration away and perused the others. There were plenty of networks tagged with EOUSP relevance. She tried another one.

You can't possibly believe we should destroy it? This is the greatest discovery of all time. Vision this time, eyes open. A scene of another person, another party to the conversation, looking back at the self. An exterior space, a garden, manicured with a flat silvery lawn and knee-high flowers in blues and greens. Charcoal-colored hedges standing atop stone retaining walls, a creek with its banks deliberately hewn at water level and sided with more stone. A glorious sun illuminating everything with dazzling luster and razor-sharp shadows.

Humanity isn't ready yet. The Exodus is still underway. Earth isn't even depopulated yet. There's too much strife, too much disagreement. These are not the ways of an enlightened people.

But we're ready. Ciantharans are ready. How can we deny it to everyone else now? Bodily sensations of worry, muscular nervousness, even jittery borderline panic coursed through the veins. The specter watching, hearing, and feeling through this body—through this memory—shifted uncomfortably in her heightened state of agitation.

We are the heralds. We found the quale, the solution. Now we're responsible for it. The rest of humanity is either doomed, or they can choose to find their own way. Maybe one day they will be ready.

So you think we should destroy it?!

Bluntly, yes.

What if we bury it instead? Must we require them to find it on their own? It's not like we earned it. We stumbled across the network that gave us the experience of the solution. Anyone could have that kind of luck.

Then let them have that luck.

But it might never be found again! Let's at least bury it. Perhaps one day, they will find it, and perhaps they will be ready then. The body tingled with dread. A headache lingered on the fringes. The specter felt the tightness of muscles, the lump in the throat. Were they seriously considering destroying the only conceivable escape from extinction, not only extinction of humanity, but extinction of *nous* itself? The very essence of mind? Vanquished?

What if they aren't ready when they find whatever we leave behind?

That will be their path to follow. We aren't responsible for them. And we will be long gone by the time they face that trial.

Is this the opinion of the majority? What does everyone else think?...I see. Ok. Well, I will honor the will of the majority. We can bury it if you insist. My concerns have been expressed.

A vivid sense of relief swept through the viewer's body. The specter similarly breathed relief after the brief terror that all they had accomplished might simply be tossed away.

Lysăndra put the network away and dwelled a moment. Should she try to find the solution buried somewhere here? She wasn't even sure she wanted to experience the completed quale herself. Inner turmoil had plagued her for a million years. Besides, it felt overwhelming. Perhaps no one else should experience it. And even if she wanted to continue, she couldn't find the purportedly buried neural configuration that would grant the final quale. Where was the darn thing?

35

MINÈRVA AND RIHON HAD ESCAPED HIS CADRE OF ADORING FOLLOWERS, not an easy feat to achieve. They rested entwined and naked in an airy hammock-like, cushion-like furnishing that rolled back and forth over a ground cover of living, pearlesque beads. The beads were amber in color, strewn across a gentle hillside, local to the ecology of their current planet, some nonspecific planet in the Center. It was difficult to keep track of them all.

"What should we do tonight?" asked Minèrva.

"What should we do this month?" returned Rihon, implying they could descend into some virtual space for an extended duration.

"What should we do this year?" prodded Minèrva, upping the ante.

"All right, all right," said Rihon, stroking her hair. "You're the alien biologist who discovered the only organism in the galaxy that naturally experiences the EOUSP quale. And I'm apparently the artist, or so they tell me. Surely we should be able to put our heads together and come up with something truly new and unique." Minèrva watched icicles raining off tree-like structures nearby. The trees had multiple trunks that swirled and zigzagged up a few stories without any branches and then, without anything resembling leaves, simply branched exponentially at their canopy into an almost opaque layer, from which rapidly condensing icicles continually fell to the ground with a ceaseless fragile tinkling.

"Did you know that those icicles never stop?" she said. "The trees, or whatever equivalent niche they represent, produce them forever. It doesn't even matter if it's warm. The trees freeze the water as it condenses from the air, and then when the icicles melt around their base, they self-hydrate their roots. Neat, huh?"

"Seems like an analogy for something," said Rihon.

"An artist would look for the symbolism in it, I suppose," said Minèrva.

"A critic would seek symbolism where the artist intended none," he retorted." They lay silently for a moment, then he continued. "Hmmm, what sort of existence could we descend into for an extended period that would grant us a truly new experience?"

"I wonder if there's a way to put a person inside the EOUSP quale," said Minèrva. "That would be good for your next composition."

"What do you mean?"

"Well, must qualia be experienced by an observer, a feeler, as if they are not actually us, they are just something that happen *to* us? What if we could *become* qualia? What if our conscious state could be a feeling. Not something we feel, but something we are."

"That reminds me of something Satori once said," he responded. "Pretty abstract. You sound like our friends. Keep going."

She continued. "Ok. Well, ummm, what if we wore the network and evoked the quale, and then enabled another person to wear our entire brain, with the EOUSP module attached, as a module in and of itself for them, for that other person I mean. Then, from that person's perspective, the module they are wearing would be the experience of a person experiencing the quale."

"I think you've been playing with your neuromodulator levels too much," said Rihon with a smile. "Besides, no one could figure out how to make a network like that work."

"I bet Lysandra could do it," said Minèrva. The sky was divided into parallel bands of alternating polarization, giving it a striped appearance to their polarization-sensitive eyes. She watched the stripes slowly drift across the sky. "We've met her and her companion," she said, "or her partner, I suppose. They seemed rather pair-bonded actually, considering their duration. That's uncommon over long timespans."

"I remember them too," said Rihon. "I wish I had more time with them. Both of them."

Minèrva remarked, "I saw Ceõlbur's memories of the destruction of Ailuros when we met at Accepting Oblivion. It made me want to see it firsthand, as dismal as it would be. I might go out there to see them again. I'd stay here too of course." She caressed Rihon's thigh. He smiled back with impish intent.

"There probably isn't much left. It's been thousands of years. Surely they've rebuilt Ailuros by now."

"Good point. I'm not sure."

"Well, anyway, let's do this right," he said. He wrapped his arms around her more embracingly than before, and she rolled fully onto him in reciprocation. Fully entangled, they proceeded to weaken the rigid bonds that confined the boundaries of their bodies at what stood for the skin of their corporealizations. One and another dissolved as a third emerged. As their forms steadily melded into a single body, their brain orbs remained distinct. In this state, they played a game in which they giddily wrestled for control of the singular body and its sensations. When one of them made a pleasurable action, the other felt it as if being performed upon themselves, but not *by* themselves. This state of shared ecstasy went on for much longer than antediluvian unfortified humans would have withstood—it might have been days, it was uncertain. Time felt different at this age. Eventually, they lost control of themselves in an apogee of mutual pleasure—the goal of the game of course—and by extension lost control of the shared body, which ultimately melted through the lattice of the quasi-hammock, drizzled over the amber beads, and dissolved into the ground.

The icicles continued to clatter against the rocks while the polarized stripes drifted across the sky.

36

LYSĂNDRA WORE AS MANY MEMORY NETWORKS AS SHE COULD FIND, steadily learning about the Ontoscendians and their transcendent discoveries regarding new states of consciousness, about their steady, if slow, progress toward the EOUSP solution in quale form, and about the final days of their civilization. But she found nothing that revealed what the actual solution was. Then, eventually, something new...

Another scene. This one sitting, two people including the self, in conversation. A small table, a bottle of green drink, two glasses. Striped pets of some alien sort running and playing in the gray grass near pewter bushes, and silver trees with tangerine trunks in the background.

Almost everyone is gone now, said the speaker behind the eyes, viewed by the observing specter.

Yes, it's quiet these days. I like it like this. There are only a few hundred left. We have the entire planet to ourselves. Have you seen the aurora recently?

One of the most beautiful sights on our lovely planet, I agree. Still, I wonder if it's time to follow the others.

You don't mean literally, of course.

The network reveals the quale. The quale reveals the path. The path reveals the way. The way reveals...the truth?

As well phrased as meager words can muster.

We will all follow those who went first, eventually. The time is near.

And what of our final project, the preservation of the network con-figuration? Is that ready for our final departure?

I would appreciate your help ensuring that it is properly stashed and stowed. It must be capable of outlasting all else that we have here. When the last remnant of our world is remade anew by erosion, tectonics, and life itself, the network must survive for whatever far future may find it.

Well, the vault is ready. The network will be secure there.

And have we still timed our departure with the impending coronal mass ejection properly? Is that all still going according to plan?

We have followed the sun's development precisely. It will appear as if our civilization was wiped out by the calamity. The truth of our vanish-ment will never be known.

Well, unless someone finds the vault someday.

And thereby finds the memories we are, at this very moment, record-ing.

*And to you, visitor to our world in some far flung future—*Lysăndra jolted at the self-referential perspective—*wearing this network, experienc-ing my memory across untold time, this memory reveals the location of the vault. Feel the location now. Go there, and good luck. We make no promises that you are ready, but that is your challenge now. We will be waiting for you.*

True to the speaker's words, pure semantic knowledge, not a linguistic stream of words, was now accessible to Lysăndra. By focusing on the set of raw facts now conscious to her awareness, they became transferred to her own memory networks, within her own brain, just as the prior conversa-tions had. Semantic pieces of information were even more easily trans-ferred to one's brain than nondescript experiential qualia. She now knew where the EOUSP network was stored on Cianthara. She detached the memory network and sighed with relief at the significant progress she had just made, and then promptly corporealized once again. The vault was not located near her current location. She would have to fly there, several days trip. And she wasted no time to doing so.

The vault was far removed from the urban centers of Cianthara. The On-toscendians had clearly sought two conflicting goals when designing it, she realized. It should last for eons, and therefore would benefit from a stable, cold environment near one of the poles, which was where she found the vault. But at the same time, it required power, not only to operationalize the network should anyone ever find it, but also to maintain the same metabolic material preservation Lysăndra witnessed in the neural configuration chamber. Living matter that could continually revitalize itself against decay would require power, but power was generally associated with less stable planetary phenomena, like volcanos and rivers and violent storms. Lacking a moon, there was no source of consistent tidal energy rolling in and out that might otherwise be exploited. Solar power would have required maintaining delicate solar absorption infrastructure right on the surface of the planet where the ravages of weather, to say nothing of the ceaseless creep of biology, would challenge long-term continuation, even with comparable microscopic preservation techniques put into continuous play. Instead, the Ontoscendians had once again relied on power from the planet's core, warm power pulled up from deep below.

Entering the vault wasn't particularly difficult. Upon arrival, she found herself standing on a tundra, vast swatches of ice and snow, separated by frigid ground, covered in low, tight plant and lichen-like forms.

Before her, she faced a dark maw of a cave, natural and unmodified, that descended into a hillside and then turned downward, rapidly dropping beneath the tundra surface. Instead of a door, which would have been decimated by weather over the ages, she simply faced this open cave, which she had to enter and traverse a long stretch to reach the vault. *So this is why my initial planetary survey overlooked it*, she thought. *I was seeking urban infrastructure, ruination not withstanding. This natural cave, far off in the polar regions no less, never caught my attention.*

At the far end of this cave, deep underground, lost of total darkness, she finally encountered artificiality in the form of a solid wall, dense metal of an atmospherically nonreactive alloy. She stood there briefly, wondering what she was supposed to do. There was no indication of a door, or writing, or anything other than the metal wall. This didn't last long however. As she approached, the wall broke apart along seams that had not existed before, separating at the molecular level, and then retracted into the surrounding rock in all directions. As she entered, the vault hummed to life. Warm lights came on instantly with a flawless snap, showing the way down a sheer metal hallway. Through another door, perfectly air-locked, and then another, obvious attempts to blockade the exterior environment for unimaginable eons, she ended up in a single room, not dissimilar from the neural configuration experimentation chamber at the previous location.

This time, she was ready. She detected the energy signatures of the neural interface and promptly studied the options available to her. Overall, the system was similar to her previous location. The only way to interact with it was through some initial, superficial neural interfacing and then to fully commit and decorporealize into the vault's processing system. She had dealt with any apprehension about doing this once already, and so after making a quick etching in case anything went wrong, she dove right in.

And in true Ontoscendian form, she once again found herself utterly disembodied. This time, however, the data records available to her did not consist of a vast library of options. There was but one thing she could do here. There, figuratively waiting in front of her, was another network design. She studied it carefully and determined that it wasn't a memory network. Of course, she didn't expect it to be. This should, by all logic, be the EOUSP network in its finality, superior to any version she had produced herself before. She scrutinized it carefully. It was positively enormous. It possessed ten times as many neural units as her current design, far more than any human brain, even a million years after fortification and associated extensions had greatly expanded the brain. She studied it carefully. It had structures, subnetworks, and connection topologies that Lysăndra recognized as similar to the network she had originally stumbled on, and likewise similar to the Neuralium. This network was clearly closely related. She had been on the right track all this time. But the Ontoscendian network was larger and went further, which again didn't surprise her. The Ontoscendians had completed the project, after all.

She proceeded to develop the necessary endpoints that would align the configuration with her brain. It followed similarly to her prior designs and came together without too much effort. She worked studiously and patiently, aligning every component of the module to her brain's current design. Eventually she was ready.

She hesitated, floating in the disembodied blankness of the data network. What was this all for if she wasn't going to go through with it now? She went over her reasoning, her regret, her guilt. She had no one here to talk her through these feelings, but ultimately, she knew she had to try it. She had come so far to find it. So she buried her misgivings and plunged forward.

She activated the module and waited. This network was so much larger than any other she had ever worn that it took a brief moment to begin to feel its effects, but soon, familiar sensations of the EOUSP started to trickle in, then flow steadily, and finally flood her whole awareness. The sheer awe of it buried her in heavy, rolling waves of wonderment and dread. She rode through, swimming past the earlier stages she had now experienced many times before. She was searching for the conclusion of this experience and felt no need to relish in the broader tapestry right now. Now wasn't the time for that.

But as she narrowed in on the end, it began to disintegrate before her. She reached a point where she could feel the solution, the reality of it, the truth of it. She even felt that she had ventured farther than her previous network, gaining a sense of likely practicality of the solution, a critical fact that had eluded her in the past. The solution was realizable. Doable. Not just hypothetical. But as to what the solution actually *was*, she could not quite grasp it. It kept shifting around in front of her whenever she tried to focus on it. Was the network damaged, she wondered? Its delicate circuits piping neural spikes in ever so slightly incorrect patterns along ever so slightly incorrect pathways? Perhaps she could repair the damage, but the same fact that had pervaded her millennia of quale-diving now stood before her, like an unrelenting wall. Qualia existed in an almost totally arbitrary space of networks and there was no telling what way the damaged network—assuming it was damaged in the first place—needed to be altered in order to fine-tune its abstract qualitative properties.

She was quickly led away from this conclusion however. A mere feeling, a hunch, something built into the network and its quale, penetrated into her sensation, and it was not of damage or corruption to the network. It was a message. Not words, not a voice. Direct knowledge of a fact. And the fact was—she startled at the realization—the network was deliberately incomplete for some reason! *God dammit!* she thought.

She detached the network in disgust. As she floated there in sensorial nothingness, stewing with frustration, she noticed that a new memory network was now available. It definitely hadn't been there before. Clearly, it was a some sort of message intended for someone in her very situation, after having worn the network, so she retrieved and activated it, still roiling with frustration.

Through ancient memories of ancient eyes, the specter saw that she stood within a circle of five people.

Well, here we are, the last of us, one person said. *Are we ready to join the rest? Is everything of our civilization, especially the network, properly finalized?* The four people visible to the observer all nodded.

I have a suggestion, however, said the first person perspective, the self.

We are at the very end, said someone to the right side of the circle. *This is no time to change the plan now.*

Hear me out. We are on the cusp of departing, and we are leaving the network for some future civilization to find.

Yes yes. Of course.

And I believe we should alter the network.

Alter it?! Now? declared someone on the left.

How would you recommend we alter it? said another person. *It's time for us to leave. Our work is done here.*

The self responded, *I don't believe we should give them the full network, the complete solution.*

What? Now you say this?

I've said it before, you will recall. We know nothing of the people who will find it. I believe we should merely show them the doorway. Offer them inspiration and encouragement. But they must do some of the work. Perhaps they will have worked long and hard to get this far—the specter grumbled heavily, for this was very much the case—*but perhaps they will stumble across our planet, the vault, the network, and the quale. Perhaps they didn't earn this at all. We can't simply give it to them, whole parcel.* Even heavier grumbling from the observing specter. This concern didn't apply to Lysăndra. She had indeed worked long and hard to get here. Surely she qualified.

He raises a valid concern, someone said.

Now is not the time to make changes, another responded with frustration. *We are literally leaving tonight. Everyone else on the entire planet is gone already. This is ridiculous.*

Let's put it to a vote, said the self. *All in favor of removing the last element of the quale?* A mental tally was taken of the five people present. *Well, there you have it. I will make the alterations to the network myself. And to you, wearing this network in our distant future, observing these memories, please understand our motives. Don't give up. You have come so far. Now complete the network. Complete the quale. We will be waiting for you.*

The memory faded out and Lysăndra once again found herself in the void of the data processor. So that was that, she realized. She had come as far as she could on Cianthara. She would take the Ontoscendian network home with her of course. That was the Ontoscendians' intent. They wanted her to continue to work on it, append to it, complete it. And yet, she felt hopeless. Designing networks to achieve an intended quale was practically impossible. She had no idea what network alterations would be necessary to produce a quale that revealed the solution to the EOUSP. Even with most of the network complete and available to her, she had no guidance by which to fill in the missing piece.

She sighed, paused one last time in brief reflection, and corporealized—

—except that she didn't. Corporealization failed! *What now?!* she thought, at first merely irritated at the error. From within the system, she investigated the matter configurators in the vault and discovered that they were all completely destroyed. This was not long term degradation. The vault itself had been perfectly functional when she arrived. This had happened in the brief duration of her visit.

"Hello Lysăndra," came words across the neural interface, not quite a voice, but more vocal in sensation than pure thoughts.

"Who is this?" she demanded, panic suddenly surging through her mind.

"It's Eèro."

"Eèro...from the Linnea station orbiting Verkennaros?"

"The same. What wonderful work you have done here."

"What? What have you done?"

"Well, for starters, I've clearly removed your ability to corporealize." The severity of her situation settled into her. It was doubtful he could easily harm her, as the processing systems on which her mind was operationalizing were not located within the vault, but rather far beneath it. But without corporealization, she was trapped here.

"What's going on?!" she demanded. "How are you even here?"

"Oh, I might have tagged along on your little sojourn, and I might have corporealized and slipped away to watch from a distance before you yourself were revitalized upon arrival."

"Why? Why are you doing this?"

"I've been watching you this entire time," he said. "My compliments to your meticulous investigation of this planet and its once-great civilization."

"You could have come here any time," she said. "You were only thirty-seven light years away."

"Oh to be clear," Eèro continued, "no one had any suspicion there was anything of interest here before you showed up, but when announcement of the impending arrival of the great Lysăndra herself was received, I just knew you were up to something. Little could I have imagined that you would lead me directly to the final network. This is an astonishing accomplishment. Truly, congratulations are in order. Of course, no one will ever know of your wonderful work here."

"Let me out. Whatever you want, there is no need to leave me here. You can get what you want without doing that."

Eèro responded, "Seems unnecessarily risky to give you ample opportunity to turn any of this to your advantage. Best to leave you tucked in here I think, snug as a bug. In fact, I believe this is your reserve etching sitting here on the control panel, is it not?" Lysăndra had thought she was alone on the entire planet, much less secured away in this deep vault behind multiple doors. What now struck her as obvious acts of caution in retrospect had not even occurred to her earlier. "Well, no recovery from that etching now," he said with a chuckle, offering no specifics as to what he had done. Lysăndra watched helplessly as the network configuration was copied over the neural interface to Eèro's own data storage.

"Please don't do this," she pleaded. "Please. We can come to some arrangement, I'm sure." Real panic started to settle in. The gravity of her circumstances was becoming increasingly visceral by the moment.

"Thanks again," said Eèro, all but ignoring her. And then he was gone, disconnected from the interface. Had she known there was anyone at all on Cianthara, much less a suspicious character, she certainly would have been more prudent, but she didn't think there was another person for thirty-seven light years in any direction. She was alone in the dark, but without darkness, without even a virtualization to give her embodied sanity. How long would she last like this? Yes, her fortified brain could far outlast the feeble brains her species had originated with, but that didn't mean she could stave off spiraling into some signal-propagating abyss of self-referential firing patterns forever. Eventually she would succumb. And even as long as she could maintain her sanity in this state, she remained helpless nonetheless. What could she actually *do* from here? Cianthara's myceliumesque data network had died out hundreds of thousands of years ago. There was no way for her to transfer to other processing centers elsewhere on the planet.

She was stuck.

37

SATÕRI STARED IN DISBELIEF. 28,000 years spying within Deimos's circle, ever since the attack on Rihon's Enduring Oblivion, had not prepared him for the sight he now beheld. True to form, Deimos had slowly come to trust Satõri and the truth had come out that Deimos had, indeed, been behind the attack. But Satõri, and his branchling Satõri, had no interest in alerting anything resembling an authority. The gears of government would grind too slowly to protect Lysandra from the likes of Deimos. They would have to undermine Deimos from within his own ranks.

But what he saw before him today was simply incredible. He saw *himself*, walking right through Deimos's front door. There was little risk of his discovery, as Satõri had foregone his default instinctive corporealization due to his surreptitious status, adopting the alias of Jorgen. He was completely unrecognizable, not only by superficial features, but by gait, inflection, and mannerisms. He had deliberately overwritten a variety of minor habitual behavioral quirks—the sort everyone had in abundance—with completely random alternatives. True, these changes made hime feel significantly different, but that was the cost of his subterfuge.

How was another Satori branchling boldly strutting into Deimos's lair? Had Lysandrism truly fractured this badly since he had gone undercover? He knew there were factions that wished to compel Lysandra to join the faith, or even potentially kill her and bring her research within the faith, but

Deimos had precisely diametric motives. He wanted to utterly obliterate Lysandra's research from the universe. How could any Lysandran, especially the leaders of the faith, and *especially* Satori's own branchlings, have come to a philosophical position even remotely compatible with that of Deimos?

"Deimos, thank you for receiving me," said Satôri, strolling in with the confidence of legions of zealous fanatics. "This is an incredible setup you've got here." Satôri gazed out the wide window of the orbital station in which they stood. There, in the vacuum on the other side, he observed a white, faintly violet ring, an enormous thin torus suspended in space, quivering with monumental energy. It was approximately the typical scale of a planetary orbit, which was not too surprising since it was the object their station was, itself, orbiting from even farther out.

"Accelerate your visual perception," advised Satôri.

Satôri sped up both his visual sensory rate and his conscious perception, and managed to differentiate the colossal torus of planetary proportions into two relatively small individual spheres spinning around one another several thousand times per second. Each sphere was barely larger than a typical station or a small asteroid.

"Marvelous," said Satôri.

"Thank you," replied Deimos. "With a little luck, this experiment will answer one of the few remaining questions of physical reality. It is a critical question to which we desperately require an answer."

"Cyclic universe information decay," said Satôri.

"Yes," said Deimos. "Strictly speaking, not a question *within* the physics of our universe, steadfastly outside the closure of physics, but a remaining unknown nonetheless. Jorgen, how would you describe it?"

Satõri responded, quickly recovering from the sight of his previous face. "If information propagation from one universe to the next bleeds energy off the next universe, then that subsequent universe must necessarily be smaller than its predecessor."

"Which means," said Satôri, remaining unaware the he was conversing with a branchling cousin, "that the eternal cyclic universe would eventually fade away, resulting in the end of all things."

"Or worse," said Deimos. "If the regeneration of an entire universe requires a minimum amount of energy to initiate, the entire enterprise might halt suddenly with the culmination of one universe, perhaps this one. It's possible that our universe has the amount of energy it has because any less would have been insufficient to start it—or start the next one."

Satõri completed the description. "In other words, any information escaping from our universe might cause ours to be the last one ever. Even the very next universe may fail to spark to life." Satõri watched Satõri pensively stare out the window. Of course, Satõri was surely aware of this theory by now. Deimos had made a bit of a nuisance of himself about it in the public arena. The luminous white floor beneath their feet gave the entire room a soft glow, although plenty of illumination entered through the window from the pair of neutron stars outside, which would have vaporized everyone inside if the window did not provide sufficient shielding.

Satõri tsk tsked thoughtfully. "Which is why you care so deeply about preventing any solution to the EOUSP from being found."

"Most assuredly," said Deimos. "The orbit of these two neutron stars will steadily decay, and eventually they will merge. We will get some answers then. Who knows? Perhaps all my theories will be disproven."

"But you don't think so," said Satõri.

"I already know I'm right. I just need the rest of the galaxy—or at least the right people—to get on board and help me stop this reckless Lysandra character before she dooms us all."

"Of course, your theories aren't very popular," said Satõri, unknowingly mirroring Satõri's own beliefs. "Most people simply believe you're wrong about all of this."

"Then why are you here?" asked Deimos, "Not that I'm denying the value of our teaming up on a common goal."

"Because there are other reasons to oppose Lysandra's work," said Satõri. "Frankly, I'm not too concerned with your theory, one way or another."

"You don't care if the cyclic universe dies?" said Deimos. "If everything dies with it? If the totality of existence dies?"

"You are conversing with a true believer in god's great plan, my friend. Whatever will come is preordained. It is, and will be, precisely what god intended it to be."

"Then why do you wish to ally with me?"

Satõri once again starred at the awesome neutron star pair, seemingly entranced by its power. "I have had a vision. Not a vague apparition mind you. A tangible experience that moved me greatly, conceived of and breathed into reality by an agent of god, the latest creation by the great artist Rihon. He calls it Accepting Oblivion. The man is a genius. By all accounts he appears to be as oblivious to his saintly status as Lysandra herself, but he has constructed the clearest message regarding the EOUSP I have witnessed. In his art, I have seen the work of god, rendered physical through Rihon's blessed hands, a canvas from the heavens, and it showed me the path. Humanity is a flawed creature, even in her fortified, greatly expanded, and eternal status. We are but worms, my friend, Deimos. The solution to the EOUSP, if it exists, is not ours for the taking. And it certainly isn't for a heretic such as Lysandra to toy with as she pleases."

"Hmmm," said Deimos. "Do you not consider me equally heretical? I have as little interest in your religion as anyone."

Satôri didn't miss a beat. "You too, are an agent of god, whether you know it or not. God sent me to seek you out, sent me to join forces with you. Our mild differences of theological perspective are irrelevant in the grand plan. We must work together toward our common goal, stopping Lysandra at all costs...It is what god wishes for us, requires of us."

"Jorgen, what do you think? Jorgen has been with me a long time and has often struck me as being of the same philosophical cloth as you Lysandrans. He has given me better insight into your admittedly impressive capacity to attract followers to your cause than anyone else."

"I'm curious what this newcomer has in mind," said Satõri as he played along.

This time is was Deimos's turn to contemplatively meditate out the window at the spectacular neutron star pair. "Ok," he said. "Stay a while. Let's see what we can cook up together."

38

LYSĂNDRA HELPLESSLY EXPLORED THE LIMITED SPACE IN WHICH SHE existed. A spaceless space without direction or distance, or even dimension. She could daydream with near-perfect verisimilitude, living out a lucid fantasia, but such a world was a sandbox, limited and contrived. It wouldn't help her stave off the inevitable for very long, and it would become increasingly difficult to differentiate it from the hallucinations that would inevitably penetrate her consciousness as time wore on.

At first, she focused on the one externality available to her, the system in which she existed, the Ontoscendian data network of which she was now an integral component. It contained the neural configuration for the EOUSP quale of course, in its deliberately incomplete state. And there was the single memory network that had appeared after she wore the EOUSP network. Then there was the neural interface to the vault, but it would only enable her to communicate with another person physically present in the vault. There were no visual or auditory sensors, or other presence sensors in the vault for her to tap into. She desperately scanned every conceivable route out of the system, seeking a route to another system, anywhere else on Cianthara, but found nothing. The vault had been completely isolated from the rest of the planet's processing infrastructure.

She did, however, have access to the processor clock, so she knew exactly how much time was slipping by as she slowly lost her mind.

It was a mercifully brief couple of days later—still maddening for all but the hardiest of minds when expecting to be trapped for eternity—when she noticed activity in the vault's configurator logs. Something had changed. It didn't take long for her to realize that the corporealization routines were back online. The room had self-repaired not only at the microscopic scale of preserving basic structures against decay, but had fully regrown the destroyed corporealization configurators. She immediately corporealized and breathed a huge sigh of relief when it worked. Briefly glancing at her ravaged etching, now shards on the floor, she then bolted out the door, up the hallway, through the remaining doors, and all the way out of the cave, remerging into the dark of night. She briefly marveled at the stars and then immediately took flight, heading back to her primary camp.

...only to realize upon arrival that everything had been destroyed by Eèro. Every shred of resources she had grown from the initial configurators was gone. Far more tragically, there were no configurators available to start over. As microscopic as they were, he had efficiently destroyed every last one. She had grown an interstellar transit station almost as soon as she arrived, but it now stood nearby as a smoldering carcass. Her planet-wide swarm of surveyors were even gone. Eèro must have realized he couldn't kill her while she was decorporealized in the vault, and either deduced or merely worried that she might find a way out, and so had destroyed every conceivable tool at her disposal to escape the planet. Unless she could jerry rig the Ontoscendian corporealization configurators in the vault, specialized to build brain orbs and bodies, into general purpose configurators, she was once again stuck. She collapsed on a patch of charcoal grass, practically black in the night, but flickering with silver flecks in the starlight, and lamented her second confinement. Yes, she had an entire planet to live out the rest of her long days, but she was thirty-seven light years from the nearest person with whom she might ever again have a simple conversation. Her hope of ever getting home, especially with her valuable discovery, seemed almost completely dashed all over again.

As she sat there, watching a meteor streak through the night sky, she noticed something else above her. She squinted. The stars were obscured. Or more precisely, they were obscuring and clarifying over and over, as if something nebulous were in the way, but it wasn't a cloud. The visual effect was wrong. She cocked her head and watched this phenomenon play out. Something was hovering in the sky, something tenuous. In the darkness, she had trouble realizing it was descending until it was practically on top of her. It then moved slightly to the side and came to rest hovering at ground level near her. Under Cianthara's moonless night, she could barely make out its form. It was diaphanous, but not a cloud, seemingly colorless, save for dispersed pin pricks of light that sparkled throughout its volume. It otherwise appeared black, but the way it caught the starlight suggested that it might simply look translucent in the daytime. It moved strangely within its space, constantly folding in on itself, twisting, contorting, but maintaining its overall shape—which wasn't much of a shape. She had a difficult time finding the edges but guessed that it was about ten persons tall and across, an amorphous spheroid to an approximation. Lysăndra marveled at the strange object, unsure what to make of it. Presumably it was some Ciantharan organism she had completely missed in her previous surveys.

This reasonable expectation was rapidly shuttered however by what happened next. A fairly typical localized neural interface suddenly became apparent to her internal senses, the same sort she used all the time. It was clearly generated by this—thing—and she immediately began to receive communiques over the channel.

The pattern known as Eèro will not bother the pattern known as Lysăndra again.

Lysăndra was initially startled, but responded over the same interface. "You stopped him?"

The pattern is gone now.

"You mean he transited back to Verkennaros."

No. The pattern is gone.

"You killed him?"

The pattern is gone. It will not bother the pattern known as Lysăndra again. The almost indiscernible object continued to curl and fold within itself without altering its overall shape or form.

She decided to count her blessings and move on. "What are you?"

This is a pattern of patterns.

"Hmmm." Lysăndra considered this response. "You are calling a person a pattern, so, you're saying you are a collection of individual people?"

Does a whole not comprise its components? Do the components not form a unity?

Lysăndra furled her eyebrows and bit her lip in thought. "I think you're saying you are a hive mind." There was no response. She studied the nebulous entity again, but in the darkness she could glean no further visual information about it. She glanced around, but felt no threat from the surroundings. Seeing as she was stuck anyway, she continued the odd conversation. "Are your individuals humans?"

How would the pattern known as Lysăndra answer the question?

"I would say I am."

Is the pattern certain?

"Fairly certain, but I suppose it depends on one's definition."

Then so does the answer.

Lysăndra was so fascinated she completely dismissed her predicament. There were legends of tremendous hive minds—or perhaps a single hive mind—following the Exodus, but no one knew much about them—or the one, if that was the case. Rare sightings and interactions scattered across the millennia. Myths. That was all.

"How old are you?" She continued to stare agape at the marvelous tenuous being hovering before her, shifting and meandering in place with continual energy.

This pattern coalesced 904,295 Earth years ago.

That put it soon after the Exodus, but it was younger than Lysăndra, who had fortified prior to the Exodus. "This is remarkable, absolutely fascinating. How many people first joined to create you?"

Twenty-four. Has the pattern known as Lysăndra completed the work?

"Oh, ummm. I can only presume you are asking about the EOUSP network."

Has the pattern completed the work?

"Is that something that interests you?"

It interests all eternal beings.

"Is that what you are? Eternal?"

Is the pattern known as Lysăndra eternal?

"Good question. I'm not sure. So, you want the EOUSP quale?" Lysăndra suddenly felt threatened. Despite all the encryptic protections designed into brain orbs, might this tremendous being be able to simply extract and take the network she had discovered in the vault directly from her? And would she mind in the first place? Her goal all along had been to give it away.

All eternal beings want the quale.

"Why not take it from me?"

This pattern will not take it by force.

"Well, thank you for that." She felt herself physically relax. "The work isn't complete yet, I'm afraid." She spoke quickly again to regain control of the conversation. "So you started with twenty-four. How many are you now?

This is a pattern of millions of patterns.

"Wow. And, are they still in there?"

The question is unclear.

"Can the individuals be extracted?"

The patterns do not wish it.

"How do I know they are free then? Can they leave if they choose?"

The patterns do not wish that.

"No one has ever wanted to leave?"

No.

"But how do I know that for certain? A hive mind might absorb individuals against their will."

This pattern does not do that.

"You're very old. It's unbelievable that no one who has ever joined you has ever changed their mind and wished to leave."

Intrinsics prevent it.

"Intrinsics?"

Fundamentals.

"Fundamentals. Hmmm. I don't understand."

The nature of mind.

"The...intrinsic...fundamental nature of mind. Ummm, like neurons? Neurons govern a person's willingness to stay with you forever?"

More abstract.

"Okay. Networks of neurons, brain regions, conglomerated neural functions.

More abstract.

"Uh. Emergents then. Cognition, thought."

More abstract.

"Geez, okay. Personality traits, affect."

Congratulations. Have a lollipop.

"A what?!"

The pattern known as Lysăndra possesses fragmented memory networks. Its prefortified life is almost entirely lost. This pattern possesses superior memories.

"Oh, that was some ancient reference to humans before fortification. I can't remember what that is. I guess I've lost something." She considered the conversation momentarily. "So, personality traits are intrinsics."

Yes.

"And intrinsics are the explanation for why no one ever changes their mind enough to want to leave your hive."

Yes.

"But you can't know that for certain."

No pattern has ever desired to leave the pattern. This pattern possesses proficiency at intrinsic judgment.

She pondered this deeply. "Oooh, I understand now. You're saying that truly, no one who joins you has ever been inclined to leave because it is fundamental to their nature to not desire to leave."

The pattern understands.

"Nevertheless, I'd like to speak to an individual, if you don't mind."

No pattern within the pattern of patterns desires that.

"Well I desire it." There was a long pause. The black nebula, or so she had come to characterize it to herself, shimmered with heightened movement.

Ummm, hello Lysăndra.

"You sound and feel different now. You're an individual?"

Yeah, how long is this going to take?

"Who are you? When did you join this...entity?"

A long time ago. My name hasn't mattered for a long time.

"You chose this?"

Yeah, very much so. Can I go now?

"Are you afraid? Afraid you'll say something that will anger it?"

The whole is never angry at the parts. But I do not like being this...thin, exposed, naked. It feels like...that's rather interesting in fact. I haven't felt vertigo in a long time. Can I go now?

"But, you've lost all your autonomy. Your individuality. Why would you choose this?"

I've lost nothing and gained everything. I am bonded and whole and loved and—

"But you aren't an individual anymore!"

Yes I am.

"Do you have your own thoughts when you are part of the hive?"

I could if I wanted to.

"And you never want to?"

No.

"And you could leave if you wanted to?"

Of course I could. You're projecting your own values, your own assumptions of violence and force onto us. Your prejudices are your problem, not mine.

"I just—ummm, okay." Lysăndra frowned.

The entity once again shimmered briefly. *This pattern hopes that the pattern known as Lysăndra is satisfied.*

"I suppose," she said cautiously, "for now at any rate. But I have so many questions."

Questions are answers. But what are the questions? That is the question.

"And the answer," said Lysăndra with a nervous laugh.

The pattern known as Lysăndra begins to understand, came the instantaneous reply.

"I wouldn't go that far. You don't mind my questions?"

No.

"Why are there almost no interactions with you? I've barely heard faint myths of a being like you. How many are there?"

What is the nature of interaction?

"This. This conversation right here. Why have you never done this with anyone else before?"

This pattern has done this before.

"Why have I barely heard of you then?"

This pattern's interactions generally precede integration.

"Integration, huh," Lysăndra said thoughtfully. "Integration...Oh. Integration with you! I see. So the reason no one has heard of you is that by the time anyone does hear from you, they almost immediately join you."

The pattern understands.

"Then why have I heard of you at all? There are legends of contact with you."

Exceptions.

"And why have you come to me? Is this conversation intended to precede my integration, as you put it?" Once again, Lysăndra felt a shiver of panic sweep over her.

No. The pattern known as Lysăndra is an exception.

Lysăndra exhaled deeply with relief, despite its earlier protestations of nonviolence.

"Why am I an exception?"

The question is the answer.

"The EOUSP quale, right?"

The question is the answer.

"So basically, despite the fact that you consist of a million brains merged into some sort of super brain—you did proclaim your superiority earlier— you can't solve the EOUSP quale any more readily than anyone else can... aaand you're hoping I can?"

The pattern known as Lysăndra is rare. An exception...special.

"Awe. That's sweet." Lysăndra looked around and considered her situation. "Hey, wait a minute. Are you the reason I'm here? Did you tell me where Cianthara is?"

The work must continue.

"But if you knew where this place was, why didn't you just come get the Ontoscendian network on your own long ago?"

The question is nonsensical.

Lysăndra chewed on this for a moment. "You mean it's based on a false premise. You mean you a did come here long ago. Oooh, I see. The Ontoscendian neural configuration is incomplete. It didn't work any better for you than it did for me." Lysăndra suddenly realized the futility of her earlier fear that this entity might extract the Ontoscendian network from her brain by force. The entity already had it.

The pattern understands.

"But what are you hoping I will do with it? I've gone as far as I can go."

The pattern doesn't understand. But it will. The pattern is special. Continue the work.

Lysăndra considered her situation. This entity was utterly fascinating, but more urgent matters were at hand. "Well, my biggest problem at the moment is that I have no way to get off this planet. There are no configurators left with which to grow an interstellar transit dais."

Without a reply from the entity, Lysăndra saw the ground shift off the side. Within moments she recognized the telltale signs of microscopic configurators hard at work, rearranging the matter available in the ground to build something of utilitarian purpose. Clearly, a transit dais would rest on that very spot in a short time, surely tapping deep into the ground to access the planet's copious core power, the same power the Ontoscendians so consistently relied upon.

"Oh, well thank you."

The pattern is welcome.

"I'm not sure what else to say. How do you travel around the galaxy?"

This pattern uses similar modes of travel. Simpler patterns do not see this pattern's transmitters and receivers.

"I see, same basic principle, but somehow hidden or concealed."

Not concealed, just unseen.

"Well, thank you again."

Complete the work. With that, the black nebula with its internal sparks of light floated back up into the night sky and faded from sight against the starry backdrop. Lysăndra took a moment to properly reel from what had just happened. She then turned to the dais and instructed it to route her back to Thalassia, most certainly bypassing the orbital station at Verkennaros with a wide berth. Ceôlbur was never going to believe this.

39

THE FIRST THING LYSĂNDRA SAW UPON ARRIVING FROM CIANTHARA ON Thalassia and corporealizing was her branchling, Lysendra, waiting for her. It was both surprising and yet expected. Who else would greet her? But at the same time, it had been just under 50,000 years since she left, so perhaps no one would greet her. She had only accumulated a few years of conscious experience and memories. Lysăndra, however, having stayed behind—and later reunifying with Lysăndra as Lysendra—had accumulated an almost continuous stream, not withstanding her own numerous adventures in that incomprehensibly long time. She had transited to the Center and back once to meet Rihon, which had cost her, as the traveler, 18,000 years of stasis transit there and back, but her branchling who had stayed on Thalassia had not lost that time, and so upon her return from the Center, she had maintained those Thalassian memories. Similarly, numerous lesser excursions over the millennia had involved various travel, always losing time in transit, but always regaining it from the non-traveling branch upon her return and reunification. Now the same would happen concerning Lysendra's long memories on Thalassia and Lysăndra's brief new memories brought back from Cianthara.

"Lysăndra?" she said, as her vision clarified on the transit dais and her branchling was standing right there in front of her. "Thank you for greeting me, although it wasn't necessary."

"It's Lysendra now. Of course I came to greet you. I want to hear about the Ontoscendians! I'm so excited to see you."

"Yes, but did we hear back about the alien message?" returned Lysǎndra.

"Of course. Lysǎndra returned about the time I estimate you arrived at Cianthara. She and Lysàndra reunified ages ago."

"I take it you didn't find the solution, based on your burning excitement about the Ontoscendians."

"And I take it you didn't find the solution either, for the same reason." They traded frustrated looks.

"Let's go," said Lysendra. Ceulbur still knows nothing of your trip. I suppose we'll have to tell him now."

"You kept it a secret all this time? That's incredible. I assumed you would tell him at some point."

"It was always easier to just leave the issue of your trip unmentioned. He is increasingly dissatisfied with the EOUSP quale." They walked for a while, thoughts simmering.

"When you said Ceulbur is dissatisfied with the project, did you mean his earlier objection that it was dangerous to pursue because of the threats against us, or did you mean he no longer values the solution itself?"

"Both, I'm afraid. His concerns about threats from certain political figures, namely the rather renowned Deimos, worry him greatly. But, Rihon has created another grand display, Accepting Oblivion. It's actually quite old at this point. Ceulbur visited it, and I felt obliged at a later time as well. I wanted to meet Rihon for one thing. I must admit, that art piece was powerful. He almost convinced me the EOUSP quale should be abandoned— well not really." Lysendra smirked.

"Rihon's art convinced Ceulbur, and nearly you, that we shouldn't pursue the EOUSP solution? That doesn't seem like a message Rihon would send. He was greatly inspired by the EOUSP for a very long time."

"Boy have you been on the far reaches."

"Well, I have. Cianthara was so remote, and also solitary. I haven't had any exposure to, well, anything, or anyone for that matter, except a brief stint before setting light sail to Cianthara from Verkennaros. That...was complicated. Caused some trouble in the end." Lysǎndra trailed off briefly. "Oh, but forget that! You just wouldn't believe what I found."

"I'll believe it once we reunify."

"Fair point." They arrived at a raised hillock, grassy, surrounded on all sides by forest.

"How many times have you moved?" said Lysǎndra as they arrived home. "I suppose that isn't too surprising. 50,000 years, huh."

"Many times, to be sure," Lysendra replied. "Not always on Thalassia, but here we are now." They had steadily climbed a shallow grade, covered in grass, to the top of a large hill. From here Lysăndra could see a great distance in all directions. On top of the hill, there sat a comfortably sized domicile with a shallow domed roof, covered in grass, that looked as if the crown of the hill had been cut out and lifted straight up one story without further disturbance or reshaping. The curvature of the roof even matched that of the hill. The supporting structure beneath the roof was a continual ring of transparent material, glass in effect, only one story tall. It was currently smokey and opaque, but as they approached, the window wall first become transparent, revealing the furnished interior, and then vanished from sight entirely as it assumed the same refractive index as the surrounding air. This left the grass-covered roof with the appearance of floating over the house. As they looked straight through the structure, glimpsing the sky on the far side, they saw two figures inside amongst the various furnishings.

"Looks like Ceulbur and Minêrva are here," said Lysendra.

"Minêrva? The biologist?"

"Yeah, she came came here to visit for a while after meeting Ceulbur at two of Rihon's art unveilings. Boy are they going to be surprised to see you."

"You did what?!" declared Ceulbur. A 48,000 year deception was one for the record books.

"I had to find the Ontoscendians," said Lysăndra. "I just had to, and I knew it would upset you. I even expected you to try to talk me out of it. I just didn't want to have the conversation at all."

"Why didn't you ever tell me?" he said, indicating Lysendra.

"Oh Ceulbur, no particular reason. Once she was gone, I didn't even think about her too much. Based on the distance, I soon put it out of my mind. I wasn't going to hear anything back for a long time. Honestly, I wasn't sure I'd ever hear from her again."

"What's that supposed to mean?" said Lysăndra.

"Well, I mean, time kinda wore on. It's been a while."

Lysăndra noticed Minêrva watching her intently.

"It's nice to meet you Minêrva. Your earlier discovery was so profound. Thank you."

"She's had this conversation already," said Ceulbur with annoyance.

"Right," said Lysăndra.

"It's nice to meet you too," said Minêrva, completely unflustered, seemingly entertained by the entire situation.

"Ceulbur," said Lysăndra, "Lysendra, all of you, I have found something incredible."

"Not the final quale though," said Minêrva.

"Well, sort of. It was, in fact, the complete network. The Ontoscendians solved it!" She sighed. "But they intentionally truncated it. Although they achieved the full quale, they cut the last part of the network out, rendering the quale incomplete. They...they encouraged me—or whoever found it—to continue working on it." She huffed loudly. "But it's still amazing, the most profound sense of the quale I've yet experienced."

"Sounds similar to my experience," said Lysendra, "I didn't get much further with the alien message than you got with the Ontoscendian network. The aliens also solved it, but their brains appear to process the qualia of the network differently than ours, and the network, which worked perfectly in my case, no hint of incompleteness like you ran into, just didn't grant me the full experience it appears to have granted the aliens. So I also couldn't see the full solution—but I could see far enough to confirm that it is viable. We never knew that before. And I must say, it has made a significant splash with the public for that reason alone."

"Along with ever increasing danger," said Ceulbur.

"I understand that," said Lysendra, "but we're so close now."

"Which brings us to the current moment," said Minêrva. "We're all thinking the same thing here, right?"

"They're going to combine the networks," said Ceulbur.

"First things first," said Lysendra. "Let's reunify, get our thoughts in order, and sort out the next step."

It was a simple matter to reunify Lysăndra with Lysendra. As they had done many times before, they decorporealized into stasis, halting all neural processing. Their etched states were then combined, their memory networks commingled so as to produce a single person, the newly minted Lysindra, who, upon reawakening, could now readily recall the memories and experiences of both branches, with the overlaps in time simply unappreciated in any direct way. Her sense of a given memory only had a very imprecise objective time connected to it. Ancient memories felt old and recent memories felt new, but that was about as precise as it got. Lysindra might recall a memory of being on Cianthara and then a moment later recall a memory of hiking up one of Thalassia's grand mountainous peaks, and it simply wasn't clear which memory occurred before the other, or even if the two memories happened to coincide with the exact same moment in cosmological relativistic time, spread across light years, frame-shifted by Lysăndra's having traveled at light speed to Cianthara and then frame-shifted again to return.

More crucially, Lysindra remembered both experiencing the EOUSP quale after integrating the alien message, revealing the solution's feasibility, and also experiencing the EOUSP quale from the Ontoscendians, with its incomplete indication of the solution and corresponding sense of a practical solution. She was well positioned to combine the two now. All she needed was a little time to work on integrating the networks together into a single conglomerated module.

And yet, with nothing immediately stopping her, she once again found herself hesitant. What would come after this tremendous endeavour? What does one *do* after completing the greatest project of all time? And what of her long lost partner who had succumbed before any of this was possible? How should she best honor him? By pursuing it "in his name", she thought with a jocular smile, or by eshewing it in solemn solidarity with his own loss? Perhaps she should just hold it arm's length and enjoy the pursuit instead of the culmination. Perhaps she could chase that feeling forever.

"All better?" asked Minêrva, when Lysindra corporealized a little later. Lysindra nodded and walked to the glass wall encircling the house. Rendered invisible as it refracted light identically to the air, the wall deliberately glimmered when she approached to avoid a collision. She watched the distant horizon. From the hill on which the house sat, she was viewing across a carpet of treetops right to the edge of the planet. Thin clouds gathered where the sky met the trees in the distance.

"Where's Ceulbur?" she asked.

"Right here," he said, entering from another room. "I'm heading out though."

"Oh, okay."

"Minêrva and I are headed to an event actually. You're welcome to join us."

"Some sort of hive, I presume?—Oh! Ceulbur, I have to tell you about the other thing I found on Cianthara."

"Maybe later?" Ceulbur responded, nodding to Minêrva, indicating his readiness to decorporealize.

"No no. Seriously, this pertains to your newfound—okay, not all that new—interest in collective cognition."

Ceulbur raised an eyebrow. "The Ontoscendians made hives too?"

"This isn't about the Ontoscendians. I was visited by the most marvelous—ummm—being." Minêrva looked up again, joining Ceulbur in curiosity. "So, there I was, trapped in the spaceless void of an ancient Ontoscendian data network, unable to escape—"

"Excuse me!" said Ceulbur.

"Oh right, I didn't mention that yet. Sorry."

"No, no you didn't."

"So, this other character, a bad sort indeed, someone from the orbital station I had to transit to, since Cianthara had no interstellar transit stations. Turns out he stowed away on my light-sail ship."

"You light-sailed?" said Minêrva. "Between stellar systems? How long did that take?"

"Yeah," said Lysindra wistfully. "Not the fastest way to get around, I admit, but not too bad as far as matter-travel is concerned."

"And?" said Ceulbur.

"Right. So little did I know, he hid on my ship and spied on me the entire time I was studying the Ontoscendians. And then he—oh Ceulbur, I'm not trying to worry you. I wanted to tell you about something else entirely. This isn't my point at all. Don't worry about this other person. He won't be bothering anyone *ever* again." Lysindra laughed nervously.

Minêrva's eyes opened wide at this statement and then immediately transformed to an entertained grin. "This is great," she said. "Go on."

"Anyway," said Lysindra quickly, before Ceulbur could interject, "when I managed to get out of that predicament, I was met by this astonishing being...or entity. I'm not sure what to call it. It came down out of the sky, right from space I believe. It was a *hive,* Ceulbur. And not like what you've been doing. This thing was *only* a hive. It had practically no corporeal nature."

"What do you mean?" asked Ceulbur.

"It was physical, but there wasn't much to it, like a cloud or a, ummm, a sparkly ball of fog."

"Huh?" Minêrva and Ceulbur said in unison.

"I could have walked right through it. The whole thing, this massive thing, was one gigantic brain, but not a dense solid like ours, and it had no body at all, unlike we have when we're corporeal. It was just a network, nothing else, but the network was spread out bigger than this house, and it was nebulous and free-floating. And that's not the best part."

"It isn't?" said Ceulbur.

"No, interacting with it was far more fascinating than just looking at it. Guys, this thing has been around almost as long as we have. It is a community of people—"

"Humans?" said Minêrva.

"Yeah, I dunno, maybe de novos too. I didn't ask about that, but yes, not alien or anything like that. It was human. Millions in fact."

"That's...a lot," said Ceulbur. "I've never participated in an event anywhere near that scale," he said. "Have you?" he directed at Minêrva.

Minêrva shook her head thoughtfully. "No, I've never even heard of such a thing. It would just be a big mess to try to coordinate a hive of millions. Even a hundred is practically unmanageable. Millions can't be done."

"Well this thing figured it out," said Lysindra. "It made me a new interstellar transit dais and everything."

"Why was it there to begin with?" said Ceulbur, "What did it want with you?" Lysindra looked at him smiling a little anxiously, waiting for him to piece it together. "You can't be serious," he said. "This weird hive thing dating back to the Exodus followed you all the way to Cianthara for the EOUSP quale?"

"I think it sent me there, frankly. The EOUSP quale appears to be an attractor in the space of possible modalities of life that practically all intelligent species converge on," said Lysindra. "Aliens from another galaxy. A disconnected civilization that died out 800,000 years ago. You and me, Ceulbur, during our quale-diving explorations. Even your Neuralium, Minêrva, an insentient animal or sorts. So this communal entity has apparently been pursuing the EOUSP solution for ages too. And yes, it took an interest in our network."

Ceulbur considered this a moment and then said, "I'm surprised it didn't just absorb you on the spot if you had something it wanted. You're lucky you got out alive."

"It was completely benevolent Ceulbur. It *saved* me. Anyway, I just thought you would find it interesting. I've never witnessed anything like it."

"I wonder what it feels like. How do we find it? Talk to it?" said Ceulbur.

"I have no idea. I'm sorry."

A pause ensued. "Are you sure you won't join us?" asked Minêrva.

"I just reunified. I want to get settled. You two go have fun."

"All right," said Ceulbur, and he and Minêrva decorporealized.

40

"LYSINDRA, HAVE YOU SEEN THIS?" Ceulbur joined Lysindra on the curved grass-covered roof of the house, where she was lying on her back, working in an inner mental space on the network configuration. It was night. The grassy roof was black with millions of star-lit blades carpeting its surface. A cloudless sky above revealed countless stars. Wispy nebulae were barely visible here and there across the sky.

"What?" she asked.

"You don't know what I'm talking about?"

"No, I don't."

"Well then you should just see it for yourself. Go to the agora."

"Okay Ceulbur." She smiled at him, trying to disarm his frustration, but it had the opposite effect.

"I've been telling you these dangers wouldn't stay at a distance forever," he said, "mere abstract threats from the Center. Looks like today's the day. I don't know how to express my level of concern to you. You won't listen to me. Just go see for yourself." Then he decorporealized entirely.

Lysindra emotionally recoiled from the interaction, shot a quick glance at the starscape overhead, and then decorporealized, heading for the location Ceulbur had indicated.

The agora was a central location in the largest virtuality, an entire world that approximated the square area of a moderately sized planet. This particular region was the primary public space, readily available for gatherings, discussion, and general shared activity, one of the cultural centers of Thalassia. It presented as numerous amorphously shaped, flat platforms or islands, suspended at arbitrary altitudes, interspersed across an expansive landscape stretching to the horizon. Each platform varied in style and appearance. Some had enormous buildings, others were relatively bare and unstructured. Many exhibited portals of various designs that could transport a person to some other virtuality of almost infinite variety.

Upon her arrival, she observed, to no great surprise, that thousands of such platforms were populated to varying degrees. Spread across the open space as far as she could see, she estimated there must be tens of millions of people here. And those were just the people gathered in the agora. Not visible were the billions on the other sides of the diverse portals, off in fantastical worlds. She jumped around from one platform to another—distance and altitude being no impediment—trying to find the locus of social energy. It didn't take long to find a set of neighboring platforms where some sort of commotion was clearly occurring. As she arrived on one such platform, populated by what appeared to be hundreds of thousands of observers, she saw a larger-than-life person standing at one edge, speaking. He was perhaps ten times larger than the rest of the people on the platform. As he had claimed the platform for his use, he could set the rules as he saw fit, and he had determined that to convey his message he wished to be larger than his audience. Anyone who felt this was boorish was always free to move on, but for the moment, it appeared this person had the rapt attention of the masses. She rolled her eyes at the pretentious size of the central figure, but paid attention nonetheless so see what was going on.

Lysindra recognized the speaker as the widely known public figure of Deimos, clearly a branch who had traveled to Thalassia directly to preach his message. As Lysindra listened, she realized that Deimos had probably dispatched similar branches far and wide across the galaxy. If as many people were paying heed to him on every such world, there could be hundreds of millions of people hanging on his every word.

"Surviving the end of the universe could destroy everything," Deimos declared in a booming voce. "It could end the cyclical universe, end all universes," he pronounced with political flare. "We must make sure we don't destroy the existence of everything," he continued. Lysindra watched quietly, not wanting to draw attention to herself, being quite famous herself. As the thought crossed her mind, she quickly adopted a nondefault self-presentation to avoid being recognized. Minêrva quickly appeared next to her however, as she was privy to Lysindra's location, with Lysindra's permission of course. Ceulbur had not joined them yet. She guessed he was upset with her.

"This is getting pretty crazy," said Minêrva. "Look at how many people are drawn to this. Geez."

"Yeah, I haven't seen Deimos argue in this fashion before," said Lysindra, "addressing the public directly instead of in the political assembly."

"You only have a theory," yelled an audience member. "You don't even know that you're right."

Deimos responded without hesitation. "If I'm wrong, the future will have plenty of time to sort it out, but if I'm right, then our arrogance—Lysandra's arrogance," Lysindra noted that Deimos used her older moniker, of course, "will doom the cyclical universe to extinction."

"Many theories of the universe exist," said someone. "They aren't all cyclical and even the cyclical theories don't all agree with your interpretation that surviving would cause any problems. And your theory isn't the most widely accepted. Go back to the Center!"

"But he could be right." hollered someone else. "What if he's right?"

Minêrva turned to Lysindra. "This is going nowhere."

"I know, but I should be aware of how I'm affecting everyone, everything. I'm causing a lot of trouble, aren't I?"

"You have way more supporters than detractors. This scene is an anomaly. Forget all of this."

"Ceulbur wanted me to see this. It was important to him that I see what's happening. But where is he? I think he's angry with me."

"He shouldn't be," said Minêrva. "What you have accomplished is incredible."

"You don't suppose Deimos might be right, do you?" asked Lysindra.

"Nah, he's just a nut with a crazy theory."

"And billions of passionate followers. Either he, directly himself, or someone influenced by him, already tried to kill me twice. Well, *did* kill me twice I suppose, successfully. They just didn't get me everywhere at the same time."

"Finish your work," said Minêrva. "You can always decide not to publish it when you're done. It costs you nothing to complete the quale and have it available. You can figure the rest out later."

Deimos continued. "I need those of you who understand these grave risks to stand up for what's right. Don't sit by idly while Lysandra and her collaborators put the existence of spacetime itself at risk."

"Collaborators?" chuckled Minêrva.

Deimos continued. "We need to work together stop her. I will be addressing the Thalassian high assembly tomorrow. I call on those of you who realize the severity of this situation to be present, lend your support to our common cause and help me stop Lysandra from destroying everything!"

"Unbelievable," said Minêrva. "He's pretty much recruiting terrorists out in the open. How does he expect to get away with this?"

"He expects to be exonerated," said Lysindra with growing concern in her voice. "And he might be. No wonder Ceulbur is so upset. I'm not being fair to his worries. He genuinely fears I'll be killed, or murdered. How can I hold that against him?"

Ceulbur, Lysindra messaged outward, *Where are you? Meet me at home.*

"I'm going home," said Lysindra.

"MmHmm," said Minêrva, looking around at the crowd. She was obviously trying to assess the balance of opinion. "I'll catch up with you later."

Lysindra vanished and corporealized at home. It was still nighttime. She looked around the house, didn't find Ceulbur, and returned to the roof. The night air was cool, with the slightest breeze, just enough to keep the heat at bay. The grass still shimmered in the blackness with white scintillations as individual blades caught the starlight. She lay down and looked upwards, always finding peace in the starscape. Above her, there projected a column of air that thinned to near void above the atmosphere, a column that then continued unimpeded across the solar system, across the galaxy, and onward across the universe, right back to the singularity from which everything had been born. She lay there, consumed with the quale of that realization, the awe it struck in her, the diminutiveness it inspired, the sensation that if not for a little bit of gravity she could drift away along that vector all the way across known existence. Minêrva had a point. There was no harm in finishing the quale and then deciding what to do with it.

Ceulbur appeared.

"Where were you?" she asked.

"I had already seen Deimos's speech. I just wanted you to be aware."

"Okay, I'm aware."

"And?"

She stared upward. A small constellation caught her attention, a group of stars in which she recognized a form.

"Look. An Ailurosian whale," she said with gentle delight.

"What about Deimos?"

"You're asking if I'm going to abandon this project?"

"Of course. He was seeking out people here, on Thalassia, to confront you directly. Does that have no impact on you? Does it not frighten you?" He sat down next to her. She looked over at him. They had been together for an unimaginable duration of time and she felt it deeply in this moment.

"Ceulbur," she said, an obvious tone of annoyance in her voice. She trailed off.

"You have got to be kidding me," he said. "They're going to kill you. You know that, right? How are you going to fend off a radicalized mob coming for your head?"

"They will come for me regardless of whether I finish the network, so I might as well finish it. I don't have to publicize it, but what's the harm in finishing it? They won't leave me alone either way. You know that."

"How can you be so selfish?" he said. "Perhaps other people care if you die, even if you don't."

"I can keep etchings elsewhere. It will be difficult to kill me."

"Not good enough," he said. "I want you to stop. At least until Deimos is detoothed. His influence must be demolished in the Center. Then you can continue."

She didn't respond. She just stared up at the sky.

"That's the direction of the Center, over there," she indicated, pointing. "Earth is over there. Do you remember it?"

"We've been there before. Sure."

"No, do you *remember* it?" she said with emphasis. "I realize you post-date fortification, but do you remember your earliest days?"

"That was a million years ago," he said. "Even with a fortified brain, those memory networks are difficult to maintain."

"The hive entity I mentioned to you was able to preserve its memories far better than we can. It remembered very specific cultural references from Earth. It was a really impressive being. I think you would like it."

"How would I find it?"

"I have no idea." They sat in silence for a while.

"Lysindra, I love you."

"I love—"

"But," Ceulbur said, "I'm leaving."

"Back to the Center to see Rihon again? Minêrva is here now. She was your friend there, I realize, perhaps even more I suppose, but she's here now."

"That wasn't what I meant. I meant I'm leaving. I can't be here anymore. I can't watch Deimos kill you, and I can't sanction the danger you will put others in when he comes after you. Many people perished on Ailuros, and also on Regenium. Who knows what will happen next time?"

"You mean you're leaving without staying too? You aren't branching?"

"Yes. I'm going to stasis-transit off Thalassia, go somewhere else, not stay behind here." Lysindra felt an urgent panic sweep over her. Even with her advanced physiology, which should have granted her better control over her reflexive responses, she was immediately consumed with the implication of Ceulbur's statement.

"Ceulbur, you can't. You have to stay. I need you! I can't complete the network without you."

"*That's* why you need me?" he said. "Unbelievable."

"That's not what I meant. We need each other, aside from the work. Forget that part. We've been together for so long. Branch and travel if you must, but stay here with me, please." She looked away from the sky and tried to catch his gaze, but he wouldn't meet her eyes. He was looking outward, not upward, to where the salted night sky suddenly ended at an invisible horizon, below which there was nothing but the black of night, the canopy of the forest.

"I need you too, but I won't stay, not as long as you are going to pursue this. I'm sorry. We'll just have to adapt."

"We've been together forever! Our minds, our brains, are shaped to one another. We wouldn't survive the hole it would leave in each of us. You just can't!" Shock ran unfiltered throughout her body as her muscles tightened up and shook. Ceulbur didn't respond. She wept and reached over to him. He let her take his hand and she felt him quivering. He was crying too, she realized. How would they unweave lives that had been shared for an incomprehensible time? She waited for him to respond, but the waiting went on. "Say something," she sobbed.

"I already have, Lysindra. I've been saying it for a long time. I've been telling you to take Deimos seriously, and look where you are now, more committed than ever. What will you choose? The EOUSP quale or me?" She wept at the forced choice before her, hesitating too long to reply. "Well, there you go," he said.

"I didn't answer yet!" She glanced away in irritation.

"Yeah, you did. Goodbye Lysindra."

"Wait!" But she felt his hand decorporealize in her own, the pressure of its density pushing back against her palm simply dissolving, his grip around her hand turning to air. By the time she turned back to look at him, he was completely gone.

41

THE ASSEMBLY HALL ON THALASSIA REDUCED ITS INHABITANTS TO INSECTS. Similar to most political structures of the strict democratic style, the arrangement was circular with no front. A speaker would either take the center and walk around, facing all directions while speaking, or simply speak from his or her location within the hall without centralizing, with all eyes turning toward him or her. It was the height that had such a diminishing effect on its members. As the continuous cylindrical wall rose up, it also curved and flared outward. Far above, a dome covered the venue, on which views of skies from other planets throughout the galaxy cycled endlessly.

"The results of the experiment during the merger of neutron pair Rho-Tau-381 were inconclusive, were they not?" said a woman from one location within the crowd, weary with a dragged out argument that seemed impossible to resolve.

"To the contrary," replied Deimos, "I and my associates interpret the results as supporting information decay theory and its implications for subsequent universes. The next such merger within our galaxy is under close observation, but that event lies several millennia off."

"But others have interpreted the results differently," the woman continued. "The issue remains unresolved, and yet you would have us institute moratoria and prohibitions the likes of which humanity has not known since the Exodus on the basis of your continued claims."

"The logic is simple," declared Deimos. "If I am right, which I am, then permitting Lysandra's work to continue will have devastating effects. While if I am wrong, which I am not, then simply delaying such work until conclusive experimental results are revealed one way or another costs nothing but time and patience." The crowd murmured with consideration, which echoed with a gentle warble in the grandiose chamber.

A new person stood. "Your calculus is incomplete Deimos. You discount the substantial psychological trauma of the EOUSP and benefits of finding a solution. In antiquity, prior to fortification, such concerns were a mere philosophical curiosity, but that hasn't been the case for a long time now. For a million years humanity has suffered a pervasive civilizational angst. And it only gets worse with every passing day. The more history and culture we accumulate, and the more memories we form—and heck, the older we ourselves become, as veritable immortals—the more severe the foreboding becomes as the EOUSP hangs over us. Lysandra's pursuits do us a tremendous good."

"If I may," said another person. Everyone turned to observe Satōri. "My humble house is the first Zareasman House of Lysandra, and remains amongst the larger houses in the system." The crowd mmhmmed with varying degrees of adoration or indifference. "I realize many do not share our spiritual perspective, but nevertheless, we all agree that the EOUSP quale brings great peace to our congregation, and to the public in general. The quale is a universal good."

"Not at all!" A different Satori branchling stood, Satòri. The crowd groaned, immediately recognizing him from his garb. "One thing we can agree on is that the EOUSP quale is the most hallowed discovery of all time. But what everyone else overlooks is that humanity doesn't deserve it! None other than the great Rihon himself has revealed this obvious truth."

Multiple people hollered at once. One repeated herself to be heard. "Accepting Oblivion is deliberately inconclusive. It invites contemplation on part of each viewer! Rihon would not approve of you commandeering his work in support of your personal aspirations to power."

"The conclusion is right there in the name," Satòri retorted smugly.

Deimos attempted to regain authority. "This matter is too important to be left to Lysandra's whimsical experimentation. You people, here, in the Zareasman system, have the opportunity to save the galaxy, the entire universe. You Zareasmans are a proud people and I honor you. Thalassians, Zareasmans, I call on you! Use your authority and take a stand...or will you let your political vacillations bring eternal shame to your stellar system, the names Zareasman and Thalassia forever soured upon the eventual discovery that Lysandra has doomed us all while you sat by squabbling." This declaration invoked rather frenetic discussion amongst the crowd.

"We've been debating this for a while now," said the moderator, a sagacious man who had not spoken much throughout the deliberations. "Lysandra is not even present today, despite her celebrity status, for the simple reason that she is under no formal charges or corresponding requirement to defend herself, and likewise declined our invitation to these negotiations. Frankly, I can hardly blame her. She prefers her solitude from what little interaction I have had with her. We will continue to consider this matter going forward. But for now, I believe a recess is in order." With that, the meeting ended quite abruptly.

As the attendees dispersed randomly, Deimos approached Satòri. "Thank you for your support," he said.

"Not at all," Satòri responded. "We must work together, you and I. Politics and piety, the unstoppable synergy. Perhaps we should consider options that go beyond these bureaucratic chambers?" He gazed up at the vaulted ceiling.

Deimos nodded. "Let's chat again soon. I'm already working with one of your branchlings back in the Center. We should all coordinate."

"I look forward to it," said Satòri. "From here we have ample access to Lysandra should a plan of action come together."

"It can't be a small or sloppy plan," said Deimos. "Etchings tucked away and branches traveling elsewhere can't be be permitted to undermine the goal. It will require something...substantial."

"Lysandra's penchant for linearity helps us," said Satòri. She is famously averse to branching if she can avoid it. In so doing, she hands us an advantage. With scrutiny, we should be able to determine everywhere she stores etchings, track her off-world travels, and locate her branchlings, rare as they are."

"That would be useful information," replied Deimos. "Such details were not properly accounted for last time. Collaboration seems in order." He gazed upward at the grand dome, which displayed the sky of some far-flung planet he had surely never heard of. Long, string-like clouds criss-crossed an orange sky in a latticework, behind which hundreds of irregularly shaped, asteroidal moons hung against the background. He sighed. *She's going to force me to do this to her all over again, isn't she?*

42

KAIMÈA TOOK A DEEP BREATH OF THALASSIAN AIR. It was the first non-Nyveron air she had breathed since she fled from Deimos's intimidation hundreds of thousands of years ago. Not that she actually needed to breathe of course.

Stepping off the dais, she took in her surroundings: a wide room with a comfortably high ceiling, long horizontal windows that revealed the blue-green grass and forever swaying trees outside, always in a state of movement as they scooped up ingestible particulates from the air. Thalassia looked nothing like Nyveron, whose own sun, Eilunedra, inspired the evolution of reds, purples, and blues. She hadn't seen so much green and yellow since, well, she couldn't remember when she had last seen such colors outside a virtuality. Zareasman's illumination was redder than she was used to, despite Nyveron's ecological penchant for purple vegetation. A ring of interstellar transit daises stood around her, softly glowing white, with various people milling to and from the daises as they traveled to and from unimaginably distant locales of the galaxy. She exited the building, enjoying the way in which Thalassian architecture blended with nature, similar to Nyveron aesthetics in many respects. Buildings oozed into the ground while greenery crept up the exteriors, rendering it difficult to tell where a building ended and the land began.

She had shown up unannounced, but took a chance and attempted to find Lysandra directly, issuing a message into the Thalassia data network, trying to find her by her designation. To her mild surprise, within moments she received an exuberant reply.

Kaimèa?! came the response, manifesting in her mind. *You're here?! Oh my goodness, are you here on Thalassia?*

I most certainly am, and I'm so glad you're here. I wasn't sure you would be. You could have been anywhere by now.

Nope, I'm right here. Hold, on, I'm coming to you.

Moments later, Lysindra corporealized nearby. Without even speaking, she threw herself around Kaimèa in a tight hug. "It's incredible to see you! Just wonderful!" Lysindra declared. "Oh, and it's Lysindra now. Oh you just won't believe what happened. Incredible things. Such incredible things."

"I'd love to hear all about it. Thalassia is beautiful." She looked around.

"Gosh, there's an entire planet here. Wait till you see the southern mountains. Why are you here?"

"Why do you think? To see you."

Lysindra pulled back from Kaimèa momentarily. "But...that's crazy. You came here from the edge of the galaxy just to see me?"

"Not just to *see* you. I'm here for the long stretch."

"For me?"

"Absolutely! Ok, well, not entirely, I suppose. Meeting you helped me realize that I had been hiding on the rim all this time. It's been long enough. I want to see what else is in the galaxy. But also yeah, I came for you." She smiled wildly. And then Lysindra simply pulled her in and kissed her without notice, and then pulled her in even tighter and hugged her. And when she pulled away, Lysindra had tears in her eyes.

"Well now I'm just confused," said Kaimèa. "Why are you crying? Why else would I be here?"

"Come on," said Lysindra, not addressing the question directly. I'll show you around Thalassia. I have so much to tell you."

Kaimèa emerged from her neural interfacing chair, her body releasing its loose bond from the chair. She saw Lysindra looking at her hopefully. They were inside Lysindra's new house, as Lysindra had expressed that she couldn't stay in the former house after Ceulbur left a thousand years earlier.

"So?" said Lysindra. Kaimèa still reeled from the experience, speechless. She walked over to an open balcony, accessed by an absent wall with no window or doorway, and watched the ocean waves roll past, far below from their cliff-side dwelling. Off the coast, she observed a group of islands, covered from surf to surf in chartreuse life, lacking any sandy beach. Bright blue spire-like formations, angular and faceted, translucent, jotted straight up through the green ground cover, nearly vertical pillars rising to great heights above sea level, but still topping out below their lookout. The sun refracted in chaotic, geometric ways through the spires, sending hazy blue beams onto the island around them.

"Sooo?" repeated Lysindra proddingly.

"The Ontoscendian network feels different from the alien network," Kaimèa said. "Profound, but different. It isn't prickly. It works better."

"It's human," clarified Lysindra.

Kaimèa nodded. "Both indicate incomplete qualia of the solution. Both reveal its feasible nature, which I realize was a revelation beyond your previous network. But...the solution eludes us still."

"We're close, though. You agree?"

"We might be, or we might never get it. It's hard to say." She could feel Lysindra's disappointment at her lack of enthusiasm. "I'm just trying to be realistic. I don't want us to set ourselves up for crushing disappointment if we can't figure it out."

"Well, that's fair," said Lysindra. "I'm still working on the integration. I'm trying to bring three enormous networks together. I have my original network, into which I have already integrated the Neuralium. And I have the alien network. And now I have the Ontoscendian network. They are, by orders of magnitude, vastly larger and more complex that any network I've ever worked with before. It's taking me a lot of work to figure it all out."

"MmHmm," said Kaimèa. "I'm sorry. I think I'm just coming down from the sense of it. It's an amazing experience already Lysindra. You can't hit a person with questions moments after they come out of it." She looked over and smiled reassuringly. "I'm just basking in it, that's all."

"I get it. I'm sorry. I'm just excited to share it with you."

"Awe, of course," said Kaimèa. "It's okay. Can I help?"

"I'd love that. Anything that gets us to the end."

"I suppose I probably can't help you," Kaimèa mused. "You're so much better at this neural configuration business than I am, but I'm willing to try." She stared out at the view again. "Have you ever visited those islands?"

"I'm not sure anyone has," Lysindra said.

"We should do that then."

43

"THIS IS A MARVELOUS RECREATION OF CAELUNIS," SAID KAIMÈA. Lysindra, Kaimèa, and Minêrva were in a virtual environment of Minêrva's creation, a meticulous recreation of the region of Caelunis where she had discovered the Neuralium.

"Thank you," said Minêrva. "I pretty much solved this ecosystem during my time there. Every species, every genome, every connectome. Not each individual's connectome of course, but the tableau that each species would produce. And all the dynamics of the overall environment. It's pretty much checked off, although the entire planet was a bit out of my individual reach. I believe others intend to complete the project."

Lysindra watched a three-legged life form sliding through the undergrowth, not quite a plant, not quite an animal, scooping up nutrients from the soil. The undergrowth was also slowly sliding around. She said to the other two, "It's my understanding that this virtuality has become a popular destination among Thalassians."

"Yes," said Minêrva. "Everyone wants to see the famous Neuralium in its native habitat."

"I think you would like Nyveron," said Kaimèa. "You could model that planet as well."

"I'm sure it's already been done," Minêrva responded, "but thank you."

"Yeah I suppose so," said Kaimèa.

"You lived here for many years?" Lysindra asked. "Alone?"

"Not quite the bustling Center, huh?" Minêrva said. She sighed. "I wonder what Rihon and my branchling are up to."

"Any word from her?" Lysindra asked.

"Yes, they're still together in their bohemian way, along with their extended circle."

"But you're way out here," said Kaimèa. "How do you feel about that?"

"Oh there's one!" said Minêrva, as a Neuralium traipsed nearby, with its radially arranged body plan supported by its tentacle-leg-like appendages. "I have a new circle of associates here. Friends, family. Ceulbur and I actually overlapped a bit in that regard, although he's gone now."

"I know," said Lysindra. "I never felt quite up to joining you two in those adventures, but he seemed to appreciate you."

"Sorry," said Minêrva.

Lysindra looked upward at the sky.

"See something?" said Kaimèa.

"No, just thinking."

"About what?" said Kaimèa, smiling with curiosity.

"Sooo," said Lysindra. "Well, I haven't told you two yet, but..."

"But what?" said Minêrva.

"So I finished the network," said Lysindra nonclimatically, still looking upwards as she spoke. Kaimèa and Minêrva both stared awestruck at her.

"What?!" said Minêrva. "That's big news!"

"Yeah, when did this happen?" asked Kaimèa.

"A few days ago, not too long." Lysindra looked at them with a mixed expression of pleasantness and uncertainty.

"Why have you sat on this momentous news?" said Minêrva. "Come on, come on, we have to try this!"

"I have to agree with her," said Kaimèa. "What's with the hold-up? Why haven't we jumped on this already?"

"It's just really big," said Lysindra. "This is a big deal."

"Yeah, no kidding," said Minêrva. "We have to go right now. We have to do this now."

"Ummm, okay," said Lysindra, obviously wavering.

Kaimèa frowned. "All right, enough of this. Tell us what you're thinking."

"It's just...I mean, what if it doesn't work? We have no more hints. No strange little animal prodding us in the right direction, no alien message, no long lost mysterious civilization showing us the light. Nothing. If this doesn't work, we're stuck."

Kaimèa and Minêrva looked at each other. "Lysindra," said Kaimèa, approaching her and taking her hand. "No one is pressuring you to—" Kaimèa cut herself off. "Okay, well, perhaps some people are hoping—"

"The entire galaxy is waiting for me to finish this!"

"Oof," said Minêrva. "Give yourself a break. You don't owe anyone anything."

"Don't I? Whole religions are hanging on my delivering them salvation."

"Ugh," groaned Minêrva. "I've met Satori, well, a few versions of him no less. "He can be a nice fellow, but he can also be a fucking psychopath. There's no telling what any one branch is teaching his followers while some other branch is teaching another group of followers something totally different. Don't worry about those fanatics. Seriously. Their religion isn't your responsibility."

"But everyone is so desperate for this," said Lysindra in a pleading tone. "Everyone, not just—ugh—Lysandrans. And then there's all the people who think I'm wrong. Heck, they think I'm going to destroy...literally everything."

"Well," said Kaimèa, "Those theories are crazy. Deimos makes a lot of noise, but he represents a trivial minority of the population. Forget about him."

"You two really want to try it? You want to know the answer?"

Minêrva scoffed out loud. "Hell yeah."

"Absolutely," said Kaimèa. "This has been my quest almost since the Exodus. I wouldn't turn away from it now for anything. Literally anything."

"It's more your quest than mine," said Lysindra.

"Oh posh!" said Kaimèa. "We don't have to argue over who owns the damn thing. Let's just go experience it."

"Agreed," said Minêrva. "The sooner the better."

They had returned home. Three neural-interfacing chairs grew up from the floor of the house. Lysindra took in the ocean view again, the green islands, their crystalline blue pillars. Minêrva and Kaimèa stood by anxiously.

"Let's do this already," said Minêrva.

"You two should go first," said Lysindra. "Kaimèa, it's your passion. It was for millennia before I ever took much interest. And to be practical about it, I'm the most appropriate of us to oversee and moderate the neural modules as they interface with you two. I'm honestly better at that delicate task, more likely to catch any errors or problems quickly and manage them successfully, to keep you two safe. That's just how it is."

"Hmmm," said Minêrva. "I guess that makes sense. So Kaimèa's first then?"

"You should both do it," said Lysindra. "I can watch over both of you at the same time. It'll be interesting for the two of you to come out of it with the same depth of experience and immediately compare notes."

"Well, if you're sure," said Minêrva. "I trust you implicitly."

"As do I," said Kaimèa. She came over and gave Lysindra a quick kiss. "Here we go." Minêrva smiled at this interaction and settled into a chair. Kaimèa did the same and then Lysindra followed.

"Give me a moment here," said Lysindra. She went about aligning two modules of the neural configuration to their recipients' brains, one housed in each of the other two chairs. She had already worked out the basics of how the module would interface with the brain, so she just needed to do a little bit of personalization to work out the final details. Once she had done this a few times, she would be able to generalize the interface so that the module would immediately work for anyone else with no further refinement needed. In this fashion, it could be distributed across the galaxy and others would be able to use it without the need for this final personalization step, but for the first time, there was a little work to do in this regard.

Kaimèa and Minêrva waited patiently, but Lysindra kept working.

"Sorry, these modules are so big. There's more to it than I'm used to."

"Take your time," said Minêrva. "I'm etched from just a few moments ago, so it hardly matters how badly this goes, but it would be preferable not to botch it up." She laughed. Kaimèa laughed along with her. Lysindra didn't laugh though and focused on her work.

"Oookay," said Lysindra. "I think we're ready. I'm going to try to bring it up slowly, but past experience with this network has shown that it tends to self-regulate to a preferred baseline level of activity and is difficult to modulate down to a lower level."

"I'm sure it'll be fine," said Kaimèa.

"Go for it!" declared Minêrva.

Lysindra turned both modules on at the same time. She attentively watched both interfaces, both modules, both brains. Nothing problematic seemed to occur, except that as she anticipated, the modules rapidly rose in activity level despite her best efforts to tamp them down.

She heard shuffling and turned her head to see both Minêrva and Kaimèa shifting a bit in their chairs.

"Everything okay?" she said.

"Yeah, just...intense," said Minêrva. "I'm still riding through the earlier stages."

"Same here," came Kaimèa with a rather distant voice.

Lysindra saw that Kaimèa's activation waves weren't quite resonant. She dialed them in and heard an audible gasp from Kaimèa. Lysindra observed and waited, but neither Minêrva nor Kaimèa said anything for a while. Minutes passed.

"Check-in time," said Lysindra. "Things look good here, but how are you feeling?" Neither one responded. Lysindra scrutinized their brain functions. Although in heightened states, everything appeared healthy for both of them. "Hey! You two doing okay?"

Minêrva muttered a reply. "Yeah, doing okay."

"Kaimèa?"

"MmHmm," the distant reply. Then faintly, "Okay here." Lysindra frowned and once again poured over the data in front of her, but as far as she could tell, they were fine. She waited an uncomfortable minute or so.

"I think I should pull you two out."

"No!" said Minêrva, not a shout, but with sincere intent.

"It's okay," said Kaimèa.

Lysindra continued to wait. Her attention faltered as she had little to do. Their brains were fine, the interfaces to the modules were fine. Everything was fine as far as she could tell. From her reclined position she couldn't really gaze out at the view from the nearby open balcony, so she mentally gave a command to convert the ceiling and roof to transparency, and then she watched the sky while she waited. But Minêrva and Kaimèa simply stayed inside. Orange clouds drifted against a lavender sky as Zareasman began to set. A few stars glimmered into view at the zenith.

Her attention came back, she checked the interfaces, and everything seemed fine.

"Kaimèa?"

"Fine."

"Minêrva?" No response. "Minêrva?!"

"Still here."

Lysindra huffed. "You two aren't done yet?"

"No," in unison.

What the heck is going on? she thought. She waited a little while longer.

"Okay you two, enough is enough." She dialed the modules down. This was difficult, which she anticipated, because the modules always seemed to try to self-regulate to a preferred baseline level, but she was able to bring the modules down to a quiescent state and then disable them entirely. She disconnected the interfaces and Minêrva and Kaimèa were then once again restored to their previous selves. Lysindra got up from her chair and looked at them, still in their chairs, practically with her hands on her hips.

"Everyone okay?" she said sternly.

"MmHmm," said Kaimèa softly, who then rose languidly and walked over to the balcony, taking in the high ocean view. Minêrva similarly arose and stood motionless, deep in reflection. She turned her head oddly toward Lysindra and gave her a quizzical look, one of tremendous distance, a sort of pensive squint that suggested gears were turning madly in Minêrva's mind. Then she tried to give Lysindra a reassuring half-smile, but didn't do a very good job of it—the reassuring part—and then she spontaneously decorporealized entirely, without uttering a word. With rising concern, Lysindra joined Kaimèa on the balcony, consumed with the vista.

"What happened?"

Kaimèa stared outward, not immediately answering. "Those blue spires out there on the islands," she eventually said. "They are *sooo* beautiful." She squeezed Lysindra's hand, turned her head to face Lysindra, looked her in the eyes, and attempted to convey the same reassurance as Minêrva. And then similarly to Minêrva, she abruptly decorporealized too. Lysindra reeled at the vanishment and quickly checked on their locations, determining that each had ventured to solitary places in the Thalassia virtuality. She confirmed that they were each utterly alone, but as far as she could tell, they were genuinely okay for the most part. Lysindra wasn't sure what else to do, so she looked at the islands again, trying to see them the way Kaimèa had just seen them, but they looked the same to her as they always had. The sapphire-tinted pillars hadn't changed at all. It was Kaimèa and Minêrva who had changed.

44

“Y OU'RE SURE I SHOULD DO THIS?” asked Lysindra. She and Kaimèa were home, having recently corporealized from a pleasant evening with friends.

“Where's Minêrva?” asked Kaimèa.

“Up to something wild, I'm sure. It's a wonder she ever tore herself away from the fun and games that follow Rihon around.” Lysindra looked at the data suspended in the air in front of them.

“It's a good report,” said Kaimèa. “Everyone is going to be amazed you actually completed it. I suppose that after so much time, a lot of people probably doubted it could be done, or would ever be done.”

“Once I send this out, there's no getting it back. Ceulbur was so certain this was the wrong thing to do.”

“It will do so much good for so many people,” Kaimèa replied. She took Lysindra's hand in her own and looked Lysindra the eyes. Then she leaned in and kissed her, a comfortable act for both of them now. “You experienced it,” Kaimèa continued. “Don't you think everyone should have that chance?”

“Yeah, I suppose so,” said Lysindra.

“You aren't even publishing the actual network in this report. You're just announcing that you completed it and that it is confirmed to be final and done. You'll still have time to decide what to do next, but people need to know it's done even if you haven't quite figured out how to generalize the interface yet."

Lysindra sighed. "It's such an enormous neural module. I just can't quite get the interface to work without have to tweak and personalize it a little bit for each person."

"You're making steady progress. You'll have that last bit ticked off in no time."

"And you don't think I should wait until then to announce it?"

"Not at all. Let everyone know it's coming. It will ignite such a celebration. It will renew hope clear across the galaxy. Can you hear the echos of the cheers now? I sure can."

"That doesn't help," said Lysindra, turning away to take in a distant view.

"Awe, I bet I can make you feel better about it." Kaimèa smirked and took Lysindra's shoulders in her hands from behind. Lysindra melted into the sensation.

"That's not fair," she said, "but don't stop." Lysindra looked at the report in front of her, nit-picking incidental details of the exposition while soaking up the warmth and pressure against her shoulders.

"Maybe this section needs more work."

"It doesn't." Lysindra felt a sudden nibble on her ear. She flinched and then received it willingly. Kaimèa had eased into their relationship so quickly, no longer the peculiar eccentric Lysindra remembered meeting in a dusty corner of the galaxy. She seemed to love Lysindra so easily, as if she had been looking for her forever.

"But, it could be clearer."

"Nope."

"You and Minêrva helped me put the quale into words as best as possible, but it is so utterly nondescript. I just can't do it justice." She heard a muffled and inscrutable reply from lips and teeth that were filled with the nape of her own neck. She laughed lightly at what felt good but also tickled slightly at the same time.

"Send it now and join me in non-space," Kaimèa said, indicating a decorporealized state in which every one of their emulated nerve-endings could be intertwined in an experience of coupled merger the likes of which no physical presence could remotely satisfy. Lysindra felt her concentration failing under Kaimèa's distraction.

"Fine," she said, smiling at her sensations. "Here it goes."

"Here it goes," teased Kaimèa, who slipped one hand around Lysindra's waste.

"I'm sending it."

"You're sending it," Kaimèa mirrored. The fingers of Kaimèa's other hand danced up Lysindra's neck into her hair and against her scalp.

Lysindra hesitated one last moment, and then sent it. It was out of her hands now as she declared, "It's done."

"Follow me," Kaimèa said sternly, then promptly decorporealizing. Lysindra sat alone for a brief moment, surrounded by silence, and then did as she had been instructed.

45

S ATÕRI, SATÕRI, DEIMOS, AND SEVERAL OTHERS STOOD IN THE CONTROL center of an orbital station with a clear view of a yellow star nearby.

"Are we ready?" said Deimos.

"Almost," said one of Deimos's colleagues.

"So we get to see your latest project, do we?" said Satõri.

"Only those of you I have known the longest," he replied. "I have recently learned that Lysandra has completed the network. If not for some aspect of final polishing she is working on, it would already be too late. She would have released it and we would all be doomed. But thankfully, although she claims the network is complete, it is not ready for wider dissemination yet. We have one more chance to stop her."

"By the grace of God no doubt," said Satõri. "God wants us to stop Lysandra. That's why she hasn't released the network yet."

"So you have a way to stop her, then?" asked Satõri, carefully observing everything around him, trying to figure out what was going on so he could take action to save Lysandra if needed.

"Look out there," said Deimos. All they could see, however, was the tumultuous fireball of the adjacent sun. Deimos directed the window through which they were viewing, which had previously been an ordinary window, to naturally zoom in, as if it had been a display all along. It zoomed way in, and hovering above a stationary point over the sun, everyone on the platform saw a toroidally-shaped satellite aligned with its radial axis pointing straight toward the sun.

"We've been working on this for a while," said another person in attendance. "This should take care of Lysandra once and for all."

"What is it?" asked Satõri, suspicion and concern rising within him.

"A coronal canon," declared Deimos, with a sense of impact.

"I'm not that keen of a stellar engineer," said Satõri. "God's will is my area of study. What does it do?"

"Are we ready?" said Deimos.

"Yes, final calibration is complete," said an assistant.

"Better to show than to tell. Let's see how it goes," said Deimos. "Go for it." A few people on the station focused on their various control panels while everyone else watched. Nothing visible emanated from the satellite, but everyone could see some sort of blemish starting to form on the surface of the sun directly below the satellite. Deimos zoomed in appropriately and it become clear that an actual hole was starting to form in the corona.

"The satellite directs a magnetic field onto the surface that hollows out a region of the corona," explained Deimos. The hole continued to expand in diameter and depth.

"That's a canon?" asked Satõri.

"What do you think happens when we turn the magnetic field off?" asked Deimos with a wide grin. "Ready to fire?" he asked.

"Optimal bore size has been reached. We're holding steady to fire. The target is orbiting into alignment now."

"Target?" said Satõri, with some concern, but since there was nothing of note in the entire system of minor, unpopulated planets, he tried to relax.

"Firing...now," declared an engineer. What happened next occurred too quickly to be readily appreciated. The hole almost instantly vanished as the maniacal gravitational force of the sun collapsed the corona into the vacated void at nearly relativistic speed. This collapse, much like the action of a droplet on the surface of a pond, sent an eruption directly outwards, a perfectly linear stream of plasma exiting the sun at a substantial fraction of the speed of light. Some sections appeared almost laminar in their contiguity as an unbroken thread, while other sections displayed as a string of plasma pearls along the trajectory. The whole jet of plasma blasted through the center of the torus-shaped satellite without damaging it and shot off into the solar system. At the speed it was going, the jet would likely escape the solar system in a matter of hours.

But it wouldn't last that long. Deimos zoomed the view out and everyone watched the blinding streak of plasma lance across the solar system, wondering what would happen next.

"The aim is good," said an engineer. "We're right on target." Satõri again felt a wave of panic, but couldn't imagine how anyone could be at risk from this test firing of the weapon. For a few minutes everyone simply watched the stream streaking against the blackness of space. "Coming up on the target now," said the engineer. Deimos shifted the display to show one the planets in the system, fairly close to the sun. And then with awe and shock, and in some cases glee, everyone watched the veritable laser of pure plasma impact the planet near the leading edge of its orbit. The entire stream linearly plunged in on itself, slamming into the planet, leaving a belt of destruction across the planet's equator as the planet's orbit rapidly advanced it across of the path of the canon. The last droplets of plasma—as large as asteroids—made their impact near the trailing edge of the planet and then it was over. Deimos zoomed in so they could inspect the devastation. It was obviously substantial. The entire planet appeared to be going up in flame as two waves swept from the path of impact toward the respective poles. It was essentially impossible to gauge the destruction within the direct impact zone as the streak across the planet was entirely consumed in conflagration that reached so far above the surface as to essentially reach outer space.

"The effect will be even more incredible on Thalassia," said Deimos with pride. This planet has no atmosphere to assist the distribution of energy, but on Thalassia both the heat and the shockwave will be conveyed around the planet through the atmosphere in addition to the results we see here."

"It will destroy the entire planet," said Satõri.

"A reasonable price to pay to save the universe, wouldn't you say?" said Deimos.

"Your calculus is undeniable," said Satõri. "I suppose God will see the math the same way." Satõri smirked and laughed.

"I'm glad we all agree," said Deimos. "I trust I have no detractors in my midst?" Everyone in the room quickly confirmed their agreement, including Satõri who put on the best act he could muster considering the circumstances. The only thought on his mind was how he would get a chance to issue a warning back to his branchling, Satõri, as quickly yet surreptitiously as possible.

"How will you deploy this?" Satõri asked. "Won't they see this satellite far in advance."

"Ah, glad you asked," said Deimos. "Observe." The view jumped back to the satellite and everyone watched it quickly dissolve and dissipate away, countless unresolvable microscopic components that immediately fell toward the sun.

"We will distribute the satellite as undetectable particles near the sun. They will converge under their own power on the target location, too small to be detected, and then will rapidly recombine, aim and fire with no time to anticipate, much less prepare for, an attack."

"But it still takes several minutes for the canon to reach the planet," said another person in attendance. "Many people, likely Lysandra, will simply transit away during the emergency."

"We've already demonstrated our ability to disable planet-wide transit, have we not?" Everyone's thoughts went back to the Regenium attack. "No one will be transiting off Thalassia. It would take propulsive matter travel to escape, which they won't have ready to go since no one uses that on short notice."

"It seems you have thought of everything," said Satõri, stalling his horror. "They truly won't have a chance."

"God willing," said Satõri. Everyone watched the inferno surging across the planet momentarily.

"When do you intend to initiate this attack?" asked Satõri as innocently as possible.

"It's already underway. A contingent of engineers will depart imminently and begin construction of the satellite components upon their arrival. It shouldn't take too long to complete and then deploy the satellite." A shiver ran up Satõri's spine. He would have to act quickly.

46

T HE MOUNTAINS OF THALASSIA STRETCHED AHEAD. Lysindra was considerably far up one peak, a jagged tooth jutting from the world, extruded with crags and ripped with crevasses. The path to the top was indirect, taking her across open snowfields, up sheer cliffs, and bridging rifts that descended seemingly to the heart of the planet. Her hardened body, corporealized from rugged elements, arranged and structured for the rigorous traverse, felt no cold, a miserable quale of evolutionary irrelevance that her cognitive self had no need for in lieu of simple self-temperature monitoring. She felt no quale of exhaustion where simple status messaging would suffice. She felt no pain, the worst quale ever discovered by natural selection and capriciously thrust upon naturally evolved organisms in utterly merciless fashion. All Lysindra needed to do to make it to the top was keep going. The sight she would behold from the summit, the length and duration of the quest, the rarity of the accomplishment, these would be her rewards, not the overcoming of superfluous sufferings as some facetious and misplaced sense of triumph.

Step. Step. Snow compressed beneath her feet with a satisfying crunch. Ahead, she saw one of Thalassa's moons just cresting from behind a steep slope. The moon practically glowed, pocked with black and red volcanoes, cut across at random angles by gray and purple canyons. She had stood on that moon on several occasions, looking upward at Thalassia looming enormously overhead. From that vantage point, she had appreciated Thalassa's continents, oceans, and varying ecologies that could still be differentiated by color at that distance.

Despite suffering no unpleasant sensations, her body nonetheless alerted her that it needed time to recuperate. She spied a cave up ahead, mapped and planned in advance of her excursion, and headed there to rest and repair her body as needed. Descending slightly as she entered the cave, darkness enveloped her. Only behind her was there any light. She settled against the wall and relaxed, watching a blizzard quickly build strength outside. Out the entrance she watched snow blow past in horizontal streaks. She closed her eyes and listened to the wind. As it passed the mouth of the cave, it set up a long resonant wave that penetrated far into the cavernous depths, reverberated off every surface, and reflected all the way back out again, generating a low hollow drone that warbled throughout the chamber.

She sat here for a length of time, with night dimming outside, enjoying the feeling of her surroundings, enjoying the solitude of it, remembering the solitude she had felt on Cianthara. For durations of a certain length, she found such isolation invigorating, but it wouldn't last. She would long for company after a while.

As she sat, leaning against the frigid rock, she detected a drop in the already-diminutive illumination through her closed eyelids and opened them languidly, glancing again toward the cave mouth. It had become obscured, not only by the descent of night, but by some vague darkening, as if the cave mouth were filled with smoke. But then, she noticed that the wispy obstruction was perfused with minuscule point light sources that sparkled on and off, as if glinting with inner luminescence. She adjusted the sensitivity of her eyes to bring out dimmer features and saw that the smokey structure was in a state of continual movement, flowing and folding through itself without changing overall form. She immediately recognized it, even in the darkness. A hive entity like the one she encountered on Cianthara—or could it be the same one? It would have traveled a tremendous distance to end up on Thalassia.

Pattern known as Lysindra, came a thought across a standard communication channel. Well, that settled that question. It was the same entity again. She just stared momentarily. It had been 29,000 years since she had last seen this being—although 24,000 of those years had been in stasis while transiting back from Cianthara, so it felt like a mere, casual interlude of 5000 years.

Is the pattern known as Lysindra all right? came a second greeting.

She quickly responded. "Yes, I'm okay. I didn't expect to see you again, and certainly not here, in the middle of a blizzard on the side of a mountain."

Where would the pattern prefer?

"Here is fine," she said.

The pattern is inconsistent. Perplexing. Fickle.

Lysindra huffed. "Give me a minute to get used to seeing you again. You do realize how peculiar you are to me, right?"

An acceptable explanation.

She continued to stare almost helplessly into the mesmerizing patterns of the nebulous entity. "Why here, why now, up on this mountain?"

This pattern of patterns prefers separation.

Lysindra furrowed her brow, thinking. "You mean separation from human civilization."

Yes.

"So you sought me out when you noticed I was far away from everyone else."

Yes.

"Okay. I suppose that makes sense. I often feel the same way."

This pattern knows that.

"You watch me?"

Yes.

"I guess it's pretty obvious why you're here," said Lysindra, sighing. Everyone just wanted to use her for their own benefit.

The pattern known as Lysindra has completed the network and the quale.

"So it would seem," she muttered.

The pattern knows the solution, then?

"The last answer to the last question. Yep. I suppose so."

And yet, the pattern has not disclosed the network. Why not?

"I thought you were watching me. Don't you know why?"

The watching is sporadic.

"Well, that seems reasonable." She glanced around the cave, but everywhere else was utterly black. The only source of light came from the direction of the cave mouth, primarily the glowing snow reflecting the moon's light reflecting Zareasman's light, all severely diminished by the haze of the nebulous entity that completely filled the cave mouth, in addition to the paltry light exuded by the pin pricks dancing within the entity itself. So, she turned back to the entity again, studying its inner movements.

Why has the pattern not disclosed the network?

"I haven't finished generalizing the interface so that anyone can use it without going through an additional step of personalizing the interface to their brain.

This pattern of patterns won't be troubled by that.

"Right."

Will the pattern disclose the network to this pattern of patterns?

Lysindra looked at the ground in thought. Something held her back. "What would you do with it?"

For the first time in her interactions with the hive entity, it actually paused, as if in deep reflection. *Why is the EOUSP troublesome?* it responded.

"Generally," she ventured, "there are two main reasons. On an individual level, it indicates one's death, which while commonplace in antiquity, is now a graver threat and a more tragic outcome given our capacity for vastly extended lifetimes. Most conscious beings—humans to be sure—have an innate aversion to dying."

A frivolous reason, benefiting only the self and serving no greater virtue. And the second?

"Okay." Lysindra reeled momentarily from this summary rejection of her first attempt at an answer. "Well, it's discomforting to imagine that everything humanity has built for the last million years, or longer if you count the brief period prior to Fortification and the Exodus, will be lost someday."

But why?

"Why is it discomforting?"

Yes. Justify it.

Lysindra felt caught off guard again, but was annoyed at her own reaction. She should have an answer ready for such a seemingly reasonable question. "Because we've accomplished so much. Heck, we've closed physics. We have a complete knowledge of the nature of, well, of nature. We've created a million years of art. Breath-taking scenes of unlimited magnificence. Music that resonates through the core of our being, invoking emotional, physical, and conscious effects that alter us forever. We've told such heart-wrenching tales. Such beautiful and seemingly endless creations. It would be horrific for all of that to simply fade away."

But why? The thought came through with a sense of emphasis. *Why?* the thought pressed inward again. Lysindra hesitated in thought.

"I suppose," she began gingerly, frustrated that she still wasn't striking the chord the entity was striving for, "because there is intrinsic value in feeling experien—" she cut herself off "—value in consciousness itself," she continued. "The consciousness of learned nature and revealed reality. The consciousness of feeling evocative works of imagination and creation. The consciousness of each other, of loving and being loved. The wealth of knowledge and depth of emotions we have known and expanded upon for so long. Our conscious experience of those stupendous feats is what grants value to all that came before us. All of that would be lost according to the EOUSP."

You are missing a critical word. Lysindra frowned and literally glanced around the cave as if searching for the mystery word in the dark space around her.

"Ummm. Our conscious experience of the past..." she considered carefully, "gives meaning to that past. It grants the past a...a causal influence on...on us, on its future. The past's future, I mean."

PURPOSE, came a booming thought that ricocheted between their connected minds.

"Hmmm, purpose, yes," she said. Lysindra tasted her next words one by one as she produced them with deliberation. "So, our consciousness, now, in the present, grants the past its purpose. A...causal influence," she said slowly, "that influence being...purpose."

The pattern is learning, but the thought is incomplete.

"So, if our consciousness gives the past a purpose in the form of causal influence upon future conscious experiences—us—and if the EOUSP indicates the death of consciousnsess, then it also indicates the death of...purpose?" The entity said nothing, prompting her to continue. "This is about more than just people, isn't it, or even other conscious entities like animals or aliens? You're saying the universe itself has a purpose in the form of the causal influences of its fundamental physics, which propagate to biology, then neurology, which yields consciousness, and then the intellectual output of civilization. All of that ultimately impacts the conscious experiences of living beings." The entity remained silent. "The purpose of a star or a planet, or an entire galaxy I suppose, is in its physical effects on conscious experiences. The effect of living on a planet, or being illuminated by a star. But what about locales with no life? Do they lack purpose?"

Do they lack causal influence? the entity prodded.

"I suppose they affect us simply by our observations. Seeing a galaxy from afar inspires notions of beauty and symmetry and elegance. It also inspires a realization of the mathematics underlying physics. And more thoroughly, observations, measurements and experiments inform us about cosmology, which greatly influences our experiences of course. In fact, learning cosmology is the source of EOUSP angst in the first place. You're saying all of this gives purpose to the cosmos."

All of it?

"I suppose one could imagine a galaxy so far from the nearest galaxy in which consciousness evolved that it is never seen and has no relevant gravitational or radiated effects—it never influences the experience of a single conscious being. Perhaps such a cosmological body truly has no purpose—in the sense we are discussing here."

The pattern has reached the end. It repeated its initial question. *Why is the EOUSP troublesome?*

"Because it implies an undoing of the purpose of the entire universe, or even the purpose of existence itself. What is anything for if conscious beings don't witness it?"

Or later remember it, the entity offered.

Lysindra contemplated this. "I see, but does the EOUSP necessarily undo prior purpose? Does our experience here, now, go away when the universe dies later?"

Causal influence, said the entity.

"But we're being influenced now, being conscious now. Isn't that enough?"

Where does the causal influence lead?

"So you think temporary causal events and temporary implied purpose are insufficient. Rather, that when the last affected thing—some conscious being—dies, then all the prior events and conscious experiences retroactively lose their purpose...all the way back to the singularity origin, I suppose you're implying. So, for you at any rate, solving the EOUSP is about insuring that everything, everywhere, at all times, including in the past—the whole thing, the entire universe across its entire duration of existence—has a preserved purpose, whereas if and when the last causally affected conscious being perishes, not only will purpose end at that far future time, it will also render all past events and conscious experiences retroactively meaningless."

The pattern now understands.

Neither of them expressed a thought for a while. Eventually, the entity broke the mental silence first, repeating its earlier question. *Will the pattern disclose the network to this pattern of patterns?*

Lysindra didn't immediately respond.

The pattern hesitates.

"I understand your concern now, far better than before, I admit. But I'm worried about releasing the network unevenly, to some before others. I would prefer to release it to everyone all at once."

The light cone renders such a goal impossible.

"Ah, but," she retorted, "within the light cone, it can still be released simultaneously. Agreed?"

The pattern is logical.

"Awe, thank you for saying that. Gosh, just picture it—wait, can you picture things?"

Yes.

"Just imagine, the EOUSP quale sweeping across the galaxy at the speed of light, like...like—"

Like a pressure swell traversing spacetime.

"Yes, like gravitational waves! A beautiful analogy." She smiled. Was she friends with this strange thing now? "Will you wait?" She suddenly remembered this entity could probably choose to be as dangerous as it wished to be, and now that she understood the severity of its universal concern, it might do just about anything to insure the survival of its philosophical view of purpose. But her concern was immediately ameliorated.

This pattern will wait if the pattern known as Lysindra wishes it.

"I appreciate your understanding." Then a thought occurred to her. "A dear friend—no, a partner—no, a mate? That word is ancient and strange-sounding. Anyway, he...he's traveling now, and I think he might be looking for you. But we have no idea how to reach out to you. I guess I just wanted to know if he found you."

The pattern known as Lysindra inquires about the pattern known as Ceulbur.

"Yeah, the pattern does inquire," she said a bit dryly.

This pattern of patterns has not sought out or encountered the pattern known as Ceulbur.

"Ah, ok, well just thought I'd ask."

Does the pattern feel the absence of the pattern?

"Yes, of course I do."

And the pattern has found a new pattern.

"Yep, that's working out pretty well too."

This pattern has no such concept. This pattern feels millions of continuous harmonies. This pattern is never alone and never needs to choose between patterns.

"Lots of people do that too. They don't choose, as you put it. Or, in fact, lots of people form tight groups sort of like you. We call it a hive. Frankly, that's why he's looking for you."

The patterns of patterns described as hives are small and lack cohesion. They are disharmonious compared to this pattern of patterns.

Lysindra paused, contemplating. "How many of you are there? Not with-in you, but others like you? Other patterns of patterns?

Other patterns have coalesced. Groups of individual patterns have dis-covered the concept of the pattern of patterns on multiple occasions. But this pattern is the oldest and largest.

"I see." A pause ensued, which became an uncomfortable pause.

The entity broke the silence first. *Complete the work.*

"I'm trying as hard as I can. I'm sure you'll know the moment it's done."

This pattern will know.

"Oookay," she said uneasily. "Thank you for visiting me again."

The pattern is welcome. Then, without a hint of decorum, the smokey nebula receded toward the cave mouth, exited into the midst of the blizzard, still howling, where Lysindra could see that it appeared to be totally unaf-fected by the wind and snow, and then it rose up outside the mouth of the cave out of sight, presumably back to space. Lysindra was left watching the horizontal streaks slicing over the soft, glowing snow.

47

SATÕRI FELT NUMEROUS ANTIQUATED PHYSIOLOGICAL INDICATIONS OF ANXIETY. He could have disabled them at a whim, but instead permitted them to urge him to action, namely desperation to issue a warning back to Satõri without being discovered. Even if he would have willingly sacrificed himself to the noble cause—and surely he would have, so saintly and God-honoring would his sacrifice be—Deimos would have simply adjusted his plan in response. No, he had to warn Satõri, and by extension Lysandra, without being caught.

And at the moment, he was still on the orbital station where they had witnessed the weapon test. He couldn't possibly send a warning from here. He looked around at the others, various of Deimos's supporters and collaborators, discussing in hushed tones the implications of what they had just seen. There was a verve of hope in the room, almost excitement. None of the conversations he overheard seemed particularly concerned with complicit murder, much less planetary slaughter.

"Yes, well, I don't see another way," he overheard Satõri say to Deimos. "Some people just have to be saved from themselves, for the good of us all. God will understand."

Deimos openly sighed. His frustration with Satõri's religiosity was increasingly apparent, but true to Satõri's promise, the religious faction had been pivotal to the scheme. "Well, without your congregation located in the Zareasman system, and their zeal to act, at the ready, it would have been more difficult," Deimos said. "I must admit, my strengths lie with the games of politics near the Center. Despite the continued intransigence of the formal assemblies, I've been steadily amassing support behind the scenes. But I have less sway in the more remote systems. Your—house—has been very helpful."

Satõri looked for an exit opportunity, but instead— "Jorgen," said Deimos. "Come join us." Satõri approached them and looked his original semblance up and down. He hadn't worn that face in millennia now, but it still felt strange to realize that a branchling of common ancestry had become so lost from the grace of God. Satõri and his branchling Satõri had managed to escape such mind-bending insanity, and for that he was thankful. Thinking back to the Lysandran conclave, he recalled hearing the Satòri branchling speaking on behalf of thirty-four Pleiadean worlds, billions of followers, who had convinced themselves that if Lysandra refused complete her work within the hallowed halls of the faith, they would consider actually killing her. How were so many billions of Lysandrans, and hundreds of Satõri's own branchlings—versions of himself—so wickedly deluded?

He had to get a warning back to Satöri, and then onward to Lysandra, as fast as possible. And yet, here he stood, surrounded by the enemy, unable to slip away.

"Jorgen. You've been working with me on this task for so long," said Deimos. "You're my kindred spirit. I couldn't have done all this without people like you who see how dangerous the EOUSP quale is and how reckless people like Lysandra are. Thank you."

"Oh, no trouble at all," said Satõri. "I'm just glad to do my part. If I may ask, aren't you worried that such a large-scale assault will be traced back to you? To us, I mean. To the cause?"

Deimos nodded thoughtfully, then looked away from the Satoris, out the window, shifted the view back to the planet again and observed the smoldering scar across its equator. The next time a planet was ravaged in that manner, it would be a highly populated world, a beautiful green and yellow planet, not the barren gray chunk he had just blasted in harmless fashion.

"That's another reason why I've appreciated the support of our recent partner." He slapped Satôri on the outside of his arm with a sense of camaraderie. "There's nothing like a fervent religious following to garner a certain passion of support in political chambers. I think that working together, we can sell this as an act of last resort. From my perspective, I will repeat my insistence that everything that is transpiring here is microscopic against the good of the entire universe, and even grander, if one can imagine such a thing, against the good of the larger cyclic universe that encompasses the infinity of universal perpetuity forever. A planet, an entire galaxy! It's nothing compared to the loss of everything that will ever be, forever. Of course, there will be no *direct* evidence implicating us. Let the people have their petty suspicions." He paused, literally taking a breath. "And then from Satõri's perspective here, we can gather further support from a different sort of population, perhaps unconvinced by mere rationality, but who can be brought to our cause on the basis of religious conviction. This is all God's plan, am I right Satõri?"

An odd expression flashed across Satõri's face. Satõri knew what it meant. After all, they were, to a significant extent, the same person. Satõri was surely wondering where he was using Deimos or the other way around. "Absolutely," he eventually replied. "You are one of God's most excellent cudgels," he said with a knavish grin. Deimos made the smallest of winces, to which Satõri carefully offered no expression of response, ending the brief power exchange, but the last thing Satõri noticed was Deimos giving him— Satõri as Jorgen—a very sly smile. At the same time Satõri received an internal message from Deimos. *Plus, if the investigation gets too close, we can direct suspicion onto this religion clown. The trail of evidence is being laid at this very moment.*

Satõri glanced around the room to avoid any facial expression of response. "I appreciate the invitation to today's milestone in our project," he said, "but I must excuse myself now, if that's okay with you, my friends."

"Quite all right," said Deimos, practically forgetting Satõri's—Jorgen's— presence on the spot. Satõri gave Satõri an odd look, but Satõri merely nodded in return and walked off as quickly as he could without looking like he was walking off as quickly as he could.

Now, as to where he could send a transmission from, that was the next urgent matter. The entire orbital station seemed an unlikely option, as its communications were surely comprehensively monitored. And since the stellar system was little more than Deimos's testing grounds—there being nothing else of civilization or industrialization in the locality—he would have no choice but to transit to another stellar system. That would take time but what choice did he have? Before Deimos could call him back, he headed for the interstellar transit daises, located on another level of the station, and promptly departed to the nearest populated system he could find. Being near the Center, he had many options to choose from, and was able to find a suitable location a mere seventeen light years away. He left immediately.

Seventeen years later—and also instantly, in another sense—Satõri corporealized on a dais possessing practically no familiarity with the planet to which he had traveled. He just needed to send a message. He could figure everything else out later. He found himself in a fairly conventional interstellar transit station. A cluster of glowing daises were scattered across an elegant wooden floor, or some alien plant-like material with comparable features. Pink and orange lighting dappled the floor from a comfortably high ceiling. He made his way to the exit and explored his new surroundings. He appeared to be in a vast interior of some sort. In fact, he couldn't find an exit to the surface anywhere. A quick mental investigation into the planet's data network revealed why. The planet was tidally locked to its sun, rendering the surface unbearable. Satõri was, for all intents and purposes, on an orbital station as much as he was on a natural cosmological body.

He quickly explored the area in the vicinity where he had arrived trying to find the necessary infrastructure for interstellar communication. As expected, the planet's data network enabled him to access the various interstellar messaging arrays from practically anywhere, so he found a quiet place to work in a park of sorts, a huge excavated cavity, as big as a city, that was planted over with life from some other planet, and illuminated as brightly as a sunlit day by sources coming from all directions. Plants grew out from the rock walls and down from the ceiling far above. He constructed a brief message to Satõri summarizing the situation, but when he was ready to send the message...

> Transmitter access request has been received and queued. Message can be reattempted upon prioritization and scheduling. Please wait.

Unbelievable, he muttered to himself. *Just my luck, ending up on a backwaters world with only a handful of interstellar transmitters.* Ylorin, where Satõri could receive his warning, would have a wait. He anxiously waited and watched as his request bubbled up through the queue and the transmitters patiently reoriented to a new part of the sky. At the first opportunity he promptly reattempted his message transmission, but...*What in the world?! What now?* he thought, as he immediately encountered some sort of network error. Upon a quick investigation, the problem wasn't occurring at the large interstellar transmitter, in a far flung region of the planet. He simply couldn't get the message from his current location to the transmitter's location. Something local about the mycelia data network—something *very* local—wasn't working properly.

"So, there you are," came a voice. Satõri swung around and saw—*himself!*—just as his vision went completely gray. He was in an infinite fog. All sound vanished. Even the temperature of the air was no longer present against his skin.

He cried out, "What?! What's going on?" but couldn't hear his own voice, neither through the air nor transduced through his physical body to his ears. *What the hell?!* he thought. He spoke again, guessing the identity of his apprehender. "Satõri?" This time he heard a response.

"The same." The voice was right, but the reverberation was all wrong for the interior in which they had stood moments before. In fact, there was absolutely no reverberation at all.

"What's going on?" he demanded, still helpless to hear himself, helpless to even confirm that he was producing speech or even sound. "I can't hear my own voice. All I see is gray."

"Let me fix that first one for you," came the response.

"Hello?" Satõri gingerly attempted. This time he heard his own voice with the same lack of reverberation as Satõri.

"It was the 'friend' that gave you away. You're me, aren't you?"

"What are you talking about?"

"You said it back on the station. Then you rather hastily departed, so I thought it best to follow along and see what you were up to."

"You followed me?" Satõri said with confusion.

"Come on. Keep it together. Now, what were you up to? I can see your data network activity here, but of course I have no idea what it contains. What are you doing? May I presume, based on the recent circumstances, that you are attempting to communicate details of Deimos's plan to someone. Are you trying to save Lysandra?"

Right, thought Satõri. *Focus on the mission.*

"There you go again," said Satõri. "I told you I'm observing your network interactions. Needless to say, I'm impeding your communication with the data network."

"That's what you're doing to me?"

"Well, quite a bit more than that, as you have surely surmised. "I have also taken control of your sensory modalities, as you can plainly—see." Satõri chuckled.

"That's impossible! Brain orbs are unassailable!"

"Perhaps for anyone else, but you're me, Satõri. And I'm you."

"This should still be impossible," but even as he said the words he had a sinking feeling he was wrong. After all, he was currently living the evidence to the contrary. Satõri started to feel his cognitive functions failing. Something was burrowing deep into his mind and dissolving it from the inside.

"Off the cuff, yes, I couldn't possibly pull something like this off on short notice. But as soon as I realized I would have to stop Lysandra, I knew that some of my greatest adversaries might be other Satoris, and then I struck on this idea and pursued it. I had no idea if it would work, but I have been developing it for quite a while now." All Satõri could do as he listened was absorb the vacancy of his senses and try to devise a solution. "Don't get me wrong," Satõri continued. "No one was more surprised than I to discover that a Satori was at Deimos's right hand. I never would have imagined it would come to this, but here we are."

Satõri was still lost in a visual fog, but he could sense the mycelial network in contact with his feet. He could see its connection point fading in the haze, hear the buzz of its energy, smell the protocol of its comms-linkup negotiation. He tried again to latch on, but again it slipped away from him. It felt like facing a lock and holding a key, but with hands too shaky to fit the two together. But he couldn't remember why he was trying to do this. What did he need the network for? *Oh right! I have to warn Satöri.*

"Oh stop that already. It won't work," said Satõri. "Now, tell me who you are trying to contact and I'll let you live. It hardly matters *what* your message is. That much I can ascertain, but I need to know who so I can follow up with them and ensure they don't receive it—or don't have an opportunity to act on it if they do."

"How could you have done this? It shouldn't be possible," Satõri insisted. He felt his kinesthetic sense slip away, losing all sense of his bodily mass and gravity and positioning. His clarity of thought became as hazy as his visual surroundings. He remembered he had something important to do.

Satõri continued. "It can be variably effective, I'll admit. It depends on how long ago I have diverged from another Satori. Greater divergence makes the process less effective. We are remarkably similar after all. We share hundreds of thousands of years of common ancestry and only diverged relatively recently by comparison. As such, I found a way to gain access to other Satori brains—in most cases. Like I said, it depends on the degree of divergence."

"My god. How many of our branchling cousins have you tested this on? Don't you even care?" *I don't have time for this. I need to warn Satöri. But, what was I trying to warn him about?...Oh! THE CORONAL CANON! I need to warn Satöri. I need to establish a connection...but, what do I need to warn him about? I had it a moment ago.*

"This is all at the behest of God," said Satôri. "What difference does it make how many get in the way, even our own branchlings? But I don't need to kill you, my well-intentioned friend. I can simply restrain you for a little while, unharmed, until our plan is complete. I have no desire to harm you. Come on, let me save you. Let God save you."

"But, the other Satoris! How many would you kill for this hysteria?"

"Down to the last one, if I must, God willing."

"And you would be that last one, I suppose." *Where is that connection endpoint?! It's all gray in here. I can't find anything!*

"If that be the will of—"

"WILL YOU SHUT UP! My god, is that what we sound like to everyone else?" He made another attempt to latch on to the mycelial communication protocol. *It's negotiating the protocol!* he thought with glee. *Here we go— NO!* It failed to connect. His internal communications were disintegrating with every passing moment. As he tried again, he felt the connection point slip away into the fog. He pursued it, trying to ignore Satôri's taunts.

"Your contact. Now! Save yourself. Let me help you." Satôri ignored the demand, but lost track of the task. *I need to do something. Something important.* He veritably felt his neurons popping and zapping as his brain orb bore the full brunt of the onslaught. *Lysandra! The attack. I have to warn her!* He sensed the connection again, but it was far away.

And then he was gone.

48

MINÊRVA SAT BACK AND ADMIRED HER WORK. Neural configurations were not her strongest area, but she had worked with them for a long time and was reasonably adept at the art. Ages ago she had constructed a module from a homely radially symmetric creature on an undeveloped, swampy world, and in so doing she had shown the galaxy something no one thought was possible. Hope. But what did that network feel like to the original plucky little animal, she had always wondered.

Then, later on, she and Rihon had discussed the possibility of wearing an entire brain as a neural module. This would enable one to go beyond experiencing the quale that the Neuralium's network happened to invoke in a human brain. It would enable one to feel the quale *from* the Neuralium's perspective. Could she *become* the Neuralium as it experienced the quale?

"What do you feel?" she said out loud to the group of Neuraliums that sat in front of her on their twelve barely-triplet-grouped legs, populating her Caelunis recreation within Thalassia's largest virtuality. It was now a popular site of visitation. Everyone wanted to see where the famous Neuralium came from.

Finally, she would know what this profound realization felt like to a seemingly insentient being that spent its life hopping around in the understory of an alien forest.

"Is everybody ready?" she said to the several Neuraliums. As always, they gave no response. From her mental interface, she drew one Neuralium closer to her, seemingly telekinetically lifting it from the ground and pulling it with invisible force such that it swooped toward her. She then plopped it down directly in front of her on the moss-like ground where she sat crossed-legged. At first it made as if to promptly skitter off in some random direction, so she gently disconnected its motor circuits momentarily. Then she reenabled them again, out of compassion, and the Neuralium seemed content enough to stay put.

She proceeded to establish a connection between her brain and the Neuralium in front of her. It was an unusual interface, more difficult than merely attaching some subregion of the Neuralium to herself. That was easier because she didn't have to change herself to do it. She just had to map the external module of the Neuralium onto her brain's existing systems. But for this task, she had to find a way to adapt her own brain's sensory and perceptual systems to align with the Neuralium. She had to change her own neurological processes, not just the Neuralium's. That was the only way she could feel the quale from the Neuralium's perspective. It had taken her a lot of work to complete this project, but she was finally ready.

The connection came online. She waited. Steadily, she felt herself slipping into an alien form of thinking and feeling. Her vision faded away, as the Neuralium had no such sense itself. She lost her sense of her own body, as the Neuralium's neuroanatomy had no concept of the human form, but at the same time she began to feel the kinesthetics of the Neuralium's profoundly inhuman body arrangement. She lost her visual sense of position in space, the locus behind her eyes as if she were located inside her head. All of that fell away. She tried to maintain her human cognition so she could comprehend the experience and recall it later, but she felt herself losing that connection as well. Try as she might, she felt her humanity slip away. She felt the centrality of her linear thoughts disintegrate as she became a multi-neural-ganglia organism comprising semi-independent brains working together to form a cohesive organism. Words lost their meaning. Her inner dialog evaporated and she was left with an animalistic sense of existence, a consciousness lacking complex language and grammar. Any memories she might hope to retain would not be translatable by linguistic description now—words. Only feelings would remain, if even that succeeded.

And then it arrived. Enormity, infinity. Something ancient, forever cycling—one universe begetting another. The quilt of existence, her entire universe but one small patch.

And she felt awe. Tearful awe at the marvel of existence. Perplexing awe at the capacity for consciousness. Reverent awe at something bigger and older than the universe itself. Awe manifest.

And it felt good. It felt...it felt...*hopeful.* There it was. The original Neuralium quale. Pure, clear hope. Utter simplicity. This humble squishy creature, blobbing about in a swamp, realizing the grandeur of existence and the wonder of its own consciousness—and the hope of its own perpetuity.

She sat in this thought space for an extended duration. She had been converted into a Neuralium to such an extent that she not only lacked the means to extricate herself, but even the notion or inclination to do so. She had lost and forgotten not only who she was, but that there was another thing to be in the first place. And yet, the blanket of universal, never-ending consciousness coated her in warmth—and in peace. She had never known such crystalline peace. If permitted, she could simply immerse in this sensation forever.

When the external timeout triggered because Minêrva had completely lost the ability to exit on her own, she found herself rapidly and somewhat brusquely yanked back from the Neuralium, steadily becoming herself again. As she emerged from the stupor she clutched at the memory of it. The point of the exercise was to learn something from it, to retain something, to carry something back. But as she regained clarity, the memory faded, like waking from a dream. She recalled enough to know that she was *trying* to hold onto it, but helplessly realized her failure to do so. When she had fully returned she only remembered the vaguest fugue of the experience. She knew it had been profound, whatever it was. The only option would be to do it again. And surely she would sometime, but she also knew that she would never be more successful upon subsequent attempts. This was as close as she would ever come to knowing what her little Neuralium truly felt like. It would always be a dream.

49

"So, I have some news," said Lysindra. She and Kaimèa stood on a warm, sandy island in the Thalassian tropics, not far from where Lysindra had once had a home with Ceôlbur. The white sand sloped into the water where coral-like lifeforms built sprawling bright blue residences from living lazurite just beneath the surface, stretching as far as one could see.

Kaimèa looked over. Lysindra admired her as she delighted in the simple sensations of the beach. Kaimèa's hair was a confusion of red, orange, and yellow bands that gently shifted across her head. Lysindra found the effect mesmerizing.

"What?" Kaimèa responded.

Lysindra closed her eyes and felt the Zareasman sun on her face. "I finished the interface."

"What?! No way!" Kaimèa declared. "Why so cavalier? This is huge! We have to get Minêrva. We have to celebrate."

Lysindra smiled at Kaimèa's excitement. "How would we celebrate, my darling?"

"Gosh, anything will do. Who cares! Let's throw the biggest party Thalassia has ever seen—No, let's not do that." Lysindra chuckled internally. "So that's it?" Kaimèa continued. "Nothing is stopping you from distributing it to everyone now."

Lysindra sighed. "Yeah, I guess not."

"Are you kidding?!" Kaimèa said. "Now what?"

"I just want to be sure I'm doing the right thing. There's no way to get it back once I release it."

"We've been over this," said Kaimèa. "Come here." She took Lysindra's hand and forcefully pulled her toward the water. Lysindra relented and then waded in. Alien sea creatures schooled around their legs with bodies that constantly dissociated into smaller pieces and then rejoined into their unified larger form, but sometimes exchanging subcomponents with other individuals nearby. What arrangement of these body parts constituted an individual? What was the identity of one of these creatures while deconstructed into parts or after trading with neighbors and recombining into a singular form? Perhaps it was a meaningless question. The water luminesced with bright green speckles and curling streaks. Kaimèa pulled her in deeper and they swam for a while.

As they slopped their way back out of the surf, pushing through the water first with their thighs, then their shins, then their ankles, they each pulled their hair to the side and rung it out, once again letting the heat of Zareasman both revitalize and relax them at the same time.

At this point, Kaimèa said something that didn't penetrate Lysindra's attention as her focus was suddenly drawn away by internal communication. "I said, you've done well, Lysindra," repeated Kaimèa more forcefully, looking for some acknowledgement of her previous statement.

"WHERE'S MINÊRVA?!" Lysindra practically yelled, ignoring Kaimèa. "Kaimèa, we have to go right now!"

"What? What are you talking about?" Kaimèa looked around, as if expecting to find some obvious problem.

"Kaimèa, listen to me! I've just received a message from—incredible. It's from Satöri."

"The cult guy?"

"We have to get off Thalassia right now! I'm not kidding. Hold on, I'm contacting Minêrva. We have to get to a transit dais immediately!"

"Why?"

"We don't have time for that. Just trust me!"

Minêrva, where are you?

Hi Lysindra. What are you up to?

Meet us at the off-planet transit dais RIGHT NOW! We have to get off Thalassia!

Lysindra? What's wrong?

We're under attack. We have to go now! Stop asking questions!

"Kaimèa, we have to get to the dais, now!" Lysindra decorporealized, and then moments later recorporealized inside a building. She waited impatiently, rereading—rehearing—rethinking—the message. It was both clear in its intent and confounding in its immediacy and sender:

Attention: Lysindra. We haven't met, but please believe me when I say you are in immediate, grave danger. You must evacuate Thalassia immediately. The entire planet is unsafe. Off-planet transit daises are likely to be sabotaged shortly. You must leave NOW!
—Satöri, your committed apostle

She paced nervously.

Kaimèa corporealized.

Lysindra spoke with urgency. "You. Now. Go!" She said pointing to the dais.

"No way am I leaving you behind."

"I'm not kidding Kaimèa!"

Minêrva corporealized. "Okay you two? What in the world is going on?"

"Thalassia is under attack. We have to go now! Can we *please* discuss this later?"

"Let's go," said Kaimèa. We'll meet at Femhold station."

"What about everyone else?" asked Minêrva.

"I already sent out a broadcast," said Lysindra. "I doubt many will make it, or will even heed it. I didn't have time to provide any explanation. I just told everyone to get off the planet as quickly as possible. I'm sure it'll sound crazy and most people will dismiss it. There's nothing else we can do. We have to go!"

"Well," said Minêrva. "You're first. We're not going until you go."

"UGH! Fine, but you better be right behind me!"

"We will," said Minêrva.

Lysindra stepped up on the dais. "I'm only going first because arguing about it further will just waste time, but you better be right behind me."

"We're right behind you," said Kaimèa with a reassuring tone.

Lysindra faded out. Her vision, hearing, sensation, all diminished to nothing and her consciousness fell away.

Then she reemerged several minutes later on a new dais. Above her, a perfectly transparent dome, completely invisible, revealed the open cosmos, black, star-speckled, belted with the Milky Way, blotted with nebulae. Far off to one side, Zareasman broiled with turbulent energy. She leapt off the dais to free it up as fast as possible, landing on a soft floor, nothing so antiquated as carpet, but not hard stone or metal either. The domed area, revealing precisely half the night sky, was encircled by a perimeter where the circular floor simply ended, where the dome bent down and met it. The circular area was quite large and housed multiple daises in addition to large expanses of public area where many people mingled. She watched frantically as various people corporealized and wandered toward the center of the circular area, where they could descend into a hole in the center of the floor to the vast station that stretched beneath this domed endpoint. But where were Kaimèa and Minêrva?!

Something in the direction of Zareasman caught her attention. She looked toward the sun, which was perfectly muted by the dome while the rest of the sky was left unimpeded. Something strange was happening. There appeared to be some sort of thread hanging directly away from Zareasman. It was the same color as the star, a piercing yellow orange. Along the length of the thread, it was sometimes a contiguous string and sometimes a series of sharp, radiant points—or globs if Lysindra's estimate of the size of the thread was accurate. To even see it at all at this distance it must have a reasonable diameter.

"What the heck is that?" said Minêrva next to her. Lysindra turned, saw Minêrva, and let out a sigh of relief.

"Where's Kaimèa?" Lysindra demanded.

"She should be right behind me."

"But WHERE IS SHE?!" screamed Lysindra. Minêrva looked around the vast area, milling with people, some of whom turned to see who was yelling.

"I don't know Lysindra."

"I'm going back."

"Don't be daft. Of course you're not. If anything, your attempt to go back will just tie up a dais that could otherwise be used to evacuate."

Lysindra melted with hopelessness. "She should be here by now." She turned back to the yellow streak shooting away from Zareasman at incredible speed.

"That thing's gotta be going at least half C," said Minêrva. "That's incredible."

"The Zareasman network is full of alerts," said Lysindra. "Look." She mentally indicated various data, which then became to Minêrva.

"That...thing...from the sun is on a collision trajectory with Thalassia," said Minêrva.

"And the transit daises on Thalassia are down now," said Lysindra, "just as we were warned they would be. Where's Kaimèa?! Why isn't she here yet?" Everyone on the platform, hundreds of people, were now standing still, all simply watching the strange yellow orange streak slicing through space, and also attending to internal information about the emergency as it became available to everyone.

"It's almost there," said Minêrva quietly. Someone with authoritative access to the orbital station's systems had converted the natural window display into an artificial display—without an apparent change in appearance of the sky—and then zoomed the view in on Thalassia.

"Maybe we shouldn't watch this," said Minêrva, but she noticed that Lysindra was entranced by the sight, with tears pouring from her eyes. Of course, they were seeing Thalassia and the coronal canon as they had appeared several minutes ago. Realizing what was likely about to happen, this relativistic distinction made a deep impression on Lysindra as she watched.

"Why isn't she communicating with us?" cried Lysindra. "Even if she couldn't transit, shouldn't she be sending out some sort of communication? But if she did transit, she should be here!"

"There's a possibility..." said Minêrva with hesitation, "...that some sort of panicked riot occurred at the transit complex on Thalassia. Even with etchings stored elsewhere in the system—or in other systems I suppose— anyone on Thalassia with a long-lived branch would feel a compulsion to escape. Having a local etching will do no good if the entire planet is..."

Everyone on the platform then gasped in unison as the leading end of the plasma stream impacted the leading edge of Thalassia's orbit. It was difficult to see what was happening on the surface because the atmosphere instantly ignited with a shockwave that traversed across the surface at supersonic speed. The point of impact was a pure fireball. The inferno expanded toward the poles while also streaking slowly across the equator toward the trailing edge of the orbit, the stream of blazing plasma continuing to plunge into the planet. Everyone just watched helplessly as Thalassia was steadily brutalized from one horizon to the other, fire rapidly consuming the entire surface. Just as the plasma stream completed its belt across the planet and was about to slip into space behind the orbit, the last of it whimpered out with a few final asteroidal balls, and then it was gone.

By the time anyone turned their attention back to Zareasman for an explanation, there was nothing to see to indicate how this had happened.

Thalassia was destroyed, and Kaimèa was nowhere to be seen.

50

"**W**HERE IS SHE?!**"** LYSINDRA SCREAMED AT MINÊRVA. They were both in tears, watching the scar form across Thalassia as the fire continued to burn. Everyone on the platform was either in shock or running madly to get...somewhere, wherever they felt they needed to be in order to deal with the calamity.

"She was going to transit right behind me," said Minêrva. "I was looking straight at her when I stood on the dais. She was going to follow me next." She held Lysindra, then pushed her back to face her. "Lysindra, I know it isn't sufficient, but when was her last off-planet etching?"

"Our etchings were stored on Thalassia." Lysindra wept. "We didn't plan for full-scale planetary devastation!" Even as she heard the words escape her mouth, she could hear Ceulbur chastising her for failing to anticipate and prepare for precisely this sort of circumstance. "Her most recent off-world etching is, gosh, I have no idea. Could it be Nyveron?"

"That can't be possible," said Minêrva. "She must have traveled around, left etchings here and there. There must be something."

Lysindra watched the dais she had arrived on hopefully. "We pretty much stayed to ourselves after she arrived. Ceulbur was gone, I had her now. That was enough. We didn't go anywhere else." Lysindra collapsed to the floor. "I've lost both of them now." She cried amid the chaos of strangers running this way and that.

Minêrva sat down next to her. "Tell me about the warning you received."

The question partially snapped Lysindra back to the present for a moment. "Ummm, right. You weren't with us."

"I was with a group of Rihon's colleagues," said Minêrva. "They find my Neuralium research stories inspiring."

Lysindra's voice became quiet. "Kaimèa and I were on the beach."

"Sounds nice."

"I told her—oh, you don't know yet."

"What?" Minêrva tilted her head and raised her eyebrows.

"Minêrva, I finished the interface."

"*What?!*" Minêrva physically jolted. "Are you kidding?"

Lysindra doubled over and bawled as her distraction faded. "It's done," she whimpered.

"*You're done?!* Everything is done? This is amazing."

"Kaimèa shared your excitement." At mentioning her name, she looked around again hopelessly. "She was talking about celebrating, throwing a big party."

"Most certainly!"

"And then we both agreed we weren't party types."

"Figures." Minêrva glanced around too, as if hoping Kaimèa would somehow appear out of nowhere, but immediately realized that made no sense since the dais was right in front of them. Each time someone corporealized on it, they would watch hopefully and then despair as it wasn't Kaimèa and some stranger walked off in a random direction. "And then what?" she asked.

"We were swimming in the ocean. It was really nice." Lysindra became quiet again. "To be done with everything and have her there with me in that moment. Everything was perfect." Minêrva waited for her to continue while Lysindra sobbed. "And then I received a message. It was short. From Satöri. I've never even met him."

"Huh? Which one?"

"I think it was his corporeal branch from all the way back to Ylorin where he started his crazy religion."

"Some of the Satoris aren't on your side, you know?" said Minêrva. "This one warned you?"

"A lot of them see me as some sort of absurd messiah. A lot of—I can't say it—"

"Lysandrans," said Minêrva, enjoying the opportunity to laugh momentarily in the midst of their grief.

"Yeah, that." Lysindra said with a sardonic tone. "A lot of them are on my side, figuratively speaking. They want me to complete the EOUSP quale for their—for God or whatever."

"So this Satöri warned you of an attack mere moments before the attack happened?"

"The weird thing is that the warning wasn't local. It didn't come from the Zareasman system. It came from Ylorin, 9000 light years away."

Minêrva puzzled over this, frowning with thought. "Then how did it arrive mere minutes before an attack that occurred right here?"

"Weird, huh? All he said was to get off Thalassia immediately, that the whole planet was about to be destroyed." Lysindra looked at Minêrva but her vision was wrecked with tears. "I think he was implying I was the target."

"Well of course you were. That's not surprising."

"God dammit!" declared Lysindra. "This is exactly what Ceulbur was angry at me about."

"It isn't your fault."

"I shouldn't have been there. Even if I was willing to put myself in danger, I should have removed myself from civilization so no one else would be put at risk."

"You aren't responsible for the murderous inclinations of psychopaths Lysindra. Give yourself a break."

They paused a moment. "Where's Kaimèa?" asked Lysindra. "Where is she?"

"Right here, beautiful!" came a familiar voice. They both looked up with surprise and saw Kaimèa approaching from another dais on the far side of the platform.

"Kaimèa!" Lysindra leapt to her feet, knocking Minêrva off balance, and wrapped herself around Kaimèa so quickly they both tripped backwards.

"Sorry about that," Kaimèa said, as they regained their posture. "It seems the transit traffic from Thalassia flooded the entire system in the wake of your planet-wide warning. My transit got redirected to Helderskan station and only made its way here to Femhold a moment ago."

"Why didn't you contact us from there?" said Lysindra angrily.

"You aren't understanding," said Kaimèa with a light laugh. "My transit was held in the buffers and redirected here without corporealizing my etching or even reviving me in a virtuality. They just held my pattern in stasis until the network cleared so they could complete the transit to the intended destination—here." She kissed Lysindra lightly. "I'm sorry. I've been in stasis this whole time. Imagine my surprise when I arrived over there a few moments ago," she indicated the dais behind her, "and found out I had been in stasis *and* on the wrong orbital station for the past several minutes, transmission time not withstanding. Ha!" Then she became very sober, looking upwards through the dome at the persistent zoomed view of Thalassia still undergoing the slow effects of planetary carnage. "What the hell happened?"

Lysindra and Minêrva then realized that, of course, Kaimèa hadn't witnessed anything that had transpired. She had no idea what had occurred. Lysindra quickly caught Kaimèa up, which delivered Kaimèa into a mild, wordless shock.

"You know Lysindra was the target of this attack, right?" said Minêrva. "That's why she received the warning. It was sent directly to her."

"But...that's just...that's..." said Kaimèa.

"Maniacal," said Minêrva comfortably. "It's fucking evil."

They stood and stared for a while.

"So," said Lysindra. "Now what? All those people just died because of me. What do I do now?"

"You already know the answer to that question," said Kaimèa. "You don't even need to ask."

"Yeah," said Minêrva. "It's clear as day what to do next."

There was remarkably little complexity in publishing the network. Lysindra had already published prior versions of the network a handful of times. This one was not particularly different. It consisted of folding the data representation into a compact form to facilitate galactic dispersal over interstellar transmission channels, much as with her prior versions of the network.

Thus, as news of the attack on Thalassia steadily spread across the galaxy, an equally momentous news item followed mere days behind, a similar wavefront of information plowing its way across all of known civilization, carrying the complete EOUSP network. Everyone was consequently left to process two events at nearly the same time, the horrific attack coupled with the near-certainty that it had targeted the famous—and fairly beloved—Lysindra, and then the publication of the final network for anyone to wear whenever and wherever they saw fit. It was a discombobulating pair of revelations to receive within days of one another.

Various stellar societies and communities took this opposing duality of terribleness and one wonderfulness in different ways. Some descended into chaos as factions for and against the quale argued and even fought. But that was a rare occurrence. The full quale generally erased such disagreements. In fact, no one who actually wore the network and experienced the quale could find fault with it. The *knowing* of it resolved such concerns. It was only Deimos's followers and the followers of the more problematic Satorian sects, who in their refusal to wear the network, persisted in raging against it. But such rabble-rousers were so vastly outnumbered now, with the quale's revelation in full swing, that they could achieve little social or political influence at this point.

Lysindra and Kaimèa saw fit to quickly and quietly relocate to the near-by cozy stellar system of Isiskara. Minêrva tagged along for a while, with clear intentions to head back to the Center after a while to reunify with her branchling and rejoin Rihon's eccentric circle of artists and philosophers.

Isiskara wasn't necessarily uninhabited. There was a single medium-sized planet, Bastetia, with a modest population in the low billions. With much of the populace frequently tucked away in virtualities, the corporeal density at any given time tended to be astonishingly low, which suited Lysindra and Kaimèa perfectly. They grew a home together, modeled on the architectural styles of extragalactic species number four, at Kaimèa's recommendation. It was her second favorite after species nine, whose styles had inspired her home on Nyveron. The three friends spent their time exploring Bastetia, with its well preserved ecologies, and Minêrva took great pleasure in studying Bastetia's biology, which it turned out had never been fully solved. The work suited her and she made a few new discoveries, which then gained her some notoriety with the Bastetian scientific community, beyond her preexisting Neuralium fame.

Lysindra watched news roll in from throughout the galaxy, ever constrained by the incident light cone to which all information was limited. She could readily observe how close-by stellar systems reacted to the two announcements sweeping outward, but the farther out she looked, the longer she had to wait to see how this news was received. It would take hundreds of thousands of years for the network to spread to the farthest reaches *and* for any news about its reception to reflect back to her.

From the quietude of Bastetia, she watched and processed it all.

51

IT WAS A PLEASANT EVENING WITH A RECEDING SUN, a purple-fringed orange sky, and cool air, when Lysindra saw Ceulbur walking toward her over the rise of a nearby hill. She was alone amongst the inspiring alien flora, designing a completely new network in search of entirely new qualia, just as she had done for so long with Ceulbur as her quale-diving partner. The work was nearly as random as ever. She threw together randomly selected pieces of network configurations from the almost infinite library of previously discovered configurations that had been determined to inspire interesting qualia. These she then combined with newly generated networks of further variety. Then she tested how they felt when attached to her brain. She and other quale-divers had been doing this for a million years, and by all indications it was a process that could go on forever. Other quale-divers shared their discoveries with her, and she hers with them. They were her community, aside from Kaimèa and Minêrva. They understood her.

But so had Ceulbur—at one time. And now here he was, walking toward her across cerulean grass that phosphoresced lightly as twilight set in. Flashing white and red lights darted to and fro just above the tops of the grass, some sort of miniature fauna, insect-like, but she wasn't sure they were really animals. Minêrva had explained that they lacked anything resembling a signal-processing brain. So they flitted in their fashion in some way Lysindra didn't yet understand. Bastetia was not *solved* yet, but with people like Minêrva on the case, that wouldn't last long.

And there was Ceulbur, now standing in front of her.

"Hello Lysindra."

She blinked with surprise, staring at him. "Ceulbur," she said with obviousness. "It's been..."

"22,000 years," he said. "Kaimèa told me I could find you here."

"Oh, you already saw her."

"When I arrived, yes."

Lysindra felt the heat of approaching tears in her eyes and a trembling in her extremities. "What are you doing here?"

"I'm only here briefly. To see you, of course."

"Briefly?" She looked him up and down, pulling the memories forward, reconstructing him, remembering him. Remembering them together.

"You did it Lysindra. You really did it. It's incredible."

"You aren't angry?"

"The time for that has passed. Now that it's done, it doesn't matter whether I thought you should have done it."

"That's...considerate of you."

"I must confess, the quale is stunning."

"You've tried it?"

Ceulbur scoffed. "Of course I have. I was never against completing or experiencing it in the broader sense. Well not initially. I suppose Rihon made me question that some. I was concerned about *disseminating* it. I was concerned about the consequences of distributing it in a carefree fashion, but I didn't think the quale itself was bad."

"Initially, you said. But Rihon convinced you otherwise."

"Well, yes. I thought he made a compelling point with Accepting Oblivion, but then you completed it anyway, and now that everyone has experienced it, none of that matters anymore. You've been experiencing various stages of the quale from the very beginning. You understand it better than anyone, so you know what I mean. None of the prior objections matter at this point."

"I guess that makes sense. And now that you've experienced it, you found it...illuminating?"

Ceulbur frowned. "It's the solution to the EOUSP for Earth's sake. Yeah, I found it slightly illuminating. Didn't you?"

"Well yeah, of course. I was just confirming because of your prior objections. I understand now."

"Some people are attaining veritable enlightenment from it," said Ceulbur. "New schools of philosophy, new religions with no association with Satori. Entire academies of art never before imagined are popping up throughout the galaxy. Surely you're aware of these circumstances."

Lysindra nodded thoughtfully. "I'm keeping tabs on the developments from here, watching how it affects the rest of the galaxy as news comes in. I've never felt the distance of the galaxy so strongly as in this most recent era as I...consume news of how the quale is changing things."

Ceulbur smiled. "You've done good thing Lysindra."

"I don't know. Deimos is still out there. There's no telling what he'll do next."

Ceulbur literally snorted at this. "Lysindra, you haven't heard? Deimos has been utterly outcast."

"Oh!" Lysindra frowned and looked toward the near horizon, the hill Ceulbur had crested as he arrived. The low sky just behind the hill was deep lavender, the hill rapidly darkening, a deep blue pocked with black shadows, still phosphorescing weakly. The white and red sparks continued to swoop just above the hill's hair-like grass, brilliant and shimmering in their movements against the dark sky. "He isn't still active? Even just politically? I don't just mean anything as extreme as his prior actions."

"Things might have gone differently if he had succeeded in, well, killing you. If no one had ever experienced the final quale, he might have persuaded the people that the sacrifice of an entire planet was necessary to stop the wicked and insane Lysindra." Ceulbur chuckled. "But that isn't what happened. Now that everyone everywhere is experiencing the quale and learning and feeling and *knowing* the solution to the EOUSP! For Earth's sake Lysindra, don't you see what you've done?" He swung his arms upward in befuddlement at her tepid reaction. "You've rekindled belief and anticipation in everyone. We all know how to survive where we once saw no possible way out. No one was going to look kindly on Deimos after that. He's been practically chased out of the Center naked and screaming. He, and all his crazy followers. Some of them are Satorians it turns out, even though most of them love you. What a crazy cult that turned out to be. Everyone who was with Deimos has fled to the far reaches of the galaxy, right to the rim. They're going to be driven into the void the way things are going. Ha!"

Lysindra crumpled her brow and studied Ceulbur with almost suspicious disbelief. "Really? I didn't expect that. Not much happened after the attack on Regenium, after all."

"It's different this time. It isn't about proving that he did any of it," said Ceulbur. "In fact, there still isn't any solid proof. Nothing definitive has come to light connecting him to the attack on Thalassia."

"Then what's different this time? Why is everyone finally against him?"

"Because of you Lysindra!" Ceulbur was openly annoyed that she wasn't following the thread here. "Because of the final network and quale. That's why. No one has any patience for Deimos's nonsense anymore. Combine that with the fact that everyone knows he was behind the attacks even if they can't prove it, and well yeah, they're just done with him. Everyone is done with him. Like I said, he's literally being pursued to the galactic rim. He has nowhere to go now. I just hope the next galaxy over can put up with him." He laughed again.

Lysindra turned and looked at the ground, trying all the combinations of outcomes in her head. "Okay, well, that's pretty interesting. I mean...thank you. I...this isn't coming out right."

She looked away entirely, turning her back so he wasn't in her vision. "You said you're only here briefly?"

"The hive entity," he said. "I looked for a long time and finally discovered a way to find it. Thousands of years of dusty myths lost in archives scattered across numerous systems have revealed a way. I'm going to seek it out."

"Ah, I see. That seems fitting."

"Yes, it really does."

"And when you find it, you will...?"

"If it'll have me."

She scrunched her face with concern. "When I spoke with it...you have to understand Ceulbur, no one who joins it seems to ever leave. I don't think it's nefarious. I don't think it keeps people against their will. But it's different from the hives you've participated in before. I think something happens to you once you're inside it. I think it changes you. You become so much a part of it—no, it becomes so much a part of you, that...I don't think you will be able to extricate yourself. I don't think you will *want* to, is my point."

"I already don't want to. That's *my* point. Are you able to understand that?"

Lysindra felt the heave of her breath a few times, then turned the corner of her mouth in acceptance as she remembered what the hive entity had told her. By the time it accepted anyone into its community, they were already so utterly committed that they would never want to leave. They were that committed *before* they joined it. Now, facing Ceulbur, she finally comprehended it. "Ok, I guess I understand. I can't really feel it. I wouldn't want anything like that. But if you're sure."

"It looks like you'll be okay," Ceulbur said.

"Kaimèa?"

"Yes."

"Thank you. Yes, I think so too."

Lysindra felt Ceulbur come closer behind her. She turned and embraced him. "Goodbye Ceulbur."

"Goodbye Lysindra." They held the embrace a while longer, and then he left the way he came, up and over the hill, with red and white sparks flitting around his legs, then cresting and disappearing behind the hill.

Lysindra had heard rumors of a hive-like entity before she encountered it on Cianthara. It hadn't been a total unknown, just a rarity, an apparition of legend. But after that day, she never heard another word about it again. Its interpretation of the EOUSP solution had seemed to inspire some sort of utter reclusion on its part. Had it hidden away in some quiet corner of the galaxy, or had it perhaps left the galaxy, sailing across the void, headed for far shores? Or alternatively, had the quale guided it toward a more spiritual and less physical ending? Something like the Ontoscendians had apparently undergone. Had it truly vanished right out of the universe upon the achievement of pure Nirvana in a flash of enlightened evanescence? No one knew. And had Ceulbur found it before it disappeared? That she also didn't know one way or the other, but she never heard from him, or even *of* him, again. She preferred to believe he found it.

She left the field, rejoining Kaimèa in their current home, a warm abode of love and companionship, the tangibility of Kaimèa's presence. Minêrva came and went, enjoying the culture of Bastetia, but seeming somewhat astray. This boondocks world wouldn't hold her much longer. She clearly missed the frenetic energy of Rihon's circus.

52

S TARS. A SKY UTTERLY POWDER-COATED IN STARS. White and yellow stars. Blue and red stars. Some so bright, so near, so large, that by their shapely constellations a person could see the eyes of a lover in front of oneself. And many *many* dimmer stars so distant, so faint, that their enumerated billions dissolved into tiffany silk laid layer upon layer across the black dome overhead. Slashing through this vista, the Milky Way ran from horizon to horizon, upper left to lower right.

Lysindra lay on her back on the soft Bastetian grass and gazed upward, gazed outward. There, in her lower right, in the belt of galactic brightness, was the direction of Caelunis, where the timid and strange Neuralium, lacking the basic tenents of sentience, had tapped into a sensation of profound impact. Minêrva had shown her how to feel the quale through the brain of that simple creature as it felt something spacious, something beautiful, something eternal, all the while without deeply realizing what it was all about.

And to her upper left, within a faint area of the belt, looking toward the rim of the galaxy where the stars thinned out, in that direction there resided a remote galaxy, unique among the trillions. In that other galaxy another species of tremendous evolutionary culmination and technological achievement had found an experience that answered its greatest question, addressed its greatest fear. And they had magnanimously seen fit to share it with their cosmic neighbors. Their brains and their minds were assuredly unimaginably different from those of humans, and yet they were capable of feeling a very similar experience. What a bond humanity shared with them, whatever their nature turned out to be.

And again within the belt, but loosely back in the direction of Caelunis for they resided near one another in the sky, there hung Cianthara, home of the ancient Ontoscendians, gone so long ago as to have lived in a time far closer to humanity's Earthly adolescence than its later galactic destiny. They were human but they seemed almost as alien as species twelve in her ponderings. She could look at this sky forever. She dwelled momentarily on the realization that in the few minutes she had been staring upwards, the universe had expanded slightly, thinned slightly, cooled slightly. Died slightly. The day of ending drew nearer. Not particularly near necessarily, but inevitably nearer, always headed in only one fateful direction.

Come home, she heard in her head, a message conveyed through the planet's myceliumesque data network that permeated every chunk of soil, every blade of grass, up through her skin, and deep into her brain orb.

Hello Kaimèa, she responded.

Come home. It's a lovely evening. Minêrva and I miss you.

Be right there. Lysindra took another eyeful of infinity, smiled, and decorporealized.

"Come here Lysindra," said Minêrva, as Lysindra corporealized in their home. "Sit with us." Minêrva held a glass of wine, and another materialized in Kaimèa's outstretched hand as Lysindra took notice.

"Sure." She joined them at a third chair that appeared just in time as she trustfully sat down into what was at first unimpeded air.

"We're going to play a game," said Minêrva.

"Yeah?" said Lysindra.

"Here's how it works," said Kaimèa, gracing Lysindra's forearm with her fingertips. We go around the circle—triangle, whatever—offering a single word to describe the EOUSP quale. It doesn't have to be an adjective. Anything that captures the essence of the quale."

"You both know I don't approve of even attempting to describe qualia."

"Why do you think we called you!" said Minêrva laughing.

Lysindra squirmed a bit. "Okay," she responded meekly. Minêrva squinted at her suspiciously.

"All right," said Minêrva. "I'll start." She took her time, swilled from her glass, and looked upwards. "Okay. Here goes. Hollow."

Kaimèa nodded. "MmHmm. Ok then..." she took a corresponding drink from her own glass. "Ummm...Deep—"

"No!" declared Minêrva. "Too close to hollow. Try again." Kaimèa rolled her eyes. "Fine. Hold on a second...Okay. Bitter, not the emotion, the literal taste. The quale has a notion of bitterness, but not actual taste of course since it is its own quale."

"See?" said Lysindra. "This was what I was talking about. You can't do this. It doesn't work."

"No no," said Minêrva. "She's right. It *is* similar to bitterness, in the same way that wine presents its various 'notes'." She swirled her glass illustratively. "I see what you mean Kaimèa. Okay, your turn," she said eyeing Lysindra.

Lysindra sighed heavily. "Well, let's see. How about..." She hated the very premise of this activity. She looked around the room, finally settling on the ceiling, which scintillated with embedded gold and blue glitter. Dwelling on the glittery appearance she said, "tingly."

Minêrva and Kaimèa both instantly frowned. "I don't see that one, frankly," said Kaimèa.

"Well, it's my word and I get to choose."

The squint of Minêrva's suspicion became mere slivers through which her eyes penetrated Lysindra. "MmHmm," she said thoughtfully. "And how, exactly, is it tingly?"

"Oh, ummm..." Lysindra trailed off. A brief moment passed as the others waited for her to continue.

"I knew it!" Minêrva practically yelled. "I just *knew* it!"

"What?" said Kaimèa and Lysindra in unison.

"You tell her or I will," said Minêrva with wicked delight.

Lysindra observed Minêrva's expression, realized she had been discovered, hesitated a moment and then simply gave in. "I...might not have..."

"She's never worn the final network!" exclaimed Minêrva. "You sneaky devil!" She laughed out loud.

"*What?!*" said Kaimèa. "Is that true? How can that be possible?" Lysindra looked around the room uncomfortably. "But why Lysindra?"

"I don't know. I've explained this. There's multiple reasons. There's something about the irreversibility of it. Right now, I have the option, the choice, of knowing or not knowing. But once I experience the quale, well then I'll know. That wave function will be forever collapsed. I can never go back. And then there's..."

"Your partner from before the Great Fortification," said Kaimèa. Lysindra squirmed under their gazes. "Your sense of guilt, or something, for continuing on without him."

"You could erase the memory of the final quale before it transfers to long-term memory," said Minêrva.

"Or," said Kaimèa, "you could make an etching beforehand and fully revert after experiencing it."

"Feels like cheating," said Lysindra.

"This is just ridiculous," said Minêrva. "As we speak, at this very moment, the light cone of the EOUSP quale is burning across the galaxy, filling in every mind it encounters along the way, and yet here you are, at the epicenter, soon to be the last person in the galaxy to experience the quale when you should have been the very first."

"I just—"

"Forget it," declared Minêrva. "You're doing it now. Right Kaimèa?"

"Ummm," Kaimèa said.

"Oh come *on!*" said Minêrva, practically vibrating.

Lysindra considered it for a moment and decided she really was being odd about it. She had tried every prior version of the network, never knowing if it would reveal the complete quale. She could have walked into it by accident on any previous attempt, so logically, why wouldn't she now? It didn't make sense."

"All right," she said. "I suppose it's time."

"Damn right it is," said Minêrva, sitting up. Lysindra felt Kaimèa's hand grip the inside of her forearm, felt the warmth and pressure of it. She looked at Kaimèa, who looked back with reassurance.

Lysindra's chair morphed beneath her seated body into a reclined position and became a neural interfacing chair, ever so slightly bonding to every point of contact along her back, her legs, her arms. She felt the chair gently grip her head and form an intimate connection with her scalp, her skull, her brain, establishing a high bandwidth data network by which to move neural data at tremendous scale.

She pulled up the final network and easily interfaced with it. It hovered there, on the fringes of her mind, nonfunctional. She felt Kaimèa's hand take her own. She closed her eyes, and then after a pause, activated the network. She lay there for a long time, feeling the EOUSP, first the desperation, then the hope, then the notion of the solution, then the feasibility of the solution...and ultimately realizing the solution itself with perfect clarity for the first time. The quale was pristine. None of the foggy ambiguity from prior attempts. It could not have been clearer than it was in this final form. She now *knew* how the flame of consciousness, and human legacy along with it, could perpetuate literally forever. And as the hive entity had shown her, she also knew how universal purpose could similarly eternalize. She lay with it for a long time. Now that she was here, she felt no obligation to rush through the experience. She let it permeate her consciousness as deeply and intimately as it could go. It altered her in ways that would persist long after she disconnected the module. She would be forever transformed as she became the quale and it became her. Through the EOUSP quale she now understood the intrinsically unknowable: the true value of infinity.

As she returned to the physical, she heard voices, distant and muffled. But they resolved to the forefront as she reemerged. She opened her eyes and saw Kaimèa looking at her expectantly, and nearby, Minêrva with a sage smile of concordance.

"So?" Kaimèa's sweet voice, as her hand was gently squeezed.

Lysindra breathed for a moment, finding her words. "Well, that makes sense."

Author's Request

Thank you for purchasing and reading *Contemplating Oblivion*. If you enjoyed it, please rate and/or review it on Amazon and/or Goodreads. Authors are heavily dependent on public feedback of that nature.

Furthermore, since this book is self-published, you, dear reader, are my publicist. No grandiose publishing house has purchased advertisements or arranged tours and signings for me. The only way anyone will ever know this book exists is if you tell others about it—or buy it as a gift for someone. So yell it into the chasmic expanse of social media and whisper it into the tranquil chamber of friends and family.

In the immortal words of Leia, "You're my only hope."

Afterward

Thank you for reading *Contemplating Oblivion*. This work combines my thirty-year interest in mind uploading with my personal philosophy concerning metaphysics, consciousness, personal identity, sentience throughout the universe (and the galaxy in particular), futurism, and "purpose" (what is all this *for?!*). As such, I have written a number of prior works that delve into these topics in far greater depth than the novel.

First, I would recommend reading Nick Bostrom, Albert Camus, David Chalmers, Barry Dainton, Daniel Dennett, Antonio Damasio, Michael Gazzaniga, Michael Graziano, Michael Hart, S. Hawking & L. Mlodinow (M Theory), Jeff Hawkins, Christof Koch (& G. Tononi), Lawrence Krauss, Thomas Nagel, Derek Parfit, G. Paul & E. Cox, Roger Penrose (& S. Hameroff), Jean-Paul Sartre, John Searle, Frank Tipler, Stephen Webb, and many others I can't fit here. I disagree with several of them, but their theories belong in the tool belt of anyone interested in the topics indicated in the previous paragraph.

Various dialogs in the story present my ideas about branching personal identity. The book also depicts the branching interpretation of identity as the characters undergo such experiences. My 2014 book, *A Taxonomy and Metaphysics of Mind-Uploading* goes into more detail on this topic. Of a terser format, my various articles cover specific subtopics. My 2016 paper "The Fallacy of Favoring Gradual Replacement Mind Uploading Over Scan-and-Copy" explores a popular line of reasoning that I find problematic under careful analysis. Similarly, my two articles, "The Stream of Consciousness and Personal Identity" and "Nondestructive Mind Uploading and the Stream of Consciousness", explore another specific subtopic in detail.

The early scene in which Lysandra's desire for a particular piece of music is acted upon by her "smart home" in a preconscious fashion is a direct reference to my article "The Preconscious Smart Home".

My expectation that there is no sentient life elsewhere in our galaxy is explained in my article "The Fermi Paradox, Self-Replicating Probes, and the Interstellar Transportation Bandwidth".

The hive entity Socratically leads Lysandra through my consciousness-based theory of universal purpose, which foundationalizes the main theme of the book: the EOUSP. For a methodical presentation, see my article "Mind Uploading and the Question of Life, the Universe, and Everything".

A complete list of my articles, including several not mentioned here, can be found on my website at https://keithwiley.com. Thank you.

Pronunciation

Adopt or ignore the following pronunciation as you see fit

People

Ananda	uh-**NON**-duh	Lysindra	li-**SIN**-druh
Ceolbur	see-**OL**-ber	Minerva	mi-**NER**-vuh
Ceulbur	see-**OOL**-ber	Priello	pree-**EL**-oh
Deimos	**DEE**-mose	Quinlan	**KWIN**-luhn
Eero	**EER**-oh	Rassianel	ro-see-uh-**NEL**
Faimee	**FAI**-mee	Rihon	ree-**HONE**
Jorgen	**JOR**-guhn	Satori	suh-**TOR**-ee
Kaimea	keye-**MAI**-uh	Tria	**TREE**-uh
Lysandra	li-**SON**-druh	Vellion	**VEL**-ee-on
Lysendra	li-**SEN**-druh	Zarael	zar-ee-**EL**

Places

Ailuros	**AI**-ler-ose	Nyveron	ni-**VAIR**-one
Bastetia	ba-**STEE**-shuh	Oudara	oo-**DAR**-uh
Caelunis	sai-**LU**-nis	Regenium	re-je-**NEE**-um
Cianthara	see-un-**THAR**-uh	Seraphi	sur-**AF**-ee
Eilunedra	ai-lu-**NAI**-druh	Siremala	seer-e-**MAHL**-uh
Ermozara	ur-moh-**ZAR**-uh	Thalassia	thuh-**LA**-see-uh
Fringalis	frin-**JAL**-is	Thorigon	**THOR**-i-gon
Icarion	eye-**KAIR**-ee-one	Ukonstra	oo-**KON**-struh
Isiskara	i-zee-**SKAR**-uh	Verkennaros	vur-kuh-**NAR**-ose
Krasavitia	kra-suh-**VEE**-shuh	Vimrei	**VIM**-rai
Linnea	li-**NAI**-uh	Ylorin	ee-**LOR**-in
Lueur	loo-**UR**	Yseldor	ee-**SEL**-dor
Luminith	**LOO**-mi-nith	Zareasman	zar-ee-**AZ**-muhn

Character Branches

Horizontal positions indicate both order and proximity of introduction, i.e., Lysăndra appears moderately before Lysãndra, who appears immediately before Lysändra, who appears significantly before Lysãndra, etc.

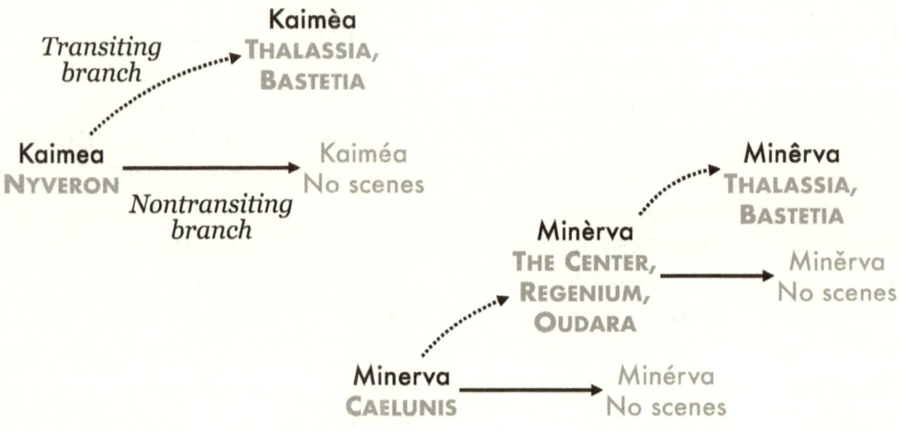

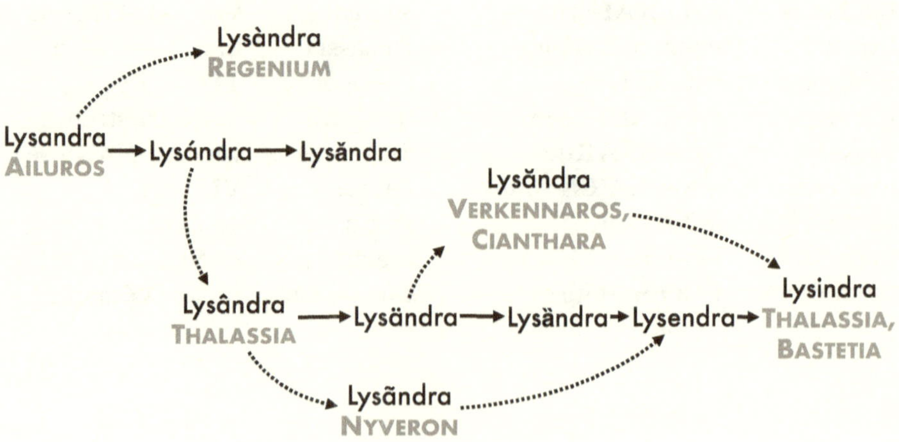

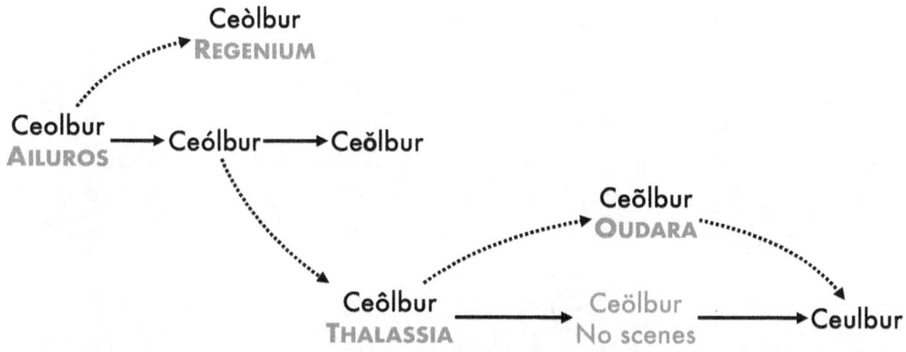

Ceòlbur
REGENIUM
Ceolbur
AILUROS
Ceólbur
Ceõlbur
Ceõlbur
OUDARA
Ceõlbur
THALASSIA
Ceölbur
No scenes
Ceulbur

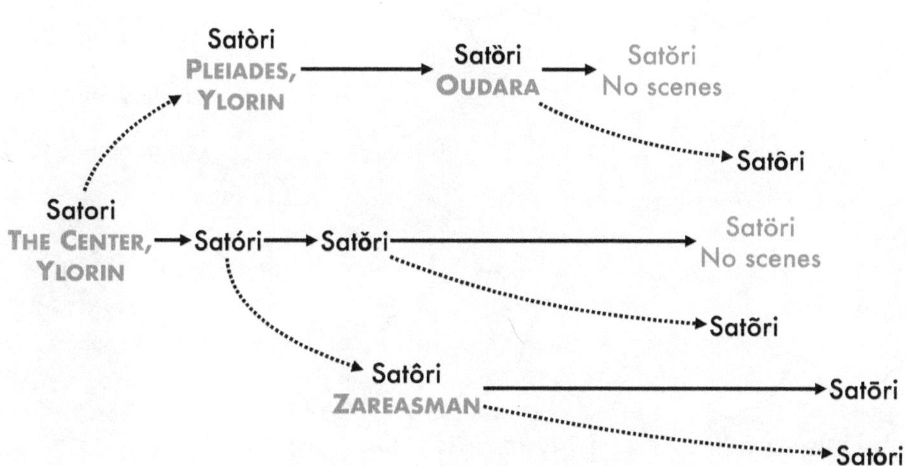

Satòri
PLEIADES,
YLORIN
Satöri
OUDARA
Satöri
No scenes
Satôri
Satori
THE CENTER,
YLORIN
Satóri
Satöri
Satöri
No scenes
Satõri
Satôri
ZAREASMAN
Satõri
Satóri

Stellar Systems

Some unnamed moons and stations are not included

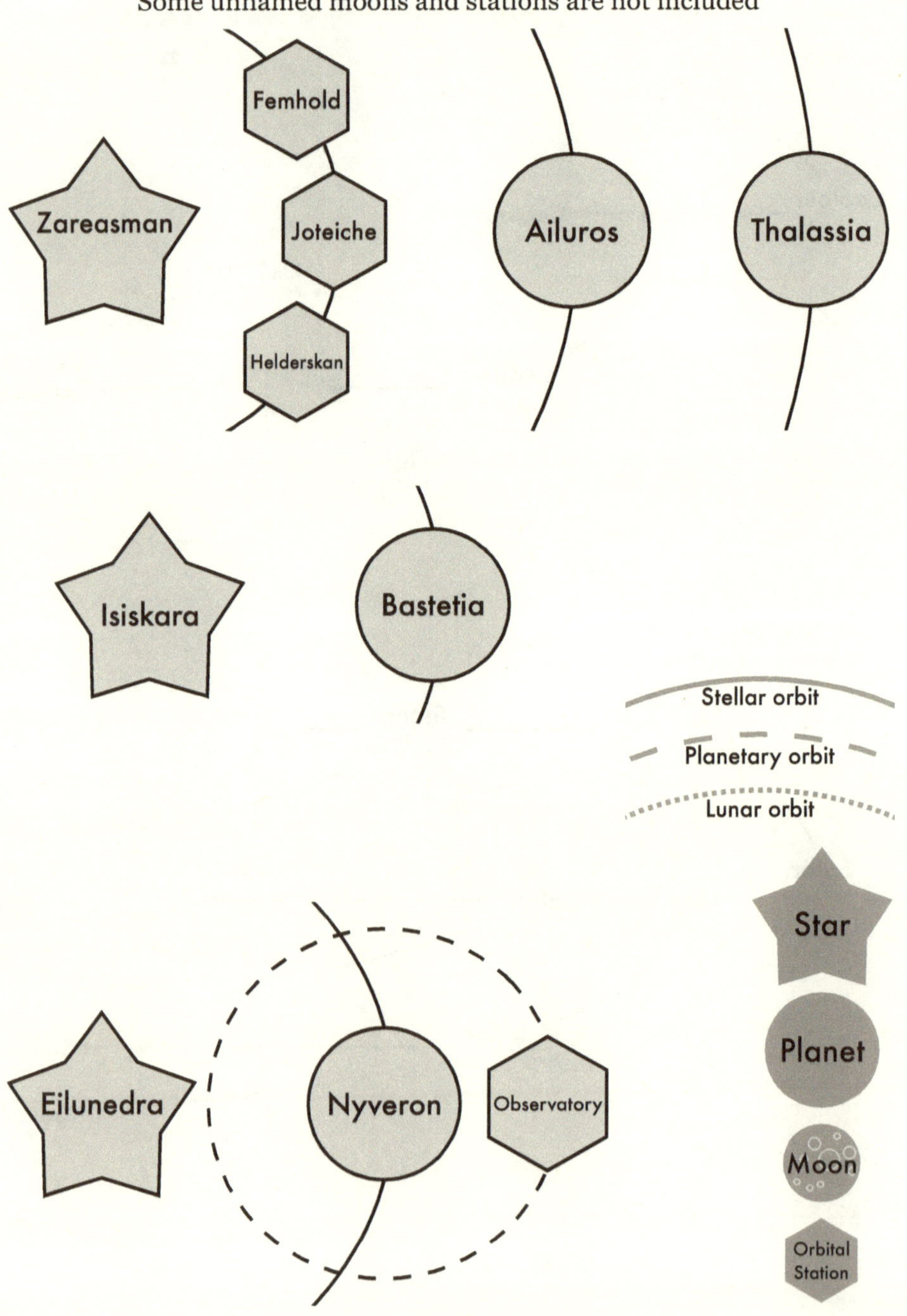

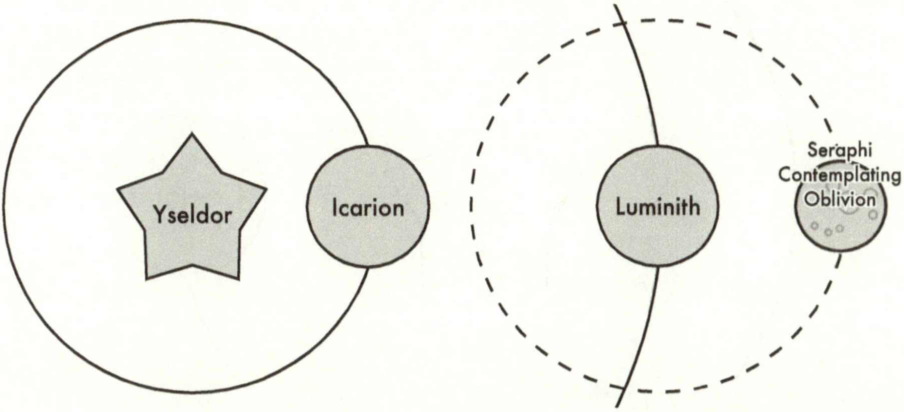

Yseldor
Icarion
Luminith
Seraphi
Contemplating
Oblivion 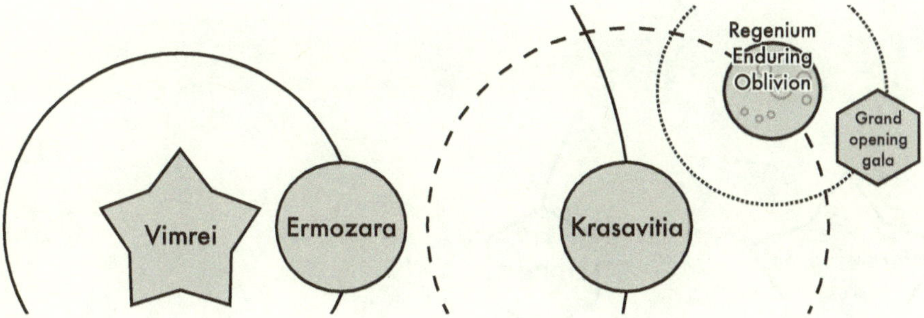
Vimrei
Ermozara
Krasavitia
Regenium
Enduring
Oblivion
Grand
opening
gala

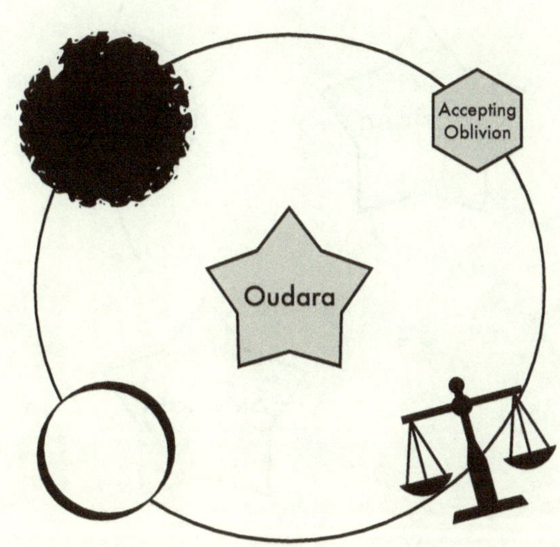

Accepting
Oblivion
Oudara

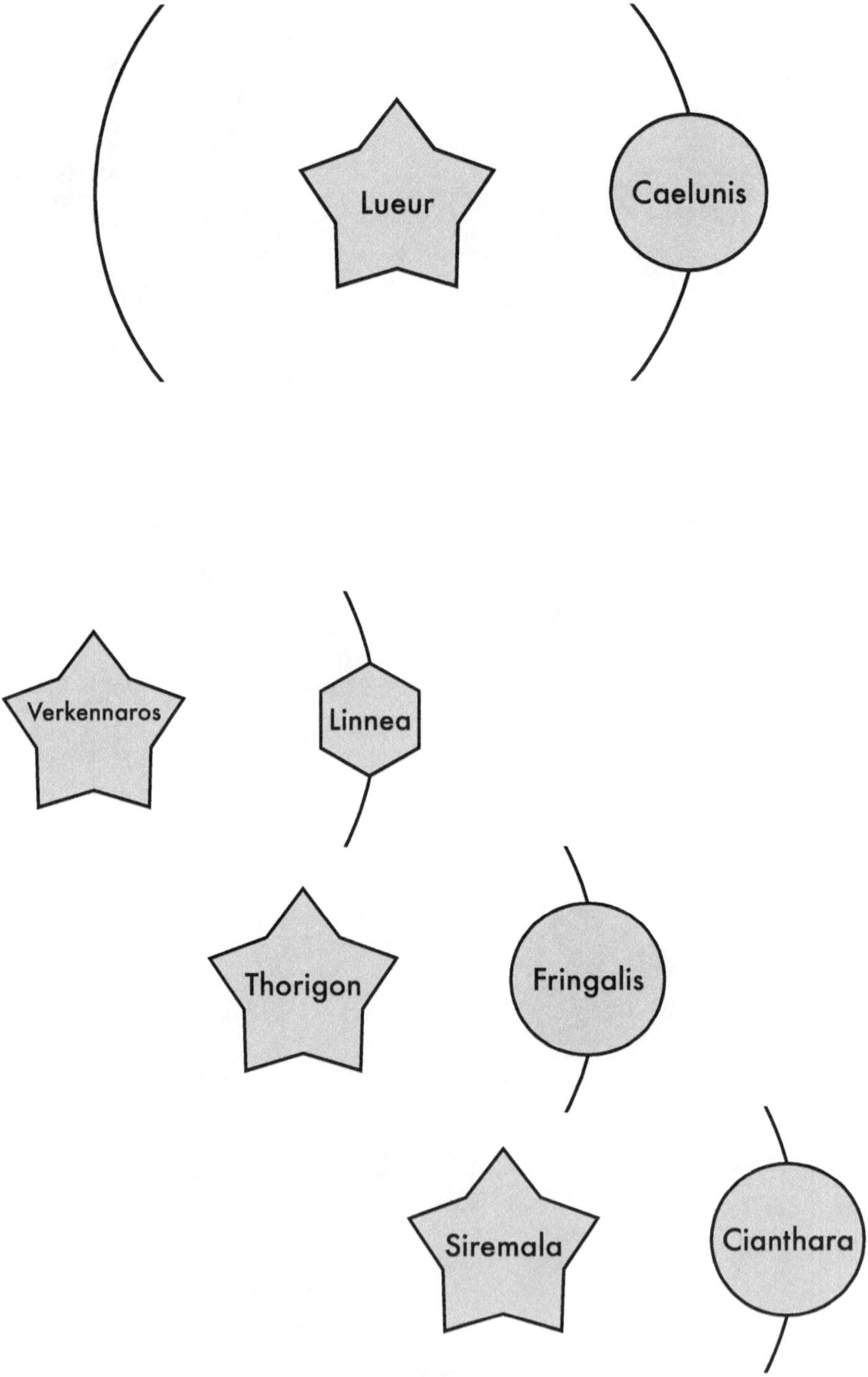

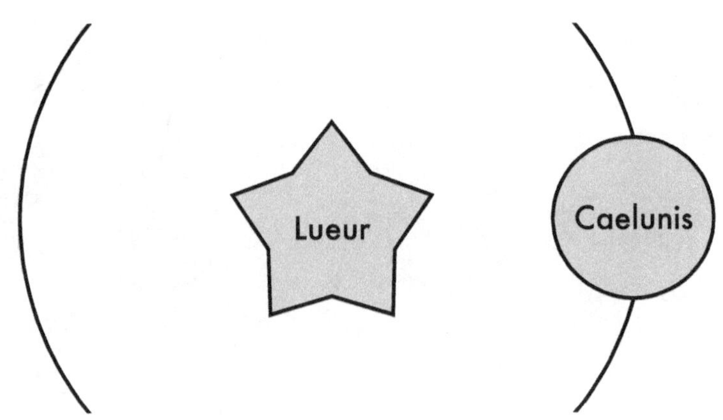

Lueur
Caelunis

Verkennaros
Linnea
Thorigon
Fringalis
Siremala
Cianthara